Songs About Life

TRISH FABER

DEDICATION

This novel is dedicated to my mom Joyce.

Even though you've been gone for so long now,

I still think about you every day,

And wonder why…

You were my loving parent, my friend, my biggest fan.

You always laughed when everyone else just shook their heads.

Thank you for showing me courage and bravery.

I hope you would be proud. I know you would be proud.

That's all I ever wanted.

I miss you and I love you.

- Trish (2006)

CHAPTER ONE

Just once, I'd like to meet that person who sits in the corner spot of the corner booth, in the dark confines of a dingy bar, and watches life happen. This person is always drunk, or at least has the appearance that he is one sip away from a total and complete lack of recognition of anything human or dead. Maybe he is dead. Or maybe he's just in limbo, waiting for the right moment, trying to decide whether or not he really wants to re-join the living, or continue to squander his time in a pit hole of puke. His name is Bobby.

Now Bobby's a good citizen. He gets up every morning and goes to work pulling cable lines for the local conglomerate, earning a decent wage. He pays his rent, telephone, and utility bills all on time, and even has a little cash left over to tip the paperboy once and awhile. Bobby never reads the paper. He stacks them chronologically in a corner of his apartment where they sit, day after day, year after year, gathering dust. An ever-thickening layer of black soot from a chimney badly in need of a sweep, envelops not only the papers, but the entire contents of the room. Bobby doesn't care, he's never there.

Sure, he sleeps a little in the lumpy old cot, which sits awkwardly in the corner, however, it's hard to get a good night's sleep when your head is always spinning and your mind is always cluttered. Poor Bobby. He is alone, but not that lonely. He has friends and they are just like him. In fact, they have a support group which meets every night from five o'clock until last call at Wilkins Place on the corner of John and Madison. Bobby, Frank, Jim, John, Dave, the same regular guys, with the same regular names, all living the same sort of lives. How do I know all this? I was walking home late one night as they departed the bar, arm in arm, singing at the top of their lungs about the glory of their lives. They were singing songs about life, and I needed to find out more, so I became "The Observer".

I began to take notice of all the little details of life as it was being lived. How Bobby and the boys shuffled their feet as they entered Wilkins Place, and danced with a light gaiety when they left eight hours later. The empty pop can that Jim would kick. Where did it come from? Did its previous owner casually drop it on the street? Maybe it was used as ammunition. A bullet shot from a speeding car, whose passenger seemed to think it would be funny to ping the homeless guy in the head. Nonetheless, everything has a story. The streets, the people, the garbage, the cries, and the laughter. I became fascinated by it all.

My life seemed simple enough. I worked, had friends, loved my family and ate three solid meals a day. I didn't really have anything to complain about. Looking hard at the events around me, I wondered why life throws so many curves to so many people, and how is it that some survive, but so many more perish, not really living, just existing? Which brings us back to Bobby. I would watch Bobby and his friends as much as the timeframe of my life would allow. I wasn't stalking, just watching. I had to pass the bar on my way home from work, so I'd peek in the window and do some undercover surveillance. Despite the need for a shave and maybe a little cologne, Bobby seemed all right.

One day, I finally got up the nerve to say "hi" just before he entered the bar. I was surprised when he gave me a slight nod of the head and a very polite, "How do you do?" From then I was hooked. Bobby and I would become unlikely friends. He with his bedraggled clothes and quiet demur, and I with an intense interest in finding out what this man was all about. I used him and he used me, but it worked for both of us.

The first time Bobby invited me to join him in the bar, I'll admit, I was nervous. This was his domain, and I was never one who strayed very far from mine. Besides, I was fairly confident I wasn't the type of girl the "boys" were used to seeing. A loud chorus of "Bobby! How the hell are ya?" greeted us as soon as we walked through the door. When I stepped out from behind Bobby's frame, the room went silent, and I nearly wet my pants with fright.

Bobby gently grabbed my hand and whispered, "Come on…it's okay…they only look like grizzlies."

It took a minute for my eyes to acclimate to the change in light, and when they did, they saw what looked indeed like a den of misfit bears.

There were big men with burly chests, and beards of tangled hair, and skinny Willy Wonka's with features so fine, I was afraid to look for fear my gaze might shatter their souls. The men were all different, yet somehow the same. With thirty sets of eyes uncomfortably cast upon me, I automatically brought my arms across my chest, protecting my femininity. I needn't have worried. Those eyes weren't looking at my body, but were searching out my own, looking, hoping for a glint of acceptance. In the strongest voice I could muster, I said "hello" and like water shooting from the blowhole of a whale, the room erupted, and I immediately felt calm. Bobby turned to me with that side-splitting grin of his.

"I think they like ya," he said.

I knew what he meant. The boys opened their hearts to me that day, and I began to learn what it was like to be the drunk in the corner.

I myself don't drink...well not really, maybe a glass of wine or two. I mean I've certainly tried, several, several times. It's not that my brain has anything against alcohol, just my body. I drink a little, think everything's okay, then my stomach starts to rumble and I know my night is done. It treats the beverages like a twelve-year-old boy surfing the internet for porn. "Access Denied". So unfriendly to the invader, my innards thrust the liquid up my throat at a furious pace, forcing me to bulldoze my way through crowds, fences and brick walls, just to find a safe and convenient place to relieve the agony. It's all quite a good show if you're a paying customer, but as the performer in question, I never come back for the encore, no matter how hard the laughs or how loud the cheers.

That first night at Wilkins, I knew I just had to take my chances. Not accepting a drink would have been a snotty slap in the face to the boys, and would have totally undermined my newfound acceptance. So I took my place at the bar, and gingerly held the beer to my lips. I hated beer, the smell alone made me gag. Bobby was watching me closely. I gave him a "cheers" and took a great big swig. The liquid burned the minute it splashed against my taste buds, and an immediate wave of hypochondriac nausea swept my entire body. I tried to hide the involuntary shudder creeping up my spine. The beer hadn't even hit my stomach.

I looked up at Bobby and smiled. "God that tasted good. I'd forgotten how good a cold beer is on a blustery January night!"

He grinned, showing a full smile of white polished teeth. If there was one part of Bobby's appearance he never let slide, it was his teeth. I was glad about that because, well I just have a thing about bad teeth and poor dental hygiene. Bobby and the boys seemed so thrilled by my chug-a-lug, I soon found myself with a complimentary refill in my left hand. The show had begun, and three more beers later, I was heading for the grand finale. I was surprised I'd lasted this long, but I knew the end was near. You can only swallow back impending vomit for so long. Believe me, I know.

We had just finished the last chorus of "Jimmy Crapped Corn" for the fifth time, when I blew. I tried to run but fell off the stool. Bobby grabbed my arm, catching my fall, and I rewarded him with a lap full of a smelly, chunky liquid. It was disgusting, and of course I didn't just throw up just once, oh no, I was a regurgitating machine. The boys tried to help, but without full fireman's gear, no one was coming close. When it was all said and done, I slumped exhaustedly on the bar, unfortunately landing in a pool of my own bile.

Bobby bravely put his hand on my shoulder, "You okay?"

"Ya I'm fine. Sorry 'bout the mess."

"Ah, this is nothing. You should have seen it the time Lester had sardine sandwiches for lunch. I swear to God, those bastards were still alive when they shot out of his mouth. Damn fool, never even chewed them. Swallowed them whole. Now that was disgusting!" I managed a laugh, which only increased the aching in my ribs. Bobby rubbed my back. "Let's get you home."

He hoisted me up on the left, and motioned for Jimmy to grab the right, and together we exited Wilkins Place. Not to a chorus of cheers but to some "take care hon" and "hope you're feeling better". Nobody made fun of me or mocked me like some of my "friends" always did. It's funny how I now describe those guys from the bar as friends, but they were. That night, me and the patrons of Wilkins shared a common bond - how it felt to be so totally exhausted and drained of life, yet somehow wanting to come back tomorrow for more. No more drinks for me, just the feeling of being amongst people who didn't judge you or expect anything more from you. Maybe that was part of the problem with the boys. They never expected anything more of each other than what they saw. But I knew deep in my heart that each man there wanted more for himself, even if he didn't realize it at the time.

The bitter chill was a refreshing change from my stench in the bar. I walked with my mouth wide open, hoping that somehow the frosty air would cleanse the violent breath lingering on my tongue. What I wouldn't do for a toothbrush. Bobby and Jimmy carefully guided me to a waiting cab and I gave the driver my address. Bobby leaned into the car to make sure everything was okay. He tucked my coat up around my neck.

"Don't want you to catch a cold now." I told him thanks and that I'd see him soon. "Hey Kid, you were a real trooper tonight. You didn't have to have that second drink...but you hung in there pretty good!"

He kissed the top of my head and then slammed the door shut. As the taxi drove away, I waved goodbye to Jimmy and he gave me a wink and a big wave. It was a strange feeling. I'd spent the night in a room full of people I'd only known for less than five hours, got really drunk, totally embarrassed myself, and yet had a wickedly good time. Then again, it didn't take much to amuse me.

I'd always had fun as a kid and would certainly describe myself as a well-adjusted, happy person. At least, that's what my Kindergarten teacher, Ms. Dennis, once wrote to my parents in my report card. That woman could pound out "Mary Had A Little Lamb" on the piano like nobody's business. She was middle aged, and middleweight, but one hundred per cent the person I wanted to be when I grew up. It wasn't until Grade Ten that I discovered she'd been banging Mr. Anderson, the Grade Six teacher my entire Kindergarten year. We'd always attributed her rosy cheeks after recess to her being a distant relation to Santa Claus. What the hell did we know or care? We were only five.

When you're five years old, nothing matters but a full belly, a warm blankie, and making sure there is always someone around to wipe your butt in case of a sticky poop. Everything's all about being independent, until the dreaded sticky poop arrives. You stand there with your pants at your ankles, bent over at the waist, screaming for help at the top of your lungs. This is one wipe you're not even going to attempt. Finally a parent arrives, or your older brother, but that's only if he's done something really bad, and you know he's in big trouble if he's having to wipe your sticky butt. Most of the time, the situation is quickly brought under control, but once every so often, the sticky poop really rears its' ugly head. Those are the times when your mother yells, "Sam, you'd better start the bath. We've got a live one tonight."

So she picks you up straight-armed in front of her, and you wonder if she really is Super Woman because she's so strong. She's careful not to touch you, and you're so thankful she's going to clean you up that you try to hug her. She laughs a little and says "yes Mommy loves you, but right now you smell like a manure pit." Okay, she doesn't really say that, but she sure is thinking it. By the time you reach the tub, the sticky poop has migrated to your arms, between your fingers and most definitely under your fingernails. But what do you care? You're only five and now you've gotten a free ride upstairs and are sitting in a bathtub full of bubbles and toys, watching the person you love most in the world, wash the shit from behind your ears. Life is great when you're five.

During story time, Ms. Dennis taught us how to sit in the circle without attempting to poke the kid beside you. It wasn't that the kid was doing anything especially wrong…sometimes they just needed poking. If you got caught poking, then you had to sit in the middle of the circle, and all the other kids would stare at you and make funny faces. This is really what most kids wanted though, to be the center of attention. Me, I was different. I had no desire to sit in the center of the circle. I preferred to sit on the edge and watch the kid in the middle make a jackass of himself. So I never poked, and the other kids never poked me. Somehow, they just knew not to. I wasn't mean, just confident.

I loved elementary school; everything about it. The colourful posters on the huge cork bulletin boards, the array of empty lunch buckets belonging to the bus kids, lined up against the hall outside of the gymnasium. It was a place to grow, learn and love. The friends you made were "best friends for life" (or so you thought). You fought over the last piece of gum in a pack, whose turn it was to throw the tennis ball against the wall, and who was the fastest runner. The only instance you ever heard the word drunk was the time Marty said "Russell drunk too much milk and it came out his nose." Life just seemed so simple then. I'm sure Bobby and the boys all went to elementary school. I wonder if they would have been friends. Probably not, but it would have been nice.

When I woke up the next morning, my head was screaming bloody murder. The only food I could think of swallowing was a cup of tea. Waiting for the water to boil, I laughed out loud remembering Big Dave doing a hula dance to that stupid song "Kokamo". He had his hips swaying so much, he lost his balance and fell sideways into poor Jimmy, who of course spilled his drink on Joe. Joe pretended to get all manly and threatened to take Jimmy outside to teach him a lesson, which was a joke because Jimmy had Joe by about seventy-five pounds. It wouldn't have been pretty.

In the meantime, Big Dave regained his balance and was now doing the twist. For a big man, he was quite agile and a very good dancer. I'd like to dance with Dave sometime.

"Hey boys!" Dave yelled. "I bet you a round I can pee straight into the shitter while I'm still doing the twist!"

"You're an asshole Dave," someone said laughing.

"Seriously…No drops or drips. Any takers?" he said sashaying his way to the john.

"I've got to see if the big bastard can do it," said Jimmy. He headed after Big Dave, several thirsty onlookers hot on his trail.

As it turned out, Dave twisted a little too far and shot wide, causing a loud cheer to erupt from the men's room. The raucous crowd spilled back into the bar, followed by Big Dave, who was still zipping up. I wonder if I was the only one who noticed the large pee spot by his zipper. Apparently, Dave forgot to shake his weapon before putting it back in its holster. He was true to his word though, "no drops or drips". He never mentioned puddles. No matter, the bar enjoyed the free round at his expense.

The kettle was whistling, so I poured the water into my favourite mug. Just drinking from this mug always made me feel better, I don't know what it was. After waiting the proper three minutes steeping time, I took the tea bag out and opened the lid of my Tupperware kitchen compost bin. I should have known better. The smell of decaying broccoli and cauliflower from Wednesday night's stir fry sent my already fragile body into head to toe convulsions. I plugged my nose, quickly threw the tea bag in the bin and slammed the lid. Grabbing the closest chair, I sat down to wait out the nausea. If I was this bad the morning after a drunk, what was I going to be like when I got pregnant? If I ever got pregnant. I wasn't in the mood to think about that today.

Slowly lifting myself out of the chair, I finished making my tea. Even though I smelt like garbage, the shower was going to have to wait. I needed my tea for strength. Samson had his hair and I had my cup of tea. I wrapped my fluffy pink housecoat tight around me and went to the front door to get the paper. Other than a few stripes on a couple of pairs of underwear, my trusty housecoat was the only article of clothing I owned that was pink. A gift from my sister to bring out my more feminine side. It certainly was feminine all right, with the ripped pocket and large coffee stain on the front. I looked like a regular fucking Playboy Bunny - all I needed were the ears.

It figured, as soon as I opened the door of my apartment, out popped Shirley Jones from apartment 3B. Yes, her name really was the same as the mother on the Partridge Family. She even wore the same hair. I didn't have the heart to tell her that the Partridge hair went out of style as soon as the Partridge Family went off the air, which was sometime in the late 1970s.

"Are you feeling okay today dear?" she asked in a hushed voice. "I heard some awfully loud noises coming from your apartment last night."

I had totally blocked out the second, third and fourth waves of pre-dawn vomiting. "Yes, I'm fine Mrs. Jones. I think I might have caught I touch of the flu, that's all."

"Oh, I thought maybe it was because you arrived home a little tipsy and could hardly open the door to your apartment. You made such a racket I had to come out and see what was going on. Here are your keys...you left them in the door. It's a good thing Mr. Jones always checks the halls for prowlers at two in the morning. Who knows what could have happened to you if someone else had found them. By the way, you look like hell this morning and what's that smell? Do you have a case of the diarrheas too? It's no wonder you aren't married, looking the way you do and wearing that dirty old pink housecoat."

"Thank you for the keys Mrs. Jones. You're my guardian angel." I bent down, picked up the paper and closed the apartment door. I could still hear her yapping her trap through the door.

"Anytime, I'm always willing to help. Have a great day!"

"Bitch."

I grabbed my tea from the kitchen counter and went into the living room. Just the short walk across the room made my head spin. Sinking into my favourite chair, I wrapped both hands around the magic mug.

"C'mon honey, do your thing".

Thank goodness it was Sunday. No work today. I hoped God would forgive me for not going to church. He'd have to since I hadn't stepped foot in a church except for weddings and funerals, in almost five years. I'd lost my faith in organized religion. Who were they to tell me what to believe, when they were so fucked up themselves? Besides, all they wanted out of me was my cash. They said it was going to help the needy. I found that hard to believe when I heard about the new state of the art multimedia system that was installed in the equally new "Praise the Lord" wing of the church. I decided from then on to give my money directly to the food bank, and I've been sleeping better ever since.

Bringing the steaming mug to my dehydrated lips, I took a sip. The taste was pure ecstasy. I could feel the hot liquid slowly drain down, soothing the searing pain in my raw and weathered throat. This time when the liquid hit my stomach, it was embraced like a long lost son, home from battle on the front. In the distance, a band played "Amazing Grace" and at once, all was right in my world. I closed my eyes and inhaled deeply, letting the steam drift leisurely up my nostrils to settle in my lungs. I felt better already.

Free from the head spins, I opened the paper. More crap about politics and the Middle East. Someone was ticked at someone else because he spat on some guys' shoe. So to get even, the next day the other guy decided to strap a load of TNT on his chest, head to the local market and blow himself up, taking a crowd of twenty innocent bystanders with him. He sure exacted his revenge didn't he? Remind me to never spit on anyone's shoes. Finishing my tea, I realized I could no longer stand my own smell. I needed a shower.

The ceramic tile was cold on my bare feet, so I hopped up and down waiting for the shower water to warm up. After five hops (I ran out of energy), I ducked behind the shower curtain.

"Shit, too hot!"

I violently flung my body away from the spray. Nobody wants singed pubic hair. Regrouping, I inched myself forward, letting my skin adjust to the sweltering heat. Finally, I took the full plunge and dunked my head under the nozzle.

"Ah."

There's nothing quite like a shower, especially when you smell like vomit. I shampooed my hair, and noticed in the little shower mirror that it was almost time to do my roots again. What I sometimes wouldn't give to be a man.

"Shit, shower, shave" my father used to say, "that's all a man needs to remember in the morning!" If it were only that easy.

Rinsing my hair, I applied my all-natural herbal conditioner. Since it needed four minutes of conditioning time (I always left it on for five to get that extra bounce), I proceeded to scrub my body from head to toe, making sure I used the proper cleansing utensil for each part. While wiping under my chin, I found a little present from last night; a gift from the depths of my volcanic stomach. I picked off the chunk, took a quick peek at the shower clock, then rinsed the conditioner from my hair. Turning off the taps, I reached for a towel.

Stepping out into the London fog of my bathroom, I could barely see and stubbed my toe on the bathroom scale. I don't know why I still kept the stupid thing. It always read ten pounds heavier than I really was. It belonged in the garbage. Grabbing my housecoat from the hook, I towelled off as I walked naked to my bedroom. Damn it was cold! I threw on my Sunday sweats, a pair of warm wool socks, and my runners. The shower had baptized me from my sins the night before, now I just needed to cleanse my soul. Pulling on my parka, I snatched my mitts from the chair and headed outside.

It was a beautiful morning. The sun was battling the snowflakes for air supremacy, with the snow handily winning out. They were huge flakes, like Christmas snow, except it was January, so the collective grumble I heard from the Sunday shoppers was no surprise. I loved the winter. I wanted to run down the street as fast as I could just to feel the cold on my cheeks and the freshness in my lungs. Snow always made me feel like I was part of something more than just concrete sidewalks and Gap Stores. I was alive. There was this huge thing going on in the world that no one could stop or even control. Mother Nature.

In Australia, people were lying on the beach in bikinis at the same moment a group of school kids were whipping down hills on toboggans over in Thompson Park. It was crazy. I might not have believed in organized religion, but I certainly believed in a higher spirit. Ms. Dennis always taught us that Mother Nature was God's little sister, and she was in charge of the circle of life and making the world a beautiful place to be. God must be very proud of his little sister. His children though, I think he's probably down right ashamed of us. We've messed things up horribly. We throw garbage everywhere, destroy our drinking water and set forests ablaze because we're too lazy to put out a campfire. Yet under all those charred remains is a new forest, just waiting to grow. All it takes is one seed. One green leaf. If a forest can regenerate itself, why can't we as human beings? We just need to find that one little seed, that one sign of life. Capture it. Nurture it. Give it hope.

A good long walk always cleared my head. I ambled along, taking my time, soaking up the surroundings. The shop windows were plastered with their "mid-January" blowout signs. The owner standing in the window, peeking out from behind the posters, trying to make eye contact with the passerby's and guilt them into at least entering the store for a look. Sheepishly, I walked with my head down, concentrating instead on the path in front of me, pretending I was Sir Ernest Shackleton exploring the surface of Antarctica. I headed down to Thompson Park to watch the children play for a while. How refreshing! Their screams were pure happiness.

Two young boys caught my eye. They were dressed in matching snowsuits, one boy slightly larger than the other. I assumed they were brothers. Both were standing at the top of the hill, each clutching a Krazy Carpet. By the bobbing of their heads, you could almost hear them starting to count. On what appeared to be two, the bigger kid lurched forward, purposely faking out the smaller one. The smaller kid threw his frame onto his Krazy Carpet and took off down the hill like a rocket. Sensing he was alone on his journey, he turned his head and looked back up the hill, which of course caused him to lose his balance, slide off the Krazy Carpet and end up with a mouthful of snow.

By now, the kid still at the top of the hill was laughing hysterically, which was more than the smaller guy could take. He grabbed his carpet, a handful of snow and charged back up the hill. The snow was deep enough that each time he stepped, he almost lost his boot. He didn't care. His older brother was going to pay. The minute he reached the top, he stormed like a raging bull towards his target. Unfortunately, his target was primed for an assault of his own, and promptly sent the bull flat on his ass. Three times he charged, three times he was sent flying. The matador waved his scarf in triumph. A truce called, both boys once again stood at the top of the hill.

"You'd better go this time," said the smaller boy.

"I will," answered his brother.

"You promise or I'm telling Mom."

"I promise, I promise."

"Go!"

The two of them shot off like a cannon, but it soon became apparent the younger brother had no intention of letting his older sibling finish the race. With great skill, he guided his carpet towards his brothers', then with perfect timing, leapt off, and tackled him to the ground. Both carpets continued their own separate race down the hill as the two brothers rolled and grappled in the snow. This time the bull was not to be defeated.

When they surfaced from the cloud of snow, the young bull was wearing the matador's scarf around his head. With a triumphant stride, he made his way down the rest of the hill, grabbed his carpet and headed across the park for home. As he turned the corner onto Keillor Street, he looked back and waved the scarf high in the air. His own personal victory parade. I looked at his brother, who by now had retrieved his carpet. He smiled at me. A little cheeky grin.

"I let him have that one. Saw him coming the whole time."

"I'm sure you did," I answered.

"Ya, every once in a while he needs to win. Boosts his confidence you know."

I laughed. "So are you going to get your scarf back?"

"What do you think?" With that he took off after his brother.

A very sudden and deep rumbling coming from my stomach broke my nostalgic mood. I was starving. I took a short cut through the park, avoiding the shops and arrived back at my apartment. Thankfully, Mrs. Jones was not waiting in the hall like a buzzard, but just in case she was lurking in the shadows, I was careful not to make a sound as I unlocked my apartment door. That woman was like a bad pimple. If you picked it, it would linger for days. Leave it alone and eventually it would get bored and go away. No wonder her husband joined the Shriners, played cribbage at the YMCA, and walked the neighbour's dog every afternoon. It was his way of keeping their marriage viable. I would have killed her by now, stuffed her down the garbage chute along with those "world famous pickled pork feet" she always peddled. Just the thought of them made me quiver. Said it was a recipe brought to Canada from the "old country". By the smell coming from her apartment when she made them, I think the feet were brought over on the boat as well. She's not a bad person, just annoying. Maybe she's just lonely. They never had any kids and the only person who ever visits, is the mailman. I wonder if she liked tea.

I hung up my parka, threw my mitts on floor, and made my way to the kitchen for some nourishment. I opened the refrigerator.

"Damn, that's what I needed to do today...get groceries."

I wasn't about to journey out again, so I captured what I thought was cheese, an expired egg and an onion that had begun to sprout. This would have to do. Heating up the frying pan, I tossed in the onion, sprouts and all. A bit of extra foliage never hurt anyone, and I figured after last night's purge, my body could use all the vitamins it could get. After the onions had started to brown, I cracked the egg (one handed of course) into the pan and covered it with a lid. The cheese required some work. I removed the wrapper and cut off as much of the greeny blue mould I could muster, leaving just enough for my sandwich. Popping two pieces of whole wheat into the toaster, I checked on my egg. It looked delicious. I sliced the cheese thinly and placed it over the egg in the pan. Instantly, it started to melt. I set one piece of my perfectly browned toast on a plate and placed the cheesy egg on top, taking a minute to stand back and admire my masterpiece, before plopping the other piece of toast on top. Pouring a large glass of orange juice, I noticed the light on my answering machine blinking wildly. The world was going to have to wait.

Although my sandwich looked picture perfect, I wasn't quite sure of the taste. That egg could have been in there since D-Day for all I knew. I did grocery shop regularly, but there always seemed to be at least one egg left over in the pack, which I would move to a smaller container. Ultimately, this would get shoved to the back of the refrigerator, where it would join the many other small half-full Tupperware containers of rice, creamed corn and spaghetti sauce.

Once, when I had arrived home late after a night out with friends, I found a leftover Caesar Salad from Wendy's. Problem was I couldn't quite remember the last time I'd been at Wendy's. I won't lie. I was tempted. I'm not sure if it was the soggy lettuce that finally turned me away or the aroma. It was worse than the time my cousin Trevor and I fed his Saint Bernard a mixture of devilled eggs and baked beans at a family picnic when we were kids. Poor Uncle Frank. He was yelled at and ripped with pine cones all afternoon for unspeakable bowel crimes, which for once, he did not commit. The dog meanwhile could hardly sit down. He would rest slightly on his rear then quickly flop over to one side and lay straight out. His dog butt must have been raw. That was the best family picnic we ever had. I brought the sandwich to my mouth. It smelled fine. Not one to linger on consequences, I took a bite then waited for a reaction. When nothing came, I dug in.

Realizing I couldn't stay a Sunday recluse forever, I checked my messages. The first one was from a telemarketer asking me if I wouldn't mind completing a survey on feminine hygiene products. They even left a 1-800 number, which I most certainly added to my speed dial. Who calls them back? Are they insane? I would rather have a job selling Mrs. Jones' pickled pigs feet door to door, than to cold call unsuspecting women to ask if they prefer pads with wings or extra-long, super thick absorbency. And on a Sunday! Wasn't that against the law?

The only time I'd ever said the words "feminine hygiene products" out loud was on a really bad blind date when I wanted to go home early. Nothing destroys romance like the word tampon. Definitely a mood killer. Oh well, better luck next time asshole. Oh, and a word of advice, lose the Jamaican accent. You're a white guy who wears a bowtie with a short-sleeved shirt on a first date (a blind date I may add – curse you Aunt Pamela). The only remotely tropical thing about you was the Jamaican Jerk chicken you ordered for dinner.

The second message was a crank from my nine-year-old niece, Paige. We have this thing whereby we call each other hoping to get the machine. If the person picks up, we hang up. The goal is not to talk personally, just leave funny messages on each other's machine. Sounds weird, but it's our thing and I cherish it. This morning she asked the old Chinese food joke.

"Do you have chicken balls?" she asked.

"Yes," she answered herself in a vintage nine-year-old Chinese accent.

"Then you sure must look funny!"

I'd heard the joke a thousand times, but laughed anyway. My niece, what an annoying little crack…I was teaching her well.

The third message was from my mother. She called to see if I was feeling better and said she would call back later…and oh, by the way, I needed to take a teaspoon of that "herbal one spoon cures all that ails ya" that Santa gave me in my stocking. I hadn't told her yet that my friend Vicky had mistaken the bag for weed, and smoked it on my balcony while celebrating New Year's Eve. She said it was the best stuff she'd ever had. I told her my Mom gave it to me. She thought that was cool. I'm not sure how my mother knew I'd been ill, but I suspected a certain neighbourhood post-menopausal jumpsuit wearing polyester princess was somehow involved.

The message light was still blinking. I hadn't been this popular since Grade Eight when I "borrowed" a pack of my older brother's cigarettes, brought them to school, and sold them off for a dollar a smoke. I made enough money from that pack to buy Christmas presents from the corner store for the entire family that year. The gig was up though when my parents opened their presents, realized they weren't homemade like usual, and wondered where I'd gotten the money, since I didn't have a job. So being the honest, self-conscious person I was, I told them how I sold off Tom's smokes for profit. My punishment was having to go to bed early on

14

Christmas night, which wasn't bad because Uncle Frank was over and once again, he was having serious bowel troubles. He really should see a specialist about that, even twenty years later, he can still clear a room with ease.

On the other hand, my brother Tom was grounded for New Year's Eve, which is mortifying when you're seventeen. He was furious with me. I agreed with my parents though, it was wrong for him to have had cigarettes in the first place, and second, he should not have left them where his younger, more impressionable sibling could find them. So that New Year's we all sat around playing board games. Tom pretended to sulk but I really think he had a good time, especially when he rolled Yahtzee twice in row. He still holds the family record and brags that when he dies his tombstone should read, Tom "Yahtzee Boy" Hanson. Magic Dice Roller. I think he needs more friends.

The fourth message was from my boss Mike. He needed me to be in Toronto bright and early Monday morning to cover some cold case crime story. Normally I only wrote a column for the city paper, but lately with all the cutbacks, I had to do some extra grunt work. I hated court reporting. You never knew how long the case was going to take, which always begged the questions: "What do I pack?" and "Do I need to find someone to water my plants?"

The last message was from Bobby. He had asked for my number in the cab but I never thought he'd remember it.

"Hey, it's me Bobby…I'm not sure if you remember but you said last night in the taxi that it would be okay if I called you today to see how you were. I've been a little worried, you were pretty sick. I'd hoped you were home, so I'd have known for sure you got there. I've already tried to reach you twice, but hung up before the machine came on. No offense, but I hate machines. Anyway, maybe I'll try back later."

Bobby was a sweet man. Kind, loyal and generous to a fault. I wondered what had happened with his wife and family, or if he even had one. One day, when I had enough courage, I'd ask. For now, I'd find some way to let him know I was fine. I didn't have his number; in fact, I didn't even know his last name. I found the phone book under the cabinet and looked up the number for Wilkins Place. I called and asked for a guy named Bobby. The girl knew exactly who I meant.

"He's not here yet. Never shows up until around seven p.m. on Sunday nights. Some meetin' he goes to or something. Can I take a message?"

I was a little embarrassed at having to leave a message for someone whom I considered a friend, at a bar, but this was Wilkins Place. It was different.

"Thanks that would be great. Tell him Alex called and I'm fine. Thank him for his message."

"Sure thing."

"Oh, can you also tell him that I'll be out of town for a while on business, but somehow I'll track him down when I get back."

"You Bobby's girl or something?"

"No, no, no...just a friend."

"Alrighty, bye, bye Alex."

"Bye."

I hung up the phone in silence. Bobby's girl? I hoped Bobby didn't feel that way. I'm sure he didn't. It's not that I couldn't fall for someone like him, in time. It was just...he was so much older than me in so many ways. Almost from a different era. No, Bobby and I would only ever be friends. I would love him though. Like a big brother. Not in a deep unconditional way like I loved "Yahtzee Boy", but in a warm and comforting way. Like a soft, cotton blanket. The kind you wrap around your shoulders at a campfire. The blanket not only keeps out the cold, but makes you feel secure. No monsters can get you now, you're safe. That was my Bobby.

I dialed my parents place. It rang five times. I assumed either my mother was out or had her hands full. My father was probably watching television. The phone was on the table beside him. I could picture the situation.

"Margaret, the phone's ringing!"

"I'm busy, can't you get it?"

"I can't reach it."

"Oh for God's sake, just a minute..."

"Hurry Margie, it's already rung five times. They might think we're not home and hang up."

"Hello!"

"Hi Mom, it's me."

"Oh hi darling."

"Everything all right there?"

"Oh sure, I was just re-potting that Boston fern. You know the one Aunt Sophie gave me when I spent the night in the hospital because that corn on my left foot got infected."

"Yes I remember the one...and Dad?"

"Apparently your father's arms have become too short to reach over and pick up the phone. By the way how are you feeling? That wonderful neighbor of yours, Mrs. Jones called me this morning and said that I might want to check on you. Said you had a rough night in the toilet. Was it only vomiting or did you have diarrhea too? Did you take the herbs...I'm sure they'll help..."

I took the phone away from my ear. She would be on the herb thing for at least another five minutes. I wondered what last night's lottery numbers were. That'd be great if I'd won.

"What's that Mom? Yes, I'm paying attention...look I just called to tell you that I'm leaving tonight for Toronto. Mike needs me to cover a story. I don't know how long I'll be gone."

"Do you need me to water the plants?"

"I'm not sure yet, I'll let you know."

"Okay, have a safe drive...what's that Sam? Oh...your father says hello."

I could hear my dad in the background. "She's probably sick because she drank too much...ha, ha, ha...remember the time she threw up at your cousin's wedding...that was a riot!"

"Yes Sam, we all remember...Alex has to go."

"Bye Mom."

"Bye Alex."

The truth was I didn't remember the wedding very much. I was sixteen and my brother thought it would be fun to keep feeding me drinks. Payback for selling the smokes I guess. It was the first time I had anything stronger than that cheap "Baby Duck" wine. I think it was rye. It could have been rum. Maybe it was both. I really don't know. My mother was of course mortified. My father thought it was the funniest thing he'd ever seen. He's never let me live it down. Every time I have a glass of wine for dinner, he pretends to shield himself from the forthcoming vomit. The joke was old and stale, but I put up with because he's my dad and I love him.

As soon as I hung up the phone, it rang. It was my boss Mike. "Oh good you're home. Did you get my message?"

"Yes, I was just going to call you back. What's going on?"

"I need you in Toronto first thing tomorrow morning."

"I was going to leave tonight."

"Perfect. I'll arrange then for the hotel. Same one as usual."

"What's the background?"

Mike proceeded to explain about the case. A forty-seven year man was being tried for a murder he allegedly committed when he was eighteen years old. A female acquaintance of his was found in her car with her throat slashed. There was evidence of sexual assault. Although, he was always the primary suspect, they could never quite pin the murder on him. Now they had DNA evidence. I was positive this wasn't going to be just an overnight trip. Great. Just the way I wanted to spend the next few weeks. Living out of suitcase. Oh well, the newspaper covered all my expenses, including a few work related "stress relieving" massages. I hated sex crimes. I was going to need those massages.

By the time I had packed my clothes and gone down to the corner deli for some driving snacks, it was five. The drive would take about two hours. I turned on the television for a last minute check of the road conditions. Sunny and bare to icy sections with some snow covered. It was going to be a long drive. I grabbed a few extras CD's and thinking of my mother, I took the blanket off the couch and the candle from the table. I always carried matches in my purse.

"It's better to be safe," she'd say.

My apartment building had underground parking, so the car wasn't snowy or too cold, which was good. I hated scraping ice. Normally, I'd just hop in the car, start it up, and drive away, but ever since I'd devoted an entire Saturday to watching The Learning Channel's car care marathon, I knew better. I reviewed Lesson Six in my head; "What to do before long trips." I topped up my window washer fluids, checked my hoses, and then walked around the car eyeballing the tires, making sure the pressure looked equal on each side. Hopefully I wouldn't get a flat; I fell asleep during that part. All I needed was gas.

I filled up the tank at the local Pioneer Station, and politely asked the attractive young man to check my oil. Too bad he was only a teenager. I myself hadn't had a good oil change in a while. Luke had been gone since last February. He didn't have to take the job in England, but he did. My girlfriends kept trying to set me up, but I loathed dating, especially blind ones, and after my "Jamaican man" I was put off even more.

"She's all lubed up and ready to go ma'am."

"You bet she is," I said under my breath.

"Pardon me ma'am?"

"Oh no...nothing. How much do I owe you?"

"Thirty-five even."

I handed him the money, then secretly peeked in the rear view mirror and watched him walk away.

"Nice ass. Momma like! Momma like!" I laughed at my own inappropriateness and started up the car. Sometimes I was just so damn funny I couldn't stand it. The Bay City Rollers were blaring on the stereo as I hit the highway. Maybe the trip wasn't going to be that bad after all. I had music, a hot coffee, and doughnuts. Life was good.

CHAPTER TWO

The trial was taking forever. It was already February 11, and I had been gone for two and a half weeks. Not that I had an overly exciting life awaiting me at home, I was just tired of hotel living. Tired of eating out. Tired of sleeping in a bed that didn't conform perfectly to my body. I longed for my pink housecoat and my mug. I guess I could have driven home on the weekends, but it seemed like such a waste of time. At least the defense was scheduled to give their closing arguments tomorrow. This man was so guilty, and the defense team was running out of options. They'd spent three whole days trying to convince the jury the evidence had been tampered with, which therefore meant the DNA might not be correct. Hello? I'd already watched this "trial of the century" years ago on CNN. But if that defense worked for OJ Simpson, why not Hector Long? Money could buy acquittals.

Hector Long sat there so smug at the defense table, casually whispering in his lawyers' ear, while his disillusioned wife sat in the family chairs. With all the hard evidence pouring out from the prosecution, you could tell her undying support for her husband was wavering. The empty beer bottle found in the back seat of the victim's car with his prints on it. His total fabrication of an alibi for that evening. His semen found on the victim. He admitted to having had sex with her, but the medical examiner's photographs showed it was a little more than sex.

The kicker came when the victim's sister was on the stand. She described in detail a missing necklace her sister had been wearing the night she was murdered. I was watching Hector's wife closely. During the description of the necklace, she slowly brought her hand to her neck, her face contorting in a creepy and discomforting way. She looked at her husband, her brow wrinkled in confusion, and then she looked away. The next day the prosecution announced the necklace had been found and entered into evidence. It was the smoking gun. Embedded deep in the locket was a trace of blood. The victim's blood. Hector's wife never appeared in court again. It was rumored around the courthouse that she'd already put their house up for sale and filed for divorce. Their poor children.

Mike wanted to me to try and get an interview with her, but I just couldn't do it. I know it was part of my job, but the last thing this woman needed was some punk-ass reporter stampeding her with questions. "How are you feeling?" "Do you still love your husband?" I couldn't even imagine how she was feeling. Her whole life shattered in the instant realization of his guilt. The man who'd slept beside her for twenty-five years, rubbed her back when it was sore, and held her hand in church, was a rapist and a killer. It wasn't up to her to seek his redemption. He would have to face God for that. Her name was Carla. Not Hector's wife. The victim, the girl he brutally murdered...her name was Carla. Carla Channing. She was just sixteen.

Since the closing arguments ran late into Friday afternoon, the judge decided to recess until Monday morning, when he would begin his instruction to the jury. With nothing to do but sit and wait, a bunch of us decided to head to Collingwood for a little downhill skiing on the Saturday. We rented a van and drove the hour and a half north to Blue Mountain. It's not really a mountain, not like the Rockies or Appalachians, just a gigantic beautiful hill, actually part of the Niagara Escarpment, a wonder of nature, left behind by the glaciers. All of us had skied before except Douglas, a reporter from Florida. Apparently, Hector Long's parents were snowbirds and much to their dismay, their son's trial was front-page news for the "Florida Sunshine" a weekly paper catering mainly to Canadians wintering in Florida.

Douglas had never even seen snow before he flew into Toronto, let alone downhill ski. "Being such a natural athlete" as he put it, "I should be able to pick this up no problem. It looks pretty easy actually." The rest of us looked at each other and smiled.

"Let's get you fitted for boots then," I said.

We all went into the lodge and rented our equipment. Douglas was having trouble walking and he hadn't even strapped on his skis yet.

"You okay there Doug?"

"Yep, just fine...are your shins supposed to hurt this much?"

"Don't lean forward so far."

I showed him how to clip on his skis and gave a little lesson in shifting his weight and stopping properly. He wasn't interested. He told me he had played college football for the Miami Hurricanes, which apparently meant he would be an expert skier.

"Of course Douglas, I should have known."

I took off with Jill, a reporter from the Vancouver Sun, and headed for the lifts. We had a blast. After the heaviness of the last couple weeks, it felt good to be so light on your feet. Sailing down the hill, the wind whipping in your face and the snow flying in your mouth because your grin is too wide to keep it out. Feeling free. Feeling powerful.

We hadn't seen Douglas all morning. Someone said that his helplessness had attracted a blonde snow-bunny. Supposedly, they were now hippity hopping on the easy runs. I was glad he'd found a friend. After some lunch in the lodge, Jill and I were just about to jump off the lift chair when I spotted Douglas and his new friend just about to take off down the hill. Jill and I exchanged worried glances. This hill was rated the most difficult on the mountain, for advanced skiers only. Sure Douglas was a jackass, but he didn't deserve to die.

"Hey Douglas, are you sure you're ready for this hill?" Jill yelled.

He turned around, smiled with his perfect teeth, mouthed a very distinct "fuck you" to the both of us, then started down the steep slope. The cold wind had whipped up causing the hills to become quite icy. Jill and I followed Douglas just in case. He was in trouble almost from the beginning. His body was moving all over with no balance whatsoever. Then it happened. He hit an icy patch with his left ski. It went one way; his right ski went the other, which is not usually a big problem, except both skis were still attached to his feet. I thought for sure he was going to spilt in two, from the crack of his ass up. Instead of gradually trying to bring the tips of skis closer together to restore some balance, Douglas panicked and jerked his right leg in quickly. His arms and poles flailing in the air, he fell on his side, with his left leg, ski still attached, pinned underneath him. He looked like a pretzel. His bunny friend had gotten too close and Douglas took her out with his pole. If Jill and I didn't know how serious the fall was, we would have laughed hysterically. Poor Douglas slid down half the hill, in a contorted jumble.

"We'd better go see if he's all right," I said.

"I guess we should."

We headed to the disaster sight. There was a trail of blood in the snow. Doug was a mess, the side of his face bleeding from being pounded into the hill and his left leg was unquestionably broken. His bunny friend had only minor scrapes, but she cried anyway. Some ski stag heard her tears, skied over and they went off down the hill. As we watched them go, nobody knew what to say.

"And here I thought I'd found the love of my life on the Canadian slopes," Doug mumbled. "Would have made a great article." We all laughed. Ski patrol was on the way. "Alex, can you show me that lesson again on balance and stopping? I must not have been paying attention the first time."

I looked at him and smiled. It was his way of saying sorry. I forgave him, besides he had great teeth. Jill went with Doug in the ambulance and once I left a message for the others in the lodge, I followed along. Jill was in the waiting room when I got there.

"They took Doug right in. He might need surgery to place some pins in his upper left leg. He's in X-ray right now."

I went to the coffee shop, picked up two coffees and some chips. Chips are wonderful crisis food. Good thing I don't experience crises very often or my ass would be the size of Mount Kilimanjaro. My favorite kind of potato chips are plain, but every once in a while, when I really have the blues, I'll buy a big bag of sour cream and onion and gorge myself. I always regret what I've done, having such complete lack of will power, but at the time it seems like the thing to do. Dealing with gut rot is a small price to pay. It's like stealing the British Crown Jewels and only being charged with shoplifting. I could deal with it.

The chips I bought for Jill and I were plain. Sure Doug was in serious pain, but it was his own stupid self-inflicted pain not mine, and therefore didn't warrant sour cream and onion. I would save those for the next time the cable went on the blink during "The Sound of Music". I should just buy the damn video. That would instantly cut back my fat intake.

When I returned, the waiting room was packed with people. Jill was nowhere to be seen. I found an empty chair as far away from the germ-infested chaos as I could, and flipped the lid of my coffee. I didn't expect the coffee to be great. It wasn't. Once in university, a guy I knew drank a shot of cat pee for a case of beer because he was short on cash and really needed the beer. I imagined my cup of hospital brew tasted like that. The chips would be better; they were pre-packaged.

I opened the bag and looked around the waiting room. It was a kaleidoscope of medical maladies. Coughing kids with mounds of snot running out of their noses, their parents needing a pail, not a skimpy Kleenex. A middle-aged woman was holding her belly and moaning constantly. I'm sure it couldn't have been an appendicitis or the nurse would have taken her back right away. I bet she was just constipated. I recognized the pain on her face. She kept moving up and down in her chair, as if she was trying to readjust her bowel without anyone noticing. I wanted to tell her that one of Grandma's homemade bran muffins, and a very large glass of water always helped me, but that might have been a bit intrusive.

There was a young man holding a cloth over a gash on his forehead. He and his buddies thought it would be cool to toboggan through a heavily forested area while loaded up on booze. Oh to be sixteen again, when your ego screams indestructibility, and common sense is about as common as homework on a Friday night. You do things that almost get you killed, just to make your friends laugh. The problem begins when the friends start laughing at you instead of with you. The harder they laugh, the harder you try; until you do something so totally outrageous, you wind up sitting in the Emergency Room with a head wound requiring twenty stitches.

Abandoned by your chicken shit friends, you now have to come up with a brilliant and believable explanation for the doctor, who's heard it all one too many times. And because you smell like you've showered in beer, the doctor is obligated to call the police. Your night finishes with an escorted walk to your parent's front door by two very burly uniformed men. As soon as the doorbell rings, you know you're dead. I don't miss being sixteen at all.

Across from the dazed teenager, a mother was holding the sweetest little girl. She was lying like a Raggedy Anne doll, draped in her mother's arms, her crystal blue eyes trying to stay open but gravity forcing them down. Her mother held a wet towel on her forehead and every once and awhile, the little girl would quiver, her body trying to defend itself against the viral intruder. My heart ached for her. She never made a fuss or cried out. She glanced over at the moaning lady and gave her a look as if to say, "lady get a grip, it's only a really big turd!"

The nurse came out with her clipboard. "Mrs. Polarski, you're next."

"That's me...Could you please help me nurse. My stomach hurts so much...I can't stand up straight."

The nurse hid a frown as she grabbed the moaning woman under the arm and helped her to the back. I looked over at the little girl and smiled. She smiled back. At least now, the waiting room was relatively quiet. I spotted Jill walking down the hall and waved.

"Where have you been?" I asked.

"I went to the washroom and then to the gift shop...oh good she's still here."

Jill pulled a stuffed bear from a gift bag and handed it to the little girl, her face brightening as she snuggled the bear against her chest. The mother smiled a thank-you, and the little girl seemed more energetic than I'd seen her. It didn't last long. A quick but weak, "Mommy I'm going to be sick," escaped from her mouth. Her mother lunged for the pail and brought it under the little girls' mouth just in time. Jill leaned over and whispered in my ear.

"I overheard the mother talking to the nurse before you got here. The little girl has leukemia and is having a negative reaction to one of the drugs."

"Why didn't they take her right away?" I asked.

"I guess she's not considered an emergency." Jill answered.

"How is that fair? She sits out here and waits while people who've inflicted their own pain get priority? It just isn't right."

I know a hospital has to have policies, but come on. I looked at the sweet little girl again. Her mother had finished cleaning her up and was now hugging her tightly, rubbing her back. She pulled back her daughter's hair and kissed her on the neck. A very large lump started to form in the back of my throat and I was suddenly having trouble swallowing. I closed my eyes against the impending burn, but a small droplet of water managed to squeeze itself out and slowly dribble down my cheek. I carefully wiped it away. I didn't want anyone to see I was crying, especially the little girl. I put my head down and took a very deep breath. Inhale, exhale, inhale, exhale. It wasn't going to work. I needed to get out of there before I really burst a pipe.

"Hey Jill, I'm going to get some more chips."

"But there's already a bag here."

"Ya I know, but I suddenly have a craving for sour cream and onion."

I walked to the vending machine and bought my chips. I lingered on the way back, taking time to compose myself. The water in the drinking fountain washed away the lump, and feeling much better, I walked back to the waiting room. The little girl was now sitting on the chair beside her mother, playing with Jill's bear.

"Are you feeling better now?" she asked me, "Mommy said you left 'cause maybe you weren't feeling well."

"I'm feeling much better, how about you?"

"Ya, me too. Sometimes I just need to throw up and then I feel better."

I knew exactly how she felt. Jill and the mother were talking.

"She's in remission but keeps having a reaction to this one drug. The doctors told us to bring her right in if she has a fever or starts feeling poorly. Other than that, they say Molly's doing quite well."

I opened my sour cream and onion chips. Molly looked at me.

"Mommy my tummy is feeling much better now. I think it's a bit hungry since it threwed all that stuff up."

I looked at Molly's mom and gestured with my bag of chips. She shrugged her shoulders as if to say why not. I guess when your kid has been through the hell that Molly has so far in her life, a few sour cream and onion chips weren't going to cause any more harm. I went and sat in the empty seat and held the bag open.

"Do you think your tummy would feel better if it had a few chips?" I asked her.

"I think it might…it might just do the trick," she said with such a serious look on her face, I couldn't help but laugh. She was a very bright and articulate little girl.

Molly and I passed the time eating the sour cream and onion chips and playing with the bear. Thankfully, some of the colour returned to her little cheeks. Suddenly, from beyond the waiting room, there was a flurry of activity. Someone was moaning wildly. There was a scurrying of footsteps followed by the slamming of a door. A long silent pause ensued. I looked at Molly and she looked at me. Shattering the pause was the longest piercing wail I'd ever heard - like a wild dog who'd been shot with an arrow. An apparent rapid explosion of several sticks of dynamite followed, ending with a huge sigh.

Dead silence filled the waiting room. No one wanted to be the first to move or talk. Eyes were searching out other eyes in acknowledgment of the event they'd all witnessed. It was sweet little Molly who spoke first. She could hardly get the words out over her giggling.

"I betcha that lady feels a whole lot better."

"Molly, shh, that isn't nice," her mother scolded, but really she was laughing too.

In fact, the whole room started to snicker. I put my hand on Molly's knee and whispered in her ear.

"I betcha she does too!"

Molly looked deep into my eyes, covering her laughing mouth with her hand. I couldn't help but love this girl and I'd only known her for a couple of hours. She showed me the simplicity of life in a complicated world. She never felt sorry for herself, never complained, just took what life gave her, and did the best she could. I never ate a full bag of sour cream and onion chips again. The happy memory of that afternoon with Molly wouldn't let me. I would eat a few and then remember Molly giggling because Mrs. Polarski blew her drawers. It always made me laugh, and once I started to laugh, I realized the huge thing I was stressed about, really wasn't that big at all. Molly became my reality check.

Finally, the nurse came out and called for Molly and her mother. As they walked to the back, Molly turned around and gave Jill and I a little wave. Then they were gone. A few hours later, Douglas came limping down the hall with crutches. He had a gleaming white cast from the top of his left leg, all the way down to his toes. Strangely, I was happy to see him. We gathered his stuff from the nurse and helped him out to the van. Poor guy was obviously hopped up on some pretty serious drugs. I felt a pang of envy. The nurse said that he'd probably be sleepy for quite some time, so Jill and I decided to take Doug back to the city that night. Jill called the rest of our ski group at the lodge. They'd already booked rooms to stay the night and were going to catch one of the many shuttle buses back to the city in the morning. It was just as well. I was tired and didn't feel like a lot of noisy commotion. As I pulled out of the hospital parking lot, Douglas was fast asleep in his makeshift bed and Jill was humming to the radio.

"You hungry?" I asked.

"I could eat."

"Sub sound good?"

"Absolutely"

There was a sub shop just before we hit the highway. Jill and I both ordered small assorted with no onions, and we picked up a large roast beef sub for Doug in case he woke up hungry. I desperately needed a cup of tea, but I hated take-out tea in a paper cup, so I scanned the roadside like a hawk searching for rabbits, hoping to spot a coffee shop.

"Over there!" Jill screeched.

I swerved into the turn lane and hit the left blinker. In five short minutes, we were on the highway, gleefully sipping steaming cups of hot Tim Horton's coffee between bites of our subs.

"Do I smell coffee?" said a dazed voice from the back seat.

Jill carefully handed Doug a medium double-double over the seat. In a little less than two and a half hours, I would be in my pajama's watching T.V. in my hotel room bed. I wondered how Molly was. I bet she wore snuggly flannel jammies with little bears on them. She had good taste.

Still feeling the wonderful effects of the happy juice the hospital gave him, Douglas didn't make it to court on Monday morning. Both Jill and I said we'd help him out with his report back to the paper. The judge finished instructing the jury just before 4 pm and immediately sent them off to start their deliberations. Now the real waiting began. You had to stay relatively close by because the jury could come back with a verdict at any moment. Good thing the hotel was only a few blocks from the courthouse. I was hoping to get in a good massage while I was waiting. I could have sailed to Sweden and back for my massage, the bloody jury took so long. Rumor had it there was one hold out who doubted Hector Long's guilt. What the hell was that all about? A guilty verdict was pretty clear-cut to me. Hang the fucker by the balls and let him rot. Finally, on the seventh morning as we were all milling about the hotel lobby, the word came down that the verdict was in. I quickly pulled out my cell to give Mike a heads up.

"Hey Mike it's me, the verdict is being read at 11:00 am."

"Good, I'll tell the guys to save tomorrow's' front page. After you tie up the loose ends, why don't you come home? The sentencing probably won't be for at least another week or two."

I wasn't going to object. "I should be home by dinner. I'll call you when I get home and fill you in on the details."

"Nah, don't bother, just e-mail me the story like usual and I'll see you in the morning. I think you need a night without having to think about Hector Long."

"Thanks Mike, see you tomorrow."

I didn't want to tell him that I hadn't really thought about Hector Long at all. Not him personally. I'd thought about his victim Carla Channing and the effects this whole trial was having on her family some twenty years after the murder had taken place. I thought about Hector's wife, their children, and even his parents, but no, I hadn't thought of Hector Long. He didn't deserve the effort.

A stern looked etched its way on the judge's face as the jury filed back into the courtroom and for the first time, Hector seemed a little nervous. After the usual preamble, the jury foreman nodded yes and read the verdict.

"Guilty on all charges."

A roar erupted from the gallery, hugs, and kisses all around. Hector slumped in his chair, his head falling forward. There was nobody there to comfort him except his lawyers, but they were too busy consoling themselves. This would be a dark blotch on their legal careers.

"You want to grab a beer?" I heard one of the defense lawyers ask.

"Ya sure…why not? We're done here." The two of them walked out of the courtroom, as guards threw shackles around Hector's wrists and ankles.

For him, it would be life in prison. Is that really enough punishment? He'll get three meals a day, physical activity and a chance to educate himself through prison resources like books and computers. Our society offers Hector more security than it does the working poor. Those law-abiding citizens work two or three jobs at a time, struggle just to get food and a place to stay, but I guess that's the price to pay for freedom. Hector will never again hear the waves lap gently against the shoreline or follow a butterfly as far as he could through a field. Then again, neither will Carla Channing. I hope she haunts Hector Long every night in his sleep. I would.

As I drove home that afternoon, my mind drifted to Bobby. I wondered if any of the guys at Wilkins Place had ever been in trouble with the law. I'm sure some of them have had a few brush-ups, but I meant something serious. Some of those guys were perennial drifters. I prayed there wasn't any Hectors' lurking in the group. You just never really knew. Hector was just a regular guy living a normal life until he got caught. I shivered at the thought.

After stopping for some much needed groceries, I pulled into the underground parking at five o'clock on the button. Needing the exercise after the long drive, I used the stairs instead of the elevator. With my arms full of luggage and plastic bags, I unlocked my apartment door and kicked it open.

"Let me help you with those."

"Oh thanks Mr. Jones, I'd appreciate it."

"It's good to have you back. We missed seeing you!"

"I missed seeing you and Mrs. Jones as well." I wasn't lying. In some strange way, I did miss them. They represented a part of my life that was comfortable and not complicated. I didn't have to share my soul with them, at least not Mr. Jones, if I didn't want to. Sometimes idle chatter could be your best friend.

"Just set them on the table there if you don't mind."

"Sure thing. That was certainly a long trial! We were following your reports in the paper every day. Heard on the radio he was found guilty, the slimy little bugger!" I laughed. Leave it to Mr. Jones not to mince any words. I agreed with him though.

"By the way, you had a nice young gentleman stop by to see you...said his name was Luke. I told him you were away, but I've been checking your door and the hallways at night, just in case he tried to come back when you weren't there. He seemed like a pretty good fella. Looked sort of like that guy who used to come around. Haven't seen him lately..."

Luke? What the fuck was he doing here? He's supposed to be in England. Not a call in over twelve months and he shows up at my door? Great, just what I needed. My life was finally beginning without him and now this. I didn't want to see him. I didn't want to reconcile.

"Thanks, Mr. Jones. I recognize the name, so you don't have to worry. Everything's fine."

"Well you just let me know if he gives you any problems at all...I know karate!"

Both of us laughed and as he walked out the door, Mr. Jones turned around and gave me a smile. I closed the door behind him and went into the kitchen to put away the groceries. Hearing about Luke made me lose my appetite. I needed some tea in my special mug. While waiting for the kettle, I went into my bedroom to unpack. My bed looked like a little piece of heaven, so inviting, just willing me to come and lay in it. A quick dump of my suitcase into the clothes hamper, made unpacking quick and simple. It was just easier that way. With the kettle whistling my favorite song, I turned and gave my bed a pat.

"I'll see you in a few minutes...I promise."

I performed my sacred tea making ritual, pouring the perfect amount of milk into the mug with one swish. Something made me hesitate bringing the liquid to my lips. The setting wasn't right. I walked back to my bedroom, put the mug on the nightstand, and stripped naked. Reaching far into the back of my bottom drawer, I retrieved my special pajamas; the ones I saved for special occasions, like watching "Bridget Jones" or "Grease". I carefully put my legs through the pant holes, making sure I didn't catch the holes in the knees with my toes. The flannel was a little worn around the cuffs, but generally, they were still in good shape. Not good enough for sex mind you, but good enough for girl time with Bridget. I'm sure she had a pair as well. Luke always cringed when I pulled out the "special me pajamas". He knew he'd have better luck pulling a sliver out of his finger with pliers than he would with me that night. I should have worn my "special me pajamas" more often. It would have served the bastard right.

I closed my bedroom blinds, turned on the television, and opened my collection of DVD's.

"Hmmm...Bridget Jones' Diary, Grease, Notting Hill, When Harry Met Sally, Pretty Woman, Shrek, The Thomas Crown Affair...hmm Pierce Brosnan's naked butt in that one...Saving Private Ryan..."

They were all worthy of watching, but given my fairly recent singledom, I chose "Bridget Jones' Diary" to bring warmth and happiness to my night. I popped it in the DVD player, dove for my covers, and wrestled the remote control until we were both safely snuggled underneath my over-sized, over-stuffed duvet. It took nearly five minutes before all my pillows were properly positioned for maximum viewing pleasure. I reached for my mug, held it firmly in my right hand like a long lost friend, then pressed play. Shit, I forgot to pee! I quickly pressed pause, put down my mug and ran to the bathroom. I'd rather force any pee out now than have to really go in the middle of the movie. It's like when you were little and your parents always made you go to the washroom before you set foot in the car.

"We're not stopping!" Dad would emphasize, even though he'd be the one that had to pee thirty minutes into the trip, and men do not know how to hold it. We'd calmly be driving along, and suddenly Dad would swoop across four lanes of traffic and onto the shoulder of the road like he had just witnessed the second coming of Christ. My mother would panic.

"Sam what's wrong...Do you have chest pains...Are you going to faint?"

"No, I have to pee."

Meanwhile, my sister and I could be in the backseat complaining for an hour that we had to go and he'd just keep on driving. The world is a man's toilet. Anywhere, anytime, anyplace. They never need toilet paper. Just shake it and bake it, and they were ready to roll. I suppose I could have peed on the side of the road like the boys, but every time I tried, no matter how hard I tried, I always ended up peeing down my leg and soaking my sock. I learned early on in life that severe stomach cramps were way better than having a pee-soaked sock. I think I probably had the strongest bladder in the city.

Having completed my bathroom duties, I climbed back into bed to watch my movie. It was six thirty. I wouldn't have to move again until eight. The perfect way to spend an evening. I had such a good time watching the first movie; I decided to make it an all-night affair. Watching Bridget spurn that egotistical rogue Daniel Cleaver made me hungry, so before I selected the next flick I made myself some dinner. At least this time I had some real food to work with. I boiled some noodles, grabbed a can of pasta sauce from the cupboard, and dumped it into the other pot on the stove. I added some sliced mushrooms, onions and a pinch of basil. As I cooked, I sang an Italian Opera song about a girl cooking pasta on a snowy February night. The composer was brilliant. All the words rhymed and the way the music flowed brought tears to my eyes. I should give up the newspaper business and move to Milan to become an operatic composer. If I could make it in my kitchen, damn it, I could make it anywhere.

A loud banging on the wall rudely interrupted my lyrical reverie. I guess my next-door neighbors didn't appreciate my musical abilities. I kept singing, but I lowered my volume and brought my glorious voice down an octave. My evening wasn't going to be ruined by a rowdy audience. I took a large sip from the bottle of red wine I'd opened, and stirred the sauce. I couldn't help but sing in homemade Italian when cooking Italian. The same thing happened when I cooked Chinese. I wasn't mocking the cultures, just the opposite. I wanted to emulate their way of life in as many ways as I could; food, song and sometimes even dance. I made sure that I was always alone during these cultural demonstrations.

With my dinner cooked and the kitchen semi-cleaned up, I headed back to my personal movie theater, with my meal perfectly laid out on the very large T.V. tray I used for such occasions. I had my bowl of pasta, knife, fork, crusty roll, tossed salad from a bag and a tall glass of grape juice. I forced myself to trade in the red wine for the juice since I had to work in the morning. It was a complete gourmet meal for one. Of course, I had enough left over pasta sitting in the fridge to feed all of Italy, but that was beside the point.

In keeping with the romantic comedy theme, I chose Notting Hill for my second movie. I just loved British movies. They're always extremely charming and witty, much like me. I carefully climbed back into bed, balancing my tray in front of me, and settled down to enjoy my dinner and a movie. It was delicious. I was just sopping up the remaining sauce with my crusty roll when the phone rang. I was going to let the machine take it, but habit forced me to pick up the receiver.

"Hello?" I surprised myself with how cheerful I was.

"Hi Alex, it's Luke." My heart sank but I wasn't going to let him know that. I had watched enough movies tonight to pick up a few acting tips.

"Luke, how are you? It's been a long time." Knowing full well that he was in town, I forced the issue. "What time is there in England? It must be late." I muffled a sarcastic laugh.

"I'm good. I'm not in England anymore though."

"Oh ya, where are you?"

"Actually, I'm standing outside your door," he answered.

"No kidding, you're serious?"

"I didn't want to totally shock you by just showing up, so I decided to call first and see if you were there. Now that I'm outside your door, you can't leave without seeing me or letting me in."

"Luke I could live in my apartment for weeks without ever leaving. You should know that."

"C'mon Alex, let me in. I need to talk to you."

"Luke I really don't have anything to say to you. You made your choice and I've moved on. Let's leave it at that."

"I'm getting married."

I almost regurgitated my pasta. I swallowed hard to regain my composure. "That's great Luke. I'm happy for you."

"Please let me in Alex, I need to explain."

"There's nothing to explain Luke. You went away, fell in love, and now you're getting married. It happens all the time."

"There's more," he replied. What the hell else could there be? Unless he was getting married to a man. Now that would make my day.

"I'm going to be a father," he said silently.

"You're WHAT!" I couldn't help it. I hung up the phone, ran from my room and threw open the front door. "You son of a bitch!" I slapped his face as hard as I could. "So that was the problem then...that's why you left...you obviously just didn't want to have kids with me."

He tried to plead his case, but I wasn't listening. I had dedicated three years of my life to him. My entire future was OUR future, until one day he informed me that he'd changed his mind about being a father. I was devastated. There was no point in me staying with a man who didn't see children as a vital part of his tomorrow. I never felt the same way about him. I still loved him, but I felt very cheated.

It was like two people training together for years to compete in a triathlon. They swim the lake side-by-side, cycle the road wheel to wheel, then one of them suddenly decides to quit before running the marathon, leaving the other one standing there, totally shocked and flabbergasted. To make matters worse, the next year the quitter decides to run the race with someone else and while they're hitting the last leg of the race, you're still trying to build up enough courage to swim across the lake. I was furious. Not so much at Luke, although if I thought I could get away with it, he might enjoy a ride down the garbage chute. I was angry with myself for letting my heart get broken again. When was it going to end?

"Babe, I didn't mean for this to happen."

"Fuck off Luke and get out of my apartment."

"Alex, I'm sorry...I'm not going to leave until I know you're okay. Look I didn't necessarily want this baby either, but it happened and I'm going to be responsible towards it and its' mother."

"Oh isn't that very noble of you." I could feel my voice begin to quiver so I turned away before Luke could see the tears forming in my once happy eyes.

"Alex...please."

"Seriously, Luke please go."

"I want you to meet her."

"Meet who?"

"Christa, the baby's mother."

"You're insane Luke." I didn't care anymore. I needed this conversation to be over immediately, so I turned around and pushed him out the door. He was surprised and his expression reflected his hurt.

"Goodbye Luke." I carefully closed, not slammed, the door in his face.

As much as I wanted to, slamming the door would have been immature and I was a grown up sophisticated lady. It wasn't until I was sure that he'd entered the elevator that I re-opened the door and slammed it shut. I was such an idiot! The last thing I wanted was for Luke to see me break down because that would mean that I still cared, which I didn't.

Suddenly I didn't feel like being alone. I looked at the clock, ten after nine. Vicki was on a date and it was too late to call anyone else. I just didn't feel like watching my happy ending romantic comedy anymore. My "special me" moment had been ruined. I needed to go out. Anywhere, a walk, a drive...no I'd had enough driving today. I'd go for a walk. I headed back to my bedroom to change clothes. I tossed my "special me pajamas" back in the drawer and threw on some jeans and my favorite gray hoody. I took the phone off the hook. That way if my mother called, she'd think I was home, and not out walking the streets alone in the dark. It's not like I had a curfew. I could go out by myself and come home as late as I wanted. Even though it was nobody's business what I did, I still didn't want my mother to know. The ensuing lecture would be hell. She'd want to know why I needed to go out that late for a walk. I'd lie about Luke. She'd know I was lying and force the truth out of me. I'd start to cry again and need another walk to calm down. It was a vicious circle, and one I desperately wanted to avoid. I put on my trusty parka and snow boots. As I headed out the door, I grabbed my safety flashlight...just in case.

Luckily, Mr. Jones wasn't patrolling the hallway, and I was able to sneak out undetected. It was a crystal clear night. The sky was a pinkish yellow reflection of the city alive below it. I wasn't quite sure of where to walk, so I just starting walking. It's funny how your sub-conscious seems to lead you in directions your conscious mind would never think to go, because before I knew it, I was standing in front of Wilkins Place. I peeked in the window. It was hopping with the usual crowd of misfits and mulligans. Tonight I didn't even hesitate; I yanked the door open and purposefully strolled right in.

"It's our spewing Cinderella. How the hell are ya darlin'"

I wasn't offended in the least; in fact, I started to laugh. "I'm fine...no actually I'm great. I missed you guys...a lot."

"We missed you too," said Bobby. He came up beside me and put his arm on mine. I gave him a shoulder-to-shoulder hug.

"Did you get the message I left for you?" I asked.

"Sure did, Betsy gave it to me straight away. I've never even asked ya. What do you do for a livin' that would take you out of town on such short notice?"

"I'm a columnist, moonlighting as a reporter for the paper. I was out of town covering a murder trial."

"Ya?...I get the paper....don't read it much though."

"Why's that?" I asked.

"I don't know...guess I sorta lost interest a while back. Maybe now, I'll start to read them again, since I know one of the reporters!" he grinned.

"Well don't start reading the paper because of me. I'm really not that good."

"Don't believe her for a second Bobby," Big Dave chimed in. "I read all those stories about that Hector Long guy. She's good, very good."

I made a silly face to hide my embarrassment. I never felt that comfortable getting compliments. "Thanks Dave."

"What was the verdict anyway?" Dave inquired.

"Guilty."

There was a collective sigh of relief from the guys in the bar. Had they been the jury, I would have been home in a day. Some of the names they called Hector Long weren't even in my vocabulary, and I have been known at times to have a serious case of trucker mouth. We talked about the trial for quite a while. The boys all wanted to know what he "really" looked like, about the victim and her family, but they especially wanted to know the graphic details of the crime. They seemed to think that the public was being kept in the dark about certain aspects of the trial. I assured them they had access to the same information I did. I was badgered for over an hour, but I didn't mind. It felt good. They genuinely seemed interested not only in my opinion, but in me as a person. That hadn't happened in a long time.

The jovial atmosphere at the bar almost made me forget about Luke and his love child. Obviously, Luke wasn't the man for me. If it were meant to be, then, I would have been the one to get pregnant, not Christa, or whatever her name was. I promised myself from then on I wasn't going to be bitter. Everything happens for a reason, and I guess my time just hadn't arrived yet. That realization didn't make my heart ache any less, but instead of being heartbroken over Luke, I was heartbroken over me.

My life was like a giant landscape puzzle, the one with a thousand pieces. I'd spent my childhood finding all the straight edge pieces and putting them together to form the shell of the puzzle. My teens filled in the varying degrees of blue-sky portions, with the occasional gray thunderstorms of teenage angst. My college days were the golden hues of prairie wheat blowing freely; their upright stocks standing tall, fiercely proud of their independence. Now in my early thirty's, I was searching for the foundation pieces for the stone century home that would stand as the focal point of the puzzle. I thought I had laid the groundwork pieces with Luke, but when I looked closely at the shapes of the pieces I was putting together, I realized that the fit just wasn't right.

When two perfect pieces are joined, they snap together, their bonds secure. You can try to pound and hammer those two pieces down, but if the shapes don't match, there's no connection. Sometimes you even try and gloss over the mistake, by adding other matching pieces to the two you tried to hammer down, but eventually that too comes back to haunt you. At the end of your life, all the pieces have to connect. They all have to match. Hopefully the frame you started building from birth is full, each piece dependent on the other. One cohesive unit that can stand on its own. Perhaps one day the landscape puzzle will hang on your granddaughter's wall; a testament to the truth that yes, it is possible to have a life where all the pieces fit. I didn't want my puzzle to end up as a broken mess on someone's floor. I would wait until I found that matching piece, even if it took a lifetime.

That's the good thing about puzzles. You can never finish a really big one in a single day, no matter how hard you try. You leave it set up on a table in the back of a room somewhere and every time you walk by, you try to fit a few more pieces in. If none fit that day, you try again tomorrow and you keep trying until you get it right. Only a sore loser gets frustrated and puts the puzzle back in the box. I wasn't a sore loser. Maybe instead of focusing so much on the foundation of my house, I'd go back and work on the wheat section. Eventually, the wheat had to lead back to the house. By then, I'd be ready for it.

I picked up my ginger ale from the table and toasted it gently to the sky. "Here's to washing away my heartache and fixing the pieces of my puzzle."

I closed my eyes and tipped the glass to my lips. As the ginger ale poured down my throat, I could feel my heartache ease. The fire that had raged in my blood only a few hours earlier, became a river of calm and transcendence. I sighed and looked around the bar. Nobody had witnessed my moment of meditation. Big Dave and Bobby were too busy hula dancing, while Fredo, a new bar recruit just in from god knows where, was chanting something indeterminable in his own special language. It was a sight to see. No, my toast was only for me. It was a cleansing of the past and a salute to the future. My future.

Feeling much better, I decided to head home. I waved to Bobby and Big Dave who seemed to be enjoying themselves immensely. I would learn how to do that, to find fun and amusement in the smallest things. I'm sure it couldn't be that hard, the boys made it look so easy. Walking home, I realized how good it felt to finally be free of Luke. After he'd left for England, I'd convinced myself I was fine, and it was for the best. Today I understood it really was for the best, and for the first time in a while, I had a jump in my step. A sudden and very compelling urge to sing opera almost overwhelmed my senses, but I held them in check and began to whistle instead.

Reaching the front door to my building, I tried to leap up the stairs two at a time. Forgetting it was the end of February, and not July, I hit the icy steps and fell flat on my ass. As I lay back, unhurt in the snow bank that cushioned my fall, I started to laugh out loud. A man and woman walking by looked at me like I was drunk, crazy or both. I played the part and gave them a goofy smile, to which they immediately turned their heads in disgust. I laughed even harder. I didn't feel like going inside yet, so I stayed in the snow bank and watched the world go by. Even with the city lights blazing, the stars managed to shine through. They were brilliant. I watched until the wetness of the snow soaked straight through my pants, triggering my bladder. I hated to go inside, but nature called and I had about five minutes to answer or I'd be dealing with a natural disaster. I took one last deep breath of fresh night air, held it in my lungs as long as I could, then bounded up the steps on route to my apartment.

CHAPTER THREE

I just made it to the toilet on time. One more second and I would have had yellow socks, which really wouldn't have mattered since I was already soaked to the bone. Even though I was cozy on the inside, I felt chilled and hopped in the shower to warm up. Safe again in my pink housecoat, I went to the kitchen for a drink. As I passed the phone, I placed it back on the receiver. It rang immediately.

"Hello?"

"Alex, who have you been talking to, I've been trying to get through for hours." It was my friend Vicki.

"Sorry... before I went out for a walk I took the receiver off the hook."

"Your Mother?"

"Ya, I didn't want to hear the lecture. What's up?" I asked.

"Oh my God...are you sitting down? Luke's home. I saw him downtown with some girl."

"I know Vicki...he's already been to my apartment. He's getting married to that girl because she's having his baby."

"Shut Up! Are you okay? What did he say?"

"It's a long story and frankly right now I'd rather not talk about. What are doing for dinner tomorrow?"

"Are you kidding? Nothing now. I'll be over after work. Should I bring some wine? Or do you have any of that stuff your Mom gave you."

I laughed, "No…you smoked the entire bag at New Years' remember."

"No…not really. That's too bad. It was good shit!"

"See you after work Vic."

"Alright, bye."

I'd known Vicki since Kindergarten when we were both in Ms. Dennis' class. Vicki was a frequent visitor to the center of the circle. Growing up, she always had to be the center of attention, with teachers, other girls, and especially the boys. I think that's probably why we were such good friends. As a piece of my puzzle, we connected perfectly. She made me do crazy fun things that I would never do on my own, and I held her back from doing crazy, stupid things that might land her in a serious mess.

Once when we were nine, I had to stay inside for recess because of the flu, and Vicki got herself in a heap of trouble. She always had this golden blond hair that flowed in bouncy curls all the way down her back. It was her parents pride and joy. Vicki could have cared less about her hair. At lunchtime, she'd complain about how her hair would gravitate towards her peanut butter sandwich and stick there. She was forever pulling long blond hairs out of her mouth. It became a sadistic playground game to take bets on how many times we'd have to stop the game we were playing so Vicki could fix her hair. She hated it and tried everything she could to ruin it, but most times, I would step in and stop her.

"Vicki, your parents will kill you."

"So what? I don't care."

"But you'll get grounded and won't be able to sleep over on Saturday night."

"Shoot! You're right."

Usually, I'd dissolve the situation before it got out of hand, but since I was inside sick, this time Vicki was on her own. In the playground after lunch, she passed out a pack of bubble gum and bet a handful of boys that she could blow a bigger bubble than they could. Of course, they all accepted. As the bubbles grew larger, Vicki burst them by throwing her head into the bubbles. Before the boys knew what was going on, all the bubbles had been popped and Vicki looked like Medusa, her hair stuck all over the place. Horrified, I watched the events unfold through the classroom window.

Vicki was walking around proud as punch of her accomplishment. The boys took off running as soon as they'd realized what had happened, and when the lunch bell rang, Vicki strutted inside, calmly took off her coat, and sat at her desk like normal. The teacher walked in the room reading a piece of paper and didn't notice. It wasn't until she told us all to settle down that she looked up from her paper and saw Vicki. She gasped. If it hadn't been for her glasses, her eyeballs would have exploded and flown across the room, quite possibly getting stuck in Vicki's hair.

"Vicki, what have you done?" the teacher asked.

Perfect at navigating through difficult situations, Vicki answered, "I'm not sure what you mean, Mrs. Garret."

"Your hair!"

"Oh, is there something wrong with it?"

The entire class started to howl. Vicki looked triumphant, sitting regally in her chair. She glanced over at me and smiled and I couldn't help but smile back. She had done it. In a way, I was proud of her but I was also glad I'd nothing to do with it. Mrs. Garret called the office and said she was sending Vicki down. As she left the room, Vicki gave her sticky tangled locks a swish, but they were too stuck together to move. The class laughed even harder.

When I called her that night, her mom said she was grounded and wasn't allowed to come to the phone. The next day, Vicki showed up for our walk to school with her hair so short you could see her scalp in some places.

"Holy crap Vicki, what did your parents say?"

"They were so mad. I think my father cried." She repressed a giggle. "My mom took me to the hairdresser's right away for an emergency appointment. She was so embarrassed. Since everybody was staring at me, I waved at the people in the waiting room as she pulled me to the back. I felt like a celebrity. It was great! She tried just cutting the gum out, but it was so sticky, the lady ended up shaving my head with an electric razor. It felt cool. Half way through, the lady asked my mother if she wanted a glass of water because her face was very pale and sickly looking."

"What's your punishment? Are you grounded for life?" I asked.

"Well, I'm not allowed to use the phone and I have to come home straight after school for a month, no friends over or anything."

"That sucks." Now I asked her the all-important question. "Was it worth it?"

"Absolutely! It'll take years before it grows that long again. By that time, I'll be a teenager and will be able to do whatever I want. It was the perfect plan."

We laughed at her brilliance all the way to school. That was Vicki, always getting into trouble. Most of the time it wasn't serious and we could laugh about it. That changed in high school.

One morning in grade eleven, she met me at my locker. She looked awful. Her hair, which had grown back to shoulder length was uncombed, and she wasn't wearing any make-up. I knew just by looking at her that something terrible had happened. When she told me that her parents were getting a divorce, I nearly collapsed against my locker. Her dad had met someone else and was moving out. She said it so matter of fact, with no real emotion, like it was an everyday occurrence, but I could feel the anger seething from her body. She was shaking; her eyes moving back and forth avoiding mine, knowing that if we made direct eye contact, she might lose her composure all together. I tried not to sound shocked and hurt. Vicki's parents were always so nice and welcoming to me. If I felt this bad, I could only imagine how torn up she was.

"It's for the best...they've been fighting a lot lately. Better my Dad goes. I can't stand to look at his face."

I wanted to reach out and hug her, but I couldn't. She looked different. That mischievous grin was replaced with an ugly snarl, ready to devour anything or anyone that got in her way. I tried to be a friend to her during the divorce, but I think I reminded her too much of all the happy times in her past, so we drifted apart. We'd still say hello in the halls, but she would never stop and talk. She started to smoke and drink...cigarettes, pot, beer, whatever she could get her hands on. She'd come to school drunk or stoned at least once a week. It broke my heart to see her like that, so I'd avoid her like the plague. I felt terrible for doing it but I was seventeen and trying my best to keep my own life on track. I'd slip a letter in her locker every once in a while to let her know that I still cared, although the only response I'd ever receive was maybe a slight head nod if we happened to cross paths. She dyed her hair jet black and wore a skull necklace. Vicki had become the antithesis of her identity. She used to make fun of girls with jet-black hair and skull necklaces; now she was one of them.

After high school, we totally lost touch. I went off to university and she hung around the local bar, looking for love, but more often than not just finding a one-night stand. She went through men like tissues; one good blow then she'd toss them aside. I had reconciled myself to a forgotten friendship a long time ago, so I was shocked when late one night, she showed up at my apartment. I opened the door and there she was just standing there. Her face was streaked with a mixture of dirt, tears and a little bit of blood.

"I shouldn't have come." She tried to turn and scamper away but I snatched hold of her arm.

"Oww!" She pulled her arm back and started to run. I was too fast for her and latched my fingers on the back of her shirt, hauling her inside and shutting the door. I wanted to handle the situation calmly. I wanted to let her explain in her own time but my emotions wouldn't let me wait.

"Vicki, what the hell happened to you? My God you're a mess. Are you alright?"

She sat on the couch and stared at me. Her eyes were glossy and sad. Gone was the fire that had driven her, the fire that had tormented her, the fire that had ultimately consumed her. The only life in her eyes was crying out in pain. Searching for help; asking for forgiveness. Her puzzle had totally collapsed.

"What do you need me to do?" I said gently. She held out her arms. "That I can do." I went over to her and wrapped my arms around her as tight as I could. The hug was as much for me as it was for her. "I love you Vicki."

"I love you too Alex."

Except for the sobbing, we sat in silence. I stroked her disheveled hair and whispered a lullaby in her ear. As we hugged, I could feel her body rebounding as if she were drawing strength from me through our connected limbs. I held her even tighter. She cried harder. This cry was different though. It wasn't the scared, staccato cry like before. This cry had depth. It had soul. It was her soul. A soul that had finally awakened to the world, and realized that no matter what had happened between us in the past it was home. I cried along with her. For the lost days of our youth, for her parents and for the condition I found her in now. The time since our paths had last crossed vanished like the smoke from a chimney, drifting away, dissipating with the wind. Finally, she lifted her head from my shoulder. She looked down at my soaked sleeve.

"Sorry about that."

I laughed and brushed the last of her tears away from her cheek. "Do you want some tea?"

She nodded her head yes, and as I lifted myself from the couch, she clasped my hand and squeezed it tight. I squeezed back. No words were spoken but the meaning of that moment was not lost on either of us. She knew that I would always be there for her and her for me.

After I helped her wipe the blood from the corner of her mouth, she told me what happened. She had caught her boyfriend cheating on her and when she confronted him, he beat the crap out of her. Vicki didn't have to tell me that it wasn't the first time he had hit her. I could read it in her eyes. For some reason, she didn't even know why, she decided to leave him that night. She'd had enough. Her parents had both deserted her a long time ago and all her "friends" turned out to be not really friends after all. She looked me up in the phone book and found my address. She was too scared to call, afraid I would just hang up on her, so she decided to just show up and pray that I was home. I was glad she did. At a time like that, I had to believe in fate. I was supposed to go study in the library with friends, but changed my mind at the last minute. Vicki hadn't even knocked when I opened the door. She just appeared.

As we talked, I noticed the colour draining from her face. When she bent over to pick up a tissue, she yelped out in pain.

"Vic, what is it?"

"My stomach...did I mention yet that I was pregnant."

"Holy shit...I'm calling an ambulance."

She didn't object and the ambulance was at our door in a matter of minutes. They wouldn't let me ride with her, so I quickly hopped in my Honda and followed her to the hospital. By the time I reached the emergency, parked the car, and ran in, it was all over. The nurse led me to her room and whispered that the police were on their way.

"Hey you." I said giving her a kiss on the cheek.

"Hi Alex...I lost the baby."

"Ya I know...I'm sorry." I didn't know what else to say.

"I'm not. I love children but bringing a child into the world I was living in would have been wrong. I was going to get an abortion anyway."

"Did the father even know?"

"No. I never told him. Somehow, I don't think he would have been overly pleased. It's better this way. Now I'm free from him forever."

"The nurse said the police are on their way. They need to talk to you about the beating. I don't think there's any way of getting around it." I wasn't sure how Vicki would react, but she seemed glad, almost relieved that all her secrets would finally be laid out on the table.

When the police came, they talked to me outside, then Vicki. She wanted me in the room, so I pulled up a chair and held her hand. She told the police everything. It was worse than I'd imagined. I didn't judge her for the things she did or didn't do, for staying with him for so long and putting up with both physical and emotional abuse. I just held her hand and fought the sickness that was growing in my own stomach.

As she relived the past few years of her horrific life that night, I noticed a flicker begin to grow from beneath the redness of her eyes. Her voice became stronger, her grip on my hand tighter. She looked over at me and smiled, and this time it was the same grin she had when she nine. She was back. My lifelong friend had returned from the depths of her hell and I was glad. Another piece of my puzzle clicked into place and slowly, together, we would begin to rebuild hers.

The doctor wanted to keep her overnight for observation, so I left and told her I'd be back first thing in the morning to get her. She would live with me until she got back on her feet. Driving home, I felt an urgent need to re-connect with my own parents. As crazy and as dim-witted as some of their antics might have been, they were still my parents and I loved them. They were the rock in my landscape; solid granite, not swayed by the wind or the rain. I could count on them always. Vicki's rock had crumbled in high school, split in two by the lightening rod of malcontent and dissatisfaction. She tried to replace that rock with an abusive boyfriend, but like the dog he was, he lifted his leg and peed all over it. That left me. I knew my place in Vicki's life was to be her rock. Plopped in the middle of her turbulent ocean, I would be the rock that jutted upright out of the water. Blasted by the surf and the wind, I would stand for an eternity. A symbol of our friendship and our love. If things became rough on her ship, she only had to look out the port side window and there I'd be; a little weathered, but still standing.

Vicki lived with me for almost four years. While I finished up university and worked part-time at the restaurant down the street, she enrolled in some courses at the local adult learning center. She had graduated from high school on time, but not with the type of marks needed to pursue any type of further education. She was a very smart girl and I could tell she was embarrassed by having to upgrade so many high school level classes.

Nevertheless, she persevered, devoted herself to her studies, and completed all her upgrades in half the time it should have taken her. All this, while holding down a job requiring her to work two or three times a week and both days on the weekend. I was so proud of her. She totally turned her life around in an instant. We still partied and had a good time, but there was no turning back for Vicki, besides, a very large boulder now blocked her old road to destruction.

Once she had upgraded her courses, Vicki applied to the University for a General Arts Degree. She had her heart set on marketing and advertising. By this time, I was working full time at the paper and able to carry more of the financial load, allowing Vicki to scale back the hours at her job so she could study. Many Friday nights, I'd come home very late from the bar and Vicki would still be up studying. She was never jealous that she stayed home while I went out. She'd just watch me stumble in, help me to bed, and in some cases hold a washcloth on my forehead while I vomited. What a friend. I think on many occasions she wanted me to arrive home a little tipsy just so that she could take care of me. She'd make us both tea and we'd snuggle under my covers and chat for hours. It was so reminiscent of the many sleepovers we'd had as children, except there was nobody around to tell us to stop giggling and turn off the light.

Vicki graduated from university on the Dean's list. On graduation day she was beaming. Her fan club included me, a couple of our friends and my parents. She was just another daughter to them now, her own parents still childishly refusing to speak to her. A friend of mine at the paper helped Vicki land an interview with a major advertising agency, and as she left for the interview all dressed up and looking so respectable, a tear fell from my eye.

"Oh for God's sake Alex, pull yourself together girl!" she laughed. "I'm the one going to the interview. How do I look?"

She looked beautiful. Her golden blond hair bounced just above her shoulders, framing her famous smile. It was her eyes I noticed the most. They were on fire with excitement; glowing with anticipation. She was ready to take on the world. I almost felt sorry for the person conducting the interview. Vicki had found her groove and nothing was going to stand in her way. We met for lunch after the interview and I could tell right away that they'd offered her the job. She tried to fake me, but I knew her facial expressions too well. I played hooky from work the rest of the day and we went shopping.

Vicki moved out six months after she took the advertising job. She joked it was time she stopped living on my sofa and took some responsibility for herself. I think she just wanted a place of her own, supported by no one but herself. She was the golden wheat in her puzzle, feeling the swaying breeze of independence. On one hand, I was sad to see her go because of all the fun we had, but on the other, I was so proud to see the woman she'd become.

A knock on the front door jarred my memory back to reality. It was Mrs. Jones wondering if I'd seen her cat Francis. I told her no and politely closed the door. Just then, I heard a soft meow coming from the closet.

"Damn cat!" I opened the front door. Mrs. Jones was still standing there.

"Sorry Mrs. Jones, Francis must have snuck in when I came home a while ago. I didn't notice her until now." I picked up the fur ball and handed her back to Mrs. Jones. I hated cats, especially Francis.

"That's okay dear. I know how Francis is...very mischievous the little darling. You seem preoccupied Alex...is it that boy that Mr. Jones saw here earlier?"

"No Mrs. Jones, I'm fine." If I hadn't known better, I'd think that she snuck into my apartment and planted that dumb cat, just so she could ask me about Luke. With a "goodnight Mrs. Jones," I closed and locked the front door.

Speaking of Luke, Vicki was coming over for dinner tomorrow night to gossip. Instead of cooking, maybe I'd stop and get Chinese food. Vicki always made up funny won ton jokes about being sweet and sour pork. As I crawled into bed, my body was racked with a sudden fit of exhaustion. Was it really this afternoon that I drove home from Toronto? It seemed like weeks ago. What a long day! I pulled the covers up under my chin to keep out all the monsters and closed my eyes. I was asleep before I'd even finished my thought.

I filed my last Hector Long trial report with my boss early in the morning, then settled down at my computer to write one final summation column about the trial. I was glad to be putting the whole thing behind me. The man made me sick. The words flowed to my fingers like magic, so I finished the column early. I e-mailed the copy to my editor, grabbed a fresh cup of coffee, and made my way to the outer offices. I'd been away from the office for weeks and had some serious girl talk to catch up on.

I started at the reception desk with Rachel, the recent journalism graduate who didn't really want to spend the day answering phones, but needed the money. She always wore a turtleneck to work, had them in at least twenty different colors. Her wardrobe defense? The reception area was very cold and the turtlenecks kept her warm. The real reason? Her horny boyfriend was a leech with his lips and left his mark as a symbol of his manpower. I knew it to be the gospel truth since I saw them in the ladies washroom at the office Christmas party. I must say, I was a little jealous of Rachel that night. I wouldn't have minded if her boyfriend sucked on my neck for a bit…he was one hot kettle of steaming manhood. Rachel was always a good sport when we teased her, especially with me. I was the only one in the office who'd seen her boyfriends' bare ass. She knew I had the goods to bring her turtleneck defense to a crashing halt.

I had also threatened her with a complete expose in one of my columns if she didn't divert all my incoming calls from Phillip, a slimy, jackass of a freelance reporter, who tried on almost a daily basis to worm his way into my pants. I think she would have diverted the calls anyway. She met Phillip once and immediately understood my pain.

Phillip was incredibly short, and not that I have anything against minute men, it was just that he was at that uncomfortable level. When he stood in front of me, his mouth was directly across from my breasts. Even then, that might not be so bad, except he always had a crusty thing on his upper lip. He said it was "a condition" he'd had since birth. As he talked, the crusty thing would move back and forth. I wanted to grab some tweezers and pull it off, but was afraid of what lurked below. It was hard to take him seriously when he spoke. I would try to look him in the eyes, but I was always distracted, his lips moving one way, his "condition" moving the other. After a few minutes of talking, a white substance would form in the corners of his mouth. If he didn't catch it in time, the froth would start to meander down the creases and eventually resurface in a droplet suspended in time on the edge of his chin.

As revolting as that may seem, his personality was even worse. He would try to impress the ladies by making jokes about the size of his weenie, which he had nicknamed Jack. Jack was apparently the "king of dick land" and "a force to be reckoned with" so Phillip thought. We girls didn't quite share his opinion. His weenie was probably more like a button on a fur coat than a ballpark sausage. Even if his weenie were as long as the Mississippi River or as thick as a python, he would still be the most revolting man on the face of the earth. Nothing, absolutely nothing, could ever sway me.

Rachel informed me that Phillip had called thirteen times while I was away and thirteen times, she had told him that he was a freak and should never call me again. It's not like we ever had any business to discuss. He wrote freelance articles about advances in technology, and I wrote columns about things people understood; like how to fend off advances from slimy roaches like him. Nevertheless, I had to give him high marks for effort, but his snake still wasn't going to lay any eggs in my den.

As Rachel and I were chatting, Wayne the sports reporter sauntered in from the elevator. We had dated a few times just before I met Luke. He was a wonderful guy, we just didn't click in a romantic way. He gave me a hug.

"Hey, how've you been? That was a long trial," he said.

We chatted about this and that and made plans to go for lunch next week. Wayne was a good friend, especially when Luke left. He made me tag along with him on several of his assignments, so I spent much of the summer at the ball stadium learning the testicle scratching rituals of the professional male athlete. It provided me with several days' worth of material for my columns. I can honestly say that I've never seen a woman scratch her boob while standing in front of fifty thousand people. It's not that women don't get itchy boobs, but we tend to at least find some cover before we scratch. Behind the apple stand in aisle three of the supermarket is always a good spot for me. Sheltered by signs, you can do your scratching in peace and sometimes it'll even work to hide a wedgie pick, but for that, you have to be really quick. Just dig and pull. You can readjust back at the car.

Men don't seem to care about the improprieties of grabbing their balls in public, and I'm sure that most men wished women would grab their own boobs more often. I'd have to try that someday, walk by a group of men and nonchalantly fondle by breasts and wait for their reaction. It could be my own personal Baywatch moment, except that I'd never walk down the beach in a bikini, let alone a street. I just wasn't that kind of girl. It's probably the reason I was still single in my early thirties.

Wayne had married his high school sweetheart as soon as they'd graduated. They divorced three years later. He told me his ex-wife expected every night to be as magical as prom night. She obviously never went to my prom. At the after party, my drunken date climbed to the rafters of the barn to sing karaoke. Imagine my pride as everyone heckled him and aimed their empty beer bottles at his head. When I left to go home, he was stripped to his underwear, passed out on the lawn. I took a pen out of my purse and wrote, "I am an idiot" across his chest, down his legs and on his forehead.

Apparently, no one had witnessed my act of vandalism because on Monday morning his best friend took all the blame. I was an amused observer in the cafeteria as they got into a huge argument that nearly ended in a bout of fisticuffs. And even after two days of constant scrubbing, there were still remnants of my criminal act on his forehead, which evoked a chorus of snickers everywhere he went in the school. I considered the pen incident to be one of my most daring exploits in all of high school, if not my life. I remembered standing over his body, admiring my work and feeling a rush of triumph mixed with a splash of naughtiness. I imagined this was how Vicki felt after her bubble gum bath.

I looked down at my watch; it was already four thirty, which meant I'd managed to flit away an entire afternoon. I loved my job. I said goodbye to Rachel and Wayne and headed back to my office to check my messages and jot down a few ideas that had sprung into my head during my prolonged coffee break. Thank goodness, it was a slow news day. My only message was from Vicki reminding me about dinner. She sounded excited, gabbing on about how she wanted all the details of Luke's visit and that I'd better not leave anything out. I sat back in my chair and closed my eyes. I needed a moment of solitude before the night began. It was always the same scenario. I was about to be cooked like a steak on the barbeque.

First, she'd grill me with some high heated questions about Luke's baby and his new girlfriend. Then she'd turn down the temperature just a little as she simmered out all the intricate details of the meeting. Finally, when I was good and roasted, she'd slap me on a plate and slice me open, forcing the juices of my soul to run free while she sat on the couch and ate carrot sticks. Vicki knew how to get to me and I loved her for it. I opened my eyes to find my boss Mike standing in the doorway.

"Having a little nap are we?" he laughed.

51

"No, just a special me moment, that's all."

"Listen Alex, I just wanted to personally thank-you for covering the Hector Long trial. I could have sent Michelle, but she's a little green in court reporting and well this being such an important case on a such a sensitive issue, I wanted the job done right."

"Thanks, Mike I appreciate that."

"Has Helen stopped by to show you all the fan mail you received?"

"No she hasn't. Was the mail good or bad? Who did I offend this time?"

"It was all good, except for the one letter written by a convicted sex offender currently residing in one of country's finest steel cages. He thought maybe you should have been a little more sympathetic to Hector. It was his opinion that the victim probably provoked Hector into the rape, then the murder. We've made a copy of the letter and are sending it to the parole board to keep on file. I'm sure with written proof of his rehabilitation; he'll be serving out his entire sentence."

"I certainly hope so," I replied.

"You done for the day?" Mike asked.

"Just finishing up a few things," I lied.

"Do them tomorrow, go home you've had a long haul."

He didn't have to tell me twice. I grabbed my coat and purse and headed for the elevator. As I passed the reception desk, I noticed Rachel's boyfriend sitting on the sofa in the waiting area. I gave him a wink and a rub of my own ass, and then entered the elevator. Turning around to face the closing doors, I saw Rachel playfully giving me the middle finger. I returned the favour and blew her a kiss just as the doors shut. I was so preoccupied with my own humor that I failed to notice I wasn't alone. It wasn't until I heard the soft shuffling of a shoe that I turned around to face the biggest hunk of burning love I had ever seen in my life. Like the twit I was, I immediately jerked my head back to face the front in an obvious attempt to hide the fact that I'd nearly drooled on his shoe. The elevator stopped.

"Well this is me," he said in a very deep and manly baritone voice. "Excuse me."

I had been frozen in place by his utter existence. His minty fresh breath wafting through the air, fighting for equal time with his cologne. Maybe he wasn't even wearing cologne. Could it be that a man just naturally smelt that good?

"Excuse me."

"Oh Gosh, I'm so sorry...I was concentrating on a piece I'm writing. I thought I was alone in the elevator...good thing I didn't start singing...ha…ha..." Could I have been more of an ass? Of course, he knew I knew he was in the elevator. I'd looked right at him. As he brushed past me, I hung my head in shame.

"Hey," he said. I looked up. "I like Italian opera." The elevator doors shut and he was gone.

Vicki and I were sitting on the couch in my apartment eating Chinese take-out and drinking wine. "He said he liked Italian opera?"

"Ya...I don't know what to think. Was it a flirt?" I said. "Or...just a witty comeback to my depressingly weak attempt at trying to hide my ineptitude with burning hunks of love?"

Vicki laughed. "It couldn't have been that bad." I gave her a frown and nodded my head yes.

"It really was Vic. I'm sure that he went to where ever he was going and said that he shared the elevator with the biggest loser he had ever seen. I'm definitely taking the steps tomorrow."

"Alex, your office is on the twentieth floor."

"I know but I'd rather arrive at my desk with sweaty armpits then risk facing him again in the elevator."

"You are extremely pathetic. Was he really that good-looking?"

"He was jaw dropping Vic. I mean he was whip off my bra and show him my tits kind of cute."

"Really?"

"Really."

"What floor did you say he got off on?"

"I didn't and nice try. You stick to your building and I'll stick to mine you smooth talking high-heeled wearing whore! Those were the rules remember."

We both started to laugh. Vicki wasn't really a whore, but we liked to call each other white trash names just for fun. After a few glasses of wine, Vicki would become Tessa, the trailer park slut and I would be Arlene, her best friend and head waitress at the local Pig and Puke bar. It really was a childish game but we always had a blast playing it.

"Arlene, darlin' would you kindly fetch me another glass of that wonderful Pig and Puke whiskey."

"Sure thang Tessa. Hey, tell me that new guy who moved into lot sixty-nine…"

"Who Bubba?"

"God Tessa, please tell me that his name surely ain't Bubba."

"Oh it's Bubba all right. And let me tell you girl…I'm thinking of calling him Big Bubba after what I saw last night!"

"Tessa, you really are the biggest whore in the entire county ain't ya?"

"Only the county! Girl I've fucked more men than Old Joe Buttons has skinned hides…and he's been hunting possums' since he was five years old."

I laughed so hard, rice came ripping out of my mouth like a machine gun. In an attempt to avoid the rice bullets, Vicki ducked and spilled her red wine all over the carpet. We laughed even harder. I didn't mind about the wine. Mrs. Jones swears she can get any stain out of any carpet no matter what. We soaked up as much as we could with paper towels just to make her job a little easier.

Vicki went to the kitchen to refill her glass. By the look on her face as she sat back down, I knew the inquisition was on its way. I quickly shoved an entire chicken ball into my mouth and pretended to have trouble chewing. She waited patiently until I was done, sipping at her wine, rubbing the rim of her glass with her finger. She was a lion, circling her prey, silent and still, lingering in the shadows. When I swallowed a little too loudly, she pounced.

"So tell me about Luke. Is he really getting married?"

"That's what he told me."

"And she's having a baby?"

"That's what he told me." I was being vague just to tick her off. She belted me in the arm. "What?"

"Tell me the details or you will die a slow and agonizing death." She was threatening me with a fork. I was completely terrified.

"All right, all right…he stopped by the apartment."

"Just stopped by…" she interrupted.

"Actually he called first, but was standing outside my apartment door when he did. He was afraid I'd totally blow him off. I really had no choice but to let him in."

"What did he say? Did he look good?"

"Actually he looked a little scrawny. I didn't find him as attractive as when we dated."

"Oh shut up…" Vicki was laughing.

"No seriously, he looked a little spent. His skin was pale and flaky. Maybe the whole marriage thing has got him all off kilter. He never was that great at dealing with stress remember?"

"Ya I remember…come to think of it Alex, he was a bit of a loser. I always thought he was too geeky for you."

"Oh sure now you tell me!" I knew Vicki was just trying to make me feel better, but honestly I didn't feel that bad. "You know, I really am okay with it…with Luke marrying what's her name. I'll admit I wasn't happy at first, but I've thought about it…and I'm fine. I think my initial reaction was fueled by jealously, not about Luke per say, but because he was getting married and having a baby and I wasn't."

"I know what you mean."

Vicki and I had the same perceptions on the subject. Both of wanted to get married and have children, but the timing just never seemed to be right.

We talked about Luke for a little while longer, then shifted gears to discuss more important things, like why on television and in the movies people always eat their Chinese food directly from the paper take-out containers using chopsticks instead of a fork. Do they not have plates in Hollywood? I don't own chopsticks and I don't know many non-Asian people that do. They frustrate me. I used them once at a fancy sit down Chinese Food restaurant Luke took me to for my birthday. The meal took almost two hours just to eat. I followed the chopstick demonstration poster to a tee. I even made the waitress show me again when our food arrived. She made it look so easy. A flick here, a flick there. When I tried, I flicked a broccoli here, and sweet and sour pork there. I even managed to add a little plum sauce to a gentleman's plate two tables over. I hoped he liked it.

The waitress finally ended my pain and brought me a fork. Luke was so embarrassed, he left double the tip, and bragged about his chopstick skills throughout the entire meal. When we got into the bright lights of the movie theatre lobby, I noticed his shirt contained enough food remnants to feed all of Ethiopia. I may have shot food on other people but at least my shirt was clean. Who looked like the idiot now asshole...all smug and arrogant, acting like he was King Ho of the Chopstick Dynasty. He made me feel like a big turd that night, and on my birthday too. We had already been dating for two years and what did he give me for my birthday? A bracelet? A watch? No, he gave me a gift certificate for a lube job and tire rotation for my car.

"You know what Vic?"

"What's that Arlene baby!"

"He really was an ass wasn't he?"

"Who?"

"Luke."

"Yes Alex, he really was."

"Why didn't you say something sooner?"

"Well...It's not that easy to tell your best friend that her boyfriend is a jerk. I mean, you seemed so happy, I thought maybe he was different when it was just the two of you. As you know I haven't always had the best taste in men, so who was I to judge...and besides, sometimes a person just needs to figure those kind of things out on their own. I sure did. It wasn't until I'd had enough of black eyes and swollen lips that I finally decided to leave."

"Ya but Luke left me remember…"

"I know, but sooner or later you would have come to your level headed senses. You just wanted it to work out so bad and you tried so hard to make everything fit, but he just wasn't right for you. We all saw it…you weren't yourself with him. It was like you were always on guard, afraid of really being you. For gosh sakes Alex, he never laughed at any of your jokes. We'd be rolling on the ground and he'd be sitting there looking uncomfortable. How could he not laugh at your Baby Suzy impression? It's hilarious."

"I guess you're right. I think he always thought I was a little immature. My type of potty humor didn't sit well with his brand of uppity sophistication."

It was late before Vicki left. We were having so much fun and completely lost track of time. That always happened with us, no matter where we were. We'd go out to dinner and plan to catch a show, but most times, we'd still be sitting at the restaurant long after the movie started. It didn't matter though. I could always rent the movie in a few months anyway, and our conversations were usually more entertaining than the films.

I wrote a short note to Mrs. Jones telling her about the wine stain on the carpet asking if she might help me out and taped it to the outside of my front door. I had no doubt that she would read it. It would be just too enticing for her, a white piece of paper covering my peephole. I'd catch hell for covering one of the most important defenses in apartment security. I could hear the speech now.

"Dear, I appreciate the note, but really you should have taped it lower. You know the safety rules. Under no circumstances should a tenant's peephole be covered."

Of course every time I heard that rule I laughed. It always sounded a little "dirty" to me, but then again I could usually find a little "dirt" in anything anyone said. I guess that was the real difference between Luke and me. He took everything at face value, and I liked to look deeper and explore the nature of words, people, and circumstances. Luke's landscape was one-dimensional like him. He would have a house with a front door, but no windows to open to let in the light and fresh air. He would cover his peephole on purpose because heaven forbid he might ever have the need to look out and notice that a world existed beyond his. That was the key disparity between us. I continually quested for the fresh air of the real world, while he was content to languish in the vapors of his own self-pitied smog. Vicki was right, had we stayed together I would have eventually choked. I hoped that Luke's new wife and baby would fare better. I prayed that he would at least let them open a window. Maybe then, he'd start to see the world in a whole different light.

CHAPTER FOUR

"What the hell?" Someone was knocking on the front door. I opened my eyes just wide enough to look at the clock beside my bed. Six thirty.

"Go away," I groaned and rolled over. The knocking continued but had increased in volume.

"Oh for shit's sake!"

I carefully crawled out from beneath my blankets, taking the trouble to preserve the cocoon I'd created while I slept. Shuffling down the hall towards the front door, I expertly collected a few more winks while I walked. The knocking continued.

"I'm coming damn it!" It wasn't until I had already unlocked and opened the door that I realized I had forgotten to grab my trusty pink housecoat from the bedroom floor.

"Alex dear, I found your note...oh my...did I wake you?" said Mrs. Jones. As she gave me the once over with her probing eyes, I believed she was actually frightened by my appearance. "I'm sorry Alex, I can come back."

"No it's okay..." I rubbed the last of the stickiness from my eyes and focused more closely on the subject of my morning sleep deprivation. She was already fully dressed in a mauve pantsuit, her hair perfectly styled, make-up impeccable. She carried a bucket full of cleaning supplies. Did this woman never sleep?

"Mr. Jones found your note earlier this morning when he was looking

59

for the cat. I would have waited until later to bother you, but a red wine stain takes a little bit of soaking-in time. I hope you don't mind."

"No not at all…I appreciate you coming so quickly," I answered.

"I could have come over last night. If it's an emergency like red wine, you can call me anytime. Now where is the stain?"

I led her to the scene of the crime. She gasped in horror and muttered something under her breath.

"If it doesn't come out," I said, "don't worry about it. I can live with it." She shot me a glance that could have pierced my skull.

"Honey, you can't live with this stain. I couldn't sleep knowing that you were living with a stain this bad."

"Maybe I could just rearrange the furniture or put a plant there."

"A plant directly in front of the couch? Alex do you know nothing about interior design?"

She gave me a "don't worry, I'll take care of this like I take care of everything else" look. I smiled stupidly and secretly hoped she didn't have to move the couch even an inch. I'm sure there was an entire colony of molecular critters living in all the other stains and foodstuffs residing under the couch. I would be so embarrassed and ashamed that I'd have to move to another apartment, maybe even another building, sentenced to live out the rest of my life in purgatory, paying for unspeakable housecleaning crimes. Worse than that, she would tell my mother. I'd have to leave town. God help me if either of them ever looked behind the stove or refrigerator. I'd be burned at the stake or forced to read back issues of Good Housekeeping magazine for hours on end.

"Dear…are you okay?" She was staring at me like I was a freak.

"Sorry…I'm fine, just thinking about the best way to tackle that stain, that's all." I'm sure she knew I was lying.

"Well, first I'll spray it with my homegrown secret concoction and let it sit for exactly two hours. Then I'll use another mixture of….." Her voice trailed off as I tuned her out.

"I'll be back in two hours Alex." I followed her to the front door. "And don't touch it dear."

Why would I try to scrub out a stain at six thirty in the morning, when she was going to come back and do it for me? Was I stupid? As I closed my door, Mr. Jones caught a full glimpse of my morning splendor from his now open door. I could hear Mrs. Jones whispering to her husband.

"Mort don't stare, she looks terrible and she's hardly dressed. She could have at least thrown on that old pink housecoat."

"Oh I don't know Shirley...she doesn't look all that bad." As he attempted to peek around the closing door, a cuff to the back of the head sent flying forward. "Damn it Shirl, I was only having some fun!"

I re-locked the door and headed back to bed. I hoped that was the one and only time Mort Jones saw me in bikini briefs and a tank top. I couldn't have looked that bad. I stopped in the bathroom to check. Fuck, I looked like hell. No wonder Mrs. Jones was frightened. It was very late when Vicki left last night and apparently, in my haste to go to bed, I had forgotten to wash my face and brush my teeth. My wine stained teeth matched my smeared mascara perfectly. My hair could have housed a flock of seagulls with all the nests in it. Wait! Why were there numerous white specks all over my head? I bent in closer to the mirror. Could a flock of seagulls somehow of flown into my room in the middle of the night and crapped in my hair? I stepped back from the mirror and shook like a dog after a swim in the lake. The white things flew off in all directions. I reached down and picked one off the bathroom floor. It was rice. I started laughing. I was tempted to eat it but threw it in the toilet instead. Probably a wise choice.

Suddenly, I heard a soft voice calling me from the distance.

"Come back to me Alex...come back to me. I am warm and cozy. Dive beneath my covers and lie in the bosom of my soul. I will protect you and cradle you. I will shield you from the morning and let you linger until the night."

I bid adieu to the bathroom; promising to clean up the rice later. Right now, I had a return engagement with a special friend. I ballet danced back to the bedroom, jumping effortlessly over last night's clothes. Ah, and there it was, the object of my desire. I crawled to its side and draped my body across its width like a princess to her king. No words were spoken; none were needed. By sliding my body under the covers, I had accepted its silent invitation and found myself nestled in a world of warmth and comfort. I looked at the clock. It was six-forty five. I had only been gone a mere fifteen minutes, but the time away had left me cold and bitter. A shiver ran down my spine. I snuggled deeper into my cocoon of blankets and closed my eyes, praying that when I awoke one hour later I would be a beautiful butterfly, metamorphosed from the opaque caterpillar of the night before. Growing up my mother had always told me I had a flair for the dramatic, but I never saw it.

My alarm went off at a quarter to eight. I rolled over and blindly smacked at it.

"Shit!" I couldn't reach it without moving. I pulled the blankets over my head in a futile attempt to block out the annoying buzzer. Whoever invented that sound was a jackass. The alarm kept buzzing, but I still needed ten more minutes of sleep.

"BUZZZZZZZZZZZZZZZZZZZZZZZZZZZZZZZZZZZZZZZZZZZZZZ ZZZZZZZZZZZZZZZZZZZZZZZZZZZZZZZZZZZZZZZZZZZZZZZZZ ZZZZZZZZZZZZZZZZZZZZZZZZZZZZZZZZZZZZZZZZZZZZZZZZZ ZZZZZZZZZZZZZZZZZZZZZZZZZZZZZZZZZZZZZZZZZZZZZZZZZ Z!"

I couldn't stand it any longer. I moved the two inches required and slammed my hand across the top of the clock.

"Did you have a good sleep?"

Yes, my clock could talk; a wonderful Christmas present from my nine-year-old niece. She thought it was the coolest thing ever, even cooler than the Barbie car that magically turned into a beauty salon. I was jealous of Barbie. The only thing my car ever turned into was a garbage pit. Bits of gum wrappers and used Kleenex littered all over the front seat. I did have a garbage pail but it was full of a partially eaten Big Mac and an empty water bottle.

Actually, the water bottle wasn't totally empty. On the way to Toronto for Hector Long's trial, I'd had a terrible coughing fit, which loosened a fair bit of nastiness residing in my lungs. I couldn't re-swallow it because that would just be wrong, and defeat the whole purpose of coughing up the phlegm in the first place. I thought of spitting out the window but when I rolled it down, the wind was blowing directly in my face. Not a good idea. I looked around the front seat of the car and was relieved to see the empty bottle stashed on the far side of the passenger seat floor. I had to hurry; the phlegm was dripping back down my throat. I was less than a minute away from spraying the entire contents of my mouth on the inside of the windshield. I checked my mirrors. I'd hate to explain to a police officer that I caused a five-car pile-up because I had to spit.

With the coast clear and my left hand holding the steering wheel, I reached down for the bottle. The car hit a small bump and the bottle rolled a little further away. I could feel a slight dribble seeping out of the corner of my mouth. I felt like Phillip. I looked back up at the road. If I didn't grab it on this try, I was going to have to pull the car over. I checked the road once more and this time with only my fingertips on the wheel, I dove for the bottle.

"Come here you little bugger," I coaxed. "One more stretch...ah ha! Success!"

I snatched the bottle and quickly righted my position in the driver's seat. I was just about to relieve my mouthful when I noticed a car had pulled alongside me; its handsome male driver staring at me as if I was the first woman he'd seen in a decade. Now the dilemma was how can I spit, and still look like a sex goddess? As I was attempting to flick my head back like a runway model, the small droplet of spit that had been pooling at the side of my mouth, escaped and flew for freedom like a caged budgie. To my utmost horror, my bodily discharge landed splat across the driver's side window. I quickly turned my head away.

"Shit!" I mumbled. "That was attractive."

I took the water bottle, put it up to my mouth, and pretended to drink its contents. The plan was to spit when I tipped the bottle down, making it look as though I was really thirsty. Everything worked to perfection until I tried to close the spit off. It wouldn't stop. The green phlegm hung from my lips, suspended halfway down the bottle. Trying to be discreet, I tried a few short spits to end the first long spit, but to no avail. My face was now the colour of a very ripe tomato. I could feel the man watching me. He may have even made a face, I wasn't too sure, but I also wasn't going to look over and check. By the time the last drop of spit finally fell into the bottle, I had hummed two verses of Baa Baa Black Sheep.

I nonchalantly moved the bottle away from my lips only to find a suspension spit from my lips to the bottle rim. I took my left hand off the steering wheel, reached for a Kleenex, and carefully dabbed the corners of my mouth, trying to be as sexy as possible. I took the same Kleenex, which was a huge mistake, and tried to rub the spit off the inside of the window. I only made matters worse, smearing the original spit with the spit in the Kleenex. The man could have swallowed a horse; his mouth was open so wide. I needed to plan my escape and fast. I gave him a half-cocked nod and a flirty little wink, put both hands on the steering wheel, then gunned the gas with all my might. I shot off down the highway like I was racing against time. So what if I made a fool of myself in front of a man? It wasn't the first time, and I was positive it wasn't going to be the last.

I turned the talking alarm clock off and pulled back the covers. I lay there half shivering, trying to decide whether to get right up or pull the covers back over my exposed flesh. I had to get up. Mrs. Jones would be back shortly and this time I would be ready for her. On the count of three, I jumped out of bed, grabbed my pink housecoat from the floor, and dashed to the bathroom. I hop scotched over the bits of rice and turned on the shower, promising myself when I emerged from the bathroom on this glorious morning, I would be a beautiful butterfly. I glanced in the mirror and had to agree with Mrs. Jones. I looked like crap. It was going to take every herbal remedy ever discovered to transform me. Since I didn't have a medicine man handy in my bathroom, I snatched a bottle of apricot facial scrub from the counter and headed into the shower.

When I finally emerged from the bathroom twenty minutes later, I was the most beautiful butterfly the world had ever seen. It took some work but I had accomplished it. While in the shower, I decided today would be a work-from-home day, since I wasn't sure how long Mrs. Jones' stain removal procedure was going to take. With the advent of technology, it was just as easy to work from home as it was to go to the office, and as long as he received my columns on time, Mike didn't care.

Mrs. Jones would be back in exactly fifteen minutes, and I still had to get dressed. I didn't want her to think I was a total slob all the time, so I put on jeans, a clean white T-shirt, and a navy blue sweater for warmth. I loved the sweater because it always brought out the blueness in my eyes. Satisfied I would pass her inspection, I headed back to the kitchen to make some breakfast. I was just sitting down to my toasted tomato sandwich when the doorbell rang. I knew it would be Mrs. Jones, but I checked the peephole anyway.

"Hi, Mrs. Jones. Just let me unlock the door."

"I'm glad to see you used the peephole Alex. Like I always say, you never know who might be calling. It's a good habit to get into dear."

As soon as I had ushered her in the door, she took off for the living room.

"Ah! Looks like we just might be able get this stain out." She seemed so pleased.

"Really? That would be great."

"I just need to clean off the first spray and then apply a different one."

She was talking non-stop as she worked and I wasn't sure she even cared if I was listening. Actually, I was surprised to find myself quite enjoying her chatter. She explained how to remove the stain, what chemicals she used and various other household hints.

"Don't you have to go to work today Alex?" she asked.

"No, I called in and told them I was going to work from home. It's too cold to go out today."

"You're lucky you can do that. When I worked as a clerk at Thompson Shoe Factory, we had to be lined up outside the front gates at seven am sharp. The owner would drive up, unlock the big iron gate, watch until the line-up of workers filed into the plant, then lock the gate behind us. If you weren't in that line-up, the only way you could enter the plant was through his private entrance on the other side of the building. He would stand outside his office door and wait for any stragglers to try to use his entrance. My desk was just down the hall from the door and I witnessed his wrath many times. He was a terrible, terrible man. I think that's maybe why I get up so early, even now. I worked at that plant for twenty years and never once did I have to try to sneak in that door. I was too frightened to be late, I guess. I never wanted to anger Mr. Thompson."

I listened intently as she spoke. It was a side of her I'd never seen before or maybe I'd just never bothered to notice. She wasn't Shirley Jones of the Partridge family; she was Shirley Jones an accounting clerk who toiled for two decades working for a man who terrified her. As she kept scrubbing, she continued her story.

She was born in Germany in 1932. Her father was a professor at the University of Berlin and her mother did odd jobs at the local hospital. She didn't have to work, as her husband made decent wages, but Mrs. Jones said her mother always felt compelled to help others. Most of the time her mother Ingrid would give her wages away to some beggar on the corner, or a needy woman with four hungry children in tow. As Mrs. Jones spoke about her parents, I could see her eyes begin to moisten ever so slightly.

"Mrs. Jones, if I put on the kettle, would you have a cup of tea with me?"

"I'd love one Alex and please call me Shirley."

"Alright then Shirley." It felt weird to call her by her first name. "Shirley? That doesn't sound like a German name at all?"

"It's not. My real name is Anke. Anke von Wangenheim. My parents changed it to Shirley Wangen when we immigrated to Canada."

"Why?" I asked. "Anke is such a beautiful name."

"Ah yes, it is a beautiful name but Anke von Wangenheim is also a very German name. When we emigrated in 1937, my father renounced all his ties to Germany. He was very unhappy with the way Hitler and the Nazi party were running the country."

As we sat at the kitchen table drinking our tea, I listened to one of the most intriguing and surprising stories, I had ever heard.

The Nazi's came to power in 1933, a year after Shirley was born, and immediately began the Nazification of Germany. All German schools from grade one to the universities were Nazified in a matter of months. Textbooks and curriculum were shoddily rewritten to enforce the new Nazi doctrine and all teachers were forced to join the National Socialist Teachers' League. Any who refused were terminated and barred from the profession all together. Kurt Von Wangenheim was a well-respected but very outspoken man.

He refused to join the Teachers' League and spoke publicly against the falsification of German history, especially the teaching of racial sciences, which stipulated that Germans were the masters of the human race and the Jews were the cause and the breeders of everything evil. Along with other great German professors like Albert Einstein, he was fired, and because he had spoken out against the Nazi party, he was considered a Jewish sympathizer and a bounty had been placed on his head.

From the moment Hitler came to power, Kurt knew he would have to gather his family and leave Germany. His need to express his opinion about all things political and humanitarian was certain to land him in jail or worse. Dead. So the day Hitler's storm troopers came calling, the von Wangenheim family was already safely in Austria. Kurt took a job as a general laborer while Ingrid cleaned houses. Their oldest daughter Freda tutored Shirley and her older brother Max in the two-room apartment they rented. Living very modestly, they purposely showed no signs of their former income for fear they'd recognized and handed over to the Austrian Nazi Party. The von Wangenheim family saved every penny they could spare. Kurt was just biding his time, waiting until he was sure he'd saved enough money to make their escape permanent.

They lived in relative obscurity in Austria, until early 1937, when it too, like Germany showed signs of succumbing to the Nazi reign of terror. From there the family traveled to England where they boarded a steamer and made the trans-Atlantic trip to Canada. While the family was living in Austria, Kurt and Ingrid taught themselves and their children to speak fluent English, so that when they arrived in Canada, they would be accustomed to the language.

They settled in Toronto, and Kurt used the rest of the money he'd saved to buy a bookstore and put a down payment on a small house. Her parents ran that bookstore and lived in that same small house until they retired. Shirley started to chuckle.

"It's funny you know. So much of my history begins with Germany, yet I don't remember a thing about it. My parents never, ever went back, not even to visit. My father said this was his home now. They were very happy, my parents…very happy Canadians."

"You never told me how they came up with the name Shirley?"

"Oh," she laughed again. "Shirley was the name of the receptionist in immigration when we got off the boat, and my sister Betty was named after the daughter of the ship's captain."

"Well I like both names, Shirley and Anke."

"Thank-you dear."

"What about your brother Max? Did his name get changed too?"

She put down her tea and closed her eyes. I could tell something was wrong.

"No, Max's name stayed the same. Father felt it already sounded English enough."

"You look sad Shirley, what's wrong?"

"Ah, I was just remembering my brother. I wanted to be just like him when I grew up. He was so smart and handsome. Wanted to be a lawyer someday."

"What happened?" Sensing her despair, I approached the subject with caution.

"Although, he respected and agreed with Father, I think Max grew tired of hearing him rant and rave against Germany. He always thought Father as a history professor, could have done more to speak out against the Nazi's, especially while we were living in Austria and Canada."

She explained how in the late 1930's in Austria, there were several underground organizations attempting to resist the Nazi regime. Kurt von Wangenheim never joined any of these movements and refused to engage in any conversation about Germany outside of the safety of his home. When the family arrived in Canada, Kurt and Ingrid desperately tried to rid themselves of their German accents, wanting no association with Germany whatsoever.

"I remember one particular argument between my brother and my father. It was in the late fall of 1943. I remember it well because the leaves on the maple trees had all turned colour creating such a beautiful landscape. They were fighting about the war. Max wanted to join the army as soon as he turned eighteen, but my Father refused to endorse his decision. He did not want Max to go to war. Max called him a hypocrite for always talking against the Nazi's but never having enough courage to stand up and fight for what he believed in. The next morning my brother was gone. He had lied about his age and joined the army."

"Before he was shipped over to Europe, he and my father did make peace. My father told him he was proud of him for having the courage he himself lacked. That's the last time we ever saw Max. He landed at Normandy on July 6, 1944 with the Second Canadian Infantry Division. He managed to stay alive during the entire Normandy campaign but was killed in Belgium on October 16 while they were trying to capture Woensdrecht. He's buried there. Somewhere. I'm not sure where though. He was eighteen years old." Her hands were trembling, so I reached out and gently took them in mine. "My father was devastated at the news. He never recovered. Not really anyway. But I'll tell you one thing...my father was the proudest Canadian ever. He never let people forget his son Max died fighting against the tyranny of Nazi Germany. I'm sure Max would have been proud of him. Very proud."

We sat there in a moment of silence. Both of us lost in thought. I was thinking about my own family. I couldn't imagine what it would be like to lose a sibling like that. I'd had enough trouble over the years trying to come to terms with the loss of two dogs, a bird, and a hamster. Sometimes I still broke down in tears looking at pictures. I looked across the table at Mrs.

Jones and smiled. There were no words of comfort spoken, I just held her hand and smiled.

"Well Alex, I'd better go check that stain," she said.

"I'll go with you."

We got up from the table and went to scrutinize the carpet. I was amazed the stain was completely gone.

"Holy Shirley, you need to market that stain removal concoction!"

"I told you I could get it out. You need to listen to your neighbors' advice more often. We're not a dumb as we look."

She gave me a playful look, but I understood the hidden meaning. She was right. I'd forgotten the Jones' had lived an entire life before I was even born, and was incredibly intrigued by her story.

"Well I'd better be leaving." Mrs. Jones said. "The stains gone and you'd better get working."

"Do you have to go? I mean, I'll just e-mail my boss one of my rainy day columns. He never knows the difference. I'd really like it if you stayed a while longer."

"Really?"

"Ya really."

She looked around the room. "Well I do see a few more stains on the carpet over there by that large plant. They look like they've been there for a while." New Year's Eve…three years ago. Vicki's date vomited up pizza and beer. It was gross. "I'll just go back to my apartment and grab some more tools and Mort's probably wondering where I've gotten to. I'll be right back."

She scurried out the door like a Mother Hen, wagging her butt as she walked. I laughed to myself. What a woman! I was looking forward to her return. I quickly went to the computer and picked a column from my stack of written but not submitted, a piece about the weather, and how I wished for the early arrival of spring. After hearing about Max, my ranting about the winter weather and how it affected my hair, seemed very inconsequential. I e-mailed the column to Mike anyway and went back to kitchen to heat up some more water in the kettle. It was going to be a great afternoon. I had just re-filled the teapot when I heard Mrs. Jones knocking on the door.

"C'mon in," I yelled. "It's open."

"I noticed you didn't have any snacks for the tea, so I brought the ingredients for us to make some muffins if you want."

"Oh how thoughtful, that'd be great. I haven't had homemade muffins in ages."

"I figured." She walked into the kitchen and put her basket of supplies on the countertop.

"I put on another pot of tea."

"Oh you read my mind Alex. Let's just check out some more of those stains before we get baking."

She hustled over to the large plant and squatted on all fours. "My, oh my...well I think maybe if I spray a little of this..."

She continued talking as she crawled around the carpet spraying any discoloration she could find. I followed behind at a short distance. When she came to the big couch, I froze. She looked up at me and smiled.

"Shall we move this out, or just let sleeping dogs lie?"

"Well," I paused trying to think of a great reason not to move the couch out and reveal the true horror of my housekeeping abilities.

"It's okay Alex. I understand. But one day, you're eventually gonna move from this apartment and like it or not, the couch will be moved."

"Are you sure you want to do that today? I mean, I can do it later," I panicked.

"Don't be embarrassed. Let's do it now and get it over with." She actually sounded sympathetic.

"Alright, if you say so."

"I'll push, you pull."

I grabbed one end of the couch and pulled as she pushed from below. I was almost too scared to look at the space vacated by the couch. Mrs.

Jones started to laugh out loud.

"Oh my gosh girl. You could feed the third world from these leftovers!" Her laughter immediately eased my embarrassment.

"I'll get the vacuum." As I hurried to the closet, I could hear Mrs. Jones playfully muttering to herself.

"Holy lord of mercy. This is disgusting!"

I snatched the vacuum and practically ran back to the living room. Problem was the last time I had vacuumed, I'd forgotten to rewrap the cord, so as I ran, it became tangled in my feet and sent me flying on my face in the hallway with a very large thump.

"What was that?"

"Nothing, I just tripped over the vacuum," I said.

"Are you okay?"

"Ya, I'm fine," I mumbled. I could hardly breathe; the pain was searing my lungs. I was pretty sure, when I looked down, the long 'corner getter' attachment would be protruding from my stomach. Footsteps pounded down the hall.

"Look at you. Are you always this klutzy?" said Shirley.

"Not always, but ya... most of the time."

As I lay there, I realized the comedy of the situation. I could read the headlines now: "Woman Impaled by Vacuum Attachment While Trying to Prevent under Couch Embarrassment." I put my head down on the vacuum hose and started to giggle. Shirley joined in my hysterical snorting, as she obviously perceived my fall to be quite humorous. She sat down on the carpet beside me.

"You remind me so much of my daughter."

"Your daughter?" I said surprised. "I didn't realize that you had any kids."

"We have a son and a daughter. One lives on the west coast and the other lives on the east. We haven't seen either for a couple of years now. Mort doesn't like to fly and well, the drive is just too long."

"Don't they come to visit you?"

"Their lives are busy. We talk on the phone sometimes but only for a few minutes at a time. They're always in a rush. The kids have soccer or music lessons or something. I'd like to visit, but I'm scared to go alone."

"I'll go with you." It was out of my mouth before I could stop it, but I wasn't going to take it back. I sat up and looked her right square in the eyes. "If it means that much to you, I'll take you. I don't mind."

"What about your job?" she asked.

"There are plenty of news stories on either coast. I go on research trips all the time, paid for by the paper."

"Really Alex, thanks for the offer, but I can't accept. It's just too much to ask."

"Well, the offer stands. You can think about it." I untangled my feet from the vacuum cord and managed to coax my body upright. Mrs. Jones still sat on the carpet, her head leaning back against the wall.

"I'm going to tackle under the couch," I said. "I have a feeling it may take a while."

She held out her hand and I helped her up from the ground. "You're gonna need some expert advice I think."

"Yes, I think you're right, I think you're absolutely right."

I willingly followed her into the living room. I had been shocked to hear she had two kids. Neither she nor Mr. Jones had ever mentioned them before. It was rather sad. I would take her on that trip if she asked. I'd be glad to go. It's the least I could do for the woman who was, at this particular moment, on all fours, cleaning my carpet.

"Need any help?"

"I'm just picking out all the coins. There sure is a lot of fried rice and popcorn under here."

"Two of my favorite foods, what can I say?"

I bent down and helped her pick out the money. We amassed a small fortune.

"What should we do with our windfall?" I said.

"Do they deliver pizza during the day?"

"They most certainly do. What would you like on it?"

"Oh it doesn't matter. Maybe pepperoni, ham, pineapple, and bacon…whatever you'd like dear. I'll eat anything. Mort doesn't like pizza, so we never order it. This'll be a real treat."

"That Mort sounds like he needs a talking to Shirley. He won't fly, doesn't like pizza. What's wrong with the man?"

"I know, he's a bit of a stick in the mud," she laughed, "but he's my Mort and I couldn't imagine life without him." When she talked about her husband, I noticed a slight shy smile escape from her lips, and despite their little tiffs and arguments, it was apparent they were still deeply in love.

By the time the pizza arrived, we had managed to vacuum the 'unspoken' area and scour and spray the rest of the carpet. Shirley was a stain genius. We talked non-stop while we worked and if it hadn't been for the lack of trucker mouth and other vulgarities, I'd have thought I was spending the day with Vicki. The pizza driver was more than thrilled with the baggie of coins I handed him. I was just about to close the door behind him, when Shirley came scurrying down the hall.

"Wait! Wait!" I reached for the drivers' arm and just caught him by the sleeve. He gave me a dirty look. "I found another quarter, here you go son," Shirley said handing him the coin. The driver reluctantly said thank-you and headed out the door.

"He didn't seem too happy, did he?" She snatched the pizza from my hands and headed to the kitchen. "This smells delicious. I hope Mort's enjoying the leftover meatloaf I took out for him." She turned around and gave me a devious grin.

"Let's eat, I'm starving," I replied.

As we sat at the kitchen table and ate the pizza, Shirley gave me run down on making the muffins, which of course was our next task after lunch. I was having a wonderful day and chided myself for not spending time with her before now. Maybe I was the weird one because she seemed perfectly normal, except for her hair. I decided not to beat around the bush and just ask.

"Who does your hair?"

"Florence on the fourth floor. Why? Is there something wrong?"

"Not really wrong. But…" She interrupted me before I could finish.

"It's outdated isn't it? I've asked Florence to spice it up a little, but I always come home looking the same."

"It just doesn't do you justice. You have such a soft, pretty face, but with your hair pulled back so severe, it makes you look so much older than you are."

"Honestly…I never thought of it that way," she said.

I hoped that I hadn't hurt her feelings and put my head down pretending to concentrate on the toppings of my pizza.

"Alex," she said.

Uh oh, here it comes I thought. I lifted my head and looked her in the eye.

"Do you think that you could help me? I mean, with a new hairstyle. I just feel like I need a change in my life, nothing drastic like a boob job, just something subtle. I think a new hair style would be just the thing."

I sighed with relief. "I'd love to help you. When do you want to go?"

"Do we need an appointment? Because I'm ready anytime." She was giddy.

"Let me just make a phone call."

I called my friend Carly at the salon. She booked Shirley in for 3 pm, which meant we had just enough time to finish our pizza, check the stains, and make the muffins. I could hardly keep Shirley from jumping up and down; she was so excited. She scrubbed those stains as if she'd been given a new lease on life. I understood how she felt. Sometimes you just need to change it up a little. Anything will do, a new haircut, a day trip, even buying a new bra. It doesn't matter if the change is hidden under a huge bulky sweater, as long as you know it's there, you're a whole new woman.

My favorite part of the day so far was making the muffins. Mrs. Jones chose bran. That way she'd kill two birds with one stone; make some snacks and help keep old Morty regular. This woman really was a hoot.

Her children and especially her grandchildren were missing out on a truly wonderful human being. I taught her how to sing Italian opera and dance ballet as she stirred the ingredients. It was mid-afternoon and we could sing as loud as we wanted, everybody else was at work. I watched her try to be nonchalant as she checked the clock every five minutes. As her appointment grew closer, she was almost unbearable, firing beauty questions at me like I was some high class runway model, which shocked me because normally Mrs. Jones was giving me grooming tips. Finally, it was time to go. Mort was out walking the neighbours' dog, so she left him a note on the door. She lied and said she was going out to get groceries.

"What Mort doesn't know, won't hurt him," she said taping the note to the door. She grabbed my hand and we set off on our adventure.

The weather was beautiful, so we decided to walk to the salon. It was only a few blocks away from the apartment building and as she walked, I could see Shirley sucking the crisp air into her lungs, inhaling then exhaling, like she was preparing her soul, readying it for the new Shirley. We didn't talk much on the journey. I was too busy daydreaming about the man from the elevator and trying to figure out what we were going to name our firstborn.

"I think we're here," Shirley exclaimed. I looked up.

"Yep, this is the place. Are you ready?" I asked her.

"I've been ready for twenty years," she said swinging the door open.

"Hi Carly."

"Hey Alex, how ya doing?"

"I'm doing just fine. Carly, I'd like you to meet Shirley. She's here for an extreme makeover." Both women started to laugh.

"Well Shirley, come on back and I'll see what I can do. Do you trust me?" Carly asked.

"If Alex trusts you, then I trust you," she replied.

"I trust her Shirley."

"So, Shirley what should we do with this hair of yours?" The two of them walked to the back of the salon.

"You two have fun," I yelled after them.

"Aren't you coming?" Shirley asked. "You're my inspiration for this makeover, so get your butt back here."

I jumped up off the chair and followed them to Carly's exclusive design room. We bantered about, discussing what look we each felt would fit not only Shirley's age, but her personality. Once the process began, I decided to run out and buy some coffee. I had a feeling we were going to be awhile.

As I was about to cross the street to get to the coffee shop, I noticed Bobby holding open the coffee shop door. I was about to yell hello, when a young boy about eight or nine walked through. I didn't want to interrupt them so I waited until they were further down the street. Who was the kid? Bobby never mentioned that he had any kids, though I guess I'd never asked him either. I watched him put his arm on the boys' shoulder and playfully jab him in the stomach. The boy threw his head back and laughed, then punched Bobby back in the arm. Bobby pretended to be hurt, but his animated smile lit up his face.

I felt a bit like an intruder, spying on them from behind a parked car, but I was glad to have witnessed their interaction. So far, I'd only spent time with Bobby within the cozy confines of Wilkins Place. It was nice to see him out in the fresh air, having a good time, without a beer in his hand and conversing with someone other than the boys. Not that I had a problem with any of the boys, it's just that like Shirley, sometimes everybody needed a little change in their lives once and awhile.

With the two of them safely out of sight, I crossed the street to the coffee shop. Still thinking about Bobby, I absentmindedly opened the door and walked in. Wham! I walked right into the chest of a man exiting at the precise moment I was about to enter.

"Sorry. My fault. Like usual, I wasn't watching where I was going." I looked up to see the burning hunk of love from the elevator staring deeply into my eyes.

"We have to stop meeting in these awkward ways," he said with that very deep, very sexy voice. My knees grew so weak, I had to lean against the door to keep from falling.

"My name's Matt." He held out his hand.

Did I shake it or just thrust it down my shirt? I was torn. Coming to my senses, I politely shook his hand.

"And I'm Alex," I spewed. Good thing my name wasn't Polly, I probably would have spit on him I was salivating so much. Even a vegetarian couldn't pass up a good hunk of meat like this.

"Not working today?" he asked.

"Actually, I was working from home, but needed a break so I escorted a friend to the hair salon over there." What a big liar I was. Although, I don't think telling him I'd spent the day cleaning the crud from underneath my couch would have been too impressive.

"Oh, I see. I thought you were just playing hooky."

"No…but even if I was you wouldn't tell on me would you?" I said.

"Of course not. I wouldn't want to get you in any trouble." He smiled as he talked. I'm sure he never realized that I was hoping he got me in a lot of trouble. And fast.

"I'm on my way out. I have to go meet a client but would you like to meet for a coffee sometime?" I almost fainted, right there in the coffee shop door.

"I'd love that…I mean, that would be great." We exchanged numbers and as he was about to walk away, he turned back.

"By the way, I love your eyes."

HELLO!!!! He loved my eyes. Well slap my ass and call me Mary! I felt the need to run home immediately and dancercise, just in case coffee led to a little late night dessert.

"Stop it," I thought to myself. "You're being awful dirty."

The whole chance encounter had only taken a few minutes, yet I would replay the event in my mind for hours and hours until we actually went out.

When I returned to the salon a few minutes later, I felt like a new woman. I had a date. I didn't know exactly when it was going to occur but it didn't matter. As long as it took place in the foreseeable future, I was happy. Carly was in the process of blow-drying Shirley's hair. It was back to the future for Mrs. Partridge! Shirley looked fantastic and at least ten years younger.

"I'd better start calling you foxy Mama! Wait till Mr. Jones gets a look at his Mrs. Jones. He's gonna want a little more than meatloaf for supper tonight."

"Alex, stop that!" She feigned embarrassment but I could tell she was more than pleased with my reaction.

"Do you really like it? I want your honest opinion now."

"Shirley I love it. It suits you so well. You look beautiful." I went over and gave her a hug. She whispered in my ear.

"I just wanted to thank you. I've had such a wonderful day." Her voice began to quiver. "It's been quite a long time since I treated myself like this. I've enjoyed every minute."

"So have I Mrs. Jones, so have I."

I told Shirley the salon trip was on me, since she'd spent all that time on stain removal duty. We both walked back to the apartment as high as the puffy clouds above us. Each for different reasons. Mort was waiting outside the apartment when we arrived.

"Where have you been? I've been worried sick. I even went down to grocery store to see if you needed any help, but they said you never arrived." Once he caught his breath, he noticed Shirley's new look. "Oh my Gosh, woman, you look beautiful. Your hair…you look as young as the day I married you." He bent down and gave her a kiss. It was so simple, yet so incredibly romantic. I was jealous. Shirley leaned over to give me a goodbye hug. Once again, she whispered in my ear.

"I should have bought a new bra too. Then he'd really be out of breath." She gave me a wink and I started to laugh.

"Oh wait your muffins and stuff." I reminded her.

"I'll get them later. I need to check those stains again later tonight. You gonna be home?"

"Unless I get a phone call." I winked back and entered my own apartment.

What a great day. So many things had transpired. I exchanged phone numbers with a man who wasn't my father or brother, uncovered another piece in the puzzle that was Bobby and most important of all, I gained a friend in Shirley Jones. I no longer avoided her when I came home late at night; in fact, I got in the habit of softly tapping twice on her front door. She said she slept better knowing I was finally home safe. Of course, the next time we'd have tea, I'd get lectured about the late hours I kept and how I needed to be careful, but I didn't mind her sermons anymore. Truthfully, I rather enjoyed them.

CHAPTER FIVE

When Shirley came over later to pick up the muffins and check the stains, she was positively glowing. She couldn't stop thanking me for inspiring her new look. I wasn't quite sure of my role in the whole transformation process, but I was glad she was so happy with the results. Speaking of results, my carpet looked brand new; the stains had been removed entirely. Since I didn't have to strategically place my furniture anymore, I spent the rest of the evening changing the room around.

I loved rearranging furniture; it was a sadistic obsession. As a kid, many a rainy Sunday afternoon was spent lugging my bedroom suite around my room. Trying the furniture at every angle and in every corner, until I found just the right combination. Of course, there was no guarantee the furniture would remain that way. I probably rearranged everything at least once every three months. It was my way of spicing up the scenery a little. Besides, it was much cheaper than constantly redecorating, and a project that didn't involve my parents or their permission.

As soon as they heard the first scrapings across the hardwood floor, they knew to stay away. I was always careful to put sliders under the legs of the heavy furniture, but sometimes the creative Gods deployed their decorative forces over me, causing me to get lost in the moment and I would forget. A stern "Alex, the floor" would resonate through the ductwork and I would quickly snap out of my trance and rush for the sliders.

The obsession never wavered, and as I grew up, it got worse. The older I became, the more adept I was at using tools. I could now actually take the furniture apart before I moved it. I could move shelves, pictures, anything

I wanted. I was unstoppable. I had moved my bookshelves so many times my walls were pocked with holes and chipped bits of drywall. By then I was teenager and able to cover the marks with posters of Scott Baio and Duran Duran. It wasn't until I moved out to go to University that my parents finally saw the damage my obsession had created.

I tried to blame all the holes on the mice that had apparently been living in my bedroom walls since I was a child, but that didn't fly. Next, I tried to tell them that I was sure I remembered the holes being there since we'd moved in. A terse, "Nice try," was the answer. They'd been living in the house for two years before I'd even been born. I'd forgotten about that. Since I couldn't think up any more brilliant excuses, I just gave in. My punishment was spending an entire Saturday filling in all the holes with a plaster mixture, letting it dry, and then sanding it down. It was the best punishment they could have given me. I had a blast and it forever forged my interest in home improvements and gave me a fresh obsession for Polyfilla.

Exhausted from moving furniture, I sprawled on the couch and relaxed in the peaceful atmosphere of my new room. I was terribly tired and needed to go to bed but that just seemed like too much work, so I reached for the converter and watched a little television. I surfed through a few infomercials. One was for a gadget promising to shave four inches off your butt in four days, without exercising. Ya right. The only thing that could shave four inches off my rear in four days was a chain saw. The second product made peanut butter from scratch. Entirely from scratch. This included shelling the peanuts before putting them into the crusher, grinder, peanut butter maker. Supposedly, the whole process took only minutes. Bullshit! It takes five minutes just to shell a single peanut, let alone crush it into peanut butter. Unless you're Martha Stewart, frankly, you really have no business even attempting homemade peanut butter.

I turned off the television and flipped the converter onto the couch. It bounced off the cushion and landed with a thud on the floor, batteries flying out in all directions.

"Oh shit."

I stared hard at the mess of electronics on the floor and tried to will it back together. After ten minutes of intense mind focus, I realized I didn't have the supernatural powers needed to put the batteries back into the converter, and would be forced to bend down and do it myself. I looked at the clock. It was ten-thirty. It had been a very long but rewarding day and I needed to go to bed immediately. The converter could wait until tomorrow. I hoisted my rear off the couch, almost wishing I'd ordered the ass-trimmer, and trudged down the hall to my bedroom. I was going to enjoy this sleep. No doubt about it.

I awoke the next morning feeling refreshed but a little stiff in the arms from all that scrubbing the day before. I pulled back the curtain and sang a little ode to the sunshine that was beating so heavenly on the windowpane. Spring was finally breaking and I was glad. The winter I loved was white and fresh, not grey and dirty like it was now. Everything was wet, slushy, and extremely mucky. I hopped in the shower and readied myself for a day at the office. I had already decided to stop by Wilkins Place for a drink after work since my curiosity was killing me.

I had to figure out a tactful way of asking Bobby who the young boy was. A series of morning meetings, followed by an afternoon writing, made for a productive eight hours. I waved goodbye to Rachel at the front desk and headed for the elevators. I fixed my hair in the strip of shiny aluminum that lined the outside doors, just in case Matt was waiting on bended knee behind door number two. I trembled with anticipation as the doors slowly opened. I tried to act cool, closing my eyes and inhaling deeply in a futile attempt to slow my heartbeat. When I opened my eyes, it wasn't my hunk of meat waiting for an Alex sandwich but Wayne.

"Hey darlin', how are ya?" he asked.

"I'm great, how 'bout you?"

"Never better…never better," he replied. "I'll catch ya later. I'm late with a report for Mike. How about lunch some time next week?"

"Sounds great." I stepped into the elevator. I shook my head. Wayne looked good. Really good. I wondered if he'd been working out. Suddenly my palms felt a little sweaty. What the hell was wrong with me? Wayne and I had already been down that road. I chalked up my nervousness to the fact that I'd been expecting Matt and not Wayne. I had to admit though; my heart did flutter a bit and that frightened me.

Bobby was already sitting at the bar with Big Dave, his head bent and cocked to one side. Big Dave was talking quietly in his ear. When he saw me, he put up his hand in a silent wave. I walked over and gently placed my hand on his shoulder. While I had already developed a strong affinity for this man, I felt even more of a kinship after I had witnessed his interaction with the little boy. I didn't know exactly how he would react, so I decided to wait until we were alone before I started my own inquisition.

Big Dave was obviously telling a joke. His arms were flailing up and down and his face kept shifting expressions. You knew the punch line was coming by the way his voice began to crescendo. He became louder and louder with each word, his body growing in animation. He took a deep breath and filled his lungs with the stale, smoky sweat, which hung from the ceiling of the bar like a pair of fisherman's old, wet wool socks. Putting both hands up in a signal for silence, he paused and looked around the room. Dave always had to make sure he'd captured everyone's attention before he hammered down the joke. Someone yelled from the back of the room.

"For God's Sake Dave we're all listening, just finish the damn joke already. I have to pee!"

"All right, all right," he answered. "You ready?"

The patrons screamed in mock displeasure. Big Dave laughed, then, finally after another short pause delivered the punch line. The crowd moaned.

"We waited an hour to hear that shit? Big man you need some new jokes and in a hurry!"

The boys came around and playfully smacked Dave across the head. Dave's jokes were never that funny and he took a beating every time, yet he continued to tell them. He reasoned that one of these days he would catch everyone off guard and tell a joke so funny they'd have to name him a comedy king. He was just waiting for the right moment. I sat down on the bar stool vacated by Dave when he went to deal with some of the hecklers in the crowd. After watching Dave amble away, Bobby turned his attention back to me.

"Hey Alex how are ya tonight?" he asked sweetly.

"I'm fantastic Bobby. How 'bout you?"

He paused a little before he answered. "I'm okay I guess."

"Just okay?" He shrugged his shoulders and stared into his glass. "What's wrong Bobby? You seem really down. You feeling fine?"

"Ya, I guess I'm just a little tired that's all. Maybe I'm catching a little of that bug that's been going around."

He abruptly stopped talking as Big Dave reached over his shoulder and grabbed his beer from the counter.

"You thought my joke was funny didn't ya Alex?"

"Sure Dave, it was a riot."

"See fellas, the women think I'm hilarious!" He kissed the top of my head and whispered in my ear. "Thanks for sticking up for me especially when I didn't even think the joke was all that funny." He snickered and walked away. I looked at Bobby. He suddenly looked uncomfortable.

"Have you eaten dinner yet Bobby?" I asked.

"Not really, only a few of these peanuts." He lined one up in his fingers and flicked it behind the bar, all the while staring into his half-empty beer.

"Well I'm starving for something other than peanuts. Why don't we go grab some dinner at that little diner down the street? It's a lot quieter and the food's pretty good too."

"Sounds fantastic. You sure you want to have dinner with a sour puss like me?" he asked.

"Positive. Let's go."

We slipped out of the bar unnoticed and headed towards the diner. The sun was just setting behind the tall office buildings of the city's downtown core.

"I can't tell you the last time I've actually left the bar while it's still light out. It's kind of nice to see the sun set." Bobby said as he looked towards the heavens. He was looking at sky as though he had never witnessed a sun set at all. "My gosh it's beautiful."

I instantly felt sad for this man. I didn't want to pity him, but I did. I watched him as we walked. He kept his eyes focused straight ahead and not once did he care to look around and notice his surroundings. I was the complete opposite. In the short walk to the diner, I saw two couples holding hands, a man almost slip off the curb and a stray dog sniff around a lamp post. Bobby noticed nothing. His expression was blank. It was like the connection between his eyes and his brain was severed causing no visual perception what so ever. He was a blind man who could see, but chose not to. I couldn't understand. It wasn't until we were almost run over by two children on bicycles that he snapped out of his trance.

"Whoa girls, be careful where you're going," he yelled out playfully. "You almost killed us!" He chuckled to himself and broke out into a wide grin. "Did you see the blue eyes on the one in the green hat? They were like the ocean...blue as the ocean I tell ya." He stood there and watched them ride away. When they were finally out of sight, he turned back around and sighed heavily. "Kids...you just have to love them. Not a care in the world those girls. That's the way it should be for kids. They shouldn't have to worry about a thing." He shook his head slowly and again was lost in his own world.

I stood there in amazement at the complexity of this seemingly simple man. Maybe he wasn't blind in life but only chose to see certain things? What made him notice the details of the young girls' eyes yet totally dismiss the large flashing neon sign that lit up the entire street? I stared at him with a look of wonderment.

"What's wrong? You've got a really weird look on your face."

"Nothing," I said. "Nothing's wrong at all." I hooked my arm in his and led the rest of the way to the diner, taking comfort in the fact that I maybe I was about to unravel the mystery of this man and maybe, just maybe I would discover how that little boy fit into Bobby's puzzle.

We took a booth in the far corner of diner and Bobby reached for the menus.

"What do you feel like Alex? I think I'm in the mood for a great big sloppy cheeseburger, some fries, and a shake. I love the pickles they have here. They're nice and sour. The one waitress always throws a few extras on my plate...she's such a sweetie."

The waitress took our order.

"Extra pickles?" she asked Bobby.

"You betcha," he answered.

"Where's Ben tonight? Too much homework?" She continued talking to Bobby as she collected up the menus.

"No, he couldn't make tonight."

"That's too bad. He's such a great kid. Always makes me laugh." Her voice tailed off as she headed back to the kitchen to give the cook our orders. I looked at Bobby and smiled.

"All right mister, enough of the mystery. Who on earth is Ben?"

"It's not a mystery Alex, I was going to tell you, but I never really know where to begin."

"Is he your son?"

"No, no," he paused. "I'm a Big Brother to Ben. We hang out together and generally just have a lot of fun. He's a good boy. A really good boy Alex. It's just such a shame." He looked out the diner window and watched the cars try to scream through the amber light. I could tell there was much more to this story but I didn't want to push him.

"Bobby, I think it's fantastic that you're a Big Brother. How long has it been?"

"Oh, almost a year I guess."

"What made you join? I don't mean to get personal but you have me intrigued."

"It's kind of a long story." He answered looking me straight in the eyes. I could tell he wanted to talk.

"Only tell me if you want to Bobby. I won't be offended either way."

A small grin crept from the corner of his mouth as he slowly nodded his head up and down. "No...I think I'm ready to talk and who better to share my secret with than you. The guys at the bar are good friends, but I don't think they'd understand about Ben."

"Why not?" I asked. "They might surprise you."

"Ya, I know, but it's always so loud in there. It's a hard place just to talk and besides, most of the guys never mention their personal lives. It's almost an unspoken rule. I didn't want to be the first to break it."

"If you don't talk about your lives, what do you talk about?"

"I dunno. Stuff, I guess. The weather, sports, sometimes politics, sometimes work...mostly we just drink. By the end of the night no one can remember what we talked about anyway, so I guess it really doesn't matter."

"Don't you get tired of it though? Drinking until you can't remember," I said.

"I suppose I do, but I don't drink to try and forget. I drink because I'm bored. Going to the bar after work is like putting on my shoes…just a routine part of my day. That's just the way it is. Nothing I can do about it," he stated matter of fact.

I didn't buy it. "Bobby, I think that's a lame excuse. You could change that routine if you really wanted to. I think you're just scared. Scared to realize that maybe there's more to life than seeing how many beers you can down without blinking. One day you're going to wake up in the morning, look in the mirror, and not recognize the face staring back at you. Promise me Bobby, that'll never happen to you. Don't piss your life away. Promise me that."

He looked away.

"Fine, if you don't want to promise me then promise Ben. I'm sure he relies on you more than you know."

I didn't want to lecture him, but I couldn't help it. Too many times I'd witnessed alcohol take control of someone's life and run. It was a tonic fuelled by pain, insecurity, and loneliness. I wanted Bobby to know he wasn't alone and I would be there to help him for whatever reason because I was his friend. He was still looking out the window as the waitress brought us our food.

"Look Bobby, I'm sorry. It's just that I care about you and I want you to be happy. Sometimes when I see you at the bar, you look sad. You smile and pretend everything is fine, but there's something missing. I can see it. The happiest I've ever seen you was when I watched you with Ben outside of the coffee shop." Oh shit, I'd blown my own secret.

"You saw me with Ben?" he exclaimed taking a bite of his cheeseburger.

"I was across the street as you were leaving. I was going to yell hi, but you two were having so much fun, I didn't want to interrupt."

"Oh I wish you would have. Ben knows all about you since he reads the newspaper. He thinks I'm cool because you and I are friends."

"I'm sure that's not the only reason he thinks you're cool."

Bobby blushed. "Well, we do get along quite well."

"So, what's his story?" I asked. "He's an adorable kid."

"He is cute that's for sure." Bobby took a big sip of his chocolate shake letting it linger ever so briefly in his mouth before he swallowed, his gaze shifted upwards as though he was trying to collect his thoughts before starting to talk.

"It's kind of a sad story. Is that okay?" I nodded. "It might make you cry a little."

That wouldn't be difficult, I cried during thirty second commercials for Hallmark Cards. "I'm sure I can handle it."

"Well…I've known Ben since he was born…"

Ben was the son of Bobby's friend Jack, whom he had met years ago when they both started working at the cable company. Jack and his wife had tried for years to conceive, so when Ben was finally born, the couple was overjoyed. Life was going great for the young family, until one morning in the shower Jack's wife discovered a lump in her breast. The couple was devastated. She struggled to fight the cancer, but the disease had already taken a strong root. After surgery and months of chemotherapy and radiation treatments, she lost her battle. Ben was five years old when his mother died. The death of his wife shattered Jack. He tried to carry on his daily routine, and keep some sort of consistency in their lives for Ben's sake, but the grief was just too much for him to handle.

He stopped showing up for work, sold their house, and eventually moved downtown to a small apartment where Ben had to sleep on the couch. He became a total recluse. Ben tried to help his Dad, but every time Jack looked at his young son, he saw his wife. Any of Ben's innocent attempts at happiness usually ended up driving his father further to the edge of his cliff. Bobby would often stop by the apartment and take Ben out for something to eat or just to play at the park. He recalled how the apartment was always dark, the windows covered with these ugly heavy purple velvet drapes left from the previous tenants.

Jack rarely took out the garbage, so a very bad smell lingered all the way out to the hallway. The sight of seeing little Ben playing on the floor with a ratty old book, while his father laid on the couch and smoked cigarette after cigarette, almost made Bobby sick to his stomach. Bobby loved kids. I asked him why he never had any kids of his own, but he just shook his head and said that story's for another night.

One night Bobby went to drop Ben back at the apartment after some ice cream, and Jack was gone. The door was wide open but the place hadn't been robbed. There was nothing to take. The only things missing were Jack's personal belongings and the picture of his wife he kept on the coffee table. Bobby didn't know what to do. He hoped maybe Jack had just stepped out and would be back, so he waited in the apartment with Ben. As midnight crept into morning, Bobby realized that Jack wasn't coming back that night. He'd spilt on his own son.

Bobby stared out the diner window. I could tell he was having trouble relieving this part of the story. He just kept shaking his head; almost as if he couldn't believe the words he was speaking.

"He just left?"

"Yep, walked out the door and nobody's seen him since. That was almost two years ago. I still have trouble understanding how a man could walk out on his own son like that. I know he was hurtin', but for God's sake, Ben was only six years old. How do you explain to a child who was still dealing with the death of his mother that suddenly his dad is gone too? I remember him asking me why his dad left, and when he was coming back. Ben handled the situation better than I did. He said that maybe his dad just missed his mom so much that he went to see her while we were getting ice cream. I believed that to be true. I'm sure Jack took his own life but there's never been any proof as to what did or did not happen that night. All I know is that any respect I may have once had for that man quickly disappeared...and he ever does show up, he'd better watch out because I'm likely to kill him myself." Bobby kind of smiled a bit. "Well I wouldn't really kill him...you know what I mean."

I shook my head yes and urged Bobby to keep on with the story. I was so involved now that I wouldn't have cared if they closed the diner up around us. Not knowing exactly what to do about the whole situation, Bobby phoned the police. When they arrived, Bobby said they treated him with great suspicion as to why he was alone in another man's apartment with a six-year boy, but once he explained Ben's background and Jack's instability they eased up.

When Ben woke up, he willingly told the police the truth, which collaborated with Bobby's earlier story and he was off the hook. The police ended up thanking him for his help, but told him he was no longer needed since Children's Services were on the way. Bobby had thought he would just be able to take Ben home with him until everything was sorted out, but the police said since he wasn't family, there was nothing they could do about it. Ben would be placed in foster care for the time being. The news crushed Bobby. It broke his heart to watch the social worker gently take

Ben's hand and lead him out of the apartment, but there was nothing he could do.

The waitress brought us the cheque and I pulled out enough money from my wallet to pay for both. Bobby protested.

"Let me pay Alex," he said.

"No way, I invited you here, so I'm paying. End of story. You can pay the next time."

He seemed satisfied with that and as we got up to leave, I wasn't sure if he still felt like talking.

"So what's on your agenda now?" I asked him.

"Nothing much," he answered.

"Well...I live relatively close by. Do you want to come back to the apartment for some coffee and dessert?"

"Sure, I'd love to if you don't mind. I mean, I'm not keeping you from anything am I?" he asked politely.

"Not at all. Spending time with you Bobby is much better than sitting home alone watching the television."

He smiled and reached for my hand. "You're so sweet Alex. Sometimes I look at you at wonder how in the world it is that you're not married or least involved with someone."

I started to feel uncomfortable, not because I thought that Bobby was trying to seduce me, which I knew he wasn't, but I always hated when people said that. It made me feel like somehow it was totally my fault I was single. I smiled back.

"Thanks Bobby, I appreciate it. I don't what the problem is. Maybe men think I have worms or something."

Bobby started to laugh and patted my shoulder. "Don't worry...it'll happen."

"Ya, ya, ya, whatever. Let's get out of here."

Using humour to deflect those types of comments was a trademark of mine. I had written many columns about the subject, trying to determine whether or not the use of self-deprecating humour was funny, or if it was just another way to avoid the real reasons I was single. Sometimes it's just easier to make fun of yourself than to dig deep and examine the truth. Humour only stings - the truth hurts.

Shirley was out in the hallway when we arrived back at the apartment. I introduced her to Bobby and she was deliberately over polite. I could have killed her!

"Have a good time tonight you two," she snickered. I playfully shook my fist at her and she laughed. I would have to go over first thing in the morning and straighten her out. I could just hear her.

"Bobby is just a friend Shirley," I'd say.

"Of course he is Alex, whatever you say," she'd answer, never giving me an inch as to whether or not she actually believed me.

"No really, I'm not lying."

"I'm happy for you. Besides, he's not so bad looking. Got great teeth!" We would end up laughing and joking, and I would forget that I was even the slightest bit perturbed with her antics of the night before. She had a way with me and I accepted it with happiness.

Back inside my apartment, I put on a pot of coffee as Bobby meandered around the living room. He was looking at the photographs resting on the fireplace mantle.

"Who's this?"

"Oh that's my best friend Vicki. We had just come back from a day at the spa and decided to get glamour portraits taken. She's not really a motorcycle queen. That was just her costume."

I started laughing. We had such a blast that day being pampered and tastefully fondled by the spa staff. It was Vicki's idea to get the portraits done. She fell in love with the leather look, and the glamour staff dressed me as an eighties prom queen. My picture lies hidden in the secret compartment of my closet, banished from the light of day. We also took a picture of us dressed as Arlene and Tessa, our trailer park alter egos. It was hilarious. I never though two respectable girls like Vicki and I could ever look so white trash sexy and trampy, but we did. That picture resides in the confines of my bedroom along with me in my "dirty pose" because like it or not, every woman has a dirty pose just itching to be scratched.

I watched Bobby looking at the picture. He was staring pretty hard at Vicki.

"What's wrong Bobby. Never seen a hot chick in leather before?" He quickly looked away from the picture, his face blushing. "Just kidding...No need to be embarrassed. I have a few pictures of leather clad men that I like to spend time with as well."

He started to laugh. "Your friend is very attractive. I just couldn't help myself."

"You should see her when she's looking respectable. She'd blow you away."

"I bet she would, I bet she would. She seems like a lot of fun."

"Fun isn't the word for Vicki. It goes way beyond that," I laughed.

I poured Bobby some coffee and told him a little bit about Vicki, leaving out the most tragic parts. He seemed very interested in what I had to say.

"You should bring her down to the bar one night," he commented. "It'd be nice to have another gorgeous woman to oogle. The more the merrier we men always say!"

I playfully smacked him on the arm, but took his words to heart. Vicki would love Wilkins Place and the men would certainly love Vicki. Bobby might have a fight on his hands. As our laughter died down, I poured him another cup of coffee and served him a piece of apple crisp Shirley had brought over in the morning.

"You never know when you're going to have guests!" she said. I think that woman was physic.

"So," I said. "I'm dying to know what happened with Ben." He looked away and suddenly I thought that maybe I'd overstepped our boundaries. "If you don't want to talk about it Bobby, that's fine. I don't want to pressure you," I added.

"No, no, I don't mind. It's good for me to talk about it. I'm just trying to remember where I stopped."

"Social Services had just taken Ben away," I said.

"Oh ya, that's right. You have a good memory."

"I remember everything. Sometimes it's a blessing, sometimes it's a curse."

"After they took Ben away I was so upset. He kept glancing back as they were walking down the hallway. His little face looked so sad and confused. I remember him peering up at the social worker, and asking her why I wasn't coming with them. It was really hard to take. The social worker, who was wonderfully kind and compassionate, bent down, looked him square in the eyes, and explained the situation honestly. Ben seemed to understand better because the last time he turned around he gave me a little "see ya later" wave. Putting on a strong face, I smiled and waved back. The social worker told me I could stop by the office in the morning for an update."

Bobby took a bite of the apple crisp and another sip of coffee.

"So, I took the next day off of work and went downtown to check on Ben. Sydney, Ben's social worker, spent the morning explaining to me how the system worked, and the different legal processes Ben had to endure since there was no known family available. I tell ya Alex, I felt helpless. There was nothing I could do. Sydney suggested that maybe it would be best if I stayed away for a little while, just until Ben became accustomed to his new surroundings. The greatest thing I could do for Ben right now was to help them find out what happened to his father. I gave her all the information I could, including the name of his sister who lived in Manitoba. I'd only met her once, and that was at Jack's wife's funeral. For some reason, I'd remembered her full name, which was surprising because I never remember stuff like that. It took some time to track her down since she had moved to the west coast, and when they finally did, she had no idea where her brother was. She hadn't spoken to him in months. Apparently, Jack had called her a while back and asked her to take Ben until he could get back on his feet, but she was in the middle of a divorce and having enough trouble dealing with the pressures of her own life and had to decline. Jack flew into a rage on the phone, yelling and screaming. Finally, she just hung up. If my brother was that upset about something, I think I'd have at least called him back later, but I guess she never did. She hadn't seen or heard from him since."

Bobby continued. The social worker informed him that Jack's sister, although she felt terrible for Ben, refused to take him reasoning that she just couldn't provide the stability he needed at that point in his life. She was barely surviving herself. She was stunned that Jack had left his child, and promised to call if she heard even the slightest whisper from him. She too was worried that he had committed suicide or was living homeless on the streets somewhere.

So Ben was shuffled into the foster care system, moving around quite a bit at the very beginning, as Sydney tried to find a family that was the right fit. He had terrible dreams, waking up in the middle of the night screaming not for his father, but his mother. Bobby tried to visit him as much as he could; however, not having any legal rights to the boy really tied his hands and prevented him from showing up unannounced. Ben always responded well to Bobby and enjoyed his visits tremendously. Sydney was the one who suggested Bobby become a Big Brother, and when he needed a reference, she spoke on his behalf. She went out of her way to ensure that he received Ben as his little brother.

"She was so wonderful to both of us," Bobby said. "Sometimes social workers get a bad rap, but Sydney deserves a medal of honour. She's just great." Bobby was beaming with pride. You could tell by the look in his eyes how much he loved that boy.

"Have you ever thought of adopting him?" I asked.

"Adopt him? They wouldn't let someone like me adopt a boy like him."

"Why not? People do it all the time."

"I know, but I'm not married."

"So what, you have a good job, you have an apartment, a car and more importantly, you love him. The relationship is already there. Any judge could see that. You could make it work. I know you could."

He looked deep into my eyes. "You really think it's even a possibility?"

"You'll never know unless you take a chance. You're always saying how much you love children. Why don't you call Sydney and make some inquiries. I'll help you in any way I can. Think it over Bobby. It's a huge decision and would mean a total change in your lifestyle."

"I have always wanted children." He paused for a moment. "Before we'd gotten married, my ex-wife promised that we'd have children, but changed her mind after the vows had been said. I spent six years trying to convince her otherwise. It didn't work. She was too busy spending our money on a lavish lifestyle…we couldn't afford to think about raising children." He sounded bitter as he spoke.

"Is that why you broke up?"

"Partly. The main reason though was the fact she was having an affair with her boss. A rich executive guy who'd made a fortune on the stock market. I couldn't give her all she needed, and she couldn't give me what I wanted, so we divorced. Simple as that. I've got more money now than I've ever had in my life and I don't have to pay alimony because she married the son of a bitch two months after our divorce became final. Want to hear the funny part?"

"There's a funny part to this story?" I said as he started laughing.

"Alex, there's always a funny part to every story...you just have to look hard. Anyway, a year after they got married, he loses everything in the stock market...and I mean everything. He put all his eggs in one basket and when the technology crisis hit, everything was wiped out." By now, Bobby was laughing hard, his infectious snorting enticing me to join along with him. "Only an idiot doesn't diversify their stock portfolio," he said.

"You play in the stock market?"

"Of course, don't you invest?" he asked.

"Not really. I'm not that sure what to do."

"We'll sit down one day and I'll give you some tips." He was serious and I was surprised. Bobby could be sitting on a piss-pot full cash and nobody would even suspect. I had to give him credit. There certainly was more to this man than I'd ever thought.

"So what happened to them? Are they still married?"

"Ya...last I heard, he'd been fired for certain disputable business practices, so the ex was having to carry their entire financial burden alone. Looks good on her I'll tell you. The greedy bitch!" He slapped his calloused hand on the table, landing on a fork full of apple crisp, which took off through the air.

"Holy shit Alex, sorry!"

We both started to howl. Bobby immediately got up from the chair and ran to clean up the spattered dessert on the floor. Since he made the mess, I wasn't about to stop him.

"Well I'd better get going," he said still giggling as he looked down at his watch. "I just want to thank you so much for hanging out with me tonight and listening to me talk."

"It was my pleasure Bobby, I mean it. I had a great time. We'll have to do it again sometime, real soon."

"You betcha darlin'. It was nice for a change not spending the night at the bar. Now that's something I never thought I'd say."

"Don't get me wrong Bobby, I love the guys at the bar, but sometimes I think a little change is good for everybody."

"I know," he answered, "it's just so hard to get out of that routine."

"I hear ya. Having a routine is what gets us through the day, but changing things up is what gets us through life. You remember those words of wisdom mister." I patted his shoulder as he put on his jacket.

"How did you get so smart?" he asked.

"Well, I watch, I listen, and I learn. That's all it takes. Plus good genetics and a million dollars' worth of schooling."

He was half way out the door when he turned back. "I am going to think seriously about Ben. I honestly would love to have that little boy in my life permanently. I'm not afraid to tell you though, I'm scared Alex. What if they said no? What if they don't think I'd make a good father?"

"Don't worry yourself with those questions right now. Concentrate on deciding whether this would be something that you truly want to do. If the answer's no, that's okay. There's no right or wrong answer here, only a feeling in your heart. I'll help you with the other stuff. I promise." I gave him a big hug and kissed him on the cheek. "Have a good night Bobby and call anytime if you need to talk."

"Thanks so much Alex. Well I'll be on my way. I've got a lot to think about."

He gave me a wave as he headed down the hallway toward the elevator. I watched him stride away and prayed that I hadn't burdened him with the suggestion that he adopt Ben. He didn't seem troubled by the idea, even though I'd just shoveled a load on his plate. I closed the apartment door, thankful that Shirley hadn't seen me hug Bobby goodbye. Then again, she probably watched the entire event though her peephole. It was going to take more than one cup of tea to explain the hug, without having to give away Bobby or Ben's life story. But, I was a writer, and one who was paid rather handsomely to shoot the shit on a regular basis. I could handle Shirley Jones. Who was I kidding? She'd have the entire truth out of me before I'd even poured the milk into my tea.

I walked back to the kitchen and scooped another piece of apple crisp. I knew I'd be forced to endure twenty extra leg lifts per side, but I just couldn't help myself, it was that good. I took my plate into the living room and settled on the couch. The three cups of coffee I just drank didn't bode well in my quest for a good night's sleep, so I thought I might as well spend some time enlightening my life by watching educational programming. I reached down and grabbed the converter, which was still lying disassembled on the carpet from the night before. Gathering all the pieces I could see, I took another bite of apple crisp, and settled back on the couch to MacGyver the converter back together. I had just gotten comfortable, when I realized I was missing a battery and would be forced to either take a break from gorging myself and get up and look for it, or I could just forgo the battery and eat my apple crisp in peace. I looked at the cheap plastic clock hanging on the wall. It was still early.

"Hmmm, what to do, what to do?"

I looked at the clock again. It hadn't moved and I was getting a little bored just sitting on the couch by myself. True, I had a friend in the apple crisp, but she was quickly being cannibalized by my sudden and ravenous appetite for anything sweet. I needed to find that battery. Because I had enough weight in my ass, gravity allowed me to hang over the back of the couch without falling and I blindly reached as far under the couch as I could. In the not so distant past, I wouldn't even of attempted to stick my hand anywhere near the underside of my couch, but since Shirley and her miraculous bag of chemicals came to visit, I was no longer afraid. I couldn't feel the battery yet, so I inched further over the couch and proudly shoved my arm in deeper.

"Ah, there you are!"

I could feel the end of the battery with my fingertips but it still lay just outside my grasp. Of course, I could have gotten off the couch, laid on my stomach and reached for the battery, but that would have been too easy. I liked to challenge myself. Push my body to the limits. I eased over the couch a little more, my pelvis resting on the very top, acting as a fulcrum for my swinging arms and legs.

"Careful now, balance...it's all about the balance. Concentrate. See the battery. Grab the battery. Dismount from the couch."

It seemed fairly easy in my head. I gathered my thoughts and took a deep breath. I felt like an Olympic gymnast going for that perfect ten on the vault. Feeling at one with my mind and body, I decided to take that final step. Slowly reaching down with my right arm, I extended my left leg for balance. So far so good. I took another deep breath and readied myself for the final descent. Creeping my left arm down the back of the couch for support, I ever so gently maneuvered my right hand to the last known battery location. It was still there. I rebalanced my legs, both of which were sprawled horizontally in the air, and with pinpoint precision, I stretched my Gumby arm out and snatched up the errant battery. It was a sweet victory.

With the treasure in hand, I recoiled my arm from under the couch. Suddenly I felt a slight rumbling coming from the inner depths of my intestines. Uncle Frank immediately popped into my head. There was no way to stop it. The gas was running through my body like an out of control locomotive. I squeezed my butt cheeks together as tight as I could, hoping that by blocking the exit, the gas would boomerang back from whence it came. It was no use. I was no match for the raging demon. It exploded into the room like a long loud firecracker, and sent a rumble through the couch so fierce, I lost my balance and fell face first on the floor. Not the dismount I had envisioned. I wasn't hurt, which was good because the whole situation would have been very difficult to explain. One of those "you really had to be there" stories.

"That would be an eight point five on the dismount and ten and a half on the fart! Good work Alex, good work!"

I crawled back around to the front of the couch, making sure I kept my head below the scent still lingering above, and slithered up on the cushions like a snake. Eyeing the apple crisp on the coffee table, I quickly placed the battery in the converter, turned on the television, and reached over to finish off the object of my desire. Before I swallowed the last bite I let it sit on my tongue, hoping the wonderful apple flavor would penetrate deep into my taste buds and sustain my craving until the morning. I closed my eyes, lost in the moment.

For me, life was all about freedom. The freedom to lie on the couch and fart as loud as you wanted. The freedom to eat as much apple crisp as your stomach could handle. But most of all, life was about the freedom of a lonely man to fall so much in love with a little boy, that he would want to change his life completely, and make that boy his son. That's what it was all about. Finding love where you least expected to, and taking that love and making it the center of your universe.

CHAPTER SIX

I wanted nothing more than to have Matt, my burning hunk of love, become the center of my universe. From a distance, he was everything a foxy lady like me could want. He was incredibly handsome, gainfully employed, had a very deep, very sexy voice, and was incredibly handsome. Did I mention that? He was like one of those pieces of cake that sat in the bakery window - perfectly frosted on the outside but you just weren't sure about the inside. It was always buyer beware. That piece could turn out to taste like the soft velvety chocolate you thought, or it could be so stale and dry, you gag and have to spit it out on the floor. The problem was you couldn't tell how the piece was going to taste until you took that first bite. Sometimes you get so used to the frosting; the actual flavor of the cake begins not to matter. That is called a torrid affair. A man worthy of marriage must be equal parts frosting and cake, with a little side of ice cream just for good measure. I didn't have a clue about Matt, but I also wasn't averse to nibbling on his frosting for a while. If his cake turned out to be sweet, then yippee for me, if not, I would continue to shop. Although I was searching for the real thing, one or two frosting flings weren't going to kill me. They might send me to Hell, but they definitely weren't going to kill me.

I had never dated a perfect frosting before and wasn't quite sure of the first date etiquette. We had exchanged numbers but I was determined not to be the one who called first. I had already made an ass of myself in his presence, and couldn't quite bear the thought of running into him again, knowing he didn't return my call. So I waited. It's not like I was obsessed about him calling. It was normal for me to carry the bulky cordless phone around in my pocket as I lounged about the apartment.

Two days went by, then three, then four. I put the phone back in the kitchen. Oh well. I was sure he regretted asking for my phone number the moment I gave it to him. He was probably out banging a blond with hooters down to her shins. His loss anyway. There were lots of cakes to be baked, and many frostings to spread. I wasn't worried, just a little down. I had been looking forward to going out, especially with someone I'd met on my own, and not some total reject sent my way via my mother.

I know she was only trying to help, but just because a forty-five year old man from the Bingo Land enjoys reading my column, doesn't mean I'm going to enjoy his company. That was the only thing we had in common. We could both read. My mother apologized profusely, saying the man had pestered her so much for my number, that she finally just gave in and gave it to him. I remember asking her whether it was appropriate for her to be giving out my phone number to virtual strangers, and she responded by saying, "no one is ever a stranger after eight hours of Bingo!" Lord Mother. What was I going to do with you?

My mom wasn't one of those people who spent every waking hour at Bingo Land. Once a month her girl's group would get together, drink a little wine, play some bridge, and every so often venture out of the house and drive to what they called the 'seedier side of town' to play some bingo. The bingo hall was respectable enough with its bright yellow door and the name 'Bingo Land' topiaried into the evergreen shrubs lining the entrance. The seediness attributed to the fantasy adult store, which had set up shop directly across the street.

I remembered having to cover the neighborhood protests when I was a junior writer. A big stink launched by Bingo Land that quickly disappeared when the company discovered many patrons of the adult store also liked to try their luck with a few rounds of bingo. More than once, something other than a bingo dabber accidentally got pulled from a purse. Even though they may not have won the jackpot, many of the regulars still went home with a little bingo on their minds. I prayed nightly to whatever God was listening, that my mother had never set foot in that store. I wasn't naïve about those things, but the thought of my own mother purchasing the latest model of dolphin pleasure made me a bit queasy. Thankfully, she never mentioned it, and I sure as hell never asked.

By the fifth day, I had completely given up on hearing from my fantasy love toy. Maybe the coffee stain on the right shoulder of my jacket disturbed him. Home from work, I flung my purse on the kitchen counter and hit play on answering machine. There it was…that voice drifting from the machine like a sultry dance. His words wafted through the air like the dense smoke of a blues club. Putting my nose to the sky, I inhaled the sweet scent. Licking my lips to taste a little sugar.

"Mmmm, mmmm delicious. Hello Mr. Sunshine. Mama knew you would call. Never had a doubt." I really was a sad excuse for a human being.

"Hello Alex. How are you? This is Matt. We met outside the coffee shop the other day. I hope you remember…"

"Hmmm…not sure that I do." I said to myself rubbing my fingers on my chin.

"…anyway," the message continued. "I just wanted to let you know that I hadn't forgotten about you, but…"

"OH SHIT….NO BUT'S…TAKE THAT BACK RIGHT NOW!!!!"

"But, I was called out of town on business. I'm actually in Vancouver at the moment…hoping to be back at the end of the week, or the beginning of the next at the latest. I just wanted to say hi, and let you know that I've been thinking about you and will definitely get in touch with you as soon as I get back. If it's not too late, maybe I'll try to call again later. Anyway, I'll talk to you soon. Bye."

I raced to the couch, grabbed a pillow, and placed it over my mouth to try and stifle the enormous scream percolating in the depths of my soul.

"Holy fuck….Ahhhhhhhhhhh. Whoa hoo for me!"

I childishly danced around the room singing my version of the soulful song Supremes' song, "I'm going to make you love me…yes, I will…yes I will." Next up was a few bars of Jackson Browne's, "She's got to be somebody's baby…'cause she's so fine." My dance ended with gyrations to Nelly's, "It's getting hot in here, so take off all your clothes." By now, I'd worked up a sweat, and had to decide whether I should hop in the shower and spend a quiet night reading, or change into my workout clothes and see if I could dance off five pounds before next week. I sprinted to my bedroom, ripping off my work clothes as I went. I threw on my yoga pants and a sloppy t-shirt.

I probably should have changed into a more supportive bra but hey, sometimes the girls liked a little freedom as well. If I was going to bust a move alone in my apartment, what did I care if my tits were flopping around like live fish on the deck of a boat? They certainly weren't big enough to knock over any table lamps. Truthfully, I was hoping the dancing might perk them up. It's a little known fact that your breasts are a direct indication of your mood. When you're happy, they're perky. When you're sad or depressed, they're droopy. My question is how do those ladies with the torpedo tits stay so happy? I bet that if I checked each of their nightstands, I'd find a wide variety of 'bingo dabbers'.

I closed the living room curtains, lit my wide variety of candles, and turned off all the lights. Before I began dancing, I needed to set the mood. I loved to work out in the dark, which is why I never went to the gym. Not only did I hate all the bright lights and waiting for the equipment, I was terrified I would unknowingly break out into song as I listened to my headphones on the treadmill. People start to stare and the situation really does become uncomfortable, especially when the chorus you're singing happens to be Barry Manilow's, "Copacabana".

I didn't care if my apartment neighbors heard me because whatever I was doing I was doing in the privacy of my own home. I'm sure I sounded ridiculous to anybody who felt the need to listen. I would try to just lip synch to the music, but every once and a while my voice would escape, blurting out scattered words like; love, lust, rock me gently and paradise by the dashboard light. I'm certain my neighbors perceived I was some sort of hoochie mama who turned into a craving, panting sex kitten after dark.

Or maybe they just thought I was weird. Sex Kitten? Most definitely. Craving? Almost always. Panting? That was just my lungs gasping for any extra oxygen they could find as I danced my mind and body into oblivion. It didn't matter how stupid I looked, or how many times I almost fell over because I'd lost my balance or tripped over my own feet trying some new move I saw on Saturday Night Dance Party. I didn't care. When the music moved me, I was inspired, and this inexplicable energy arose in my body, forcing me to shake what my mama gave me. Sometimes when Vicki was over, we would dance together as only best friends could.

But for the most part, I liked to dance alone. I loved going out to clubs and dancing, but it was different. Unless you'd had a whole bunch to drink, you had to restrain yourself, and homemade dance routines were definitely taboo. I took pleasure in honing my skills in the living room, so when the day did arrive, and the time called for dancing, and I mean real dancing, I would be ready. I danced for my make believe hotties that sat on the sofa drinking shots of tequila and watching my tits bounce. I danced for the high school cheerleaders who would never let me join because they thought I was too clumsy. I danced the tango for my future Latin lover, and I danced the twist to help with flexibility issues. But most of all I danced for me because I could and it made me happy.

After Matt's phone message I danced for two hours straight, and believe me when I went to shower later, I had never seen my breasts so perky. Happiness drenched my body like water on leaves after a rainstorm. The dew wet on my brow, my skin glistening with sexiness. Not only did I feel fantastic I knew I had to look fantastic. My vision was shattered as I gazed in the mirror. My face was purple and splotchy, certainly not the sun kissed colour I had envisioned, my t-shirt was soaked with sweat, and my hair...well I'd rather not discuss it.

Because I danced so gracefully, I needed to wear the big, bulky headphones, not the little ones that were supposed to fit snugly in your ear. I found they always fell out during my forward leap in "It's Raining Men" which frustrated me to no end, as I would have to stop dancing, replace the headphones, and then try to find my momentum again. With the larger headphones I could jump, twirl and scissor kick (my own personal move) with ease, never having to worry about losing the beat. The main drawback of the larger fully ear-covering headphones was really bad hair. But if that was the price to pay for dancing freedom, I would gladly oblige. A ballerina had her deformed toes and I, the queen of the apartment disco, had my bad hair. At least my hair woes could be cured with a shower. I would hate to go through life never being able to wear sandals.

Before I showered, I sat on the couch and hydrated my thirsty body with what seemed like a pail of water. I must have sat too long because when I went to get up my freshly toned gams had turned to Jell-O, and I fell back on the couch pouring the remains of the water down my chest. As the icy liquid penetrated my shirt and touched my skin, I witnessed an immediate burst of steam rise from my scorching flesh. I was hot. In every sense of the word. I sat in my candle lit room for a minute longer, waiting for my temperature to even out and my legs to regain their strength. I looked at the clock. It was only eight. I'd thought for sure it had at to be at least midnight. The rumbling in my gut reminded me that I hadn't eaten dinner yet, so I forced my wonky legs to stand straight and I ambled into the kitchen.

As I walked, I could hear the water swishing around in my empty stomach. I looked in the cupboard for something that wasn't only quick and easy to make, but would absorb some of that liquid. Something to try and stave off any explosive incidents that might be waiting in the wings. I wasn't overly hungry, the exercise having curbed my appetite, so I chose some instant apple and brown sugar oatmeal. I heated the mixture in the microwave and took the bowl to my bedroom stripping off my sweaty clothes and covering up for now in my trusty pink housecoat.

I loved oatmeal. It was one of those foods you didn't even have to take time to chew. Just spoon it in and swallow. It was the perfect remedy for an exhausted body. I could hear the oatmeal splash as it hit my stomach and like a vacuum, begin to suck up its swampy surroundings. I liked my oatmeal thick with no milk. That way I could squish it through my teeth without dribbling down my chin. The same rule applied to mashed potatoes. They had to be thick, smooth, and creamy. Lumps made me gag. I shoveled the last of my oatmeal into my mouth and sauntered off to the bathroom to take a shower. I had to pick up the pace though; I was quickly losing strength in my legs. Since I wasn't having sex that night, I didn't need to shave, and consequently I was back in my bedroom dressed in my pajamas in a matter of minutes.

The oatmeal must have done its trick because I suddenly felt thirsty for a large glass of orange juice. Walking back to the kitchen, I realized I'd forgotten to extinguish the candles that surrounded my dance floor. I hardly had enough breath to blow them all out. My body felt like it weighed a tonne. To be honest, I think I spit on most of them. It seemed to work quicker. I downed my juice, brushed my teeth, and headed for my bed. It was still early so I crawled under the covers, intending to watch some television, but ended up just lying there in the dark cradling the converter to my chest. The sound of the phone ringing sent me flying through the roof.

"Who the hell calls in the middle of the night?"

It was only nine-thirty, which meant I'd been asleep for roughly forty minutes. That couldn't be. It just couldn't be. I felt like I'd been sleeping for hours. The phone was still ringing. It was probably Vicki. She usually called at this time of night so we could discuss the current installment of our favorite show, which I had of course missed because I'd been napping like a baby. I struggled for a moment to wipe the cobwebs from my brain before I picked up.

"Hello?" I tried not to sound annoyed.

"Hi Alex?" It wasn't Vicki. "Is that you? Your voice sounds different. It's Matt. I hope I didn't wake you."

"No, not at all. I'm just getting over a bit of a cold…that's probably why my voice sounds a little groggy."

It was a blatant lie but telling the truth in this situation wasn't the best thing to do. I didn't want to scare Matt away by informing him that yes, I was sleeping, but that was only because I had exhausted myself from dancing with excitement over his phone message. Nobody but me needed to know how pathetic I really was.

"Oh that's too bad. I hope you're feeling better soon. If I was there, I'd make you some chicken noodle soup. That always makes me feel better," he said.

Ahhh! What a sweetie. No man had ever offered to make me soup before. I was in love. I faked a cough to keep up appearances, and asked him what he was doing out in Vancouver. It turned out he was a financial planner/broker and his boss had sent him out West to smooth a clients' feathers after a botched business deal. Matt was very articulate when he spoke about his job. He loved what he did, and he especially enjoyed the power that came with dealing with millions of dollars. Unfortunately, he said, none of the money was his, but he was moving up quickly and not to worry. I thought it was rather odd for him to discuss his salary aspirations during our first phone call, but I figured he must have been so used to talking about money it was just second nature.

I didn't care too much, whether a person had money or not, and it certainly wasn't one of the main things I looked for in a man. In fact, I hated it when men were flashy with their money. Driving a nice car was one thing, but pulling out a wad of one hundred dollar bills to pay for a coffee was another. To me, that showed insecurity and always red flagged the relationship. I had witnessed too many of my girlfriends in university chase after the rich frat boy, get used, and then recycled like an empty case of beer. The most attractive rich men were those who were either shy about their wealth or very nonchalant, refusing to let their money run their lives. I tended to fall for the guys who had no money whatsoever, but I didn't care. You could marry for money, but what happens if one day the cash runs dry and you suddenly realize that your husband is as smart as a block of wood?

Sure, you have all those cars, jewels and a huge house, but when has any of those material things ever held your hand walking on the beach or told you how pretty you always looked first thing in the morning? As long as we could pay our bills and maybe have a little bit left over for an occasional evening out, I would be satisfied. If I was forced to make a choice between a life of wealth with a dim wit, or a life of peanut butter and jam sandwiches with someone I loved, respected and could talk to, my answer would be clear. I loved peanut butter. It was as simple as that.

"Did you get my message?" Matt asked.

"Yes, I did. I'm glad you called."

"You weren't thinking I wasn't going to call were you?"

"No…I mean…that's a trick question." I could hear him starting to laugh on the other end of the phone. "You want me to say I was, when the real answer is I wasn't, but then it would seem as though I was expecting you to call. Very sneaky line of questioning. Are you sure you're not a lawyer?"

"No," he snickered. "I thought about it at one time, but that meant another four years of school on top of the six I already had. I needed to get out and find a job. Find my place in the world. You know what I mean?"

"Absolutely…the thought of having to go back to school for any reason makes me cringe."

"So you work at the paper? Forgive me…but I asked the girl at your front desk. The one you flipped the bird. I hope you don't mind."

Mind? I can't believe Rachel didn't tell me. That girl is dead meat. No wonder she's been a little cheekier with me lately. She had a secret and I didn't catch on. I was losing my touch.

"Mind? Of course not. I hope Rachel didn't give you any trouble. She can be a brat sometimes. All in good fun though!" I laughed. "I'm actually surprised she told you the truth. Wait…what did she say I did at the paper?"

"She told me you emptied the trash and ran the paper shredder."

Damn her! The turtleneck cover-up was going front page. It was war.

"Of course," Matt continued, "I didn't believe her. I knew you were a writer. I recognized you from the picture in your column. Besides someone who collected the garbage wouldn't have been dressed as sexy as you were that day in the elevator."

Hello! I think I need to dance again.

"Oh please," my voice was suddenly sultry and suave. "Stop. I thought for sure I'd made a total ass out of myself that day."

"You did," he said, "but you still looked sexy."

I wasn't quite sure how to take that last comment. I didn't expect him to agree with me out loud. Then again, I brought the subject up and he answered honestly. Moreover, he did end the sentence with another reference to my incredible sexiness. I let the comment slide.

"Yes I'm a writer, and it's a known fact that writers are the sexiest people around. Sexier than strippers." What the hell was on my mind? I never talk like this on a "get to know you" call. It must have been the Cosmo Magazine I'd read earlier in the day.

"Sexier than strippers, I don't know about that. Show me your routine and maybe I'll have to change my mind."

"Alrighty, enough of this dirty talking," I said, "I hardly know you." Matt started to chuckle. My god even his chuckle was smooth and sexy. Suddenly I felt a deep compulsion to run to the cupboard and rip the lid off a can of instant frosting. Damn the spoon. I would use my fingers.

"Well Alex, I have to get going. I'm due to meet with another client tonight."

"Sure no problem. And really thanks for calling, especially long distance."

"It was my pleasure and don't worry…I'm not paying for the call. Are you kidding? This is a company conversation don't you know. Anyway if I get a chance to call again I will, otherwise I'll talk to you when I get back."

"Sounds great. Good night Matt."

"Good night and sweet dreams."

The dial tone clicked off but I kept the receiver glued to my ear. Good night and sweet dreams! I'm sure Matt didn't realize what a loaded statement that was. I placed the phone back on the hook and let my head flop on my pillow. For some reason I felt a little dizzy. I thought the conversation had gone extremely well. He seemed interested enough and there certainly weren't any of those long awkward pauses that often accompanied many of my "get to know you" calls. It was an encouraging sign. I'd even managed a bit of wholesome flirting. Okay, maybe it wasn't so wholesome, but it's not like my mother was listening in and besides, I was a woman of the new millennium and could be as nasty as I wanted to be. I reached over and turned out the light. Any further nasty thoughts were going to have to wait until the morning. I was bagged. I snuggled under the covers, pulling them tight around my chin and closed my eyes.

"Good night and sweet dreams" he had said. I sighed heavily. "I'll do my best honey. I'll do my best."

I slept like hibernating bear. It wasn't often I woke up in the morning with my body in exactly the same position as it was when I went to bed. I felt great…until I went to stand up. As soon as I tried to swing my legs over the side of the bed, I knew I was in trouble. They didn't seem to want to move on their own. I hooked an arm under each one and slid them horizontally across the mattress like a bulldozer moving dirt. The entire process took almost five minutes, as I had to keep resting my weary arms along the way. It was all Matt's fault that I was so stiff and sore. If he hadn't have left that very sexy message, I never would have danced like a crazed monkey for two hours. Curse that man and his voice!

I finally managed to place both feet firmly on the floor. I gripped the edge of the mattress and attempted to hoist my sorry ass up, rocking back and forth a few times, trying to gain some momentum. On the first attempt, I only managed a few inches before a twinge of muscle ache burned through my thighs. The second attempt wasn't much better. I was determined to make it on the third. I took a deep breath and dug my fingers into the mattress. I rocked back once, then twice and on the count of three, I thrust my body forward tweezing by butt as hard as I could.

"Ow shit!" I screeched as I landed upright, quickly throwing my hands out for balance. I stood there frozen as the blood rushed to my toes causing intense fire throughout my legs. I needed to go to the bathroom, but from where I stood, I had a better chance of wetting my pants then getting my legs to move in an orderly fashion. I took a small step and cringed with pain. I felt like Bambi. "He's a little wobbly ain't he," Thumper the rabbit always said.

I took a small step followed by another and another. Through sheer grit and determination, I made it to the toilet but was devastated when I realized I would have to sit down (not that I'd forgotten a woman has to sit when she pees). I slowly backed up to the toilet like a dump truck making those "beep, beep, beep" noises as I went. I knew the final ascent to the seat was going to be cruel. I inched down my pajama bottoms and braced one hand on the countertop and the other on the windowsill, which hung just to the right of the toilet. Gingerly I began to squat. I only made it halfway before the tingling sensation in my thighs forced me to stop. I looked down and judged the remaining pee distance. I snickered. Not a problem. I'd certainly peed from higher positions, not trusting the cleanliness of some of those seedy bars I'd visited many a Saturday night's during school.

I shuffled my feet a bit to get a better angle, and turned on my internal faucet. I must have swallowed a lake the night before because I swear I stood in that position for at least an hour. I could have read the entire Reader's Digest without getting the red toilet rings on my butt. It would have been ideal. With a last little spurt, I was finished. I wiped, flushed, and washed my hands. As I brushed my teeth, I stretched my legs on the countertop almost gagging on the toothpaste when I tilted my head back too far. I turned on the shower and stripped naked, purposely checking to see if my breasts were still perky.

"Shit. That didn't last very long." Flexing my arms and legs in a couple Ms. Universe poses, I admired my firm butt. "That dancing certainly did the trick," I said stepping into the steam.

As soon as the beads of hot water pulsed against my body, I felt revitalized, my muscles gleefully twitching with the instant massage. I could have stayed in the shower forever, but realizing I had responsibilities other than ensuring good hygiene, I forced myself from its soothing comfort and readied myself to face to the day.

Matt didn't end up returning from Vancouver until Wednesday, but he called almost every day. I was glad we were able to get to know each other over the phone before our first real "face to face" date because it allowed me to find a comfort zone with our conversational skills, without the anxiety of his physical presence looming across the dinner table. Believe it or not, I had carried my intense childhood shyness with me into adult life like a terrible case of bad breath. I could try to mask its appearance by constantly chewing on spearmint gum but it always seemed to rear its ugly head at the most inopportune times. Dating was one of those times. I always tried to make a first date short and sweet and either in the afternoon or in early evening so if things weren't going too well I would have an escape plan ready.

"Gee Alex, are you sure you have to get going?" the loser would ask as he discreetly tried to pick a hard booger from the edge of his nostril.

"Ya, real sorry but I promised my young nephew, I would stop by and tuck him in. He broke his leg playing hockey and had to have surgery. Poor guy, he's in tremendous pain and I wouldn't want to let him down. I gave my word. Sorry, what can I do? I hope you understand."

"Sure, I understand," my date would say, the booger now dangling in plain view. "It's too bad, we were having such I great time weren't we?"

"Oh ya, just the best. Again I'm really sorry."

"No problem. I'll call you later then?"

"Ya sure, you do that." I'd lie.

Thank the Lord for call display. Most guys usually got the hint after a few ten-ring calls but some dates needed over a week. I hated that. Once I screened every call for two straight weeks after a rather horrendous outing to the zoo with a prospective mate. I knew I was going to have a problem the minute he grabbed my hand and tried to have a moment at the polar bear exhibit. His hand was soft, squishy, and a little moist. I almost threw up and prayed he hadn't noticed the instantaneous shudder that ripped down my back like a violent roller coaster. I tried to nonchalantly wiggle my hand free, but this guy had me in a vice grip. My only escape was faking a sudden need to use the ladies room. I waited in the washroom for an eternity, not caring what he thought I was doing, planning my escape. He even asked a few strange women who were entering the washroom to relieve their own needs, to check on me.

Thankfully, one lady took pity and offered her help. We contrived a plan to send my date on an expedition for ginger ale to help calm my "upset stomach". She relayed the message to stud man, who immediately took off for the nearest pop machine. She then watched closely as I snuck out the bathroom door, shielded by her body and ran full steam the other way. I know, it was a horrible thing to do, but sometimes when you've exhausted all other means, horrible becomes the only option. I'm not sure how long he waited outside the door, nor did I really care, except for the sick and cruel part of me that was dying in suspense, wondering what he did after he realized I wasn't in the bathroom. Did he wait all night? Maybe he even went into the women's bathroom to check himself. That would have been fun to see. Hopefully he didn't wait too long (I would have been satisfied with five hours, one for each of the clammy fingers I had to endure) before he got in his car and drove home.

That's why I always insisted on taking separate transportation to and from first and second dates. If two cars ended up in the motel parking lot of Jumping Joe's at the close of the night, that was fine, but I refused to let myself get stuck in an uncompromising situation just because I needed a ride home. Even Wonder Woman had an invisible jet, which of course begs the question as to why none of the other crime fighting superheroes never told her that only the jet was invisible, not her. Oh well, she was still cool.

Polar Bear Paul called fourteen days in a row, leaving these long poetic, desperate, and pathetic messages on my answering machine. I unhooked the machine after two days, but he kept calling. Finally after three hundred and thirty-six intolerable hours, I picked up the phone and in my finest East Indian accent informed the gentleman caller that "the lady Alex you are referring to got a job in the Yukon stripping pinecones from big trees to make festive displays. She moved last week. I am her landlord Sangi."

"Will she be coming back?" asked Polar Bear Paul.

"No, I do not think so. Apparently her festive displays were a very big hit at the Great Bear Lake Festival, and she obtained enough orders to keep her busy for the next year."

"Oh, I wish she would have told me of her plans. I'm her boyfriend."

"Her boyfriend! Oh dear…well that is a shame now isn't it? Maybe she will send you a display for Christmas. Good day to you now sir!" I hung up. My boyfriend? Nice try buddy. Take another trip to the zoo. Trust me…you'd have better luck with a monkey.

Talking to Matt on the telephone was like having a relationship with a blind man. All the superficial elements were eliminated, at least for now. He couldn't tell and certainly didn't need to know that for most of our conversations I was clothed in ratty pajama pants with an equally ratty top, my hair pulled back with a bandana so it wouldn't interfere with my cleansing oatmeal facial mask. If he wanted to picture me lying naked on my bed, wearing only a few strategically placed tissues to ward off the chill, and playfully twisting the phone cord between my perfectly manicured toes, that was his choice. Wait maybe that was my vision of him? The telephone was a wonderful tool to get to know somebody.

We talked about everything freely and easily. I began to recognize what some of his voice variances represented, especially when he was angry. Not at me, but at his client. He was having an extremely difficult time trying to convince him that he needed to change his business plan in order for his company to survive.

"Damn it Alex, he just won't listen to me. It's like he's not accepting the plan just to piss me off."

"Matt, I'm sure it's not about you. Maybe he's just not ready yet to take his company in that direction. You have to remember, he built it from scratch. This can't be any easy decision for him."

"Ya but it's the right decision."

"In your eyes yes, but those aren't necessarily the eyes that matter here."

"I know, but it still peeves me. I didn't go to school just to have some old guy tell me I'm wrong."

"And he didn't work his butt off for thirty years, putting all he had, physically, emotionally and financially into his business to be told by some young smart ass graduate with a degree that everything he had done was wrong."

"Well it was," Matt responded.

"That's your opinion. I mean what's more important, helping this man regain his life or collecting a huge payday?"

"What do you think?" he answered bluntly.

To tell the truth, I wasn't sure. My heart wanted to believe that he would go out of his way to help this man, but my mind was pretty certain he'd take the money. It was one aspect of his personality that bothered me, and I hadn't been able to get a good read on any deeper thoughts he may have had. While we had talked quite a bit, it was mostly about everyday things like the weather, work, entertainment, or sex. I wasn't asking him to bear his soul, just give me a small glimpse and so far, I'd gotten nothing. But I enjoyed his company and conversation immensely, which was more than I could say for Polar Bear Paul or Luke for that matter.

Luke wanted to talk about everything. If I had menstrual cramps he'd ask me to describe the pain so he could share in the experience. To start, I told him to take a pair of tweezers, nip them along his penis, and see how that felt. Then add a wicked headache, nausea, severe back pain and the worst fucking bitch on, and then maybe he would be able to share in my "experience". He never brought up the subject again.

But at least if Luke had something to say, however stupid he may have sounded, he would have said it. With Matt, I didn't know. When he did say something meaningful and not sex related, his words seemed very contrived and calculated, and he almost never said anything dumb. Me, I said dumb things all the time. I even wrote dumb things in my column from time to time. It didn't bother me. Sometimes I stuttered when I was nervous. It was human nature.

Matt was different and I hadn't quite been able to pin point what the difference was over the phone. I was anxious for him to come home, so that we could go out, not just to have coffee, but do something fun and adventurous. Maybe his body language would give him away. The two times I had actually seen him up close were very brief, and with me being so enthralled with his good looks, I never got the chance to sit outside of the circle and observe. I would make a point to do that.

You could tell so much about a person through body language. I didn't mind a little swagger in the step as long as it was followed by a desire to truly get to know someone, and not a self-indulgent parade of one's attributes. Nothing offended me more than a man who strutted his way along, with his head held high and his eyes firmly staring down the future - not caring that he just elbowed an elderly lady in the chin, or squished some other man's sandwich with his steps. These were the types of men who cheated on their wives and neglected their children, all in the name of career advancement. Some had even married their trophy wives, but in the end, they ended up cheating on them as well.

I preferred a man who had his head firmly on his shoulders and his eyes focused on the world around him. My guy could try and strut, but maybe he would end up tripping on the crack in the sidewalk. I would help him get back on his feet and he would welcome my help with open arms. He would give me the freedom to strut, but would also be there to pick me up when I fell. Falling didn't bother me; it was never having anyone there, willing to stretch out an unconditional hand to help me back up. Luke used to grab me by the shirt and pull as quickly as he could, hoping nobody had noticed that I'd even lost my footing. My life and dreams must have been a real embarrassment to him. Maybe that's why he always gripped my arm so tight when we walked. That way I'd have to go where he led. I should have tripped him before he tripped me.

Matt was a toss up. He strutted but hadn't quite lost his footing. I had hope, the relationship was still in its infancy, and although I could form an opinion, I wasn't going to judge his character on the basis of a few phone calls. It's a sad commentary when you hope for someone to falter, but in this case, I needed to see if Matt was real and evaluate his intentions. I was never going to be a trophy wife and I most certainly wasn't a plaything. If he still needed time to discover himself, then I wasn't the woman for him. I didn't want to wake up one morning and realize that the man sleeping beside me, as beautiful as he may be, wasn't the piece of the puzzle I needed. I had already done that and couldn't go through it again. Matt seemed like a good candidate for the cornerstone for my house, but I proceeded with extreme caution.

Luke once told me "the first time you get burned by a fire, it's an accident. The second time it's your own fault". Back then, I wasn't sure of the meaning, and how it applied to my life, but now I made the connection. It was like Vicki and her penchant for abusive men; in order to overcome that, she had to totally regain control of her heart, body, and soul. My body and soul were fine, it was my heart that always got me into trouble. But closing my heart would drain my body of life, and turn my soul into a ghost-like waif, floating in existence until it was time to die. Some people lived like that. Not me. My heart was my body and my heart was my soul. Together they formed the trilogy of my life. They all co-existed, independent yet dependent, each looking out for the other.

Matt may freely win my heart and I may willingly allow him to use my body, but it would be a cold day in Hell before I gave him, or any man my soul. I wanted a soul mate, not a soul keeper. Think of a figurine on top of a trophy. It may look all shiny and beautiful, but it's only a trick. Underneath the gold or silver plating is a lifeless piece of clay. Drop it on the ground and it shatters into pieces. Why does it shatter? It shatters because it has closed its heart, and it splinters because it has no soul. That's why I could never be a trophy wife.

I opened my heart to people and even though I might have sometimes felt destroyed, I would never totally break. My soul kept me alive. It's up to you to rid your life of the things that cause your heart to close and your soul to dissipate. It may make you feel horrible doing it, but sometimes it's the only choice. It's your trilogy. You were there when it was born; you nurtured it and helped it grow. Heart, body, and soul. I had the freedom to give them as I pleased, but more importantly, I had the right to reclaim them if I ever felt they'd been violated or endangered. I thought I had given my soul to Luke. Thankfully, I was wrong. It had always been with me. Hidden in the depths, waiting for me to blow away the cobwebs in my brain and set it free.

CHAPTER SEVEN

Matt and I made plans to go out for our first real date the Saturday night after he returned from Vancouver. Yes, we'd already talked quite a bit, but I still found myself waking up early that morning with a belly full of butterflies. I tried to keep my mind occupied by doing chores around the apartment, but there wasn't much to do. I found myself bored silly by ten am so I called Vicki.

"Hey Alex, what's up?"

"Nothing much. Just bored."

"You bored? I don't believe it for a second. Tonight's the big date isn't it?"

"Yep."

"You're not nervous are you?"

"No. What makes you think that?"

"Because you're calling me at ten o'clock on a Saturday morning, breaking the unwritten rule, which you devised I might add, that clearly states, 'no calling before eleven in case the night before was heaven'. That way, any unexpected guests who may have needed a place to sleep for the night would have had a chance to clear out so we could talk freely about them." Vicki started to laugh. "Besides, I know you too well. You always get nervous before a date."

"I do not," I said, trying in vain to defend myself.

"Ya, whatever you say Alex. I guess it wasn't nerves that caused us to pull over three times on our way to Toronto to meet those two guys at the theatre."

"How many times do I have to tell you? It was the three bean burrito I ate at lunch the day before, not nerves thank you very much."

"That was one of the longest drives ever. We drove for fucking miles in the back country looking for a rest stop."

"Don't remind me," I added.

"And you made me pull over so you could use one of those portable shitter houses for the construction guys."

"I said I didn't want to be reminded."

"I can still picture you hiking up your sexy evening dress as you gracefully stepped over the pile of cement blocks. I've never laughed so hard in my life."

"…and I caught my nylons and fucking ripped them from the knee all the way down. I ended up whipping them off to use as toilet paper. It was either that or take my chances with a very questionable roll of yellowish-brown tissue that was lying on the floor of the stall. I used to make fun of you for always carrying an extra pair of nylons in your purse, but that night you saved my ass."

Vicki was laughing so hard she was having trouble talking. "Can you imagine the guy who dumps the full shitters though, seeing a pair of nylons in there? Especially at a construction site? I'm sure he had a hell of a time trying to figure out which tough guy was feeling silky smooth under his pants."

"I'm sure they don't look at it Vicki."

"You never know. You just never know," she answered. It took a few minutes for both of us to settle down before we could resume our conversation. "So what are you wearing tonight?"

"I don't know yet."

"What do you mean you don't know?" She shouted into the phone. "It's the first face to face and you're not sure what you're gonna wear. Don't give me that shit. You've been thinking about it for a week! I know you."

"Fine…if you know me so well then YOU tell me what I'm going to wear smart ass," I replied knowing full well that she would probably guess my outfit correctly, right down to the underwear.

"All right. Where are you going again?"

"We're going to that little bistro across from Thompson Park."

"Oh, that's a nice place. Anyway…for starters you'll wear your tan colored pants, the ones with a little stretch because they make your butt look smaller…with your navy blue open neck sweater because it makes your eyes sparkle and is cut low enough at the front to show a little of the goods, but reserved enough to say your goods are not for sale. You'll wear your black bra just in case the night goes well…with the black undies that have that little lace flower on the front. I know you'll wear the black combo because they make you feel sexy and even a little dirty."

"Shut up…" I interrupted.

"Finally, you'll wear those nice brown shoes with the slight heel."

Damn it! She guessed right. "I was not going to wear those shoes bitch." I could hear her snicker in the background. "I was going to wear my brown boots, so there!"

"Holy fucker, stop the presses…"

"What? Would you prefer I wore something different?" I said, actually hoping she would suggest something. "I really don't have much else except for work clothes. I need to go shopping."

"Let's go then," she squealed. "I'll find you a sexy new outfit and we can have lunch. I can meet you in a half an hour. What do you say?"

"Fine, I'll go shopping, but I'm warning you right now, I'm not buying a thong."

"Yes you are."

"No, I'm not!"

"I really think you are."

"Goodbye Vicki."

"See ya in a bit, you sexy bitch."

Every time Vicki and I went shopping, she tried to get me to buy a thong, and I of course refused. I'm a pure cotton jockey girl, sometimes a little lace, but mainly just cotton. I like to buy the three pack low waist, mid-leg cut briefs, in white. Now and again if I feel a bit adventurous, I'll buy a pack that contains a solid colour, say purple, a striped pair, and a white pair. That's how I ended up with the black ones; they came as a bonus Christmas special in my pack of whites. I can't wear skimpy underwear. They drive me crazy. I think my butt crack must be magnetic because the moment I walk, it sucks the material in and hugs it tight like a vice. If I can't stand that, I'm almost positive I couldn't stand a thong. Vicki's always going on about how sexy and comfortable they are but I think she's a liar. Sure, a smooth ass may be sexy, but having a long thin piece of material shoved up my ass is definitely not my idea of comfort. She tries her best though.

I remember running my purchases through the cashier one day only to find Vicki had hidden a very tacky leopard print thong in the pocket of the jacket I was purchasing. Not only was I mortified because the sales clerk was male, but I was almost arrested for shoplifting. Vicki quickly explained that she had been the one who put the thong in the pocket, not me. She was hoping that I wouldn't notice him ring it in.

"I'm trying to get her to buy a thong, but she refuses." Vicki looked him squarely in the eyes and smiled. "Guys like girls who wear thongs don't they? I bet your girlfriend wears one."

The teenaged clerk, still holding his hand on the security phone turned a bright pink. Vicki went in for the kill.

"She does, doesn't she? I can tell by the look on your face. I was only trying to help my poor friend here. She's just had a break up and needs a little excitement. I swear I wouldn't have left the store without paying for it. Honest. Would I lie to you?"

I was ready to faint. Vicki was leaning so far over the counter, she was practically sitting on it. The guy was so flustered he couldn't speak.

"Please let us go. Here's twenty bucks for the underwear. You keep it. Give it to your girlfriend. Someone might as well have some fun." Slowly he took he hand off the phone and reached for the twenty dollars. He rung in the underwear and handed Vicki the change.

"Sorry ma'am, I can't accept any gifts. It's against store policy. Give them to your friend. Looks as though she could use them."

Vicki seductively reached to capture the thong from his hand, making sure her fingers brushed up against his. "Thank-you so much. You are just the sweetest."

I could only stand at the counter and shake my head in disbelief at Vicki's sickening use of her feminine wiles. She looked at me and winked, forcing me to fake a coughing fit to hide my laughter.

"Oh, dear," she said. "We'd better get you home and take care of that cough. Bye now."

Vicki snatched up my parcels, grabbed my arm, and flitted the young man a wave over her shoulder as we quickly exited the store. Once outside we both busted a gut.

"What the hell was that?" I asked her.

"I didn't want you to go to jail."

"You are too much," I said as we model-walked down the street.

"At least you have a thong now." I shot her a look of death and she burst out laughing again.

I never did wear the thong. One night after too much red wine with friends, I secured a walnut in the front with an elastic band and flung it off the balcony, while reciting 'Ode to A Thong'. As I ran to the balcony door with the thong held high in my hand, Vicki tried to tackle me, but I was too quick. I was Spiderman, leaping on furniture, plants, and speakers avoiding her grasping hands at every turn. I left her lying in a pool of her own tears. It wasn't until daylight that I realized the puddle wasn't tears, but Vicki's red wine, which is why I used to have a large planter sitting almost in the middle of my room.

Vicki looked sick as she longingly watched my leopard thong hurling through the night sky. I was sick when I heard the crash of my neighbors' stained glass window two seconds later. Luckily, they were on holidays. I felt bad and hoped it didn't rain. Admitting the thong weapon was mine, in a face-to-face meeting, would have been far too embarrassing, so the next day I typed a short note and put it, along with one hundred dollars cash in an envelope, and shoved it in their mail slot. That night it rained. Hard. Damn that thong.

Vicki was waiting for me by the time I had made my way downstairs.

"Holy shit, you were quick!" I exclaimed as I hopped into her car.

"I told you on the phone I was already ready."

"I know, but you're never on time. My five minutes is twenty minutes in Vicki time."

"I'm not always that late am I?" I looked at her with raised eyebrows and nodded yes. "Well," she continued, "I never mean to be. Any particular place you want to go to buy your thong?" she asked, trying to keep a straight face.

"No."

"Good."

"Would you have taken me there anyway?" I enquired.

"No."

I knew I should have driven. She gave me one of her playful grins, which reaffirmed my notion that the afternoon was going to be classic Vicki and Alex. Who knows, maybe Arlene and Tessa, our trailer park alter ego's would even show up. Vicki had that look in her eye and I had to admit I was a little frightened.

"You all set?"

"Yep!"

"Let's plough." She rolled down the windows, cranked up the radio, and hit the gas, veering her way out into traffic. We were too fucking cool…singing at the top of our lungs and bobbing our heads to the beat of the music. It didn't matter we both butchered our attempts at high "C" during the chorus, we rocked and we knew it.

Vicki steered the car toward the Third Street Market. I adored this part of town. It made me feel like a tourist visiting some exotic locale, with all the different vendors displaying their wares on make shift racks set up on the sidewalk. The only thing missing was a stray goat or chicken. Vicki parked on a side street and as I exited the car, I felt inspired by the warm sun as it caressed my ivory skin, gently awakening it from a long winters solace. I closed my eyes, took a deep breath, and smiled.

"What are you smiling at?" Vicki asked. "Pretense to getting laid?"

"Oh fuck off," I laughed. "I was just enjoying the brilliant sunshine."

Vicki laughed and closed her car door. "I don't mean to interrupt your moment here, but we have some work to do. We need to find you a fuck me silly outfit."

She grabbed me by the arm and together we waded into the sea of people. There were vendors everywhere, selling everything from homemade sausages and clothes, to the finest jewelry ever stolen off the back of a truck. Temptation surrounded me like a dense fog, blurring my vision, forcing my willing body to veer off in unknown directions. I could feel Vicki's hand on my arm pulling me away from the object of my desire. She was Satan.

"Alex, do you really need another piece of pottery?"

I pretended not to hear her as I ran my fingers over the handcrafted teapot, lovingly reading the perfect imperfections in the clay with my highly trained fingertips. I could almost taste the cup of tea this wonderful pot would make. The steam would meander through the spout like a lazy river, slowly releasing its aroma to the air like the river empties into the ocean, freeing its contents to spread over the earth for eternity. I was in love; seduced like Eve by the poisonous fruit. She ate apples. I drank tea. I had to have that pot.

"Alex!"

"What!" The venom spewed from my gnarled lips as I pulled the pot protectively into my bosom.

"God damn girl! What the hell was that face all about?" She looked a little scared.

"Isn't this just the best teapot you've ever seen?"

"Yes Alex, of course it is. It's even nicer than the one you bought here last time we came."

"I didn't buy one last time did I?" Vicki nodded her head as I tried to recollect the pot. "No, I'm sure I didn't Vicki."

"It was painted blue."

"Oh ya, now I remember, but I gave that to my mother, so it doesn't count," I said in a very ha, ha, ha voice.

Vicki looked at me as only a best friend could and pulled out a twenty to pay for the pot. She gave the woman the money and snatched the pot out of my hands so it could be wrapped.

"I could have paid for it."

"I know," Vicki said, "but I wanted to look at some of the other stores today." The woman handed her the bag. "You can buy lunch," she added as she tugged my hand, trying desperately to lure me away with the thought of food. It worked. I gave the pottery table one last quick glance then took my precious cargo from Vicki as she led me away from my sin and back onto the path of righteousness.

Despite my moment of evil possession at the pottery stand, we had a wonderful day together. We scoured the shops for things we didn't need but bought anyway, and had lunch in this little outdoor café that specialized in serving whopping sandwiches on homemade grain bread with a side of the sour pickles. With Vicki's help, I did manage to find a new outfit for my date with Matt, which apparently made me look both sexy and sophisticated. I even bought a pair of strappy sandals, although now I had to concern myself with proper toe etiquette. Bright polish, clear polish or no polish? Vicki wanted me to paint them red to reflect the passion that burned in my soul, but I generally preferred a precise clipping with no polish at all. It's not like I had hammer toes or anything, but why bring attention to a body part that really has no business being looked at? The same goes for crop topped belly shirts.

I'd always been a tuck in kind of girl, which I suppose is the reason I detested belly shirts. I didn't mind maybe an inch or two of flesh showing but anything over that should be outlawed, especially if that inch or two is dangling over the top of your waistband like a Jell-O slinky. I'm not against the freedom of personal expression, only against just how much personal expression that some people, male or female, allow to roam free. Nowhere in the Ten Commandments does it state that "middle aged men shall be allowed to remove shirts while cutting the grass or walking the dog". Fellas, give the ladies a break and at least strap on a good fitting bra, it'll do wonders for your posture. Better yet, put that shirt back on; even Moses wore a cloak while he wandered forty days in the desert.

I decided to go way out on a limb for my date with Matt and wear a dress. Vicki found the perfect one hanging on a disheveled sale rack at the back of one of the shops. She knew I'd refuse to pay top dollar for any type of clothing, so she concentrated her efforts on the bargain bins and misfit shelves. The dress cut close and sexy around the bodice, flaring out a little at the bottom, just above my knees with the neckline dipping low, but not low enough to give the girls any ideas about making any unscheduled appearances at the dinner table. The silky material had an abstract pattern of reds, oranges, browns and blacks; not the most attractive sounding colours, but it was one of those patterns that made perfect sense for a flirty dress. When I tried it on, I felt like Venus, Greek goddess of beauty. I twirled a few times in front of the mirror and model walked down one of the aisles.

"Damn Alex, that dress is hot."

"You think?" I answered, pouting my lips in a sexy pose.

"Absolutely!"

"Good, I'll take it." I gave myself one more wink and sashayed back into the change room. I had to agree with Vicki, I did look good. I paid for the dress and tucked it carefully in the bag beside my beloved new teapot.

"What do you want to do now?" Vicki asked.

"I dunno…what do you want to do?"

"Are you done shopping or do you need another outfit for much later in the night, just in case you get dessert to go?" she laughed.

"Oh shut up…I'm done shopping, if you are. What time is it?"

Vicki pulled up the sleeve of her red cotton shirt and checked her watch. "It's time for us to get you home for a little pre-date spa treatment."

"I like the sound of that."

We headed back down the street toward the car, stopping briefly to buy some fudge from the lady at the corner stall. It was always our last stop, a Third Street shopping ritual. She made the best fudge I had ever tasted and I certainly had tasted my fair share of fudge. We each bought two pounds of chocolate mint and I promised myself I'd take at least a pound over to Shirley and Mort as a treat, but realistically I knew that would never happen. I'd eat almost half a pound in the car on the way home, knowing I was going to feel sick, but doing it anyway because I had no willpower when it came to fudge. The other half I'd probably eat later in the night or early the next morning. Depending on how my date with Matt went, I was looking at the prospect of eating two complete pounds of chocolate mint fudge in a span of twenty-four hours. It was a disgusting, yet real possibility. I hoped the date went well, not just for my emotional well-being, but my physical well-being too. My ass was already made of fudge and didn't need two pounds worth of company.

"Is it just me or what? I'm exhausted!" Vicki sighed as she collapsed into the drivers' seat.

"No, I'm tired too...shopping always makes me tired," I replied.

"And hungry..." Vicki reached into her parcel and pulled out her fudge. "This'll perk me up." She broke off a rather large chunk and shoved it into her mouth. She could barely chew.

"That's very attractive Vicki."

"I know...it's a wonder I don't have men screaming down my door," she said quickly grabbing a tissue to wipe away the fudge juice that was escaping from between her teeth as she talked. "I mean, what more could a guy want?" She gave me a big chocolaty smile and I laughed.

"I don't know Vic...I don't know." She dropped me off in front of my apartment. "Have a good time tonight. Don't be nervous. Look great. Act sexy and most importantly, call me in the morning. I'll want details honey, details."

"Ya, ya...thanks for going shopping with me."

"No problem. Anything to help the cause. See ya later."

"Ya bye Vic."

I slammed the car door shut and watched her drive away. She waved in the rear view mirror and I waved back. Today was just the type of day I needed before my date. Instead of the intense nausea I usually felt in the hours, if not days leading up to a date, I surprisingly felt relaxed and calm. That was the Vicki effect. It was still early though. Butterflies lived year round in my stomach.

I had two types of butterflies living in my stomach - the good kind and the bad kind. The good kind fluttered about when I would kiss a man, especially for the first time. I could feel them flying through my body, awakening every nerve and sensation as they made their way up my throat and into my brain. I would close my eyes and take a deep breath to try and keep them from totally conquering my senses, but most times I would be too late, and my knees would begin to buckle ever so slightly. That was a wonderful feeling. Purely spontaneous and definitely uncontrollable. Those butterflies were my friends.

The bad butterflies were always self-inflicted, the result of too much worrying about whether or not the good butterflies were going to appear later in the evening. They tickled about in your stomach flapping their feather-like wings as quickly as possible, a constant reminder of their presence. The only way to banish these demons of hell was to meditate silently over a burning candle, stowing away the nervousness they represented and replacing it with peace and harmony. If that didn't do it, a few glasses of wine would. I crossed my fingers in a vex against the bad butterflies and bounded up the steps into my apartment building.

Seeing Mort patrolling the hall, I decided to give him one of my pounds of fudge. He thanked me and immediately opened the package and broke off a chunk.

"I'll tell Shirley, it came with a piece missing," he gave me a coy wink and continued down the hall.

I unlocked my door and went inside. Carefully placing my new treasured teapot on the kitchen table, I ventured over to the answering machine to investigate the blinking message.

"Oh no, I bet it's him. He wants to cancel. Damn it! I bought a new dress and everything. I was even going to bikini wax just in case." I hovered my finger over the play button like a helicopter trying to land on a windy day. It nervously swayed to and fro, indecisive of its next move. "You idiot! Just press the button."

"Hello baby...It's Matt calling..." It was Vicki. She must have called from the car as soon as I got out. She was trying to talk in a deep sultry voice but couldn't keep from laughing. I was relieved.

"...wear something sexy tonight...maybe a little dress and some strappy sandals...and a thong...that would make me very happy!" I started to laugh. "Well, I'll see you in a few hours baby...and don't be late...and if you do throw up before hand, make sure you brush your teeth."

"You are such a bitch," I said as though Vicki could really hear me.

"Did you just call me a bitch?" Vicki's message responded. She knew me far too well.

"Anyway Alex," she said dropping her horrendous impersonation, "have a great time tonight and try not to be nervous. You'll do just fine. I had a great time today psycho teapot lady. Talk to you tomorrow morning, after eleven of course. Hey munch a carrot for me will ya." The message clicked off. That girl was a piece of work, with a very dirty mind I might add. I loved her.

I checked the clock. Dinner wasn't until eight and it was only four thirty. Since I had some time to kill, I decided to test out my new teapot and maybe get a head start writing one of my columns. While the kettle heated, I went to my computer to check my e-mail messages. There were fifteen. Seven of them were porn, which had inexplicably began appearing after I had helped my niece Paige do an internet search for a school project on the origins of the hot dog. Mistake! Up came pictures of wieners in buns, wieners on sticks, wieners as a stick and wieners in women. Although, I must say, I bookmarked the "wieners as a stick" site to check out after Paige went home. Pure smut. Took me the whole night to get through the volumes of "hot guys" who willingly let it hang for the camera. I was so disgusted I had to invite Vicki over the next night to show her.

Three of the messages informed me that some stranger from Nigeria wanted to give me his twenty million dollar fortune, if only I would "help him in his time of need"; three others were jokes and the last two were work related. I opened the jokes first. The first one I had already seen, the second one was really dumb and the third one was from Wayne.

"Hey Alex...thought you might like this one since it's a little dirty. Talk to you later, Wayne. P.S. Baseball season has started again...let me know if you want to go hang out on the field. I know how much fun you had the last time...Ha! Ha!"

"Ah, that was sweet of him."

I opened the message and burst out laughing. Wayne was right. It was a little dirty and I did like it. Without thinking, I e-mailed him back, thanking him for the dirty picture, telling him I'd be happy to accompany him to the ballpark anytime he wanted me to. It wasn't until I had already pressed send, that I had second thoughts about my response. What if he took it the wrong way? I'm sure he meant as friends. I shook my head at my own arrogance and went to the kitchen to make my tea. I wonder if Matt would enjoy going to a game, especially having press access to the field and the players. Wayne wouldn't care, he'd be happy I found Matt.

I knew as soon as I poured the boiling water into the new teapot that this was going to be the best cup of tea ever. I wasn't wrong. Taking my mug back to my desk, I slumped in the chair to begin writing. Stumped on what to write, I read some of the online newspapers, especially the advice columns to try and jog my mind into writing something provocative. One of the papers had a very interesting letter to the editor. This woman was complaining about how the amount of dog poop at the local playground was affecting her child. Bingo! I had my idea.

I reached for my mug and took a great gulp, which of course burnt the back of my throat.

"Damn that's hot!" I quickly swallowed and took another gulp. I was a glutton for punishment. The words flowed like a waterfall from my brain. While not mentioning the lady directly, my column was a comment on the lack of respect shown by dogs for crapping in the playground sand. Have they no decency? Why can't they poop in toilets like humans? If humans have the technology to send probes to Mars, surely they can devise some sort of devise to keep the dogs from pooping in the park. I agreed that her child's welfare was in danger. Many times, I've come home from a walk in the park with dog poop squished on my shoe and it's gross. Damn the dogs. It's not the owners fault. They can't do it all. It's hard to talk on a cell phone, smoke a cigarette, and pick up poop all at the same time. Like I said, damn those stupid dogs.

I finished my tea as I re-read my masterpiece. Sometimes I had trouble believing I was paid good money to write this crap. (No pun intended). I leaned back in my chair, placed my hands behind my head, and sighed. As I tipped my head back, I noticed the clock on the living room wall.

"Holy shit!" I had to hurry. I must have spent more time than I thought surfing the web, trying to spark my creative juices. I quickly saved my column and tore off for the shower, discarding clothes as I went. It was six-thirty. Not that an hour and a half wasn't enough time to look stunning, but ever since my unfortunate shower incident, I always liked to give myself those few extra minutes.

I had just finished belting out the ending to "Wind Beneath My Wings" when I stepped on the soap, (which I had dropped earlier in the song), and fell forward, smacking my head on the towel rack. I sat dazed in the empty tub while the hand held shower hose went into convulsions, spraying steaming water all over the bathroom. (During my descent, I had tried to steady myself by grabbing the shower curtain. Unfortunately, it wasn't strong enough to catch my fall, the rod landing half on me, and half on the countertop). I was never sure how long I sat there, but I can certainly say that when Vicki came to pick me up to go see a movie, she was very surprised to find me lying half-naked on my bed with a bloody towel on my fore head. We missed the movie and she cleaned up the bathroom. I didn't need stitches, but truly felt like a dork walking around the next few days with a massive black eye and bandage right above my eyebrow.

This time, I showered without incident and was ready to go in about forty-five minutes. I liked my dress. It made me feel sassy, twirling, and flitting about as I walked. I checked my look in the mirror one last time, snatched my keys and headed out the door. Mort and Shirley were in the hall loaded up with groceries.

"Good evening neighbors," I announced.

"Wow, look at you," said Shirley, "he must be someone special if you're wearing a dress."

"I'm not yet sure if he's special, but he does have potential," I answered, giving Shirley a playful twirl.

"He'd better be special," Mort chimed in, "only the best for our girl."

"Thanks, well I'd better scoot. Don't want to be tardy on the first date. Might not make the best impression."

Just as I was about to walk away, Shirley reached for my hand and gave it a squeeze. "Have a good time Alex."

"I will."

"You promise."

"I promise."

I gently squeezed her hand back and gave her double thumbs up as I walked away. Suddenly I began to feel a few butterflies awaken.

"Shit, I knew I should've had a glass of wine while I got dressed."

As I reached the outdoors, I stood for a moment in the fresh night air to collect my thoughts and take a few deep breaths. The restaurant was within walking distance and since it was a beautiful night, I let my feet be my guide. Normally on a first date, I would drive, but it was just down the street and I felt safe in my own neighborhood.

When I arrived at Franco's Bistro, Matt was nowhere to be found. I checked my watch. It was seven forty-five; I was fifteen minutes early. Not wanting to seem over anxious, I ducked into a nearby store to wait. Like a secret agent spying on a suspect, I picked up a magazine and pretended to read, all the while keeping one eye on the front entrance to Franco's. As the time drifted by, I could feel a wave of sickness surfing in my stomach. What if he didn't show up? I wasn't sure I could handle it. I checked my watch again. Eight-o-five. Maybe I had missed him and he was already sitting in the restaurant waiting for me? I mean I wasn't a professional spy and the article in the Wood Worker's Digest was very interesting. Feeling guilty for reading the magazine without buying, I quickly went to counter and threw five dollars on the counter.

"Keep the change," I said.

"I'd love to," the clerk answered, "but the magazine's ten fifty."

"Ten-fifty?"

"It's a special anniversary edition," he responded.

Great. Just my luck. I put another ten on the counter and headed out the door, taking my four-fifty in change with me.

"Hey you."

Startled I looked up. It was Matt and he looked fine.

"Hi," I said.

We exchanged polite hugs and cheek kisses. He smelled like a God.

"I'm not that boring am I?" He gestured to the magazine.

"No, no. I went in to buy some gum and saw this issue. I've been waiting for the anniversary edition to come out."

"Is there no end to your talents? Writer and carpenter? My god, you might be more than I can handle." He put his arm around me and began to laugh.

"Ha, ha, it's for a friend at work. He asked me to keep an eye out for it." My lie was deepening.

"Where's your car?" I asked, changing the subject.

"I walked. It was such a nice night and I don't live too far away," he answered. "What about you?"

"I walked too."

"I guess that means we won't be getting' it on in the back seat of a Chevy tonight eh?"

"I could always run home. I have a Honda. Will that work?" He pulled me closer as we walked towards the restaurant laughing all the way.

"By the way Alex, you look gorgeous tonight."

"Thank-you. You look pretty good yourself."

The hostess led us through a maze of people to our table.

"Everybody's looking at you," he murmured in my ear. "I can't blame them."

It felt good to walk into the restaurant with Matt. Not just because he was so good-looking, but because he made me feel comfortable. The way he gently placed his hand on my back while we walked, and how he kept whispering funny comments in my ear. I didn't expect that. So far, the date was going well.

We sat down at the table and ordered drinks. I was surprised at how easily the conversation flowed, like we were still talking on the phone. He told me a funny story about his plane ride home, even making animated hand gestures for emphasis and I was mesmerized by his voice.

"You're a very funny girl Alex."

"I hope you mean my sense of human and not that I'm weird," I answered.

"Well, you are a little weird, but aren't all writers a little off beat? Isn't that part of the creative process?" I gave him a dirty but playful look. "Don't get me wrong," he continued, "I like weird. I find it very attractive to spend time with someone who's not afraid to be a little different. Not purple hair and nose ring different, but someone who looks outside of the box and can be themselves...Like the first time I saw you in the elevator when you were giving that girl the finger. You don't see that every day. I could tell by the look on her face that you two were kidding around and having a great time. I love that you don't take yourself so seriously. I wanted to ask you out then, but I wasn't about to ask a married woman on a date. That would be inappropriate, so after I finished my business meeting I went back up to ask about you. She was extremely helpful."

"I'm sure she was," I laughed.

"So tell me, why were you giving her the finger anyway?" Matt asked.

"Oh just girl stuff…a little dirty office humour."

"I like dirty office humour."

With drinks already on the table, we paused the conversation to choose something from the menu. I decided on a pasta dish with a side salad while Matt ordered some sort of fish.

"I've been obsessed with fish ever since my trip to Vancouver. Usually I'm a steak and potatoes guy but I ate fish almost every day out West and really enjoyed it."

"I'm not much of a fish person myself," I said. "Although I do enjoy shrimp."

We discussed the merits of eating fish versus beef, and tried to discern whether or not I was a picky eater just because I liked shrimp, but wouldn't eat fish. It was some of the best pre-meal conversation I'd ever had. We laughed like teenagers and it felt wonderful. Matt didn't seem embarrassed when I dribbled a bit of my wine down my chin. In fact, he leaned over and very seductively wiped the drip away. Luke would have given me his 'damit I can't take you anywhere look'- he was so good at giving. Matt just smiled and tried to make me feel better.

"Don't worry about it," he said, "when you were in the washroom, I spilt my entire glass of water on the table, and the waiter had to come and change the tablecloth."

"You did not," I replied.

"You're right, I didn't…but it could have easily happened. Maybe next time it will."

"Next time?" I thought to myself. If he's already mentioning a next time, I must be doing okay, despite my lip malfunction. Our meals came and we bantered with small talk about the weather, sports and the crisis facing today's male: boxers or briefs.

"So are you a boxer or brief guy?" I asked him between bites of my salad.

"What do you prefer?" he asked me right back.

"Since I've never worn either, it seems my opinion on the matter is of no consequence. Frankly, I prefer my men wearing neither."

"Your men?" he asked coyly. "You have several?"

"I have a whole harem don't you know. I keep them locked away in closets until I need a little lovin'. They all provide full service and maintenance. I already assumed you had a harem of women yourself."

He laughed flirtatiously. "No, no. I'm a one woman man Alex."

"That's good," I replied. "I'd have to break-up with you if you weren't." Shoot! I used the words break-up before we were even officially going out. He's going to assume that I think we already are. Then he's going to panic and decide that I'm hopelessly starved for male affection and dump me anyway. I quickly shoved a spoonful of pasta into my mouth and tried to change the subject.

"My good god! This pasta is delicious," I said. "You should try it." I pushed my plate toward him.

He looked up from his own plate wearing a devilish smile and a wee bit of salad dressing. "Sure, I'll try it," he said, reaching over with his fork. "You're right, it is delicious and by the way…"

"Oh shit here it comes," I muttered to myself.

"…could you save some space in the bedroom closet for me? I have to tell you though; I tend to get a bit claustrophobic. I'm not sure how long I could be locked up without going crazy."

"Oh, I think I could manage to let you out quite often. If you were good of course."

"I'd be better than good. I'd be grrrreat!" he said sounding like Tony the Tiger selling Frosted Flakes. We broke out laughing, so loud that the surrounding diners looked up from their own intimate conversations to see what all the fuss was about. "Oops, I guess that came out a little louder than I expected. Sorry if I embarrassed you."

"Embarrassed me? You're going to have to do a lot worse than raise your voice in a restaurant to embarrass me. Usually it's me doing the embarrassing things."

Matt reached across the table and took my right hand. "I don't think I could ever be embarrassed by you."

"Thanks for the vote of confidence, but you haven't seen me drink more than two glasses of wine yet. Just wait!" I replied.

"I like you Alex Hanson. You make me laugh." He paused. "Yep, I like you a lot."

It was a good thing I was sitting down because the sound of his voice and the look on his face made my knees weak. Was he for real? I was beginning to believe he was. We took our time with the rest of dinner, ordered more wine, and had some dessert. We didn't talk too much, having found comfort in each other's company. When the cheque came, I pulled out my wallet to contribute my share, but Matt would have none of it.

"Are you sure?" I asked. "Just so you know I'm not the type of woman who expects the man to pay for everything."

"I'm glad to hear it," he answered. "You can pay next time."

"I think Tuesday's are $1.99 Big Mac Day's at McDonald's if you're interested?"

"You're on!"

Matt held my hand as we walked through the restaurant and out into the night air. The street was a buzz of activity.

"Don't you love this city?" I asked him, snuggling into his shoulder as we stood.

"I do. There's always such a great vibe, especially at night. Do you mind if I walk you home or would you rather I hail you a cab?"

"No, I'd love to walk. It's not that far, if you don't mind?"

"Lead the way."

Still holding hands, we strode off in the direction of my apartment building. Every once and a while Matt would fling my hand into the air like we were five years old and I would laugh. I felt like I was five years old again, not caring about anything in the world except the man who was walking me home. It was a tremendous feeling. I was somewhat surprised at how our first date had turned out. I knew I was physically attracted to Matt but I was never able to get a good read on his personality over the phone. Tonight he exceeded my expectations. He was funny, generous, and very down to earth. He never mentioned money or his career aspirations once, except to say that his training in financial management always helped him figure out the tip. He was even able to laugh at himself, a quality that I admired and found totally lacking in Luke. Too soon, we arrived at the entrance to my building. As much as I wanted to ask him up, I didn't want to seem too desperate or slutty on the first date. Maybe the second.

"Well here we are," I said.

"So here we are," he answered pulling me close.

"I had a fantastic time Matt, I really did." I could smell his wonderful manly scent. I was in heaven.

"So did I. You're very refreshing Alex."

"Thank-you, I appreciate that."

"Can I see you again?" he asked softly.

"Absolutely. I'd love that."

"Good, I'll call you then."

"You'd better."

"Don't worry, I will."

With those words, Matt held me tight to his chest. Not being able to help myself I looked up and found myself staring into his stunning brown eyes.

"Can I kiss you?" he asked.

"I don't know…can you?"

I tried to act coy but I was dying for him to kiss me. I could feel the butterflies begin to stir in my belly.

Teasingly, he brushed his lips against mine as the butterflies almost shot out my ears. He paused for a split second then gently, ever so gently placed his soft lips on mine. It was a good thing he was holding me so tight because my legs had gone numb and I was about to fall over. He finished the long kiss with a few short ones on my cheeks and finally one on my forehead. Trying to catch my breath, I leaned back slightly from his embrace.

"Good night Alex."

"Yeh, good night Matt."

He released me from his grasp and turned to walk away, still clutching my hand. I didn't quite know what to do. After staring at each other for an eternity, Matt finally let go of my hand and began to head off home. He took a few strides before he turned back.

"Did I tell you how great a time I had tonight Miss Hanson," he said rather loudly as I blushed. "I mean what more could a man ask for? Good food, better wine, and the finest woman around. I'd say it was a pretty good night…"

He kept talking as he strolled down the street; turning every so often to wave, and I watched him until I could no longer see his sexy silhouette in the night. With a great sigh, I reluctantly entered my building and headed to my apartment.

I needed a drink of water terribly, since all the moisture in my body had seemingly evaporated with that kiss. Throwing my purse on the floor, I skipped to the kitchen. That man was amazing. His kiss was so gentle and sweet, yet packed the punch of lightening rod. My skin was still tingling and my knees, still a little shaky. He had barely even touched my lips. What a weapon! If it so happened that we ever did have sex, I think he might kill me, but I would be willing to take that chance. This was one piece of cake that wasn't going to be left sitting on my kitchen counter. I had tasted a smidgen of icing and it was good. I had visions that cake itself would be better.

I went to bed a little horny but very satisfied with my day. I'd almost forgotten that I'd even spent the morning with Vicki. I was sure she'd be calling first thing tomorrow for details and thankfully I'd have some good ones, no boogers, no moist hands, no extraordinarily long nose hairs. It had been a good date and for the first time in a very long time, I began to let myself hope. Hope that maybe I wouldn't have to spend eternity alone and haggard, dancing naked by myself on a Saturday night. Like I said, there was always hope.

CHAPTER EIGHT

I woke up the next morning still drugged by the passion of the night before. I lay in bed just snuggling under the covers, replaying the events of the night before in my head. It almost didn't seem real, and I was glad that Matt and I hadn't spent the night together. The kiss and the close snuggle told me more about his character than a night of wild sex ever would have. He was a romantic and I was definitely smitten. I rolled over and looked at the clock, ten fifty-eight; Vicki only had to wait another two minutes. I closed my eyes, took a deep breath, and yawned. The telephone rang.

"Hello?"

"How did it go? Is it safe to call? He's still there isn't he?"

Just as I suspected, Vicki bombarded me with questions.

"No, he's not here. He didn't stay the night."

"Really? I thought he'd have you between the sheets before dessert," she laughed.

"Turns out Vic that he's very much a gentleman."

"He didn't even try to cop a feel of your boob? In that dress too? What is he blind or…no…he's not gay is he."

"Would you shut-up Vicki," I said returning her laughter. "No, he didn't try to feel my boob, yes, he loved the dress, and told me I looked extremely sexy and a definite no on the gay part. No gay man kisses a woman like that."

I held the phone away from ear as Vicki shrieked at the top of her lungs and began singing some seventies disco tune. "Are you finished yet?" I screamed into the phone.

"Sorry, I just had to do a little victory song and dance." She was out of breath. "Seriously, did you have a good time?"

"Vic, I had the best time in the world. He wasn't at all what I'd expected in person. Turns out he's actually a bit shy."

"Ahhhh…isn't that sweet…and scrumptious," she taunted into the phone. "I need more details. I'm coming over."

"Fine. I'm still in bed though," I answered.

"That's okay. I'm still in my pajamas too."

The doorbell rang.

"Hang on Vicki, someone's at the door."

"I know," she replied, "it's me. Don't get up. I'll just use my key."

About two seconds later, Vicki came running down the hall and dove onto the bed landing heavily on my torso.

"Be careful," I playfully shouted. "I have to pee!"

"I can help that!"

She wrestled and wiggled on top of me, all the while trying to press on my bladder with her hands or butt. I was laughing so hard that I almost did involuntarily soak my sheets.

"Stop it," I said giggling, finally grabbing a hold of her arms, and flinging her off to the side. "How bloody old are you?"

"Old enough to want to hear every detail about last night. Spill it honey."

"Let me go to the washroom and pee. Can you wait that long?" I asked her.

"I guess, but hurry up."

When I came back from the washroom, Vicki was snuggled under the covers drinking a coffee and munching on a whole-wheat bagel. "I picked up some breakfast on the way. I wasn't sure if you'd have enough energy to make your own."

I threw my hairbrush at her. "Smart ass."

Vicki just smiled and pulled back the rumpled covers, handing me my coffee. I purposely took my time pulling back the tab on the plastic coffee lid and reached into the bag for a bagel. I could tell she was losing patience, so I very slowly took a long, deliberate slurp from the cup.

"Would you hurry the hell up! I didn't come all the way over here in my pajamas to watch you slurp coffee."

"Alright," I snickered. "By the way, did you go into the coffee shop in your pajamas?"

"Of course. How do think I bought the coffee."

I shook my head in utter disgust and told her about my night. I had to repeat everything at least twice so that she could "get a good read" on Matt's actions or inaction. She especially liked how he protectively guided me through the restaurant.

"Alex, he sounds too good to be true."

"I know and that's what scares me."

"Don't be scared, not all men are dogs; just the ones you and I usually date!" she said. "Seriously I know you're terrified at getting your heart broken again, but please promise me you'll at least give this guy a fair chance. Don't cut him loose on the second date on a mere technicality."

"Moist hands are not a mere technicality," I responded.

"No, you were right to ditch that guy, and the one in the Hawaiian shirt. They were nasty."

"Thank-you," I said smugly.

"Is he going to call you?"

"I have no reason to believe that he won't."

"Alex I'm so happy for you. How did the night end?"

I told her about Matt walking me home and the kiss.

"It was that good?" she asked.

"Felt it all the way to my toes."

"Wow, that is good," she said.

"You said it Tessa."

We spent the rest of the morning and half the afternoon lounging around in bed talking. It was the perfect way to spend a Saturday. I had to go to dinner at my parents that night so I invited Vicki to come along.

"Are you sure your Mom won't mind?"

"Of course not, my family loves you. If it makes you feel better, I'll call her right now."

"Hello Mom."

"Hi dear, you're not cancelling for tonight are you?"

"No, I just called to see if Vicki could come too."

"Of course Vicki can come. I already assumed that she was."

I gave Vicki the thumbs up sign.

"Thanks Mrs. Hanson," she yelled.

"Tell her she's welcome," Mom replied. "I'll see you around five then?"

"Do I need to bring anything Mom?"

"No, I think everything's set. It's nothing special, just a barbeque."

I said goodbye and hung up the phone.

"Your family's so sweet," Vicki said getting out from under the covers.

"Ya, they're not too bad."

"I'd better scoot. Can't wear my pj's to a barbeque."

"I'll pick you up about four o'clock," I walked her to the door. "Thanks for breakfast, and try to be ready on time."

"I will, I will," she answered.

I locked the door behind her and blissfully headed to the washroom to have a shower. I loved barbeques, especially family barbeques. The sun was shining like a beacon of hope on the lingering afternoon. Surprisingly, Vicki was waiting outside when I arrived.

"Holy crap, is that really you?" I said checking my watch. "I'm sure you must be some sort of impostor! What have you done with my best friend Vicki?"

"Oh shut up bitch," she said nose flicking me.

"Ouch!" I retaliated with a crisp clean forehead flick.

"Okay, we're even!" she laughed grabbing my hand before I could get in another shot.

"Look what I brought," Vicki reached into her purse and brought out a small container. "It's lavender body spray, just in case I'm cornered with your Uncle Frank."

I looked at her and smiled. "Lucky for you, he's up at the cottage and won't be able to make it."

"Thank goodness. I love your family, but that guy is a piece of work."

"I know he's the family shame. He's our version of the modern day eco-terrorist, but instead of using chemical gases to poison the environment, he uses his ass gas, which frankly I think is much more potent and powerful. His ass is a weapon of mass destruction all by itself."

"It should be registered with the government or something," Vicki added.

"I hear ya."

When we arrived at my parent's suburban house, the street was lined with mini vans and sport utility vehicles. I squeezed in the driveway beside a shiny new black convertible.

"Tom must have a new girlfriend."

"Why's that?" Vicki asked.

"He's driving a new car and lately it seems that every time he gets a new girl, he changes cars or vice versa."

"How do you know that the convertible's his?"

"Please, you know my family. Who else would drive a brand new convertible? Certainly not my sister Janey, she has the kids and all their crap."

"I wouldn't be commenting too harshly about crap in cars," Vicki replied holding up a used Kleenex she'd retrieved from the floor. "I hate to say it but your car is a shit hole."

"And yours is better?" I shot back. "Bear in mind Vic, I'm the clean one remember."

"Ya, ya, whatever."

We exited the car and made our way into the packed backyard.

"Hello dear."

"Hello Mom," I said giving her a hug. "Remember Vicki?" My mother shot me a disgusted look.

"Your father's over by the shed talking to Uncle Smitty...go say hi." She gave us a polite shove and walked toward the house.

"Do you want a drink first?" I asked Vicki.

"What do you think?"

I caroused by the makeshift outdoor bar and made a couple of lime margaritas.

"Already double fisting are we? It's not that bad." It was my brother Tom.

"No, one is for Vicki."

"I thought that was her. She looks hot."

"Give it up Tom, she thinks you're a pig with women, and I even though I love you to death, I most certainly agree. So where's this month's little tart?"

"Talking with Janey."

"Why does Vicki think I'm a pig? I'm a nice guy."

"Ya...a nice guy who habitually fools around and enjoys doing it. She does think you're a great guy but lately you've been nothing but a shit Tom. Girls like Vicki see you and run the other way...but it's girls like Vicki you want to marry, not that twiggy blond thingy over there."

Janey looked over and gave Tom the 'what and the hell did you bring this twit to a family barbeque look'. Tom started to laugh, "I think Janey wants me to rescue her."

"You think?"

"Alex I know where you're coming from but right now I'm just having some fun." He kissed my forehead. "It's not like I'm going to give her a ring or anything!" He smirked and quickly ran toward Janey before violence ensued.

My brother Tom. He really was one of the sweetest guys in the world, but ever since he broke up with his long time girlfriend Melissa a few years ago, he's been the king of one-night stands and short-lived flings. I think it's his way of protecting his very shattered heart. He always insisted that the break-up with Melissa was mutual, but I heard through the grapevine that she threw him to the curb like a sack of garbage, which was ironic because I'd always thought she was the trash in their relationship. Tom was crushed. He'd been planning to marry her.

At the time, I was still supposedly happy with Luke and selfishly kept Tom and the details of his sad-sack life out of mine. It wasn't that I wasn't concerned for my older brother, just too pre-occupied, and wrapped up in my own happiness to let outside distractions bother me. That changed the minute Luke dumped me like a sack of trash, and I was the shattered one reaching out to anyone that would listen. In that instance Tom became much more than my brother, he became my friend.

We spent many evenings sitting on his patio drinking beer, and discussing the collective horrors of our love lives. It was almost like talking with Vicki except we never discussed any intimate dirty details, because discussing those types of sexual matters with your male sibling was just wrong. I thought I knew my brother, however spending those nights together just talking made me realize how much we'd grown apart over the years. Sure, we saw each other at family gatherings, but those were always fun times when it was acceptable for an older brother to pelt a younger sister with frozen peas in the kitchen. Our contact was humorous and familiar. I'd ask how he was and he'd ask how I was. We'd both say fine…even if we weren't because sometimes it's easier to lie than to tell a family member your life's a complete wreck. You'd rather suffer in silence than to let your family down or see you as a failure.

Everyone has a certain role within the family unit, and if one person breaks down or changes their role, say from "strong rock" to "sappy basket case," the fear is that somehow the whole family will fall apart. In some cases it does, but generally in a solid family atmosphere, one member will always step up and fill the vacated role until the former member is ready to return. At least that's how my family worked and I was genuinely thankful.

Looking back, I could never imagine not growing up in my family. We all lived our separate lives yet remained deeply connected by the red passion that flowed through our veins. It was our bond, our glue and our protection from loneliness. As playfully nasty as he was to me growing up, Tom Hansen would always be my brother. I knew it, he knew it, and nothing in the world would ever change that.

Unfortunately, the passage of time acts like a curtain on your life, allowing you to open and close it as you please, shutting out those who happen to be on the other side. For some inexplicable reason I had closed the curtain on Tom or maybe we had closed it on each other. I wasn't sure. We were both adults, and it was time for me to pull back the curtain and see my big brother in a different light. When I finally did, I was surprised to find that Tom had grown up and faced the same challenges and uncertainties in his life as me. We both thought we were alone. We were both wrong.

"Tom really brought home a winner this time," said Janey rolling her eyes. "Why can't he find a nice sensible girl?"

"Leave him alone. Dating isn't as easy as it looks you know. You're lucky. You already have a husband and three wonderful kids. You hopped off the rotating fuck buddy carousel a long time ago. Tom just hasn't quite found his way yet."

"And what about you?" she asked. "Any prospects?"

"As a matter of fact, I am seeing someone."

"Is he real? Or did you buy a blow up doll?"

"Fuck off Janey." I gave her a half-hearted laugh. Married people always thought they were hilarious.

"Alex, enough with the language. You're not in college anymore. Act like a lady," said my mother placing some more potato chips on the table.

"Ya Alex act like a lady."

"You should talk Vicki. You're the one who taught me all the bad words in the first place."

Vicki looked at Mom and shook her head in denial, "Mrs. Hanson, now you know that isn't true."

"Of course dear." Mom smiled and walked away.

"So Alex tells me she's dating someone. What's he like Vicki?" said Janey.

"I don't know. Haven't met him yet. She's keeping this one under wraps."

We spent the rest of the night eating food and drinking too many margaritas. Since neither one of us was able to drive back into the city, we hauled our sorry asses up the stairs and crashed in my old bedroom. Except for the wicked bed spins, it was déjà vu to fifth grade. We were laughing so hard Vicki almost fell off the bed, and my mother threatened to ground us both if we didn't shut up and go to sleep, which of course made us laugh even harder. Surprisingly, I made it through the night without getting my face washed in margarita smelling back splashed toilet water, which was a bonus and made the barbeque much more memorable.

"I think I kissed your brother last night," Vicki said nonchalantly as we were driving home.

"What you mean, you kissed him goodbye…"

"No, I think I stuck my tongue down his throat."

"What!" I nearly lost control of the car. "You think or you did?"

She paused for a moment, "No, I'm sure I did."

"I don't understand…how'd it happen? Where was his date?"

"I don't really know how it happened. We were in the kitchen getting more ice for the bar and next thing you know, I've got my tongue down his throat."

"Did he kiss you back?"

"Yep…he certainly did!"

"Shit Vicki. I don't know what to say."

"Are you mad?"

"No, I'm not mad. I'm just shocked that's all."

"Tom's an attractive guy Alex. He's got a lot going for him."

"Ya I know, but he's my brother!"

"You're mad. I can tell."

"No Vicki, really I'm not mad…I'm just, I don't know. Is that it? Just one kiss? Or?"

"We're going to dinner on Friday night."

I didn't know how to feel. On one hand, I was happy for them because they were both good people and deserved to be happy, but on the other hand, I was worried about the consequences if it didn't work out. Would I have to choose a side? What if someone's heart got broken? I didn't want to be in the middle. I loved them both. Vicki reached over and put her hand on my arm.

"It's only dinner Alex. I promise we won't do anything foolish. I have to be honest though. There were definite sparks in that kiss. I'm a little scared."

I dropped Vicki off at her apartment and headed home to digest her revelation over a cup of tea. I met Shirley in the hallway.

"Just getting home now?" She peered down at her watch.

"Vicki and I stayed at my parents last night. It was the annual 'Hula Luau Barbeque'. Good times, good times. So how have you been Shirley? We haven't had tea in a while."

"I know I miss you," she answered.

"I miss you too. How about now? Let me grab a quick shower. Say fifteen minutes."

"Have you had breakfast yet?" she asked.

"No…not really."

"I made some carrot muffins earlier this morning. I'll bring them."

"Perfect."

I was just stepping out of the shower when I heard Shirley knocking on the front door.

"C'mon in, it's open." I threw on my trusty pink housecoat and met her in the kitchen.

"Honey, we really do need to get you a new housecoat. That old thing is a ratty piece of crap, excuse my language."

"I know but it's like a second skin to me."

"Even snakes shed their skin every once and a while. You should try it sometime."

"If you insist. The kettle should be hot. Help yourself."

I hustled into my room and threw on an old pair of jeans and my favorite grey T-shirt.

"So Shirley let me ask you something," I said picking up my teacup. "How would you feel if you found out your best friend kissed your brother? Not a little peck on the cheek but a full throttle tongue down the throat kind of kiss."

"Oh my…" she giggled.

"I know…except I said a little more than oh my."

"I bet you did!" She paused for a moment to collect her thoughts and take another sip of tea. "I assume you're talking about Vicki and your brother Tom?"

I nodded in agreement. "Vicki kissed him last night at the barbeque."

"I can see where you're coming from there," said Shirley. She put down her cup and stared straight into my eyes. "Something tells me you're not all that happy they kissed."

"It's not that I'm not happy. I know both of them so well and I just don't want either one of them to get hurt. Vicki hasn't had the best luck with men and to be honest, Tom is going through women like fireworks...a few sparks, one giant kaboom, and then they sail off into the night sky, never to be heard from again. I love my brother, but he's been on a rampage since he spilt with his ex, Melissa. She broke his heart, and because he's so afraid of getting hurt again, he refuses to open up and get serious with any of women he dates."

"Like brother, like sister."

"That is so not true Shirley, I'm willing to open up and get serious with someone. I wasn't going to tell you yet, but I'm dating somebody right now."

"You are? Good for you. Who is he?" She was practically dancing a jig on the kitchen floor.

"I'll tell you when I'm ready, and not a minute before. Let me go on a few more dates before you start planning the wedding."

"Alright, alright...I won't bother you about him...just tell me his name."

"Matt," I answered.

"That's a very manly name...have you slept together yet?"

"Shirley Jones that's a very personal question, and one I certainly choose not to answer at the moment."

"I take it that's a no," she said grabbing my hand. "I'm just having a little fun with you honey."

"Of course you are. So enough about me, what should I do about Vicki and Tom?"

"I didn't realize there was anything you should do Alex. Frankly, I don't think it's any of your business. They're grownups and can do as they please. Besides from what you've told me about both of them, they'd probably make a great couple."

"I'm not denying that. They're perfect for each other, I just don't know if the timing's right."

"Alex, when is the timing ever right? Sometimes when opportunity knocks, you have to open the door and take a chance. So the circumstances aren't perfect, who cares? You're the one who taught me that never taking a chance in life wasn't really living. So what did I do? I took a chance, embraced change and I couldn't be happier. Let them take a chance on each other. Maybe it's their time."

"I know you're right...I just have my reservations about Tom being ready for another serious relationship. I talked to him earlier that afternoon before the kiss, and he seemed intent on just fooling around and having fun. You should have seen the date he brought. I'm sure he picked her up at the Playboy mansion on the way."

"He brought a date?"

"Ya, that's what I mean. He's in the kitchen smooching Vicki while his date was in the backyard. He's just not ready."

"You don't that for sure Alex, and I must say you're being awfully judgmental this morning. How do you know what your brother wants when you're not even sure what you want? You think you know, but are you really sure? You can spend a lifetime searching for that perfect person only to discover he's been staring you in the face all along. Tom and Vicki have known each since they were kids, am I right?" I nodded. "Maybe they've always harbored a secret crush on each other and just never told you."

"Tom has always said how cute he thinks Vicki is."

"There you go. Don't fret so much about this Alex. If it's supposed to work out then it will. You need to concentrate on Matt and finding yourself a new housecoat, just in case he does sleep over one of these days."

"I'm not that bad Shirley...I do have more appropriate after sex wear you know!"

"You need to wear it more often then."

"That would imply that I need to have more sex."

"You said it Alex, not me. You're a beautiful young woman, and not that I condone sleeping around, but a few overnight guests here and there wouldn't kill ya."

"Shirley you're being awfully dirty this morning. What's gotten in to you lately?"

She looked at me and grinned, "Mort."

"Okay, enough said about that."

"Just because we're getting on in age Alex Hansen doesn't mean the wheels don't spin anymore. Sometimes Mort just needs an extra crank or two to get him going!" I laughed so hard I almost choked on my muffin. Shirley got up from the table and put her dirty mug in the sink, "I'd better run. Mort and I have a euchre game scheduled this afternoon with the Stevenson's from the third floor, and we still need to go over our signals. Thanks for the tea Alex and don't worry about Tom and Vicki. What's to be is to be! You just need to have some faith."

"I know, I know. Good luck this afternoon. Are you playing for money?" I asked.

"No, we're playing for dinner. See ya later."

I gently closed the door behind her. Maybe Shirley was right, all I needed was a little faith. Faith in what though? That the relationship would work out or faith that it wouldn't? I just wanted Tom and Vicki to be happy. If they were happy, then I'd be happy.

I flopped on the couch and reminisced about my own kiss with Matt. It hadn't been a tongue thruster but that was okay. I preferred a gentler, kinder first kiss anyway; the kind where your lips barely touched but the tingling sensation lingered forever. That was so much more romantic. If however, Matt chose to stick his tongue down my throat on our next date I wouldn't complain. The phone interrupted my sexual reveries.

"Hello?"

"Hi Alex, it's Bobby."

"Hi Bobby, how are you?"

"I'm doing terrific. I was wondering if I could ask a favor."

"Sure, what's up?"

"Well, I took your advice and contacted a social worker about Ben."

"Bobby that's fantastic!"

"There's one problem. She wants to set up a meeting at my apartment, but my apartment's a mess. A real mess. She'd turn me down for sure.

149

Would you be able to help me?"

"Of course I'll help you fix it up Bobby. When do you want to start?"

"Luckily she's on holidays for a few weeks. Do you think that'll be enough time?"

"Should be...but I'd have to see the place first."

He gave me his address and we arranged to meet later that evening. I was proud to be a catalyst in hopefully bringing Bobby and Ben closer together. No one should have to journey through life alone, especially not a young boy traumatized by the death of his mother and subsequent desertion of his father. Bobby deserved someone to love who was going to love him back. Ben could be that someone.

Suddenly feeling the need to write, I quickly changed my clothes and headed into the office for a while. The newspaper was open seven days a week.

"Good afternoon Alex," Rachel said as I walked pass the reception desk.

"I was working at home all morning," I answered.

"Ya right...Who cares? It's Sunday. I'm only here because it's my Sunday to work. What's your excuse? Hey by the way, Phillip's on the prowl. He was in a meeting with Mike earlier, but I'm not quite sure where he is now."

"Thanks, I owe you one."

"Damn straight you do."

I tip toed down the hallway carefully peeking in each open door as I went. Phillip was nowhere to be found. Relieved, I quickly ducked into my own office.

"So Babe, how 'bout I just ravish you right here on your desk!"

"Phillip what are you doing in my office?"

"Waiting for you...so can I?"

"Can you what?"

"Have sex with you on your desk?"

"No! Absolutely not you pig!"

"Can I touch your boobs then?"

"You can try, but I'd have to kill you. Nobody touches Alex but me." It was Wayne. He gave me a big smile. "Lay one hand on my girlfriend, and I'll squash you like the insect you are."

"Since when is Alex your girlfriend?" said Phillip.

"For a while now...we've been keeping it quiet." Wayne walked over and put his arm around my waist. It felt good.

"I don't believe you," Phillip muttered.

"Do you believe this?"

Wayne took me in his arms and touched his lips to mine. As he drew me close against his chest, I could feel my heart pound like a jackhammer. He parted my lips and kissed me in a way usually reserved for lovers not friends and before I could stop myself, I kissed him back.

"Holy God, would you two get a room already and can I watch?" Phillip stammered grabbing his crotch. "That was hot."

Wayne gently pulled away and looked at Phillip. "If you ever bother Alex again...talk to her...look at her funny, make even the slightest nasty comment, I will find you. Do you understand?"

"Ya I get it," Phillip answered as he headed for the door. "If you two will excuse me, I have to go to the washroom. That was really hot..."

"Hopefully he'll never bother you again." I couldn't speak. "Alex, you okay?"

"Ya, I'm fine."

"Sorry about the kiss. It was the only thing I could think of on such short notice," Wayne laughed nervously.

"No, it was fine...I mean thanks for helping me with Phillip. He's such a slimy little piece of shit."

"It was my pleasure. See ya later?"

"Sure, ya, later..." I mumbled. "Close the door on your way out, will

151

you?"

Wayne closed the door behind him and left me standing alone and very confused in the middle of my office. We were friends, just friends. But was I missing something? Was that kiss just a spur of the moment thing like Wayne said, or had it been lurking deep inside both of us? And for how long? The few times Wayne and I had gone out romantically in the past certainly didn't end with a passionate kiss like that one. Still feeling the weakness in my knees, I reached for my chair and sat down. There was a knock on the door.

"C'mon in," I said, hoping it wasn't Wayne. I needed more time to sort my feelings out.

"What the hell did you do to Phillip? He was all sweaty and gross when he got in the elevator," laughed Rachel. "You didn't kiss him did you?"

"Hell no, Rachel take that back. It frightens me to even think about it."

"What happened then?"

I didn't particularly want to tell Rachel about Wayne, but I was bursting at the seams.

"Wayne kissed me to make Phillip jealous in hopes that he would leave me alone once and for all," I said trying to sound nonchalant.

"Really? Wayne kissed you. That's so sweet. He's such a good guy." Rachel turned to walk away but abruptly stopped. "Wait a minute...why are you blushing so much?"

"Close the door," I replied. "Wayne kissed me on the lips...I mean really kissed me on the lips...and I kissed him back...really kissed him back."

Rachel's eyes nearly popped out of her head. "No way. I don't believe it...actually that's not true. I'm surprised you guys kissed in the office, but I'm not surprised you kissed."

"What the hell are you talking about?" I clambered.

"Oh please," Rachel said sitting on the corner of my desk, "it's so obvious that there's a little somethin' somethin' going on between you two."

"That's so not true," I countered.

"Whatever...there's some serious heat happening every time you and

Wayne are in the same room."

"I never really noticed," I replied.

"Well open your eyes then."

Rachel hopped off the desk and sauntered out of my office like the Queen of Egypt. Who did she think she was, insinuating that Wayne and I were anything more than friends? That was nonsense. We had already tried the dating thing and there was nothing there. No heat, no passion, not even a little spark. Pouring an entire drum of lighter fluid over our bodies, then throwing a match still wouldn't have ignited the flames. I closed my eyes and leaned back in my over-sized office chair. If only Wayne wasn't so nice and gentlemanly. I could have handled Phillip on my own; I'd certainly done it many times before. Wayne didn't need to run into my office and rescue me like I was some sort of damsel in distress. I pounded the desk with my fist. What was I talking about? Wayne was only trying to help. He was only being a friend. A good, caring, and honest friend. But why did he have to kiss me? And if he was just a friend, and there really was nothing going on between us, then why were my knees still weak, and why was I having trouble catching my breath?

I was utterly confused. Just when I thought I had my love life all straightened out, along came another bump in the road to throw me off course. I couldn't take the roller coaster ride much longer and right now, I didn't want to be presented with choice. I wanted to focus my attentions on one man and one man only, Matt. Wayne's kiss was just a blip, a manufactured moment taken straight from the pages of Cosmo. Matt was my choice of cake, and I had to at least have a bite before I even thought about moving on.

I turned on my computer and got to work. I needed the distraction that working on a column entitled, 'How to Survive That Mid Life Crisis' would bring. Not that I knew much about the subject. I definitely wasn't middle aged and wasn't having a crisis. Or maybe I was. Maybe my entire life was one big crisis and I just didn't know it. Everyone had a different opinion on what constituted a midlife crisis. For some it was a total need to change everything in their lives, jobs, houses, cities, husbands, or wives. For others, it was a newfound commitment to exercise or finding their spiritual being. One particular woman I interviewed had her midlife crisis when she ran out of Tide laundry detergent and had to switch to Sunlight. She claimed after that day her outlook on life suddenly became 'lemony fresh', and she was able to see things in a much brighter way.

By the time I looked up from the computer, the clock on my desk read six-thirty. I never worked this late, that's one of the reason's I became a writer. That and my complete disdain for anything mathematical. I was okay with electronics; just don't ask me to multiply anything not in groups of ten. I typed a few more lines to finish my thought, then shut down my computer for the night. Most of my colleagues left their computers on all the time, but the last thing I wanted was for some night cleaning guy to start nosing around in my system (which I know they did) and find all my "dirty girl" files. Those were the files containing bad jokes, dirty web site links, and naughty pictures. My computer was definitely password protected.

I reasoned I had just enough time if I hurried, to run home, grab some dinner and change before I was supposed to meet Bobby at his apartment. I walked into the kitchen and immediately put some water on the stove to boil. It was going to be an instant mac and cheese night. Again. I liked cooking, but I loved instant macaroni and cheese. It was like a warm blanket on a cold January night, the stuff childhoods are made of. Besides it only took three extra ingredients, water, milk and margarine. Those I always had on hand. And if I didn't, Shirley did.

While I waited for the water to boil, I changed into an old pair of jeans and T-shirt. I really wasn't sure what to expect at Bobby's. He didn't seem like the type of guy who left shit stained underwear in the middle of the floor but then again, how well did I actually know this man? As I ate my macaroni, I became extremely apprehensive about going to his apartment. I definitely wanted to help him in any way I could, but on the other hand, I hoped I wasn't getting involved in a situation that was way over my head. As much as Bobby was my friend, I didn't know a whole lot about him, which made the task of helping him go through some very personal items both intriguing and a little bit intimidating.

I was just about to head out the door when the phone rang. Thinking maybe it was Bobby wondering where I was I picked it up.

"Hello?"

"Hey what are you up to?" Vicki asked.

"Actually, I was just heading out the door. You remember me telling you about Bobby?"

"I think you've mentioned his name before."

"Anyway, I'm helping him out tonight with some stuff at his

apartment."

"I bet you are you sneaky bitch."

"No, nothing like that Vic. It's kind of complicated, but I'm really late. So I'll call you later or tomorrow. I'm not sure how late I'll be. By the way, Wayne from work kissed me on the lips today."

"What?" she screamed.

"Sorry, gotta go."

I hung up and started to laugh. Vicki was absolutely going to kill me for hanging up without elaborating. Oh well, it served her right. It was retribution for her not telling me she kissed Tom the moment after their lips separated. I could be such a bitch. As I stepped into the hall and closed the apartment door behind me, I heard the phone ringing again. Poor girl. She was going to have a long night.

I set the wrinkled slip of paper containing Bobby's address on the dashboard and took off. He didn't live that far away, but I was already late and didn't feel like walking. I drove past Thompson Park and turned down Foxborough Avenue. There was a large warehouse on the left hand side, right next to Miller's Old Glass Factory. Thinking I was lost, I pulled over and read the slip of paper again, 514 Foxborough.

"I'm on the right street…I just don't see any apartment buildings."

As I got out of the car to look around, I noticed a man waving from one of the windows in the warehouse. It was Bobby.

"Holy shit…he lives in a warehouse…not a good sign."

I waved back and walked towards the building. Bobby met me at the door wearing a pair of overalls and dirty old work boots.

"Hi Alex. Thought you were lost eh?" He chuckled.

"A little…I'm not back in the warehouse district much. I couldn't read any of the addresses on the buildings. Are they all abandoned?"

"Not all. Some bigwig city official owns the one on the other side of Miller's there. He wants to tear it down and put up an ungodly office high rise, but the council and other city developers won't let him on account of the petition signed by the entire neighborhood, especially around Thompson Park. Myself, I'd like to see all these old buildings turned into apartments and lofts, keeping the existing building exteriors. It'd be a shame to tear it all down."

I looked around and had to agree with him. The buildings did look a little shabby, but they definitely had promise. All they needed was a little tender, love, and care.

"Couldn't you just picture a nice little park over there," he continued seemingly lost in his explanation, "and who wouldn't want an apartment overlooking that?"

"You've got some good ideas Bobby. What does your landlord think about the whole thing?"

"I am the landlord," he said sheepishly.

"You're the landlord? You own this building?"

"And the one over there." He pointed to the abandoned glass factory. "R.J. Miller was my great-grandfather on my mother's side. He pretty much owned this entire block of land. My mother sold the business to the Earthenware Company from California awhile back."

"If she sold the business, how to you still own the property?" I asked.

"Earthenware didn't want to buy the property, only the rights to the business and production secrets and all that. My mother was a smart lady. She gladly sold to Earthenware for an inflated price, knowing all along that the land was worth more than business. When she passed on four years ago, everything became mine. I'm an only child and I never knew my dad. He died in a car accident when I was three."

I stood there shocked at what Bobby had just revealed. He was sitting on property that was probably worth well over a million dollars. If not more. Bobby was rich, really rich.

"You look like you need a drink," he grinned. "I know it's a lot to take in and it's certainly not something I mention to many people. People treat you different when they know you have money, so I just never tell."

"What about your ex-wife? Didn't she leave you because you had no money?"

"Yep."

"I don't get it Bobby. You've got me very confused."

"C'mon in, we'll grab a drink and I'll explain."

He took my hand and gently led me up the stairs and into the warehouse. I did need that drink. Badly. The night was still young and Bobby had a lot of explaining to do. Hiding one's wealth to seem like a regular guy was admirable, but also a little sad. And just when I thought I was beginning to get a sense about my friend Bobby, he threw me for an enormous loop. I guess today was just one of those days. First, I find out Vicki kissed Tom, then Wayne kissed me, and now Bobby announces he's worth more money than all of us put together. This had to be one of the longest, most intriguing days of my life. My brain was tired but Bobby was about to sing me a song about life who's lyrics I didn't want to miss.

CHAPTER NINE

I tried not to gasp as I looked around the musty little apartment. It was a filthy mess. Newspapers were stacked everywhere, along with a couple of chairs and the remnants of more than a few take-out meals. Stretched out in the corner of one of the rooms was a lumpy old cot, covered with a blue denim duvet. I was in shock. Bobby had no chance whatsoever in securing a foster placement for Ben, living in stink hole like this. I turned my head and sighed.

"Bobby...I don't know what to say."

"I know," he answered. "It's awful isn't it?"

"You can say that again. I don't understand. You have all this money, yet you live not only like a pauper, but like a pig. I don't mean to be rude but man, this place is absolutely disgusting! How can you live like this?" I walked over and picked up one of the newspapers, blowing off the dust to read the date. "This paper is two years old and it doesn't even look like it's been opened let alone read. What's up with that?" Bobby looked away. "Look, I'm sorry if I'm hurting your feelings Bobby but I'll be honest with you. If the social worker sees this place, she's going to walk the other way as fast as she can."

He sat on the edge of the faded green couch and put his head in his lap. "I know Alex, I'm doomed. I just can't seem to do anything right."

"Bobby that's not true and you know it," I said putting my hand on his shoulder. "We'll figure this all out. I promise. Now how about that drink. All this clutter and dust is making me thirsty." He started to chuckle, his blue eyes sparkling like a sun-kissed river. He grabbed a couple of beers from the refrigerator and we both made ourselves comfortable on the couch.

"Before I can help you Bobby," I said taking a swig, "I need to know one thing. Why?"

"I don't know really," he answered sheepishly.

"Sure you do. Give it a try. I need to understand this if I'm going to help you in any way. Please Bobby, help me to understand. What's with the whole I'm a poor guy, working as a cable guy for a living routine? By the sounds of it, you could wear Armani every day."

"It's not a routine," he replied. "I do work for the cable company…have for a long time now. Growing up I never saw much of the money from the factory. We lived in a very modest home in a working class neighborhood. Mom never wanted to be rich, and certainly didn't want others to think we were rich, especially the people she employed. By the time I finished college, the factory was sold…"

"Wait," I interrupted, "you went to college?"

"Degree in math, but since the demand wasn't too high for math degrees, I applied at the cable company and got hired right away. I've been there ever since. Love my job and the people I work with, and I'm not ashamed if that's what you're thinking."

"No, Bobby honestly it's not. I just didn't figure you for a college boy. My mistake. I'm sorry."

"No need to apologize," he laughed. "Looking around this apartment, you'd think I was still in college. No…Mom never gave me a cent, and I never asked her for one. I'm glad too…taught me how to survive on my own. I guess that's why I live like I do now. It's the way I've always lived."

"What about your wife?" I asked. "Did she know about the money?"

"No, I didn't even really know about the money until Mom died. I knew she had some, but when her lawyer told me how much, I just about shit my drawers."

"I bet."

"Connie, that's my ex-wife's, she would die if she knew that the entire time we were married, Mom was sitting on a fortune."

"Didn't Connie know about the factory?"

"No, Mom had sold it by the time we were married, and Connie never asked anything about anyone unless there was some way she could benefit. I made good money, but it was never enough for her...she always wanted more."

"Do the guys at the bar know?"

"No, the subject never came up. We don't really talk about stuff like that." He got up from the couch and walked to the fridge. "Do you want another beer?"

"No, I'm good thanks. You know what happens when I have more than one."

"That I do darlin'. So what are we going to do about my apartment here?"

"Can we burn it? Just kidding. How long have you lived here?"

"I moved in after the divorce. It used to be office space for the factory. I haven't really done much with the place as you can tell," he laughed.

"No kidding. I'll say this much. It's going to take more than two weeks to make this apartment liveable. Can I make a suggestion? You need to find somewhere else. Rent another apartment for a while, even buy a small house in the area. You're going to have to spend some money to even have a chance at Ben."

"That's fine. I'll do anything it takes."

"Good. I'll call a real estate agent tomorrow morning and see if they can give us a run down on any of the local properties. You're definitely going to want something with two or even three bedrooms, that's hopefully close to the park. Even if you only live there for a few months. Anything's better than this place. In the meantime, you can clean this place out and build it into a real apartment. Restore the buildings like you wanted to. Hell if they turn out nice, maybe I'd even rent from you."

"If this works out with Ben, I'll let you live for free."

"I'm sure you would," I said laughing. "But seriously Bobby, you need to do this. For Ben and for you."

"It's not like I haven't thought about it. I just never seemed to have the drive or find the time."

"You never had the drive because you only had to care for yourself. Having Ben changes all of that. Take the plunge. Put your money to work. Make the apartments low-rent if you want. It's totally up to you. Put the money to good use. You can't take it with you when you die, so you might as well spend it!"

"That's true," he said thoughtfully. "There really is so much I'd like to do to the place. Like I said before, lofts, maybe low scale office space...not necessarily corporate offices, but small businesses. Maybe even a daycare center, not for profit though. I'd only charge enough to cover costs. I hate that daycare costs parents so much. My problem is Alex...I just don't know where to begin?"

"That's where I can help. I have enough friends and contacts around the city that I can call."

"Can I ask you something personal Alex?" Bobby said reaching over and putting his hand in mine. "Why are you doing this? I mean don't get me wrong, I appreciate it, but I have trouble understanding sometimes. Connie never did anything kind unless she was getting something in return. What do you get out of all of this?"

"I was hoping to help a friend, but if you're accusing me of helping you because I want some of your money, then you don't know anything about me or about friendship." I was offended and Bobby knew it.

"I didn't mean that at all Alex. You were a friend to me before you ever found out about the money. It's just that I've never quite met anyone like you," he smiled. "You've become that sister I never had but always wanted. Thank-you." He reached over and gave me a kiss on the cheek. I hugged him as hard as I could.

"You're welcome Bobby and thank-you too."

"Why are you thanking me?" he asked.

"Because you've not only shown me a whole other world by inviting me to be one of the 'boys', you've made me appreciate my life and all the people that dwell in it. I'll be honest Bobby; I used to look down on people like you and Big Dave. Guys who spent their lives in one big drunken stupor, melting away like an ice cube in a glass of water. The ice cube starts out as the central point in the glass but bit by bit it gets absorbed by the water until there's nothing left and you can no longer distinguish what was ice and what was water. I still don't agree with how much time you guys spend at the bar, or how much you drink, but I understand it. I'm a lucky girl, I have a wonderful family. You guys want the ice to melt. You want to blend in. It's easier that way. You said it yourself...you don't really talk to the guys about important stuff, only small talk and jokes. None of you are willing to stand up and face any of your fears. To be a rock in river only creates rapids, and I'll bet that's just too rough for any of you to handle. Since I've met you, I've been forced to examine my own life and the choices I've made and continue to make. I've decided to be a rock. I want to stir up you, and the guys at the bar. It's become a bit of an obsession. You asked me before what I got out of helping you. I guess that's it. I refuse to see you waste away on a barstool. You have so much to give and I don't mean your money. All of you guys do. You're probably some of the nicest, most genuine people I have ever met, and it's time you all got off your asses and let the world know it. Let your friends be friends and help you. I think you'll be surprised at their reaction."

"Wow, are you done?" he said smiling from ear to ear.

"Yes, I think I am," I answered smugly, "sorry, I didn't mean to preach...it just sort of spewed out that way."

"You weren't preaching but I have to admit, you're good. Really good and I get it," Bobby answered.

"Good because I'm not even sure I get it, and I said it!" I laughed. I got up from the couch and headed for the front door. "I'd better get going before I say anything more. I'll make a few real estate calls in the morning and let you know."

"What do you need me to do?" Bobby asked.

"Start clearing out some of this junk. Maybe Dave and Joe can help. And Bobby...tell them about Ben. You don't have to tell them about the money yet, but tell them about Ben. It's important."

"Alright, I will. I just don't how to approach it."

"How about you just say, 'hey guys, wanna hear my good news?' and go from there," I said.

"That sounds fairly simple," Bobby replied.

"It is. I'll see you later."

I walked out the door and into the humid night air feeling quite positive about my night. I hoped I wasn't too hard on him, but Bobby needed to hear those things out loud. To throw away an opportunity like Ben out of plain fear and laziness was ludicrous, and I wasn't going to let him do it. I couldn't live with myself if I did. And the money! That certainly threw me for a loop. I had to give Bobby credit for not letting the money rule his life or change who he was. I only hoped that if some monetary fortune bestowed itself on me, I would have the same self-control.

I awoke the next morning with vigor and a renewed sense of purpose. Wanting to get an early start to the day, I put the kettle on and quickly hopped in the shower. By eight-thirty I was dressed and sitting at my computer drinking my tea and chomping on a bagel. I was proud of myself; normally I wasn't even awake before nine, let alone ready to face the day. I called Marissa, a colleague who worked in Classifieds at the paper and she hooked me up with a real estate agent known for quick and easy sales. Bobby didn't have to love his new place, he just had to tolerate it until he got Ben, and the warehouse was finished.

The real estate agent had some listings she thought I might be interested in so we made an appointment to meet at one o'clock. I didn't know how to get in touch with Bobby at work, so I called Vicki who was more than happy to take an extended lunch break to help me house hunt. Her office was located in a very busy part of the city. Hordes of noon hour pedestrians were braving the intersections as the cars zoomed by, weaving in and out of the people like they were pylons. I pulled up in front of Vicki's building; a forty story high rise that had about as much architectural design as a ruler, which was surprising since it housed some of the city's most well known and profitable design companies. Vicki was flirting with Dino the hot dog vendor when I drove up.

"I'll go out with you next Friday Dino!" Vicki bellowed as she reached for the car door.

Shaking his head but grinning from ear to ear, Dino replied, "you say that every week!" He playfully threw his hands in the air and turned away to serve a hungry customer.

"One of these days you're going to have to keep your promise Vicki. He'd probably have a heart attack if you actually said yes!" I said maneuvering my car out into the chaos.

"Dino's a good guy. He's married you know!"

"Really?"

"Ya, I've met his wife a couple of times. She sometimes helps him out in the summertime. Wonderful lady. She knows we flirt back and forth. She thinks it's a riot. Dino's all talk. Those two are so in love it almost makes me sick!" Vicki reached in her purse and put on fresh lipstick. "So why are we going house hunting? More importantly, why are you house hunting for a man that isn't even present?"

"It's for Bobby," I stated.

Since Vicki already knew a little of Bobby's story, I filled her in on the rest, including his pot of cash and his plans for the warehouse.

"Wow," Vicki said sounding rather shocked, "how did you respond? I mean what did you say to that?"

"There really wasn't much to say. I was too astounded to even make sense I think."

Vicki leaned back into the seat. "Holy shit Alex...is he cute?" I shot her a dart with my eyes. "Settle down girl," she said, "I was just kidding!"

We both went quiet for a moment, letting our minds wander. Vicki broke the silence. "Actually, I'd like to see the warehouse someday. If it turns out half decent, maybe I'll finally quit my corporate job and set up shop on my own."

"I'll believe that when I see it. Here we are."

I pulled into the driveway of a very tiny red brick home. The shutters needed painted and the garden was severely overgrown but at least from the outside the house had potential. The real estate agent hadn't arrived so we sat on the porch steps and busied ourselves trying to squish ants with our high heels. We had just settled into a left shoe, right shoe pattern when the real estate agent bounded out of her car, apologizing the entire time for being late.

At first glance, the house looked dingy. Not as bad as Bobby's apartment, but dingy none the less. As we toured around, I began to change my mind. Three bedrooms, two baths, decent sized kitchen, family room, den, and basement. It fit all of Bobby's needs. The backyard was the clincher. It was beautiful. A small concrete patio, a well-built wooden shed, and best of all, a gigantic maple tree with a tire swing. I gave Vicki an excited smile. While the agent answered her cell phone, Vicki and I went back in the house.

"The layout's perfect," I said. "Most of the rooms could stand an interior design update, but that's nothing we couldn't handle."

"We?" Vicki replied. "Since when did I become involved in your little scheme?"

"When you kissed my brother and didn't tell me right away," I said laughing. "You owe me a pound of flesh but we'll talk about that later. What's the problem? You love redecorating. With a few more hands, we could have this place ready in a few weeks at the most." I gave her my 'best friend ever' smile and a cute little shoulder shrug.

"Don't give me that look Alex. You think you look all cute and everything..."

"Please," I begged.

"All right, I'll help. But before I do, I'd like to meet this Bobby guy. He seems to have you wrapped around his little finger."

"No he doesn't. He's just a sweet guy who needs a friend or two. You'll like him. His smile and his sparkly blue eyes will hook you. I promise."

"Sorry about that, ladies," said the real estate agent closing the back door with a bang. "I don't usually answer but it was my son's school. He fell from the monkey bars at recess and smacked his leg. Apparently, it's so swollen he can hardly stand. I tell ya, it's always something with him. Broken arm, stepped in glass. He even rode his bike into a fence once. On purpose! I love him, but he's going to put me in the nut house. The school wants me to pick him up as soon as I can, but he can wait until we're finished here. So how do you like the place?"

We talked about the house for a while, and the purpose it would serve for Bobby and eventually Ben. She agreed that it needed some cosmetic work, but assured us the house itself was solid and virtually maintenance free, handing me a copy of the house inspector's report.

"It really is a good property. Hasn't even been on the market a week. With a little work, I'm sure you could make a tidy profit on resale."

"I do like it...but I can't make a final decision without Bobby seeing it as well, even though I'm almost positive he'd say 'if you think it's right, then go ahead and make the deal'. I won't be able to get a hold of him until later on this afternoon. Could you at least hold the property until then?" I asked.

"Absolutely. Call me on my cell after you talk to Bobby, and we can set up another showing. As you can tell, the house is vacant, so I'm free to show it when I please. Later on tonight is fine too."

"What about your son?" Vicki inquired.

"I can drop him off at his father's. We're divorced but share custody. Luckily, we've remained friends. It makes it so much easier on Michael." She locked the front door behind us and waved as she drove away in her sparkling red SUV.

"She seems nice," I said starting up the car.

"Oh no," Vicki replied, "What is going on in that head of yours? I can see the wheels turning."

"Nothing. I just think she was really nice."

"And?" Vicki prodded.

"And...when I talk to Bobby, I'm going to tell him to make sure he freshens up before we see the house again. How stupid of me, I didn't even catch her first name, did you?"

"I think it was Carrie," Vicki said reaching into the front pocket of my purse for her card. "Ya, Carrie Stevenson." We both looked at each other and in unison began to sing.

"Bobby and Carrie sittin' in a tree. K I S S I N G. First comes love, then comes marriage, then comes Bobby pushing a baby carriage."

"He'd love that," I said.

"What? Kids of his own?"

"The whole loving family thing. Kids especially. I think he may actually be more desperate for love and companionship than me."

"Wow...worse than you? I don't believe it," Vicki said. "I'd like to hear more about this Bobby guy. He sounds pretty interesting."

"Do you have to go back to work or do you have time for a coffee?"

"I told them I had consultations all afternoon on this new account I was trying to nab. So I'm good."

After dropping my car off at home, we walked a few blocks and spent the majority of the afternoon sitting on the patio at Sam's Café. I told Vicki as much about Bobby's life as I could without crossing any friendship boundaries between Bobby and me. Vicki seemed genuinely touched by his story and was more than willing to help in any way she could.

"I want to meet him," she said between sips of her lime margarita. "I'd like to be there when he sees the house, if you don't mind. I've got some decorating ideas for some of the rooms, especially the cute back bedroom with the big window."

"No, not at all. It's about time I introduced you to the Posse."

"The Posse?" she questioned. "You mean Bobby isn't the only one?"

"Shit no. There's Big Dave, he likes to dance, and Joe and Jim. There's a whole room full of them. They drink too much and smell a little sour, but generally they're pretty good guys."

"Why'd you pick Bobby? I mean, what drew you to him more than the others?"

I set down my drink, tilted my head to the left, and stared off into space. I thought better this way.

"I don't know...there was just something about him that pulled me in. Maybe it was his twinkling eyes or his smile. I trusted him right away and he seemed to trust me. He has this scruffiness about him but he's one of the kindest most caring men I've ever met and the way he talks about Ben...it breaks your heart that they're not together."

"Did you ever think about dating him?" Vicki asked seriously.

"No, I've never had those sorts of feelings for him at all. He's more like a brother."

"Speaking of brothers...are you okay with Tom and I and that whole kiss thing? We never really talked much more about it."

"I'll be honest Vicki. I was angry at first. Of all the guys in the world, you had to kiss my brother. But I've had some time to think and ya, I'm okay with it. I think you two would be great for each other. My biggest concern is what happens if it doesn't work out and I'm put in a situation where I'm forced to choose between my best friend and my brother."

"That would never happen Alex and you know it."

"Can you give me a guarantee?" I countered.

"You know I can't."

"Fine," I said, "just promise me when he breaks your heart, you won't blame me."

"Alex why do you think he's going to break my heart?"

"I don't know Vicki…he's become such a player since he and Melissa broke up. I'm worried about him."

"Can't you see it's all an act? It's the male defense mechanism for commitment. I've known Tom almost as long as you have, and I know he wants the wife, the house, and the family just like we do. He's just not ready to admit it right now. I'm not saying that I'm the wife, but maybe I can at least help him open his eyes to see beyond the big boobs and pink fingernails he's seeing now."

"I hope so Vicki. I just want everyone to be happy."

"And you," she asked. "Are you happy right now?"

"I think so. Things finally seem to be going my way. At least for this week! Who knows what's going to happen next week? It may all fall apart in a second."

"You are so pessimistic sometimes, especially about your love life."

We poked away at our rapidly dwindling margaritas with our straws. Suddenly Vicki lifted her head and stared me.

"You bitch! You never called me back last night. I forgot all about that. How long were you going to let me stew before you let me in on the details of your little smooch with Wayne?"

"Honestly Vicki, I forgot all about it. By the time I got home from Bobby's place, it was late, and all I could think about was him and the fact he had just told me he owned almost an entire city block! I totally forgot about the whole Wayne thing until now. Maybe I was subconsciously trying to block it out."

"Was it that bad?" she asked.

"No, it was that good…"

"Spit it out Alex…tell me exactly what happened. Every word, every movement, every expression. I need all the details so I can analyze the situation properly."

I ordered some more drinks, and proceeded to tell Vicki about my encounter with Wayne. When I had finished, she seemed as confused as I was.

"So what does it mean?" she asked.

"I don't know. Nothing I guess."

"It doesn't sound like nothing to me. Besides, you're blushing."

I quickly put my hand to my face. "It's just the alcohol," I replied.

"No I don't think it is Alex. What's up? Do you have feelings for Wayne?"

"I really don't know. I didn't think so but now I'm not so sure. I'm terribly confused. I have this great date with Matt, which ends with what I thought was the world's most perfect kiss, then Wayne lays one on me so sweet, my knees buckle, and I almost fall flat on my face." I shrugged my shoulders and tossed back the remnants of my drink, tilting the glass just far enough to free the last chip of ice from the bottom.

"What are you going to do?" Vicki asked.

"Nothing for now. I'm not going to make some rash decision about Wayne based on a single kiss. I really want to see where things are headed with Matt. We had such a good time the other night." I smiled. "Wayne already had a couple chances to sweep me off my feet."

"Or maybe," Vicki interrupted, "you had too much lead named Luke in your feet last summer. You were pretty bitter. Maybe Wayne tried but you just failed to notice. It wouldn't have been your fault or his, just terrible timing."

"Maybe, but I still want to see Matt again."

"Absolutely. Play the cards you're dealt."

"Problem is both guys are aces. Wayne is definitely the Ace of Hearts and Matt with all his flash and glitter is the Ace of Diamonds. But what's trump? Who do I bet all the chips on, the Heart or the Diamond?"

"It's a tough call Alex. One I'm glad I don't have to make."

She smiled and squeezed my hand. I appreciated the gesture and squeezed back. Vicki would always be there to cheer from the sidelines but I knew I had to play this one alone. What I couldn't understand was why there was even a hand to play. I didn't have any feelings for Wayne. Or did I?

It wasn't until later that evening when I was comfortably snuggled on the couch watching television, that I realized it had been two days since our date and Matt hadn't called yet. I could have called him but I was stubborn. For some strange reason, I didn't feel that sense of panic every time the phone rang or that sense of torture when it didn't. I certainly wanted him to call but I also realized if he didn't, it wouldn't be the end of the world. Sure, I'd be upset, but I reasoned I could still be a useful member of society without a burning hunk of love on my arm. Matt was just a guy and maybe he was the one, but then again maybe he wasn't. Maybe I was growing up. Or maybe spending time with Bobby in the last few days made me realize that there are other ways to fill your time and your heart. If Matt called, I'd be happy, if he didn't, it would be his loss.

The next day after work, I picked up Vicki and headed for another meeting with Carrie. We were going to show the house to Bobby. I'd left a message on his machine to meet us at the house, and told him to make sure he shaved and wore a clean shirt. When we pulled up Bobby was standing on the porch talking to Carrie. Vicki looked at me and smiled.

"Just be careful Vicki. He's very shy. I don't want him to feel uncomfortable or anything. He's here to look at the house. If we all have to go out to dinner so he can sign the papers, then so be it."

"I won't say a thing Alex but it looks to me like they're already getting along quite well."

Vicki pointed to the porch. Carrie had nonchalantly placed her hand on Bobby's forearm and they were both laughing.

"Hi ladies," Bobby said as we approached the porch. "Carrie was just telling me a story about her son. Funny lady here!" Carrie blushed and turned her head.

"Bobby this is my best friend Vicki. She's offered to help me help you."

Bobby held out his hand. "Thank you so much Vicki and it's a pleasure to meet you."

Carrie led us inside and showed the house as only a professional could. Bobby seemed impressed but I wasn't quite sure if it was the house or Carrie that had tattooed a permanent smile on his face.

"I like it," he said cornering me in the kitchen. "It's perfect and just the right size. Ben would have his own room and did you see the backyard? Unbelievable! That would have to impress Social Services. Alex, do you really think we could get the whole thing fixed and cleaned up in a couple of weeks?"

"I'm certain of it, Bobby."

"I've got some holiday's saved up which I can use at any time," he answered rambling on like a little boy. "I wonder what colour to do Ben's room. He likes sports and camping. Maybe we could make it a sports theme but he likes the ocean too....fish, whales, all that stuff, especially dolphins. He loves dolphins. Oh Alex, I'm so excited!"

I put my arm around his shoulder. "Me too Bobby. You know you're going to have to spend some money."

"I know. I'll spend whatever it takes. It's only money." I gave him a hug just as Vicki and Carrie returned from viewing the upstairs once again.

"Hey what's going on in here?"

"Nothing Vicki," I answered. "Just giving Bobby a celebratory hug." Carrie's ears perked up.

"You thinking of purchasing the property Mr.....I'm sorry I didn't catch your last name." Carrie looked to me for help. Trouble was I didn't know it either.

"It's Reed. Bobby Reed. And yes, I'm very interested in purchasing the property. Shall we go over some of the details over coffee Carrie?"

"That sounds great Bobby. There's a little shop just around the corner. Let me gather my papers from the living room."

"Bobby...you dawg! What's gotten into you?"

"Nothing Alex except I think she's funny and nice. She's cute too."

"Well I think it's a great idea," chimed Vicki. "Alex, I'm sure Bobby is quite capable of handling the details on his own from here."

"I'll be fine ladies. Thanks so much for your help."

"You're welcome." Vicki shook Bobby's hand. "It was so nice to meet you and I look forward to seeing you again."

"Thanks Vicki. Likewise." Vicki left Bobby and I alone.

"Are you sure you're going to be fine?"

"Yes Mother, I'll be fine," he grinned and kissed my cheek. "Thanks for caring so much."

"I can't help it. You've captured me. Have fun with Carrie and call me later so we can finalize plans for starting the reno's and stuff."

We met Carrie on the porch. "You ready?" she said locking the front door and smiling at Bobby.

"You bet. Wanna walk? The shop's only around the corner right?"

I watched them walk away as I got into my own car. I had only ever seen Bobby walk with that much spring in his step once before and that was with Ben. Maybe things were turning his way. I hoped they were. He deserved it.

CHAPTER TEN

I heard the phone ringing the minute I stepped out of the elevator.

"Shoot!" I took off running towards my apartment, readying the key in my right hand for one quick insert and turn of the door lock. 'Click'. It worked to perfection.

"Hello," I answered panting desperately. Apparently, I needed to increase my cardio workouts.

"Hi Alex. Where on earth have you been lately? You are a very difficult person to get a hold of."

"Hi Matt. Sorry about that. I've been helping a friend with a housing issue the last couple of days. He needed to find a place in a hurry so I've been running..."

"He?" Matt interrupted.

"It's not what you think."

"Better not be...I couldn't stand to think of you spending time with another guy."

"Get used to it. I'm an extremely popular girl! In fact, I spend most of the work day with other men."

"That's not the same."

"Maybe, maybe not." I answered. I really wasn't in the mood for this type of discussion, and found myself feeling a little annoyed that Matt was already concerned about me seeing other men. "You know Matt, there's no need to be jealous."

"Who said I was jealous? I was just kidding. What's with you anyway? You sound a little grumpy."

"No, I'm not grumpy just tired I guess. Sorry."

"That's okay. So listen I made reservations for us on Thursday night at Luey's Pub. It's their special once a year steak festival. I usually make it a guy's night because the portions are so big but I thought after seeing what you ate for dinner the other night, I'd take you!" He started laughing and I pretended to laugh along but deep inside I didn't share his enthusiasm.

"You're real funny Matt. It was a big plate of salad remember. I hope I didn't embarrass you?"

"Geez Alex, I was just kidding." He paused. "So I'll pick you up at seven-thirty."

"Ya sure, sounds great."

"Alex, did I do something wrong? I'm sensing something going on here."

"No Matt not at all. I have a lot on my mind. Sorry. I promise to clear my head before Thursday."

As I hung up the phone, it occurred to me that I'd apologized to Matt three times during the conversation. Why did I feel the need to apologize at all? Spending time with Bobby wasn't a crime. I should have lied and said I was helping a girlfriend. Matt pretended to joke but I was beginning to think there was some underlying sense, a hidden meaning to his words. He was letting me know in no uncertain terms that spending time with other guys, friend or not, was unacceptable to him. I read the message loud and clear. I didn't dare tell him about Wayne. He wouldn't understand. I didn't even understand.

I spent the rest of the evening looking through catalogues and searching the Internet for design ideas. Decorating Bobby's house was going to be fun. Hopefully we could get some of the guys to help. I jotted down several ideas and made some preliminary sketches of the kitchen, family room and bathroom. The drawings were terrible but at least I had an idea of how I wanted to decorate. I paused and shook my head. What was I talking about? How I wanted to decorate? It had become my little project, a great distraction from my own life.

Sometimes you needed a distraction, something to pull you away from your own reality and selfishness. Lately my life had been one big soap opera. Which man do I choose? Who was the better kisser? Questions, I'd actually pondered in the last few days. My life was a boring pathetic excuse of existence. I needed a new focus. My landscape had become cloudy and I was losing my way. Helping Bobby for a few weeks would hopefully clear the fog and set me back on track. I was always up for a challenge and this was certainly going to be a challenge.

The next two weeks were a blur. I spent each morning at the office writing like a fiend so I could leave at lunch to help Bobby at the house. Vicki would join us around four or five and together we would work until at least midnight. I was exhausted but the house was coming along great, and we had so much fun, that the time and the days just flew by.

We had only planned on a quick coat of paint for the walls and some new furniture, but once we got started, the project became a little more encompassing. Bobby, who turned out to be quite the handy man, started out by accidentally putting his hammer through a wall in the kitchen. Before we knew it, every cupboard, countertop, appliance, and even the yellow stained linoleum floor was piled on the front lawn.

"I think we might need some reinforcements," Bobby laughed.

Later that evening as Vicki and I were scrubbing the mildew from the bathroom walls, we heard a booming car horn. I ran to the window and peered into the street.

"Vicki, you've got to see this!" Bobby was standing proudly by a brand new shiny black pick-up truck, his excitement almost uncontrollable.

"Girls, hurry down and check out my new ride!" We were down the stairs and out the front door before he finished his sentence.

"Bobby, what's gotten into to you?" I laughed.

"I figured a truck might come in handy with all the garbage and stuff. Besides, it's pretty cool isn't it? I just couldn't resist. Ben's gonna love it. He's been begging me to get rid of that old beater I drive."

"You used to drive," added Vicki. "Hey, who's that?" She pointed at a second truck that had just pulled into the driveway.

"Joe and Jim! Wow Bobby you told the guys?" I gave him a hug. "I'm so proud of you."

"Ya sorry, that's why I was late tonight. I bought the truck this afternoon and then went around to Wilkins Place to show it off. The guys wondered what I needed a truck for, so I told them."

"What'd they say?" I leaned in with anticipation.

"They were pretty surprised...but happy for me."

"Did you tell them everything?"

"Everything...the money, the warehouse, my plans, and I told them about Ben." He looked away as his blue eyes began to gloss over. "Those guys are really something."

I kissed his cheek. "I know Bobby. So are you."

"Would you two quit smooching and introduce us to this fine young lady."

"Joe, this is my best friend Vicki. She's been helping out with the house." Joe took Vicki's hand.

"I'm not sure you want to kiss it Joe," Vicki laughed. "I've been scrubbing a nasty looking bathroom wall." Joe looked at her hand and kissed it anyway.

"I'm sure I've kissed worse in my lifetime!" He bellowed a hoot so infectious we caught it instantly.

"What's all this laughing about?" Big Dave yelled out his car window as he parked on the street. "Could use some help here with the pizza, boys"

"Dave you shouldn't have."

"I know I shouldn't have, but I did anyway. You got a problem with that Bobby? I say we eat now and then get to work."

"Dave you always want to eat first!" said Jim.

"Can't work without a full belly."

"I'm a little worried Dave...if you put any more food in that belly...I think it might explode!"

"Shut your trap Joe. You should talk."

"How 'bout you all shut up so I can show you inside the house." Bobby grabbed a pizza box and headed for the front door.

Vicki pulled me aside on the way in. "Are they always like this?"

"Yep...wait 'till they start drinking. It'll get worse. Much worse! There might even be dancing."

"Dancing?"

"You never know with this crowd Vic. You just never know…"

Since the house was devoid of any real furniture, Vicki and I sat on empty milk crates and dug into our pizza.

"Darlin' are you sure you're even chewin'?" said Dave.

"Sorry to gross you out Dave, but we're starving. Washing all the shit off those bathroom walls is hard work."

"And I'm pretty sure in some spots it literally was shit," Vicki added. "It's one of the most disgusting things I've ever seen."

"That's nothing," said Dave, "you should see the men's washroom at work. Now that's disgusting. Pee, shit, puke..."

"Okay Dave," Joe interrupted, "we get the picture."

Bobby was leaning up against the living room wall smiling like a monkey, enjoying every minute of the razzing. His messy chestnut colored hair flopped loosely over his ears and for the first time I felt a slight twitter in my stomach as I watched him. He looked so happy, so at ease with himself. It was an attractive quality.

Vicki and I finished our pizza and headed back up to the bathroom. The boys went outside and started loading the garbage into the trucks. You could hear them laughing and telling jokes the entire time. I was glad to see that Bobby had some true friends. Guys that would be there when he needed them the most, no questions asked and no judgments made.

"Thanks for all your help Vic. I know Bobby appreciates it and so do I. It means a lot to me."

"No problem. I hate to admit it but I've had fun. Who knew cleaning up poop could be such a rewarding experience."

"No seriously Vic, you're always there for me."

"No Alex, we're there for each other. It's called a support system. Besides, with the debt I owe you. You saved my life once."

"All I did was answer the door! You did the rest."

"You did more than answer the door Alex. You rescued me from myself. You know there's nothing I wouldn't do for you."

"Well now that you mention it...I was just about to scrape some unknown substance from behind the toilet here." I turned my head away and waited for the ensuing smack. She didn't disappoint.

"You bitch! Fine! Where's the Pinesol?"

"How 'bout you clean the left side and I'll clean the right," I said throwing her the bottle.

We worked late into the night and finished the bathroom completely. Despite the ugly 1970's gold countertop, the room looked pretty good. Bobby was ecstatic. He figured that a sparkling bathroom would make a positive impression on Social Services. I guess for a man, proving that you could pee into the big white bowl and not beside it was a mark of growth and maturity. Bobby promised he would keep the bathroom clean, especially after Ben arrived but Vicki and I had our doubts. Every pistol misfires once and while. We left a cleaning bucket and the Pinesol under the sink just in case.

The next afternoon we tackled stripping the purple striped wallpaper off the walls in Ben's room. It turned out that the purple paper was only the first in a long list of patterns, floral, and more stripes.

"My gosh what were these people thinking?" Bobby muttered. "I've never seen anything like this before. The steamer's isn't even working. We're gonna have to do the entire thing by hand."

I checked my watch. "Damn it...and you're going to have to do it without me. Sorry."

"Oh ya," said Vicki, "big date tonight at the all you can eat beef buffet!"

"Oh zip it! I've got to go. Matt hates it if you're late. Shit Vicki, Matt would have killed you by now."

"Matt huh? So that's his name," said Bobby, "I knew there was someone. I'd heard you two talking the other day."

"You're not jealous now, are you Bobby?" I winked.

"No, but he better be good enough for you Alex. I mean it or he'll have to deal with me!"

"Thanks, I'll see you guys later!"

"I won't call tomorrow until after eleven, just in case," Vicki yelled.

"You'd better not. 'Cause nothing makes me hornier than a big old plate of beef. Medium rare!"

I closed the door and sprinted to the car. It was already quarter after six. Matt was going to freak if I wasn't ready. I had just stepped out of the shower when the doorbell rang.

"Shit! You've got to be kidding me!" I threw on my housecoat and turbaned my sopping hair. "Maybe it's just Shirley." I peered through the peephole.

"Nope." I quickly glanced at my image in the front hall mirror and after wiping away a foot long mascara smudge from under one eye, I opened the door.

"Hey Matt, c'mon in."

"Hi beautiful." He sauntered in and gave me a kiss. I could see Shirley peeking out her door. She smiled and gave me the thumbs up. I smiled back and closed the door.

"You smell incredibly delicious tonight," Matt said.

"Thank-you. It's my peach body wash. It's incredibly expensive so I only use it for very special occasions."

"I feel honored."

"You should be. Consider yourself a lucky man tonight!"

"That's kind of what I was hoping." He grinned and reached for my housecoat.

"Hey," I laughed jumping out of the way. "Stop that childish behavior!

You're a grown man."

"...with grown man desires." He caught the back of my housecoat and reeled me into his arms. I had to admit he felt good. Strong and yummy. We kissed forever, only stopping when I finally realized my housecoat was hanging wide open at the front.

"Okay mister, I'd better go get dressed." I said gently pulling away. "We're going to be late for our reservations." I quickly closed the front of my housecoat and walked toward my bedroom. "There's an open bottle of wine in the kitchen. Help yourself. The wine glasses are in the cupboard over the stove. As you can probably tell from the half-emptied bottle, I've already had a few glasses. I promise I'll be out in a minute. Make yourself comfortable."

I knew I was yammering nonstop but I couldn't help it. His passion had caught me by surprise and I was incredibly nervous about his intentions for the evening. Besides a few one night mistakes, I hadn't been with a man I'd cared about since Luke left. Sleeping with Matt would be a big step for me. It would mean that I've moved on. I cared about Matt. I enjoyed his company and he seemed to enjoy mine. What would be the problem? It's only sex. Ah...but that was the problem. It wasn't just sex. Not in this case. We would go from uncomplicated dating to being lovers. Lovers...what a stupid word. It implies that somehow you're suddenly in love with the person. I knew I wasn't 'in love' with Matt. At least not yet. He certainly had potential and there was no denying we had a definite sexual magnetism.

Dressed only in my special black bra and matching underwear, I opened the top drawer of my dresser and rummaged around trying to find a pair of nylons that didn't have a run in them.

"I hate nylons. They are a complete and utter waste of time," I mumbled.

"So don't wear any."

I dove for my housecoat. "Matt you scared the crap out of me. How long have you been standing in the doorway?"

He didn't say a word as he walked closer and closer, never once averting his eyes from mine. My heart was beating so fast I could feel the blood rushing like a faucet through the vein in my neck. Trying to be cool, I turned my back and continued to look for a pair of nylons.

"Ah here we go. Brand new. Not even out of the package yet." I knew he was standing directly behind me but I didn't have the legs or the courage to turn around. So I waited, matching his silent expectation with my own. I could feel his breath on my neck and that smell. He was one of the finest smelling men I'd ever known. I couldn't take it anymore.

"Matt, I really need to finish getting dressed."

"I know," he answered. "I just came in to see if you needed any more wine?"

He reached over me and filled the empty glass that was sitting on my dresser, purposely brushing my neck with his shirt, then walked out of the room. I picked up the glass of wine and collapsed on the edge of the bed, my knees no longer able to sustain any weight.

"Holy fucking mother! He is one smooth piece of ass."

I closed my eyes, took a deep breath, and chugged the wine in one gulp. I put my head down and tried to steady my breathing with thoughts of angels, sunny days, calm waters, peace, and tranquility. It was no use. Satan's little demon had stirred up some very disturbing thoughts that no Bible preaching pulpit could ever forgive. I was a sinner and needed to repent, but since that demon was still patrolling my house wearing a very nicely tailored Armani suit, I reasoned I could repent in the morning and let the devil have his dues tonight. I quickly finished getting ready and moseyed into the kitchen.

"What cha' looking for?" I said calmly.

"Wow baby, you look beautiful!" he said closing the fridge door. "I was thinking maybe if you had enough stuff, I'd make some dinner, but..."

"I know the cupboards are a little bare. What about our reservations and the all you can beef?"

"We can go if you really want," he laughed, "I just had the impression from our phone conversation that you weren't all that excited about the prospects of eating a great big slab of meat."

Cow meat no. Matt meat yes! Please God tell me I didn't blurt that thought out loud. I know I've had some wine, but let me retain a little dignity.

"What about ordering in Alex? We could light some candles, put on

181

some music, and just relax. Do you like Chinese?"

I could definitely go for a little yufuckme ifuckyu right now. Stop it Alex! You're ill! I could hear Satan laughing.

"Alex?"

"Huh? Oh sorry Matt, it's the wine gone straight to my head. Chinese sounds great. In fact, I love Chinese. What's there not love about Chinese? The Cantonese Chow Mein, egg rolls, sweet and sour pork. I love everything."

Matt gently took my hand and led me to the couch. "You sit down, I'll order."

I didn't know what was wrong with me. I wasn't drunk, but my stomach was turning somersaults faster than an Olympic diver. I needed food. There's nothing better than a gut full of rice to soak up the stomach acid.

"Food should be here in about a half an hour," Matt said plopping himself beside me on the couch. "Is there anything I can get for you? How about a glass of water?"

"Sure that'd be great. I think I'm just a bit over hungry. I was working at my friend's house most of the afternoon."

"That guy right?" he said handing me a glass of ice water.

"Thanks. Ya Bobby. The three of us. Vicki was there too. We were stripping wallpaper in the living room. You wouldn't believe the mess. The previous owners had just kept pasting new wallpaper over the old stuff. I'm not kidding, there had to be at least five or six layers. It was horrible." I took a sip of water and waited for Matt to respond. Nothing, so I took the leap, "look Matt, Bobby and I are just friends. I'm helping him out right now because he needs me and besides I want to. It's all for a good cause."

"And what might that cause be?"

I figured it would be better to clue Matt in on Bobby's situation, than to have him always questioning our relationship.

"He's trying to become a foster parent to a very special little boy in hopes that one day he can apply to formally adopt him. Bobby was living in a small typical bachelor place that wasn't suitable for a child. I helped him find a house to buy but it needed a little bit of fixing up. He only has a few weeks to get everything done before the social worker gets back from vacation and sets up a viewing."

"Wow, a foster dad. That's pretty heavy stuff. Sometimes those kids are all messed up. I hope he knows what he's doing?"

"He does."

"I know I never could."

"What…be a foster parent or be a father?"

Matt paused for a moment to think. "At the moment…both. I mean I like kids enough but the situation has to be just right. It's a huge responsibility. You have to give up a lot."

"But Matt, don't you think you'd gain a lot as well?" I didn't like where this conversation was going. I wasn't in the mood to find out the guy I'm seeing doesn't want to be a father. I gulped down the rest of my water.

"Alex, I want to be a father. Just not tomorrow," he reached over and caressed my hand, "and I think you'd make a wonderful mother. You're so kind and giving. What you're doing for this Bobby guy is fantastic. Way above and beyond what a normal friend would do."

"Thanks. I have to admit, I'm enjoying the decorating and renovating work. All the scrubbing and scraping is helping build up the old upper body. It feels good."

"I noticed that in the bedroom." He inched closer on the couch and placed his hand on my thigh. "You looked good. Real good."

"More wine?" I said skirting off the couch like a jackrabbit. Matt sort of chuckled. "What?" I said, "Why are you laughing at me?"

"Because every time I get close to you tonight, you run away."

"Do I? Oh sorry, I didn't mean to," I said lying through my teeth, "I suddenly had the urge for more wine."

"What are you afraid of Alex? Me? I'm not going to hurt you."

I cracked another bottle of wine and refilled our glasses. "I'm not afraid of you…I guess I'm afraid of being hurt again." There, I had said it out loud. I was afraid of getting hurt again.

"Alex, you have to let someone in at some point."

"I know. It's just hard."

"Of course it's hard. So who was the guy or don't you want to talk about it?"

Feeling somewhat relieved at admitting my own shortcomings, I snuggled up beside him on the couch and told him about Luke. Matt was a good listener, and as I talked I could feel my muscles relax and loosen, like the calm water downstream from a set of river rapids. It didn't hurt that Matt was also massaging my shoulders with those big strong hands of his.

"What an ass!" he said.

"I know. But I'm done with him. Moving on to bigger and better things." I lifted my head and kissed his chin. "I'm glad we stayed in tonight."

"So am I," he said returning my kiss with a tender one of his own.

The tender quickly turned into a full out passionate slob session, and if the doorbell hadn't rung, I'm not sure what Satan's little demon would have had me do on that couch. I lit some candles and we settled down for a makeshift Chinese picnic in my living room. The conversation was casual, with me mostly answering questions about my family and childhood. Matt was less responsive to my inquiries and I didn't push it. The night was going well and that's all that really mattered. I figured he'd tell me more about himself when he was ready.

"You look like you're feeling better?" he said spiking a chicken ball with his fork.

"I am. Thanks," I said sipping my wine, "I knew I was just over hungry. I always get light headed. Plus I don't think the wine helped too much. It's my own fault. You'd think I'd know better by now."

"So this isn't this first time it's happened?"

"Ha! I wish. No Matt, I hate to say it but I'm a cheap date and a lousy drunk!"

"I'll have to keep that in mind!" he laughed.

We ate the rest of the meal joking around and enjoying each other's company. I was feeling much more comfortable and actually looking forward to the prospect of getting a little lucky tonight. It had been awhile! If it worked out long term with Matt, great. If not, there was no harm in practicing a little bedroom aerobics. The exercise would do me good.

Matt laid down his fork and pushed back his plate. "Wow, I'm stuffed."

"I know me too. And I'm very proud of myself. For once all of my rice ended up in my stomach and not strewn across the floor. Then again, I was being extra careful since I have special company."

"So I'm special company am I?"

"Of course you are. It's not very often I wear a formal dress and nylons to eat dinner on the couch. I'm feeling rather overdressed."

"You could always take something off. I wouldn't mind. But only if you're comfortable of course."

"You mean like these?" My nylons landed on his shoulder.

"That's a start." His voice was surprisingly shaky. I, on the other hand was suddenly feeling empowered. A woman with a purpose. I leaned over and began tugging at the knot in his tie.

"You know I'm all for equal rights…and tell me something…how useful is this tie really?" I playfully pulled the tie from around his neck.

"Apparently not very."

I kissed his neck as I unbuttoned his shirt. "And this shirt. While I quite like the quality of the material, a very fine cotton, I think it would look better like this." With both hands, I pushed the shirt open and looked him straight in the eye. "Yes, much better."

I rubbed my hands across his chest, familiarizing myself with every inch of his chiseled muscles. I heard him moan a little when I straddled his legs and began to kiss his soft skin. He was at my mercy and I loved it. For once, I had the power. I had the control. I was just about to undo his belt when in one swift move, I was lying on my back and he was kissing my neck. So much for being in control. Oh well, I wasn't complaining, especially when I looked up and saw my bra hanging off the lamp.

"How the hell did that happen?" I wondered. "God he's smooth. Real smooth." He ran his hand up my thigh. "Not here Matt."

"Yes here. Right now."

185

"No seriously. I can't have sex on my couch. It's not right. Maybe somebody else's couch but not my own. My sweet neighbor lady has tea on this couch and talks about flowers and the poor kids in Africa…and my mother. She would know. She has a sense."

"What about the kitchen table?" he asked.

"You're kidding right?" He answered me with a passionate kiss. "Guess not, in fact if it really must be on the couch then so be it. I suppose it really wouldn't be that bad…I mean sex is sex right? Wherever you do it!"

Matt looked up from between my breasts and smiled. "Are you going to babble the whole time? Or am I going to have to find some way to shut you up?"

"Well what did you have in mind? How about you try it and then I'll let you know?" Then he did something so spectacular I have no words to describe it.

"How was that?" he asked.

"Let me catch my breath and I'll tell you." I lay there and took two chest-heaving breaths. I mean I was sucking air from the fucking Grand Canyon. "Ya that wasn't bad. I think you may need a wee bit of practice though. Maybe it's the technique that's a little off."

"Oh shut up," he laughed, "it looked to me like you were enjoying yourself."

"I'm a great actress. What can I say?"

"Fine, I'll just do it again smart ass." This time I thought for sure I'd died. I was no longer a conscience being in the world.

"My God Matthew, where did you learn to do that?"

"Promise you won't laugh?"

"Why would I laugh? That particular sexual act is a serious matter."

"One summer vacation in high school, I was so bored I spent an entire day rummaging through a box of old books in our basement. This one book had the cheesiest cover ever. Two people stranded on an island…you get the picture. Anyway, I randomly opened it and started reading. And the guy from the cover was doing it to the girl. I couldn't believe it! It explained the technique word for word. I was shocked my mother even had a dirty book like that."

"You'd be surprised what kind of books and other things your mamma keeps hidden in the basement," I said playfully.

"You're dirty."

"I know and you like it," I said licking his ear.

"Yes I do."

"So, tell me when did first put this move into action? Because you've obviously done it more than once."

"No baby, you're the first! I promise," he teased.

"You're so full of shit."

"It was shortly after I'd read the book. My girlfriend and I were tired of just kissing and she wasn't ready to go all the way yet, so I asked her if it was okay if I tried something new."

"How old were you?"

"Fifteen."

"Fifteen! Holy shit man! I certainly wasn't doing that at fifteen."

"But yer' doin' it now aren't ya!"

"Making up for lost time!" I said accepting his outstretched hand. "Where are we going you man whore?"

"To the bedroom, my dear. You think I'm only a one trick pony? I'll show you just what I've learnt since high school." I took off running to the bedroom and slammed the door before Matt could get in.

"Give me one minute," I asked.

"You look great honey."

"Thanks, but it's not me I'm concerned about. It's my room. I need to do a quick pre-sex clean up. I wouldn't want to embarrass myself or anything."

I could hear him laughing on the other side of the door. In the meantime, I threw all the shit that was on my floor into my closet, closed the door, and lit some more candles. I took a few seconds to collect my thoughts and steady my breathing. I had to admit I was having a blast tonight, and not just because I was about to get laid. Matt and I got along well. We had fun and that was important to me. Sex tonight wasn't going to be an obligation but a pleasure. I pulled back the sheets and hopped onto the bed. It took me a minute to perfect my now totally naked pose but it was worth it. I looked damn sexy. Realizing that I had forgotten to brush my teeth, I reached on the night table and quickly tossed a piece of spearmint gum in my mouth.

"Can I come in yet?"

"Not quite." Chew...chomp...chew...chew...spit into garbage pail. I did the back into your hand breath test and was satisfied that Matt would only taste me and not Chow Mein when we kissed. I repositioned myself on the bed, took a deep breath, and told him to come in.

"Well hello there big dawg. Isn't it about time you chewed on mama's slipper?"

CHAPTER ELEVEN

The work on Bobby's house was almost finished and everything looked spectacular. The kitchen had doubled in size and Bobby had installed all new cupboards and stainless steel appliances. I would have liked to have the kitchen myself. Ben's room was perfect. Bobby knew a guy who did a little custom carpentry and got him to build Ben a set of cool bunk beds. Since Ben liked camping and the outdoors so much, Bobby thought it would be a great idea to shape the beds like rowboats. The carpenter was a creative genius adding features that Bobby hadn't even ordered, such as the tent flaps, suspended over the middle of the top bunk, and draped to the floor. They could be rolled up or down, whatever Ben wanted. It was Vicki's idea to put glow in the dark stars on the ceiling to simulate the open range concept. Bobby was so thrilled at how the room turned out I thought he was going to cry.

The social worker was scheduled to arrive the next day at three in the afternoon. We were confident that she would find the living conditions more than suitable for raising a child like Ben. The deciding factor would be Bobby himself. How well would he do in a formal interview? He said he wasn't nervous but I could tell he was just trying to be strong. If things didn't work out with Ben, I'm not sure how he would react. He had planned his entire future around this little boy and if it worked out that would be fantastic. But what if for some stupid bureaucratic reason he was turned down? Who would Bobby turn to, to help pick up the pieces? I knew the answer before I'd even asked myself the question and while I would never turn Bobby away, I selfishly only wanted happy things in my life at the moment. Who was I kidding? When my friends are sad I'm sad, and I'll do anything I can to make them happy, even if it means jeopardizing my own happiness. It was my blessing and it was my curse.

189

Vicki and I were sitting on the brand new deck drinking some lemonade, relaxing before we finished the last bit of dusting and straightening. Bobby had gone to get groceries. Vicki thought a well-stocked pantry and refrigerator would make a good impression on the social worker.

"The place looks fantastic doesn't it?" Vicki said.

"Yep, everything finally came together at the last minute. I'm glad we talked Bobby into hiring a work crew to do the major installations. I don't think we could have pulled it off. I'm exhausted now." Vicki gave me a mischievous grin. "What? Why are you laughing?" I asked.

"It's not working on Bobby's place that's making you tired girl."

I tried to hide a sheepish grin. "I have no idea what you're talking about."

"You are so having sex with Matt and you didn't even tell me about it bitch!"

"Damn her!" I thought, "She knows me too well."

"So spill it, Alex. What's he like?"

"He's great if you really must know. We've slept together almost every night this week. So there!"

"You slut!"

"Oh shut up!" I said laughing. "It's so funny. It's like we're having this clandestine affair. I call him on the way home from here and he meets me at my place. Then we have the best bone-rocking sex ever. Then he goes home and I go to sleep. It's simple really."

"You're kidding me? That's not like you."

"I know and I was really shy and nervous at first but then I said what the hell, Matt's a nice guy who's totally fucking hot. What was my problem? So I jumped right in, literally, and now I am Sheena, Goddess of the bedroom, or kitchen, or living room or almost the stairwell outside my apartment." I paused to give Vicki a chance to catch her breath. "And," I said holding up my forefinger, "he is Rex, Master manipulator of the Sword of the Truth, and Keeper of the move that caused the angels to fall from heaven." I sighed. Just the thought of it sent a chill down my spine. I needed a cigarette. Too bad I didn't smoke.

"Who are you?" Vicki laughed in complete astonishment.

"I know I can't believe it myself. The guy is incredible and he's says I'm pretty damn fine myself. All Luke used to do was roll over and put his watch back on. Matt actually says thank-you before he leaves."

"He hasn't stayed over yet?"

"No...why?" I answered.

"Nothing, it's just that you'd think he'd get tired of always going home after. By the sounds of it, I'm surprised the both of you aren't dead yet! Have you even suggested he stay over?"

"No, but the one time he didn't leave until three in the morning, so that's almost like staying over isn't it?"

"No Alex, nice try."

"Funny thing though Vic, I'm okay with the way things are right now. I've been so busy lately. It makes things easier. I'm sure now that the house is done and things settle down, we'll do more couple stuff like talk!"

"You don't even talk?" she asked.

"Not too much lately...like I said, we're pretty much just having a ton of sex."

"And there's nothing wrong with that."

"So what about you? How's my brother?" Vicki put her glass to hide her face, but her smile still managed to creep out the sides. "By the look on your face I'd say things were going well," I said.

"They're going better than well Alex," she paused, "I'm so excited. I mean we're both taking it really slow, just seeing where things go. That last girl hurt him bad. He admitted he was a mess and just fucked around with anyone for the sake of fucking."

"No kidding," I said.

"Ya, he's kind of embarrassed about the whole thing now."

"He doesn't need to be embarrassed," I said, "we were all just worried about him that's all. He's my brother, I'll love and accept him no matter who he sleeps with." Vicki started to giggle. "And I'm now assuming that's you?"

"Do you really want to know?" she asked.

"No, but you're going to tell me anyway right?"

"He's so gentle and kind Alex. So different from any other guy I've ever been with. He actually seems to care about me. And he cuddles. Isn't that cute?"

"Well he always did sleep with a big teddy bear named Scruffy growing up. I guess some habits die hard."

"Ahh Scruffy, what a cute name!"

"Okay Vicki I'm about to gag!"

"Sorry Alex, I'll shut up now." We sat in silence for a moment, enjoying the fresh air and our lemonade. "Can I say one more thing?" I rolled my eyes and nodded my head. "He's good...I mean he's really good."

"Okay! Not listening anymore...nunnna, nunnnnna, nunnnna," I said cupping my hands over my ears.

"What on earth is going on out here?" Bobby smiled as he walked out onto the deck.

"Alex is grossed out because I told her Tom is a wild jungle man in the sack," Vicki laughed.

"Well that would do it I suppose!" Bobby answered.

"I'm just kidding," I said placing my hands down on the table, "I'm glad they're happy. I truly am. Did you get all the groceries you needed Bobby? I would've come you know?"

"I know I did fine on my own."

"Bobby, did you put the ice cream in the freezer?" a voice said from inside the house. Vicki and I smirked liked we'd seen Santa Claus.

"Oh hi ladies how are you?" Carrie said from the doorway. "Bobby, the ice cream, I can't find it. Did we leave it in the truck?"

"No I already put in the freezer in the basement."

"Oh, I didn't think to look there," she said going back into the kitchen.

"So I've been replaced have I Bobby?" I joked.

"You could never be replaced Alex," he said tussling my hair like I was a puppy. "It's just that Carrie lets me kiss her on the lips."

"Bobby, you dawg!" Vicki said smacking his arm. Bobby only shrugged his shoulders and grinned like an idiot.

"What can I say? All the women want me!"

"All the women want you? Fat chance mister!" Carrie said as she sat down at table. "Cookies anyone?"

"I was only kidding Carrie," Bobby blushed.

"So was I." There was a definite bolt of electricity flying through the air when Bobby and Carrie looked at each other. Bobby snatched one of the cookies and shoved it into his mouth.

"Mmmm these are delicious."

"Thanks," said Carrie. "I made them last night. I thought it might make a good impression if you had some fresh home baked cookies on the table tomorrow when the social worker came. That way she'd at least think you were domesticated and not the bachelor bum that you are."

"Ouch, that one hurt," Bobby laughed, "but you're right and thank-you. Hey maybe you'd like to teach me some of those skills sometime. I'm a very eager student." He winked at Carrie and I could tell that she too had fallen prey to his eyes. "Anyone need a fresh drink?" We all nodded and Bobby went inside.

"Girls I want to tell you how much Bobby appreciates all the work you've been doing. He may not show it but he really is thankful."

"It's been our pleasure," said Vicki. "I love doing this sort of stuff. I work in advertising but I love to do design as well."

"Really? I'll keep that in mind. Do you work independently or at a firm?" Carrie asked.

"Right now I'm working at 'Persuasion Inc.' but I'd eventually like to go solo. A lot of risk but I also think the rewards are better. I'd love to keep the hours that one over there does." She pointed to me and laughed. "She's never in the office."

"That's not true," I argued. "I'm there most days…just not all day. I'm flexible shall we say. As long as I get my column written and my required research and editorial work done, my boss is fine with it. Most days he prefers I work at home. I seem to get more accomplished there than at the office. At the office I tend to chat a bit."

"Don't we all," said Carrie.

Bobby came back with a tray full of drinks. "I hope you don't mind, I doctored them up a bit."

Carrie took a big sip and screwed up her face, "I'll say you did. What's in them?"

"Just a wee bit of Vodka."

We sat on the deck and chatted for the longest time. Carrie was one cool lady. Intelligent and well-read with a wicked sense of humor. It was easy to see why Bobby was so smitten with her. She had such a casual laid-back demeanor and a smile that could crack even the hardest veneer. No wonder she was one of the top real estate agents in the city. Bobby could hardly take his eyes off her the whole time. In his defense, she was an attractive woman, but it was more than her physical beauty. She had a wonderful spirit about her. The attraction certainly seemed mutual, as she was forever reaching over and grabbing Bobby's hand or affectionately rubbing his arm. I wondered if they'd had sex yet. I wasn't even sure how many times they'd actually been out. It was none of my business but still fun to guess. Besides who was I to talk, I'd been having sex like a rabbit lately. I looked down at my watch.

"Shit, it's getting late and I still have to finish vacuuming the carpets."

"Don't worry about that Alex, I can do it," Carrie said.

"Are you sure? My plans aren't until later tonight. I still have time."

"Much later Carrie," Vicki chimed in. "In fact I'm pretty sure it'll be dark before Alex's company arrives."

"Oh shut up Vicki," I laughed and turned my attention to Bobby who was looking rather confused. "Ignore her please. She has no idea what she's talking about. Look, I'll stop by after work tomorrow to see how things went." I paused and thought that maybe he'd want Carrie there instead. "Or if you're busy, you could just call me."

"No Alex, I'd love it if you came by. You are the reason all of this has happened. You should be there."

I kissed him on the cheek. "Okay then, I'll see you later. Carrie it was so great getting to spend some time with you. I hope we can do it again sometime."

"I'd love to. Maybe next time we can leave the penis at home and just have a girl's night," she smirked.

"Sounds good. Vic are you coming?"

"Yep, just finishing my lemonade. See you later guys. Bobby good luck tomorrow. Don't be nervous, you'll do just fine."

"Thanks."

Vicki was meeting Tom, so I headed home. I wasn't sure what Matt was doing. I'd tried both his home and his cell and there was no answer. Oh well, I was tired and maybe a night off would do me good. You know replenish the sexual juices or whatever they're called. I'm sure mine were getting pretty low in the tank. I took the stairs up to my apartment because now that Matt was seeing me naked on a regular basis, I thought I'd better keep in shape. Every little bit helped. As soon as I opened the door of the stair well I heard it, and was hit with a wave of terror.

Matt's laugh bellowed through the hall like a hyena, followed by Shirley and Mort.

"Oh no they've captured him and he's being tortured. Worse yet, she's interrogating him," I panicked.

Maybe I could just sneak by their door and enter my own apartment without them knowing. I could pretend I hadn't heard a thing. Matt wouldn't know the difference, but Shirley, that woman could sense the presence of a fly landing on the roof. It was no use. I had no escape.

"Alex, it is you!" Shirley said popping her head out of the door. "I thought I heard someone coming up the stairs. Funny you normally use the elevator."

"Hi Shirley. What's new with you tonight?"

"Don't give me that bullshit Alex," she whispered. "You know he's in here don't you? And you're scared shitless."

I couldn't help but laugh. "Shirley, you are one of a kind."

"Hey everybody," Shirley said throwing the door wide open. "Look who finally decided to stop by."

I stepped in the apartment and waved. "Hi Mort. Matt! Hi! What a surprise. I didn't know you were here?" Shirley pinched my ass from behind. "In fact what are you doing in my neighbors' apartment?"

"Hey babe. Mort here saw me sitting out front waiting for you and he invited me up. What a great guy! We've been playing cards."

"And drinking some beer I see," I said looking at the row of empty bottles on the kitchen counter.

Mort just grinned. "We need a fourth for euchre. Sit down and join us."

"I'd love to but Matt and I really should be going. Shouldn't we honey?" As much as I loved them, the last thing I felt like doing tonight was playing cards with Mort and Shirley. They were sharks and would wipe our butts clean.

"C'mon Alex. It'll be fun and I'm having a great time," Matt said while giving me his sexy eyes. He was so drunk that instead of looking sexy, he just looked cross-eyed and stupid. Even Shirley couldn't hold in her laughter.

"Alright, alright, you win. But only for one game," I said sitting down at the kitchen table.

"Woo hoo, let's play some cards!" Mort cheered.

"Mort's been drinking a little too," Shirley whispered as she handed me a glass of her homemade apple wine.

"Really Shirl? I hadn't noticed."

One game of cards quickly became two, which turned into three and so on. Matt just kept drinking and drinking. He didn't seem to know when to stop. Shirley could tell I was getting annoyed, especially when he knocked the half-full bottle off the table and broke into hysterics. Trust me it wasn't that funny.

"Well Mort we should let these two youngsters get going. I know it's past our bed time," Shirley said while reaching for the mop.

"Shirley let me do that please," I said.

"Ya Shhhhirrley, let Alex do it," Matt slobbered. "She's a hell of a lot younger than you!" I thought Shirley was going to clock him over the head with the mop. Even half-baked Mort sat up in his chair. I had to get Matt out of there in a hurry.

"C'mon Matt I think it's time to go."

"Not yet babe, I think Morty's still got a few more brews in the fridge."

"No Morty's all out," Shirley said rather harshly.

"Oh that's too bad. Okay." He tried to get off his chair but fell.

"Oh great," I mumbled to myself, "here let me help you." He reached for my outstretched arm and purposely pulled me down on top of him.

"Babe, I know you want some but not here," he laughed while trying to kiss my neck and unbutton my shirt.

"Matt stop it, you're being a real asshole."

"I was just having some fun Alex. You should try it sometime." I managed to get the both of us up and out the door.

Shirley gently grabbed my hand, "If you need me, please call."

"I'll be fine thanks. Sorry about this. I've never seen him drink this much."

"He doesn't handle the liquor so well does he?" she smiled.

"Apparently not. I'll see you later."

Shirley watched me lug Matt across the hall and into my apartment. At the last second, I caught a glimpse of her shaking her head in disgust. I didn't disagree. There was nothing worse than a bad drunk. It was so unattractive, and right now, gorgeous Matt was about as appealing to me as a dog who'd rolled around in his own shit. I didn't want him near me, so I tilted his body toward the couch and let go. He missed and fell on the ground. I laughed.

"Ow babe, you trying to kill me?" He looked so pathetic lying there on the ground too drunk to move, and too stupid to care. I threw him a blanket.

"Good night Matt."

"Good night Alex. Hey wait," he slurred, "no goodnight kiss or anything? C'mon I'm feeling a little horny...I'll do it...that thingy you like...I promise...Please Alex..."

"No. You smell really bad right now. See you in the morning."

I left him lying sandwiched between the couch and the coffee table and honestly didn't care. I was exhausted. I'd spent a great afternoon at Bobby's and was looking forward to having a peaceful night. Instead I find out my boyfriend becomes a gigantic jackass when he drinks too much. What a wonderful quality to have. I wasn't impressed and would wait until the morning to see what he had to say for himself. It's one thing to drink and enjoy yourself but when you're personality starts to change it's time to stop.

I climbed into bed and was about to call Vicki to dish when I realized she'd probably be with Tom right now. I sighed and put down the phone. Tom would never do what Matt did tonight, especially at a virtual stranger's house. Tom was a cute drunk. He'd be snuggling with Vicki, telling her jokes, trying to make her laugh. Vicki was lucky to be with my brother. He was a great catch. Then again so was she.

I was sleeping soundly until I heard Matt get up to use the bathroom. I could tell he was trying to be quiet, that is until he sat down on the toilet and set forth a noise from his rectum that shook the bloody windows. Now normally I don't have a problem with a good fart, but this one was disgusting. It was wet and sounded like there was spray. I heard him snicker. I wanted to puke.

"That is so fucking gross," I said rolling over so my nose was nowhere near the bathroom door. "That better not smell." No such luck. Matt didn't just fart, he exploded into the toilet, and it went on for an eternity. There was going to be definite splash back.

I buried my head under the covers and started to laugh. I had to admit it was funny. I wondered how I was going to face him in the morning without breaking up. I'd try and be a grownup because Lord knows I've had my own issues with explosive diarrhea. He flushed. Twice. Then went back to the living room. Hopefully he knew enough to sleep on the couch this time instead of the floor.

The race to the toilet went on all night. I started to feel bad for him. His ass must have been burning like the sun. I didn't want to embarrass him, so I waited until the coast was clear, plugged my nose, and ventured into the bathroom to find some poop pills for him.

"Oh my God." I couldn't breathe. I needed air. Fresh air. I quickly rummaged through the bottom cabinet for the pills. I grabbed the Pepto Bismo too. He needed all the help he could get. I left them on the countertop and ran back to my room. The smell followed me. It was like the angel of death. It lingered on my pajamas and in my hair. I had to defend myself. I snatched my kiwi body spray and went to work. When I was through, my room smelt like the make-up counter at Sears, but at least that was better than the barnyard. I climbed back into bed and went to sleep. I only heard him a few more times and they almost sounded more like precautionary visits and not the real thing. He must have found the medicine. Thank you Jesus.

I woke up the next morning to find Matt staring at me.

"Hey Alex, don't get up. I've got to get going. Early day at work today. I just wanted to apologize for my behavior last night. I was having so much fun, and I guess I didn't really realize how much I'd had to drink." He leaned over and kissed my forehead. He still reeked of beer. I instinctively turned my head away. "Sorry, I know I smell. I'll call you later okay. Go back to sleep. I'll let myself out."

He looked embarrassed and I was glad I didn't say anything about the diarrhea. The poor guy probably couldn't wait to get home and have a shower. I hope he bent over and let the water shoot up his butt. It needed some freshening. When I finally got up, the first thing I did was venture into the bathroom to open the window. It was already open - wide. Bless his heart, he must have done it this morning. I also noticed two of the poop pills and quite a bit of the Pepto Bismo was gone. I laughed again. Poor guy.

I put on the coffee pot and went into the living room to wait. Matt had folded up his blanket and laid it nicely on the arm of the couch. The room smelt like stale beer. I opened the windows and sprayed the room with air freshener. When I opened the front door to get the paper, I noticed

Shirley's door was ajar. I was betting I'd have company any minute. Knock. Sure enough. I held open the door and waved her in.

"Coffee?" I asked.

"Sure."

"He's gone already."

"I know Mort saw him leave this morning."

"Do you people ever sleep?"

She laughed. "So how was he? Did he cause you any trouble?"

"No he passed out on the floor in front of the couch. I threw him a blanket and let him sleep there."

"Good for you!" We sat in silence for minute at the table.

"Look Shirley I'm really sorry about last night. I had no idea he was that bad of a drunk. I was terribly embarrassed."

"There's no need for you to be embarrassed, he's the one that acted like a moron."

"He did, didn't he? I couldn't believe some of the things that came out of his mouth. I'm hoping it was just the alcohol." Shirley tried to smile. "You don't like him do you?" I asked.

"It's not that I don't like him. We had a very good time while we waited for you to come. He was nice, almost too nice. He seemed to know exactly what to say, and when to say it. Until of course the alcohol kicked in."

"I know, he's real smooth. But then in the middle of all the cheese, he throws out something that always makes me shake my head. I just don't know Shirley. I really like him. The chemistry's fantastic but I just don't know."

She reached over and gave me a hug. "I understand completely. It's still early in the relationship. Maybe just give it a bit more time."

"Ya maybe we just need some more time. He does have his good qualities," I laughed.

"I noticed the new housecoat Alex. I'm assuming that's one of his good qualities." I only smiled and shrugged my shoulders. "One word of advice honey. Be careful. I just can't put my finger on it yet."

"I will and thanks."

Shirley left and I went to the office. Matt called after lunch and wanted to make amends. He suggested we meet for dinner but I put him off for a couple of days. I needed to think. Besides, I was going to Bobby's after dinner. That was more important. I didn't tell Matt the truth and he sounded hurt that I brushed him off. I refused to be one of those ladies who are the beck and call of their man. I had a life before Matt, and if he didn't like it, that was too bad.

I could hardly work that afternoon, I was so nervous about Bobby's appointment. I had no reason to think the meeting wouldn't go well, but there was always that chance. Bobby had changed so much since I first met him. He had opened up his heart not only to me but to Ben and now Carrie. I was so proud of him. It was there all along, he just needed a push, and I was happy to oblige.

When I pulled up to the house I noticed Bobby and the social worker sitting on the new wicker rockers on the front porch. They seemed to be talking amicably and Bobby had a smile on his face. There weren't many times these days when he didn't. I pulled the car further up the street and waited in the car. Bobby was going to make a great dad. He had all the qualities. I could just imagine him trying to discipline Ben for something non-consequential like leaving his bike on the front lawn instead of putting it away like he was supposed to. Bobby would talk in a deep voice and stress the point about Ben needing to be responsible, then he would feel bad about getting angry and take the kid out for pizza. He would love Ben until the day he died and Ben would love him right back.

I put my head back and closed my eyes. Wow, I was bagged. Not one of my better sleeps. Matt said he was feeling great today on the phone but I think he was full of shit. No, I take that back, my toilet was full of shit. Just thinking of the night made me laugh.

"What's so funny?"

"Bobby, geez you scared me."

"Sorry about that. Hey I want you meet Sydney."

"How'd things go?" I asked getting out of the car.

"I think it went well, very well. She's just talking to her supervisor on the phone right now."

"Are you sure I should be here?"

"Of course, you're my friend. I already asked her when I finally noticed your car. You'd make a great stalker."

"You think?"

We waited on the porch for Sydney to come back. I think I was more nervous than Bobby. I couldn't sit still.

"Would you settle down," he laughed.

"I can't help it. I'm nervous for you."

"Look Alex, whatever the answer is, I'll deal with it. If it's no, then I'll just keep trying."

I grabbed his hand and squeezed as tight as I could. "Here she comes."

"Hi you must be Alex, I'm Sydney."

"Hi."

"Well Bobby, I'm afraid that Ben won't be able to come…"

Bobby's head dropped. "That's okay, at least you tried," he interrupted.

"You didn't let me finish. I was about to say he couldn't come until at least the end of the week. It'll take that long to get the paperwork done. Everything's so backed up. Is that okay?"

"Okay? That's fantastic!" He shook Sydney's hand then wheeled around, picked me up and gave me a bear hug.

"It's going to be at least six months before we can petition the courts to start formal adoption proceedings. I'll be in touch though, and once again, congratulations Bobby." They shook hands and Sydney left. Bobby watched her drive away and when he turned around, I noticed his eyes were wet and shiny.

"I can't believe it," he said, "I'm going to be a father." All we could do was hug and cry. Bobby let it all out.

"Alex I can't tell you what this means to me. I've waited my whole life to do something important, you know something that was going to have an effect…and know this is it. I'm going to be a parent."

"And may I add you're going to be a fantastic parent."

"I hope so."

"So what's next?" I asked him.

"Well I was thinking that I should get some fun stuff for Ben, likes toys and that, but I don't really know what to buy."

"What are we waiting for? Let's go."

"You mean it? Oh thanks Alex. Just let me lock the house up. We'd better take the truck just in case. You never know what I might buy. I'm so excited."

We hopped in the truck and headed to the mall. Bobby was like a little boy running from store to store, flashing bills like they were leaves on a tree. We were both starving, so Bobby bought me dinner at the food court. He wouldn't shut up the entire time and I was happy to share in his excitement. He bought Bobby DVD's, CD's, electronic games, and regular board games because they were Ben's favorite. He took his time picking out each item and drove me nuts with his funny questions about what kids nowadays liked, because apparently I knew.

It was dark when we got back to his place. I helped him carry in all the presents and even though he offered me a drink, I had to decline.

"I've got to hit the road Bobby. I had a crappy sleep last night and I want to drive home before I hit the sleep deprived wall and pass out."

"Hey Alex before you go, I want you to have this."

He handed me a small package. "Bobby what is this?"

"Just open it."

I lifted the lid and inside was a beautiful gold necklace, one of the thick kinds. The kind that cost a lot of money. "Holy smokes Bobby, I can't accept this."

"Yes you can and you will. I didn't know of any other way to say thank-you. For everything." His eyes began to mist up again. "You've changed my life, and made me see things that I never ever bothered to look at before. You've made me a better person and I'll always be grateful to you for that." I looked at him in stunned silence. He reached up and gently brushed away the tears that had begun to trickle down my cheek.

"I don't know what to say."

"Don't say anything. Just lift up the back of your hair so I can put this on you. Wow, you're one beautiful girl."

"Now you're trying to make me blush," I said giving him a kiss. "Thank you Bobby. I love it and I love you."

"I love you too! Now get out of here before I start crying like a woman again."

I gave him one last hug and walked out the door. I wanted to tell him how much he meant to me as well but for once I didn't have the words. Not only did he expose me to a world that I never knew existed, he invited me in with open arms and accepted me for who I was, not who he wanted me to be. I found a home in this world. I was comfortable. Bobby also showed me courage by taking a huge gamble with Ben. He'd risked his heart and found happiness. He also proved to me that happiness didn't always occur in a traditional sense or in the places we searched so hard to find it. He showed me that sometimes, simple happiness could be found in the joyful tears of a grown man.

CHAPTER TWELEVE

"More wine Alex?"

"No thanks Matt."

"What's wrong you've hardly had anything to drink tonight?"

"I know my stomach's feeling a little queasy already. I don't want to compound the problem with alcohol. I'm sure I've already mentioned that sometimes alcohol and don't get along too well."

"Yes you have. I think that's hilarious. Oh well more for me." He motioned for the waiter to bring another bottle.

"This restaurant's fabulous," I said. "The atmosphere's very romantic and the food's good too."

I had forgiven Matt for the episode at Mort and Shirley's. He'd already apologized, brought me flowers, and had now taken me to this incredibly fancy and expensive restaurant. His apology was convincing. He said he'd had a horrible day at work, and then gotten into a fight with his sister on the phone. He didn't tell me what they fought about and I knew not to ask. He said he just needed to relax and blow off some steam and Mort was more than willing to keep his glass full. He really did seem to feel bad, and I refused to judge or label him based on one bad experience. Besides, he looked incredibly sexy. What was a girl to do?

After dinner, Matt invited me back to his apartment. It was the first time and I don't know why, but I was nervous. But maybe being in his apartment would shed a little more light on his life and his family. It probably wasn't any of my business, but I still wanted to know.

His apartment was in the snooty part of the city, where the people who thought they had money and prestige, (but really didn't) lived. The lobby was covered with marble and had these huge grotesque statues guarding the elevators. It all seemed a little pretentious to me. As soon as we were in the elevator, Matt started to grope me like a chimpanzee.

"Matt stop. Can't you at least wait until we get upstairs? Or is sex in the elevator what you had planned?" He grinned and pulled me closer. "Seriously stop, I'd be embarrassed if someone saw us."

"Why? Are you ashamed to be seen with me?"

"What a stupid thing to say. I'm just not that comfortable fucking in an elevator for everyone to see."

He laughed and gently caressed my shoulders. "Fine I can wait...I guess."

"I know baby. It's hard not to want me all the time. It's my curse," I said purposely flipping my hair in his face.

The elevator stopped and the door opened. "This is us," he said taking my hand, "I'm just down the hall."

"Pretty ritzy hallway," I said looking around.

"Nice huh, a lot better than the stained walls at your place."

"What the hell is that supposed to mean?"

"C'mon Alex, your place isn't exactly five star?"

"So what's your point? I like my place. It's homey and welcoming."

"I'm just kidding babe, settle down." He opened his door and led me inside.

The apartment looked like it should have been on the cover of a magazine. Designer couches, high-end television and electronics. Everything was colour coordinated to perfection. The perfect painting in the perfect spot, beside the imported Egyptian vase full of fresh flowers. I was almost afraid to touch anything. It was nice, but definitely not homey.

"Wow, Matt great place!"

"Ya not too bad eh? It'll do for now. There's a place I've been looking at over in the Ivy building."

"The Ivy building? Those places are expensive. Why would you want to live there?" I asked.

"Because it's the Ivy building, and that's where young successful people live." He went into the kitchen. "Hey do you want some wine?"

"Only half a glass please" I said surveying the living room a little closer. There were a few photographs sitting on the mantle. One was of Matt sitting with a bunch of guys, and in another, he had his arm around a girl. I picked it up for a more in depth look.

"It's a friend from college in case you're wondering," Matt said handing me my wine.

"No, I was just looking. I thought maybe it was your sister or something," I said trying to dig for a little information.

"Leave those and c'mer and sit down. I feel like I haven't seen you forever."

"It's only been a couple of days," I said setting my glass on the coffee table.

"Coaster…"

"What?" I said.

"Coaster. Put your glass on the coaster please. I don't want any water stains on the wood."

"Oh sorry," I said quickly moving my glass. I thought Matt was going to have a shit. Talk about someone needing to relax!

We sat on the couch for a few minutes sipping at our wine and enjoying some small talk. Of course, Matt was attempting to get dirty and I was having fun making him wait. Not because I didn't want to have sex, but because I could. It was driving him crazy.

"Why won't you let me touch you?" he asked.

"Because," I laughed, "my boobs aren't sore at the moment and don't need any massaging.

207

"But they work so hard," he said as I playfully shook my head no. "Well at least let me massage your shoulders…with your shirt off."

"Fine, but the bra stays on."

"Of course, I wouldn't dream of it."

"I find that hard to believe," I said unbuttoning my shirt.

"Let me do it. I love undressing you." It wasn't until he pulled my shirt back from my shoulders that he noticed the necklace. "Holy shit, nice necklace. Is it new? I've never seen you wear it before."

I froze. I'd meant to take it off before I went out. I had to stall or change the subject.

"Okay if you really want to massage my boobs, go ahead. I'll deal with it."

"No seriously Alex," he said, his eyes bearing down on mine. I couldn't lie.

"It was a present from a friend."

"Who…Vicki?"

"No."

He tilted his head and closed his eyes. "It's from that bar guy isn't?" he said sounding annoyed.

"His name is Bobby and he's not that bar guy. He's a good friend. He gave it to me as thanks for all the help I've been giving him."

"Ya right Alex. That necklace looks pretty expensive. A guy doesn't give a girl something like that to just say thanks. He definitely wants something more."

"Matt it's not like that, I promise. We're just friends."

"That's what you think…besides this must have cost him a couple months' salary. What does he do again? Collect trash?" I pulled my shirt back over my shoulders and got up to leave. I was pissed. Matt immediately grabbed my arm. "Alex I'm sorry. I didn't mean to offend you. Please don't go. I was only kidding." I don't know why, but I let him pull me back on the couch. "I just can't stand the thought of you being with another man. I get a little jealous."

"You think?" I said resting my head on his chest. "You have nothing to worry about. I'm here with you aren't I? Are we going to have to discuss this again? Because if we are I'm going to have to leave. Matt...Matt." He had begun to smooch the soft spot under my ear. "Matt are you listening?" He mumbled something but now I was the one who couldn't hear and frankly didn't care what he'd said. I loved being kissed under the ear and he knew it. Damn him!

We fooled around on the couch for a while then eventually made our way into his bedroom. He sat me down on the bed and I readied myself to be ravished.

"Wait here for a second. I almost forgot." He went into another room and came out with a box. "Screw that Bobby guy. I got you a present too."

He handed me the box and encouraged me to open it. I lifted the lid and almost died. Inside was the tackiest black silk teddy with matching fish net stockings. I tried to smile.

"There's more on the bottom," he was incredibly excited.

"More? Matt you shouldn't have." I set the teddy and stockings on the bed and pulled out a fire red silk housecoat with a black monogrammed A.H. on the front. I almost gagged. First of all, I hated silk. It's not practical and stains quite easily should something happen to spill. Second, I'm not a lacey sort of girl, and this teddy was full of lace and fringy things that hung off the front. It was the ugliest thing I'd ever seen.

"Go put it on."

"Right now?"

"Ya."

"But aren't I just going to have to take it off again in a few minutes?"

"That's the whole point babe. I want you to strip for me."

"Excuse me? You want me to strip for you? I don't think so."

"Oh come on, it'll be fun. You'll see. Please..." He was practically down on his knees. I didn't want to but he started kissing my neck again and I was lost.

"Fine, but you can't laugh."

He had this funny look on his face. "Why would I laugh?"

Maybe because I'm going to look like a fucking stripping bar maid from the wild old west. I went into the bathroom and purposely closed the door. He had to be kidding. I sat on the toilet and stifled my laughter in a towel folded on the tub. I was not the stripping kind. Problem was the towel smelled like Matt, and the more I covered my laughter, the deeper I inhaled, and the hornier I got.

"Nobody is ever going to know about this. Not even Vicki. I'm taking this one to the grave," I mumbled as I stripped naked and put on the 'outfit'. I caught a glimpse of myself in the mirror and did a double take. Apparently, I could pull off the cheesy, stripper look. I hated to admit it, but I looked good.

"Are you coming?" Matt said through the door.

"Not as much as you're going to..."

"What? Sorry I didn't hear you," he said.

"Nothing...I was just talking to myself. I'm almost ready."

"Good because everything in here is set to go."

Everything in here? What did he suddenly bring in a stage with a pole and some back up dancers? I needed more alcohol and fast. Luckily, Matt's bathroom had two doors. One opened up into his bedroom and the other into the hall. I peeked out the hall door. The coast was clear. I tip toed into the kitchen and found the opened bottle of wine. I snatched it off the counter and made my way back to the bathroom. I locked both doors and tilted the bottle to my mouth. I didn't care about the consequences of the liquor in my body; I just wanted to forget the fact that I was wearing fish net stockings and lingerie with a snap closed crotch.

"Lord help me," I prayed and pleaded.

I finished the bottle and set it in the tub. I was pretty sure I'd be making another appearance in the bathroom in a couple of hours, and I didn't want any visual reminders of the poison I'd shoved down my throat. I'd see enough when it came back up. I turned off the bathroom light and took a deep breath. I practiced a few moves in the dark, got disoriented, and had to turn the light back on to find and unlock the door.

Getting into character, I flew open the door and stood in the doorway. Matt had filled the room with candles and was lounging on a reclining chair in the corner. He was wearing a black silk housecoat and a great big smile. Some jazzy sex music was playing on his clock radio.

"Well hello there…" I panted in a husky voice, "My boss told me to come to this address. It seems there's a lonely cowboy living here who needs a little lovin'."

"Oh my God, you look fantastic."

"Shh, I'll do the talking if you don't mind," I said putting my finger to my lips, then licking it very seductively.

I heard Matt breathe deeply. I was in total control. This was fun. I began swiveling my hips to the music and moving my arms like a goddess, unfortunately as I moved, the stockings, which were already halfway up my ass, began to creep uncomfortably higher. I tried to dance my arms near my butt to pick them out but was unsuccessful. As I danced, I pictured what I must have looked like in my head and began to laugh. I couldn't help it. I looked ridiculous and stopped.

"Matt I can't do this," I blushed, "I feel stupid."

"Yes you can! You're doing great! Keep going!"

As I turned to walk back to the bathroom, he quickly jumped off the recliner, but his foot got caught and he tripped. The next thing I knew he was flying through the air toward me, housecoat wide open, his baggage already looking like it had been handled. He landed with a flop on the floor. I didn't know what to do. I wanted to laugh but he looked like he was hurt and that would have been inappropriate. So I waited. He groaned and rolled over. Damn it. He wasn't laughing. I was going to have to be serious. I ran over and knelt down beside him.

"Are you okay?" I asked.

"No… I'm hurt."

"Where?"

He pointed to his penis. "I think it needs some mouth to mouth."

"You pig! You are so full of shit! I'm certainly not touching that thing now," I laughed.

"You mean you were going to?"

"In your dreams." He grabbed me and pulled me down on top of him. "Now just a minute sir, my boss never said anything about me having to ride the horse, I was just supposed to strip."

Before I could count to ten the lacy contraption was laying on the floor and the fishnet stockings were hanging from the chair. The horse was ready to gallop but until he strapped on a saddle we weren't leaving the barn. I'd done some foolish things tonight, but I wasn't about to ride bareback and wind up with a colt in nine months.

We had a great ride, and ended up back in the stall a little while after. It wasn't until I'd gotten off the horse, hosed him down in the shower, and laid out some fresh straw that I began to feel the effects of the wine.

"Please God," I said taking a deep breath. Don't let me be sick. Not here. Not in front of my stallion.

With the stallion fast asleep, I ran to bathroom and deposited the contents of my stomach into the toilet. I didn't bother flushing because I knew there'd be another round in a few minutes. No point in wasting the water. As I waited, I decided to be nosy and snoop in Matt's cabinets. I knew it was wrong but I had the opportunity, so I took it. I thought I had a lot of grooming and skin care products. He had everything and all the expensive stuff too. No 'bonus fifty percent more' shampoo bottles like I had. He even used the highest quality of toilet paper. I never understood that. You used it to wipe poop, who cares about the quality? If it's too thin and you're afraid there might be a finger break then you just use more. It's still cheaper in the long run. I felt the second wave coming and readied my naked body over the toilet. It was quite a skill to vomit with limited sound, and over the years I'd become somewhat of a master.

I still felt nauseous so I ventured into the kitchen to muster up a cracker or something to nibble on. All I could find was a package of 100% Whole Wheat and Oat Thins. Geez, that sounded real yummy. I took one out and it looked like something I would feed a horse. Maybe that's why my man just won the Alex Derby. I took a small bite and as I chewed, I could feel my mouth instantly drain of moisture. It was gross. I couldn't finish it. I spit the fiber gob into the sink, turned on the water, and washed it down the drain. I just prayed that it wouldn't clog the pipes.

"Who eats this shit?" I mumbled. "Whatever happened to the good old white salted cracker? I guess maybe that's the cracker of the common man."

I crawled back in bed with Matt and tried to fall asleep but the next few hours were awful. The nausea wouldn't go away and I just wanted to go home. There's nothing worse than feeling like a bag of dirt in someone else's yard. Exhausted, I closed my eyes. I must have dozed off because the next thing I knew I was awakened by the smell of bacon and eggs.

"Morning baby," Matt said setting the tray on the bed, "I made some breakfast."

"Mmm thanks. It looks delicious," I lied. Just the sight of it made me quiver.

Matt climbed in beside me and started eating. I didn't want to insult him by not eating, so I picked up a piece of bacon and gingerly took a bite.

"You're not eating much."

"I'm sorry Matt. I'm just not a big morning eater."

"No? That's the most important meal. You need to fuel your body up for the day...and it helps keep weight off too."

"Ya I'll keep that in mind," I said sarcastically.

I suddenly realized I was still naked and began to feel awkward and self-conscious. I could feel his eyes on me when I went to the bathroom to rescue my clothes. Sure, he'd seen me naked when we were having sex but this was totally different. It was morning. There was light. I had nowhere to hide. He was yapping on about breakfast the entire time I was getting dressed. I could feel the bacon grease hit my empty stomach and immediately stir up trouble. I had a small window of opportunity to get the hell out of there and into the safety of my own bathroom.

"Aw what'd you do that for?" he asked as a walked out of the bathroom fully clothed.

"I've really got to get going Matt. There's an article I've been working on and I just have to get it finished before Monday," I lied, "I'll talk to later okay. And thanks, I had a really good time last night." I kissed him goodbye and practically ran out of the room. The smell of eggs on his breath almost did me in. It wasn't until I was in the cab and safely on my way home that I remembered I'd left my 'outfit' in Matt's room. That was a shame.

After a plate full of real crackers and a few hours of solid sleep, I felt much better. Not great, but better. I was just making some tea when the doorbell rang.

"Holy, you look like shit!"

"Thanks Vic. Feel like shit too," I answered.

"What happened? I thought you swore off the excessive alcohol?"

"I did but there was a situation." I tried not to but I started to laugh. "Want some tea?"

"Sure, but quit trying to change the subject. What do you mean there was a situation? Did Matt hurt you?"

"Oh god no, nothing like that," I paused. I was already embarrassed enough about last night and I wasn't sure I wanted to relive the events even for Vicki.

"Would you spill it! Something happened and you know I'm not leaving here until you tell me."

"Fine, but you can't laugh," I said.

"Have I ever laughed at any of your situations?"

"Oh please, it's more like when you haven't laughed."

We sat on the couch with our tea and I proceeded to relay the events from last night. She was laughing as soon as I told her about Matt groping me on the elevator. It was going to be a long afternoon.

"He gave you what?" she said when I told her about the outfit. "How cheesy is that? Did you actually put in on?"

"Well this is where the story actually gets interesting." I refilled our mugs and brought out some chips. She almost spit out her tea when it came to the stripping part, and by the end of the story we were both in hysterics.

"No wonder you kept drinking. I would have too."

"Vic, I mean you know me. Am I really the stripping kind?"

"No...not at all. Well maybe when you're dancing by yourself, but definitely not in front of a man. You don't even like wearing a bikini. Was it fun though?"

"It was after he fell. It sort of broke the ice so to speak."

"Well if you had a good time, why are you complaining?" she asked.

"I'm not complaining. I'm just embarrassed."

"Don't be embarrassed. We've all done something like that once or twice before."

"Ya but you've always been a little more trailer trash than me," I laughed.

"You are such a bitch!" she paused, "I must admit though, the whole scene plays kind of creepy and weird."

"That's what I thought too. I think that's why I was so uncomfortable. I don't mind role playing but the whole costume thing...definitely not me."

"How's the sex?"

"Fantastic. That's part of the problem. I want the relationship to move forward but we can't ever seem to get further than the bedroom. Don't get me wrong, it's great, but I want more. I can't imagine just cuddling on the couch watching a movie. Matt would want sex. In fact he would expect it."

"I don't know what to tell you Alex. If he makes you happy then stick with it. If not, let him go."

It's not that I was afraid to be alone because I wasn't. Sometimes I was happier being alone than having to worry about making a relationship work, especially if I was the one doing all the work and making all the compromises.

"I am having fun Vic. Despite all the sex!"

She grinned, "Ya that's a horrible problem to have Alex."

"I'm not willing to throw in the towel yet," I said, "there is potential. I know it."

"Good for you. That's the spirit." She put her cup down on the table. "That being the case then, when are we going to meet him? I know that

Tom is anxious, and frankly so am I. I need to see the man that has turned my best friend into a fucking machine."

"Wanna double date or something? Nothing very formal though. It has to be fun," I said.

"What about going bowling?" Vicki suggested.

"Bowling? That's a great idea. It's fun, non-threatening and I can kick your ass!"

"Ya whatever, geek girl."

"Just because I manage to throw the ball in the lane and not in the gutter does not make me a geek. It makes me a skilled athlete. Your athletic skills on the other hand leave a lot to be desired." She was laughing because she knew I was right on the money. I loved the girl but I had to admit she'd be my last pick for anything requiring hand eye coordination.

"Do you think Matt will go?" she asked.

"He will if I promise to kiss the creature."

"You are soooo bad! You'd do that just to get him to go?"

"No, of course not, but he doesn't have to know. Just the anticipation will get him through the night," I said.

"You crack me up!"

"Thanks. Hey speaking of kissing the creature, how are things going with my brother?"

Vicki immediately turned red and smiled, "Fantastic…we've spent so much time together just talking and getting to know each other as adults you know? He's such a great listener, and I feel so comfortable around him. I could tell him anything."

"Has he opened up to you yet?" I asked.

"Almost from the beginning. He's really honest, and I know you're going to laugh but he's really mature. We talk about adult things. Politics, sports, work, family…It's so refreshing."

"I bet," I said with a big sigh, "it would be nice to talk like adults sometime. The horny teenager thing gets a little stale."

Vicki smiled. "But you're so good at it."

"I know I'm a dirty vixen!"

We chatted for a while about girl stuff then turned our attention to more important things like which celebrity was cheating on the other, and would it affect their next movie. It was great to spend the afternoon just hanging out with Vicki. Since Matt came into my life and Tom into hers, we'd put each other on the back burner. No matter though, she would always be my best friend. No one could replace her. She was special. She danced across the floor to put the DVD into the player, pirouetting midair as she went. All I could do was smile. She was that kind of girl.

I made some popcorn and we settled in to watch the movie. It was a sad one and both of us were balling within the first hour. It felt good to cry. Especially since the reason I was crying had absolutely nothing to do with my life. Or did it? Was I crying because the daughter lost her mother to cancer in the movie, or was I crying because I had subconsciously put myself in the daughter's shoes? What would I do if my mother was diagnosed? How would I react? Would I be strong enough to handle it? Thinking of these questions only made me cry harder.

"Are you okay Alex?" Vicki reached over and took my hand.

"Ya I'm fine. I was just thinking about how easily this movie could be real life."

"I know!" Vicki answered, "I was thinking the same thing except I was using your mother instead of mine." She shrugged her shoulders. "My mother could die and I probably wouldn't know until I read the obituary."

"Vic," I said.

"No seriously, it's true. Nobody would call. I don't even know where my parents are living these days. It doesn't matter anymore. To me I guess they're already dead. If they don't want to be a part of my life, that's their choice."

"And their loss," I added, "I think they'd be surprised how their angry teenage girl turned out. They just never gave you a chance to adjust."

"Ya they turfed me out at the first sign of trouble. I was a rotten kid. I guess I can't blame them."

"You were not a rotten kid Vicki, quit saying that! If your parents had acted like parents and not children, you likely wouldn't have gotten yourself into the mess that you did. It wasn't all your fault. Sure, you made some dumb choices but you were a kid Vic! Just a kid!"

"Ya I know but still…" She turned her attention back to the television but I could see fresh tears welling in her eyes. "Sometimes though I just….I just miss them. I don't want to…but I do." She was doing all she could not to completely break down and cry. I wanted to comfort her but I knew it was best to let her be. A hug now would open the floodgates, and that was the last thing Vicki needed or wanted. She was a strong, independent woman who would deal with her tears in her own way.

"Popcorn?" I said picking up the bowl and shoving it in front of her face.

She took a handful and smiled. "Thanks." She knew I was there for her now and would be there forever. We watched the rest of the movie in silence each lost in our own thoughts but knowing we were in each other's.

"That was a good movie," Vicki sighed wiping away a final tear. I on the other hand had begun balling again.

"It was just so sad though," I said.

"Ya but at least the end was a good sad…you know what I mean?"

"I know…but now that I've started crying…I can't stop," I sniffled. Vicki just looked at me and laughed. She knew. I used to cry during every episode of Little House on the Prairie. I still do.

"Some things never change," she said patting my knee as she stood up. "What's for dinner?"

We rummaged through my cupboards and scraped up enough ingredients to make spaghetti. My stomach had even recovered enough to crack a bottle of wine. It was movie night with Vicki. There had to be wine. We made our spaghetti, drank our wine, and had a wonderful time. The phone rang while I was stirring the sauce.

"Vicki can you get that?" I asked.

"Hello?" she said. Her face suddenly went beat red and she held out the phone, ready to explode with laughter.

"What?" I whispered.

"It's Matt. At least I hope it is or you really are a whore!" she whispered back holding her hand over the receiver. I quickly grabbed the phone.

"Alex? Alex? You there?"

"Ya sorry Matt, I dropped the phone and didn't hear you. What did you say?"

Before I could stop her, Vicki reached over and put Matt on speakerphone.

"You heard me alright. I could hear you breathing heavy on the other end. You just want me to repeat it because it makes you horny too."

"You're right," I lied, "please just repeat it. Please."

"Fine. I said, hey baby…I'm lying naked on my bed, fresh from the shower and I was thinking about you and your spectacular performance last night. I'm still so turned on.' How 'bout you baby?" His voice was all deep and husky. Vicki had to leave the room she was laughing so hard.

I didn't really know how to respond to the question so instead I answered, "So what's up?"

"Me baby, why do you think I'm calling." I was absolutely mortified. Vicki was dying.

"I didn't mean that in a dirty way Matt, and you know it," I said.

"I know but I couldn't resist. So seriously, are we getting together tonight or what? I really need to see you."

I turned off the speaker; I think Vicki had already heard enough. "Not tonight. I'm just chillin' with Vicki. We're actually making spaghetti at the moment."

"Blow her off Alex…c'mon. You can spend time with her another day."

"No Matt. I'm not going to blow off my best friend just because you're horny."

"Fine," he said. "What about tomorrow? Or are you knitting with the neighbor?" His voice was drenched with sarcasm.

"Actually, I'm driving out to my parents for a family dinner."

"Oh God! That's even worse. You can get out of that can't you? It's only family."

"Matt…this may be difficult for you to understand but I actually enjoy my family and am looking forward to going. We have fun together."

"Ya whatever."

Vicki had stopped laughing when she saw the scowl that'd crept over my face.

"Don't whatever me! Just because you don't get along with your family doesn't mean I can't get along with mine."

"Who says I don't get along with my family?"

"I don't know…Me!" I said, "I just assumed that since every time I ask you about them or even mention them, you have a hissy fit."

"I do not."

"Ya, you pretty much do." The other end of the phone was silent. "Look Matt," I continued, "I don't want to fight okay. I have to go, my spaghetti sauce is bubbling over. I'll talk to you later. Matt?"

"Ya I'm here." His voice was quiet.

"I'm not trying to pressure you about your family. If you don't want to talk about it, I understand. I can live with that for now. But in the meantime, you can't get pissed off when I want to see mine. Family's a big deal for me. It's the most important thing in my life."

"I thought I was the most important thing," he said in a sweet kind voice. I think he was trying to be funny. I wasn't buying it.

"Matt you are important. But I've known you for what? A few months? Don't kid yourself. Besides all we ever do is have sex!"

"I know…isn't it great?"

I shook my head in disgust. "Ya wonderful…just wonderful." Vicki handed me a scrap of paper. "By the way, we're going bowling with Vicki and my brother sometime next week."

"Bowling? Sounds like lots of fun," he said sarcastically, "I'll talk to you later then baby."

I slammed the phone and sat down at the kitchen table. That man infuriated me! I couldn't get a solid read on his personality and it was driving me crazy. Vicki brought over a plate of spaghetti and set it in front of me.

"Wanna talk about it?" she said digging her fork into her own bowl and swirling it around.

"No I'm fine." I played with my food while I cleared my head. "I just can't figure him out Vic…"

"Quit trying Alex and just enjoy the time you spend together. You're making it harder than it should be. From the bit of conversation I heard, he seems like he's a lot of fun." She turned her head away so I wouldn't see her smiling.

"Oh shut up and eat your spaghetti!" I tried to sound harsh but was having trouble and Vicki knew it. She was ready to pounce.

"No man ever called me while he was naked, lying spread eagle on his bed. I thought only women did that sort of thing."

"Oh Vicki. You'd be surprised at some of the things that man says and does," I said. She smiled and showed me her mouthful of chewed spaghetti. "You are so disgusting…"

"I try!" she answered.

We didn't talk about Matt or Tom the rest of the night, which was good because I needed a break from men. It was nice to just sit and enjoy another movie with Vicki. I didn't have to worry about my hair or make-up or even if my breath smelled like spaghetti sauce. Vicki didn't care, she smelled just as bad. Relationships were hard work, and sometimes I wondered if in the long run it was worth all the trouble. Why do we kill ourselves trying to be someone we're not just to impress someone that may not even care? I guess that was part of the game. Part of the puzzle. You never find the right piece on the first try. But you keep trying until you get the one that fits. Problem was, the game was getting exhausting and the puzzle more complicated with every piece I tried to fit. I was starting to think that maybe my puzzle pieces got mixed up in someone else's box. It certainly would explain a lot of things.

CHAPTER THIRTEEN

I didn't speak to Matt for the rest of the weekend. He called on Sunday afternoon but I was purposely screening the telephone. I'm sure he called just to make sure that I really did go to my parents' place. The whole family dinner thing was a lie to start with but he didn't have to know that. I needed a day to relax and catch up on some laundry and other work. I picked up the phone to call him back on Sunday night but couldn't bring myself to dial the number. All I really wanted was a hot bath, a cup of tea and a good book. I didn't mind reading about someone else's juicy sex; I just didn't want talk about my own.

In fact, I avoided the phone completely for the next few days. I was in one of my writing marathons and didn't want to be disturbed. The more articles and columns I wrote at once and stockpiled, the more free time I had later on to do nothing. That was the beauty of my work. The answering machine was blinking when I came in from getting groceries.

"Hey Alex…It's Bobby. I just called to tell you that Sydney dropped Ben off on Sunday night. I've been meaning to call you sooner but I've been so busy with Ben. Anyway we were wondering if you'd come to dinner tomorrow night. Ben wants to make his 'special dish'. I'm not quite sure what that is yet. Please bring Vicki. That girl's crazy and I think Ben would really like her. Let me know okay. Bye."

I'd never heard Bobby sound so excited. I put the milk and the ice cream away and picked up the phone.

"Hello?" said this sweet little voice.

"Hi Ben. It's Alex calling. How are you?"

"I'm fine Alex. Are you coming for dinner? I'm gonna make macaroni and cheese. It's my favorite. Not the stuff in the box though…the real homemade kind." I heard him take a deep breath then yell. "Bobby! It's Alex. I asked her about dinner. I think she's coming."

"Hi Alex. Sorry about that. He's pretty excited."

"You sound pretty excited yourself Bobby. I'm so happy for you."

"Thanks. We've been having a great time already and he just loved his room. He can't stop talking about it."

"I'm so happy to hear that."

"I know…I'm happy too. So what about dinner tomorrow night?"

"That sounds good to me. I haven't talked to Vicki yet but I'm sure she'll come if she doesn't have any plans," I said.

"Oh Ben will be so excited. He's been wondering when we were going to have company."

"What about Carrie? Has he met her yet?"

"No," Bobby answered, "Carrie thought it might be a good idea to let Ben get settled before she came over. She didn't want Ben to think that he had to share me right away."

"I don't know Bobby, I think you should introduce her as soon as you can. I think Ben would really like her."

"I suppose. Well, I'll let you go. I promised Ben I'd scoop him some ice cream. I'll see you around six tomorrow then?"

"I'll be there Bobby."

I picked Vicki up on my way to Bobby's place. She was going to have dinner with Tom but he thought it was more important that she go to Ben's dinner party. Who knew my big brother was such a cool boyfriend. Matt on the other hand would never have understood. He'd have given me grief about not spending the time with him. What he didn't know certainly wouldn't hurt him. Bobby and Ben were sitting on the front porch when we drove up. Ben jumped off his chair and bolted toward the car.

"Slow down Ben!" yelled Bobby. Ben slowed for two steps then started running again. Bobby laughed and shook his head.

"Hey Ben," I said shutting the car door, "how ya doing?"

"Good. Wait till you see the macaroni and cheese. Bobby said you really like cheese so I added extra. I hope that's okay?"

I put my arm around his shoulder. "That's perfect Ben. Hey, I want you to meet my best friend Vicki. I'm warning you right now, she's a little crazy." Vicki made a funny face and Ben laughed.

"I'm pleased to meet you Mr. Ben," she said holding out her hand.

"You don't have to call me mister. I'm only a kid. Pleased to meet you!" He took Vicki's hand and shook it with all his might.

"I like this kid Bobby. Firm handshake. Big smile. He means business." Vicki tussled Ben's hair as she walked toward the house.

"Do you like macaroni and cheese?" Ben asked her.

"It's my favorite. Why?"

"We're having it for dinner!" Ben said enthusiastically.

"No way!" said Vicki. Ben looked up at her and nodded his head. "How cool are you Ben?"

He just laughed and skipped ahead. "C'mon! Are you guys coming?"

"Yes Ben, we're coming. Sorry ladies, he's a little enthusiastic. I'll just warn you about the macaroni. He made it from a recipe all by himself. So I'm not quite sure how it's going to taste."

"Guys!"

"We'd better hurry before he grounds us all," Vicki laughed.

Ben had already set the table when we went inside. He had even poured four gigantic glasses of chocolate milk.

"Ben this looks great," said Vicki taking a seat at the table.

"Hold on Vicki, there are name tags on the plates." Ben leaned over and pointed.

"So there is. I'm in the wrong spot then."

"Ya you're over here. Alex you're here and Bobby you're in the middle. That way it goes boy girl boy girl and everybody's sitting beside someone they know."

"Ben that was very thoughtful of you," said Vicki, "I think this is going to be the best dinner party I've ever been to."

Vicki was so good with kids. She always knew what to say and never made herself look like the bumbling adult. She treated children with respect and they immediately connected with her. She was awesome and kids love awesome. One day she was going to make a great mother. I wondered how often she thought about the child she'd lost. I couldn't imagine the pain she must have felt. It's one thing to lose a child through miscarriage because there is something wrong with the fetus or the pregnancy; it's another to have a child die inside your womb because of violence. I looked over at my friend. She was busy showing Ben how to make a sailor's hat out of a napkin. She must have sensed me staring because suddenly she looked over and gave me a funny look.

"What?" she said.

"Nothing," I answered, "Nothing at all." All I could do was smile.

"You're weird Alex," she smiled and turned her attention back to Ben. "There, now just flip this piece under here and you're done." She put the hat on Ben's head.

"Wow, Vicki that's sweet." Ben's eyes filled with wonderment and admiration as he took the hat off, looked at it, and then looked at Vicki. "Know any more tricks?"

"I know plenty young man but I came here for dinner and I'm starving," she said pounding her fists on the table.

"Oh ya the macaroni." Ben scooted off his chair and into the kitchen.

"Hold up there Ben. I'll help you get the casserole from the oven. It's hot." Bobby quickly followed Ben into the kitchen leaving Vicki and I alone at the table.

"Isn't this cute?" I asked Vicki.

"I know. They both seem so happy." She paused for a moment. "Hey why were you staring at me before?"

"Sorry, I didn't mean to stare. I was just watching you with Ben. You're so good with kids that's all."

"You're not bad yourself Alex. I've seen you with Janie's kids. They think you're just the coolest thing on earth. Much cooler than their own mother."

"Vic, is it really that hard to be cooler than Janie?" I laughed.

"No I guess not."

"Here it is ladies!" Bobby said putting the piping hot casserole in the middle of the table. Ben was close on his heels with a bowl of salad. The boys took their spots at the table and just as Bobby was going to dig into the macaroni, Ben started coughing. After the first few coughs, it became apparent that Ben was totally faking and was trying to send a message to Bobby.

"Ben are you okay?" Bobby asked.

"Grace!" Ben said as he pretended to sneeze.

Bobby tilted his head and wrinkled his forehead. Then his eyes lit up. "Ben I'd be honored if you would say grace."

Ben reached out his hands and motioned for me to take one and Vicki the other. Bobby looked a little uncomfortable as he shrugged his shoulders and held out his hands for us to hold. Satisfied that everyone was holding hands Ben began.

"Dear God. Thank you for food we are about to eat, especially since it's my favorite...and thank you that Alex and Vicki came to eat tonight too...and I know I've said it before but thanks that I can live with Bobby...and oh ya...thanks for my new room."

Half way through the prayer, I could feel Bobby squeezing my hand tight. It must have been an involuntary reaction because both Vicki and I glanced sideways at the same time. Bobby's head was bowed and his eyes closed but I sensed there was something going on in his heart that was much greater than being thankful for a bowl of mac and cheese. Vicki sensed it too because a small smile crept from the corner of her mouth.

"Amen."

"Amen," we answered.

"Okay everybody, now we can eat!"

Ben had one of those giggles that started in his toes, rumbled in his gut, and then shot out of his mouth like sputtering car engine. He was adorable. Vicki was on fire with kid jokes and antics. Ben had to plead with her to stop because he had a stomach ache. Even Bobby got animated during a game of charades, jumping up and down like a man with his ass on fire.

"What a great night?" I said to Vicki in the car on the way home.

"It was. I had a blast! Sometimes I think it's beneficial to spend some quality time with a kid every now and then. It gives you a good reason to act like an idiot and nobody cares. Kids don't care who you are or where you came from. They only care about the here and now. For them it's all about living in the moment. As adults we could learn a lot if we cared enough to pay more attention to them."

Vicki was right. Kids were the best. It sounds cliché but it's true that children are the innocence of the world. You'll never convince me that the newborn baby lying in her mother's arms knows the difference between black skin and white skin. As long as they have food and a clean diaper, their world is perfect. Adults teach children to hate. It's adults that point out that white is good and black is bad; or black is good and white is bad. Children don't care. They just want to be loved and accepted. As adults that should be our job. Unfortunately, there are too many adults in the world needing to be fired.

"So," Vicki said, "did you set a date with Matt for bowling? Tom said anytime is good for him. I'm the same."

"Well I mentioned it to him the other day but I haven't talked to him since."

"Seriously, you mean you didn't have a Sunday shut in sex-a-thon."

"No," I chuckled. "I needed some space. I haven't talked to him since you were over. He's called again but I haven't picked up."

"Alex, you can't avoid him forever."

"I know but I'm allowed a weekend aren't I?"

"Absolutely…but let me know about the bowling. And don't even think of breaking up with him before I at least get the chance to meet him. That would be so unfair of you."

"I'm not going to break up with him. I guess I'm just not used to all this attention. And the maintenance, everyday, pits and legs to shave, waxing the bikini line. I'm bloody exhausted!"

"Ya keep that up. He doesn't seem like the type of guy who appreciates the wild, natural side of beauty. I'm surprised he hasn't asked you to shave everything. Or has he and you're just not telling me?" She was staring at me with tiger-eyes.

"No, he hasn't asked and even if he does, it's not going to happen. Do you know how itchy that gets? I'd go insane trying not to scratch in public."

"You mean in pubic!" Vicki chimed in laughing.

I dropped her off and headed home. It had been a great night, but I was tired and looking forward to a hot bath and a good night's sleep. I was a little surprised no one had called while I was out. Okay, I was surprised Matt hadn't called. I was glad I wouldn't have to deal with it, but I guess it also left me wondering whether he was angry with me for not calling him back before. I was so mixed up. I didn't know what I wanted and at this point, it would have been my own fault if he didn't want to see me again. Maybe I was reading too much into the situation. I had a tendency to do that. I tried not to worry as I lathered my legs with shaving cream and got to work with my razor. The last thing I needed was to cut myself; that would be embarrassing. Besides a large bandage might snag on my fish net stockings.

The next day I was sitting in my office working away when the phone rang.

"Hello Alex Hanson," I said with fake cheeriness.

"Hey baby, how are ya?"

"Hi Matt, I'm good. How are you?"

"I'm wonderful. Hey I tried calling you on Sunday but you weren't home."

"I know, I told you I had to go to my parents place for dinner. I didn't get in until late," I said.

"What about last night? I called again but you weren't home. I didn't bother leaving a message."

"Oh, I was out with Vicki for a while. We were running errands and stopped to get a coffee. Sorry, the time went by so quickly…"

"That's okay," he said, "I just thought maybe you forgot about me."

"Forget about you. You know better than that. I just had a lot to this weekend. That's all." I didn't dare mention that Vicki and I were at Bobby's last night, even if it was for Ben. I knew Matt wouldn't understand, and he'd be more than ticked knowing I blew him off in favor of a young kid and a dish of some of the best macaroni and cheese casserole I had ever tasted.

"Look Alex, it's almost noon. How 'bout we get some lunch?"

I was getting hungry. "Sure that sounds great. Can you hold on for a second Matt, someone's knocking on my office door." I held my hand over the receiver. "Come in."

"Lunch is served."

"Matt! What are you doing here?"

He held up his cell phone. "I was outside your office the entire time. I wanted to surprise you with lunch."

"That was really sweet of you. Thanks," I said giving him a smooch.

"Wow Alex, you look fantastic today."

I made a model pose and said, "Thanks. It's my new shirt. I think it brings out the blue in my eyes."

"It certainly does," he said smiling. "Where can we eat? I brought sandwiches and salad. I hope that's okay?"

"It's perfect. Here let me clear off some space on my desk."

He opened the bag and pulled out two sandwiches, a bowl of salad, and two wine glasses. "I figured it probably wasn't a great idea to drink in your office, so I brought some sparkling grape juice. There's a roast beef sandwich and a ham sandwich. Have whichever you like; it doesn't matter to me. I brought some packets of mayo and that. I wasn't sure what you wanted so I didn't put anything on the sandwiches this morning when I made them."

"You made them? I thought you just picked the stuff up at the deli."

229

"No, I made the salad too. Here's some dressing and a fork."

I was pleasantly surprised by our impromptu lunch. The fact that Matt had made everything himself was very sweet and it showed me a different side of his personality. Maybe he wasn't as selfish as I'd thought. We drank our grape juice in wine glasses and had a wonderful conversation. He even asked how the family dinner went. I slouched back in my chair to let my food settle.

"You can't be full yet!" Matt said enthusiastically, "there's dessert!"

"Oh Matt, seriously, I'm stuffed."

"Too bad," he said placing a small box of chocolates in front of me on the desk. "Just open them up."

"Fine," I said. "But I only want the ones with nuts. I'm not a big fan of the strawberry mushy ones."

"Try the one in the middle; I think you'll think it."

When I opened the box, I was in complete shock. There in the middle of the box wrapped in pink tissue paper was a diamond pendant. It was huge and I was speechless.

"I'd recommend you didn't try and bite that one. You might break your teeth." He was almost giddy.

"Matt, my God! I don't know what to say. I certainly didn't expect this. I really was just looking for the walnut."

Matt started to laugh. "I figured that since you've become so attached to that necklace of yours, I'd give you something to hang on it. That way you'd remember me too." He took my necklace off and hung the pendant on it. It looked massive. "You're awful quiet. Are you okay with this?"

He reached down and lifted my face toward his. His eyes bearing down on mine, so soft and gentle. Of course, I'd started to cry. He just smiled and leaned over to put the necklace back around my neck. He smelt so good and as he leaned in, his hair brushed my cheek and I thought I was going to die.

"Matt thank you. You didn't have to do this."

"Alex sweetie, don't you get it? I wanted to. You make me happier than I've been in a very long time. It's not about Bobby and the necklace…it's about you and me."

By this time, he was whispering in my ear and kissing my neck. I tried to resist him but once again, I had about as much willpower as a pig in a mud puddle. Maybe it was the sparkling grape juice or the sandwiches, I didn't know, but this man had a power over me that I couldn't control. Maybe I just didn't want to. I met his lips with mine and the romp was on. I swear to God he was trying to retrieve some of the sandwich I'd just eaten with his tongue. It wasn't until I felt his hand under the shoulder strap of my bra that I'd realized he'd unbuttoned half my blouse.

"Matt…stop. Not here. We're in my office for God's sake in the middle of the afternoon," I protested rather weakly. He kept at it and I let him. Pretty soon my blouse was wide open and he was grabbing my boob like it was a water balloon.

"Alex…Mike needs you to check these…Oh my God!"

"Rachel!" I said quickly pushing Matt off me. "Have you ever heard of knocking?"

"I did," she said trying to contain herself. "You obviously were too busy to hear me. I'll come back later. Oh, I'll close the door again. You might want to think about locking it next time."

She walked out and I could hear her laugh like a fucking donkey. I was mortified! To be caught at work almost literally with my pants down was unacceptable. I was more mature than that. But to make matters worse, Matt had resumed his assault on my balloons.

"Matt seriously stop!" I said pushing his forehead away from my chest.

"Oh come on Alex! Don't let a little interruption spoil the good time we were having. I thought it was funny."

"Well I didn't," I answered angrily.

"You are such a party pooper. Sex at the office is fun."

"Obviously you've done it before. I should have known."

"Of course. You haven't?" he asked.

"No I usually try to be a reasonably mature person at work. It helps me keep my job."

"Oh please…like they would fire their star, just because she was going down on her boyfriend behind her desk?"

"For your information Matt, I wasn't going down on you…"

"Ya but you would have," he interrupted.

"No I wouldn't have. And besides, what makes you think I'm their star? Apparently, you haven't read my column that often. I'm really not that good." I only said that to see how he would answer. I knew I was a good writer but I had this sneaking suspicion that Matt had never even read my work before.

"Maybe so…but you're hot! Isn't that what matters in the entertainment industry?" he answered.

I knew it! "The entertainment industry? Matt I work for a daily newspaper and a very respectable one at that. We report the news not the gossip."

"But isn't your column about chick shit?" he asked.

"No. Okay yes, I sometimes write about subjects that pertain more to women, but I've also written lots of stuff on the environment and social issues. I was also the lead reporter in the Hector Long trial earlier this year."

"Who?"

"Hector Long! The guy who was charged with murdering his first wife…" I looked at him in shock. How he didn't know about the trial was beyond me. It was everywhere. Newspaper, radio, television. You had to pretty ignorant of life not to have heard.

"The thing is," Matt began, "if it doesn't concern me or affect my life in any way, I really could care less."

"What an awful thing to say Matt!" How self-centered could one person be? I wondered.

"Sorry, but that's how I feel. Except for business. I read everything about business. If it'll help me make a buck, I'll read it."

I just shook my head and started to re-button my shirt.

"Need some help?" he asked with a devilish smile.

"No I think I can manage on my own. Although I'm still not too sure how you undid it so quickly?"

"Here, I'll show you." Before I could say no, the three buttons I had redone were hanging open again.

"God, you are good!" I sighed and sat back in my chair. I must have been sight, sitting back in my office chair, blouse wide-open, undone bra pushed above my balloons. Matt was sitting on the edge of desk looking a little ruffled himself.

"I better go before I change my mind and ravish you right here whether you like it or not!" he said getting off the desk and whispering in my ear. "But you'd like it wouldn't you?" He kissed my neck again and made his way to my mouth.

"Well I wouldn't necessarily be disagreeable to the idea," I said breathlessly before meeting his lips with my own.

Matt started to laugh. "You talk too much…"

We kissed for a few moments before Matt lifted his head and said, "I'd better get back to work."

"Hold on one second," I said. "Can you just help me redo my bra? It's a little hard to reach without taking my shirt off completely."

"Of course, I'm here to help." He stuck his hands in my shirt, reached around my back and redid the clasp taking full advantage of my vulnerability to cop another feel. I slapped his wrist.

"What?" he said kissing me again.

"Alrighty then," I said, "thanks for the sandwiches and stuff. They were great. And Matt…really thanks for the pendant. I love it."

"I was hoping you would."

He was almost out the door when I remembered to ask him about the double date with Vicki and Tom.

"Bowling? Shoot I'd thought you'd forgotten." he said.

"Friday night."

"Alright sweetie. Anything for you."

I watched his fine tight ass walk out the door. It had been a good lunch and even though we'd had an argument, it was only a fun one. I wasn't even upset that he hadn't read any of my columns. I mean I certainly hadn't read any of the reports he'd written for his job, nor did I care to. We didn't have to have everything in common or always enjoy the same things. That would be boring.

I pulled my chair up to my desk and began working. It wasn't until I felt a slight breeze on my chest that I realized I hadn't buttoned my shirt again.

"You ass!" I said laughing to myself. "You are so easily distracted these days." I had just finished my shirt when there was a loud knock on the door.

"Come in!"

Rachel popped her head in and looked around. "Is it safe to come in or is he coming back for round two!"

"Oh shut up!"

"Seriously Alex, I'm sorry for barging in before. I honestly didn't know he was in here."

"That's all right Rachel, but I swear to God you're dead meat if I hear even a whisper about this around the office."

"I guess this means we're even? My turtlenecks cancel your bare chest." Rachel held out her hand.

"We're even," I said sealing the agreement with a hardy handshake.

"So tell me about the guy. He's incredibly hot! I think I might have even paid to watch had you let me stay," she laughed.

"Ya well, I'm not quite into the whoring business yet, despite what you might have seen. His name is Matt. He works in Finance. And yes he is a burnin' hunk of sweet molasses love."

"I'll say…"

"Rachel get that look off your face. You're creeping me out!"

"Sorry, I couldn't help it. I just kept picturing his face…your boob…"

"Alright enough!" I said, "What did you want anyway or were you bored and decided you needed a visit."

"Oh ya. I wanted to discuss the office Christmas party."

"The Christmas party? Rachel…Christmas isn't for months."

"Okay fine you got me. I saw a cute guy go into your office and well…I needed more information. Not quite the amount you showed me but…"

"I knew it!" I interrupted. "You nosy bitch!"

"Sorry," she said walking toward the door. "By the way, you missed one of your buttons," she cackled and walked out.

"What was that all about?"

"Wayne! Geez doesn't anybody knock in this place." I quickly swiveled my chair away from his wondering eyes so I could fix my button.

"Sorry Alex…Rachel told me to go right in."

"Ya I'm sure she did." Button fixed, I turned around to face Wayne. He was smiling.

"I hope I didn't interrupt anything important. You look flustered," he said.

"No…everything's fine. My…ahhh…boyfriend…or friend I should say stopped by for lunch. We were just finishing."

"Boyfriend eh?"

I could feel my face turning the colour of an over ripe tomato. I don't know why I had trouble telling Wayne that Matt was my boyfriend. It was no big deal. Or at least I thought it wasn't.

"Was that him I saw leaving a few minutes ago?" Wayne asked. "Dark hair, kinda tall?"

"Yep that's Matt."

"Well he seems like a nice guy. We chatted for a minute in the hallway."

"You chatted?"

"He said he recognized my picture from the sports page. We talked a little baseball and football, then he left."

"Speaking of baseball," I said desperately wanting to change the subject. "Would you still be able to get me a few field passes before the end of the season? I'll buy them."

"Sure…but you don't have to buy them. I get them for free. Who you taking? Matt?"

"No, no, they're actually not for me. Remember me telling you about my friend Bobby? Well he was finally able to secure a foster placement for Ben. I think both of them would love being able to be on the field for batting practice," I said.

"Wow Alex, that's fantastic! Bobby must be thrilled?"

"He is! The two of them together are priceless."

"Instant Dad…I'm not sure if I could handle that."

"Oh you'd be a great father Wayne. I know it."

"You think?" he said pausing. "Ya you're right, I'd be a great Dad. Not right this moment though. There's a few things I need to do first."

"Like what?"

"I'm not at liberty to say quite yet," he laughed. "But I'll let you know as soon as I can."

"Fine, be secretive. What do I care?" I teased.

"The reason I stopped by…would you be able to drop by my office later and help me go over this one article? There's something missing and I need your expertise."

"No problem. Just let me finish what I'm doing."

"No rush. I'll see you later then."

He gave me a cute little wave as he walked out the door. I wondered what plans Wayne had up his sleeve. Maybe he was dating someone? I hadn't heard but a woman would be crazy not to want to date him. He's a model boyfriend. Kind, caring, compassionate and strangely enough getting cuter as the months went by. It's funny how that happens. The best-looking guy in high school always ends up bald and fat at the twenty-five year reunion, while the average guy has suddenly become adorable. Go figure?

My office was a mess. There was lunch debris all over my desk and floor. No wonder Rachel and Wayne were smirking. I collected all the garbage from the desk and put in the wastepaper basket. The only way to pick up the bits of lettuce and tomato from the carpet was to get down on my hands and knees. I immediately locked my office door. I wasn't taking any chances this time, especially since I was wearing a tight pencil skirt that wasn't very conducive to crawling around on all fours. I hiked my skirt to mid-thigh level and set to work. Nobody was going to accuse me of being a messy sex addict. I might be a dirty one, but certainly not a messy one.

I was almost finished when I noticed some more paper under the desk. The only way I could reach it without hiking my skirt up any further was to try and nab it with my ruler. I was hoping to shoot the paper forward into my waiting hand but of course, I used too much force and instead the paper whacked off my knee. Except the paper wasn't just paper, it was the box that contained the pendant. Matt's pendant. The one I was now forced to wear around my neck at all times. It was nice, but huge. One of those 'look what my money can buy' sort of pendants. No wonder my knee hurt. I was hoping it wasn't a sign. The pendant was already causing me aches and I'd only been wearing it for less than an hour. I tossed the box into the garbage and fixed my skirt. The air in my own office suddenly felt stale and close like I was trapped in a thick fog of uncertainty. I needed out. I needed to breathe. Maybe the air in Wayne's office was better or maybe I was just fooling myself.

CHAPTER FOURTEEN

Matt was true to his word and went bowling with us. Vicki and I had decided we'd all bowl a few games first and then catch a late dinner and drinks. I hadn't been bowling for ages and was looking forward to night of pure fun. I definitely needed it. The last few weeks had been stressful. Full of sex but stressful nonetheless. The alley was packed when we got there, some old timers league. Matt of course fussed about having to wear a rent-a-shoe but I really didn't care.

"Relax, they disinfect them after each use," I said handing him his pair of red and green beauties.

"It's still gross," Matt grimaced. "What if the person before had athlete's foot or something nasty like that?"

"Then you'll need a prescription. Now shut up and put them on, Vicki and Tom are waiting."

"Fine but I want it to go on the record that this isn't my idea of a good time."

"Ya I know all too well what your idea of a good time is," I said sarcastically. "You've had a good time almost every night since we started dating. Now I'm not going to deny that I enjoyed myself as well but tonight I want to go bowling with my friend and her boyfriend."

"Isn't he your brother?" Matt asked with a slight tinge of annoyance in his voice.

"Technically yes, but tonight I'm treating him as Vicki's date, and this is a double date, so as women we can act as women do on double dates."

"And how is that?"

"I'm sure you'll find out soon enough. Now come on." I grabbed his hand and lugged him off the chair.

"Alright! Alright!" he laughed, "I'm coming!"

Tom and Vicki were already practicing when we got to the lane.

"Get ready to have your ass whipped again missy!" Vicki triumphed.

"Vicki please. You beat me one game out of what a hundred?" I snapped back playfully. "You should know better than to taunt the master."

"The master?" Matt asked.

"Ya…Alex likes to call herself the lane master," Tom said. "She used to bowl all the time as a kid. Was pretty good too but don't tell her I said that."

"You don't have to," I said kissing Tom on the cheek. "I heard you."

"Shit! Now I'm going to have to listen to stories of our youth the entire night," he replied.

"Not all night…just the ones where I beat you at things."

"Alex, I wouldn't be too proud of the fact you spent your youth in the bowling alley if I were you," Tom smirked. "Us cool kids had better things to do right Vicki?"

Vicki smiled and nodded.

"Ya well look where that got you both," I said. "I have a room full of trophies and you two have vague memories of booze, sex, and pot. It's all about the choices people!"

Vicki and Tom were smiling sheepishly.

"Well sorry babe," Matt piped in, "I'd have chosen the booze, sex, and pot too. No offense, but you sound like you were kind of a nerd. I'd have stayed clear away from you back then."

"Matt, sorry to break it to you," Vicki said, "but in case you hadn't realized it yet, she's still a nerd."

"Shut up Vicki. I'm not a nerd…just an intelligent woman with a creative flair."

"You should see how creative this woman can be!" Matt said grabbing me around the waist. "Most guys would kill for a nerd who did the things that she…"

"Okay who's first?" I said interrupting. "Fine no takers? I'll go then. We came here to bowl, so let's get bowling." I picked up a ball and waltzed onto the lane. I didn't want to turn around because knew my face was beat red. How embarrassing! My brother just heard that his little sister was incredibly adept at raising the flagpole while striking the V-pose. The night was off to a flying start.

"Strike! Beat that bitch!" I said slapping Vicki's hand on the way by. She didn't have to say a word. Her sideways smirk and raised eyebrow told the story. She felt my pain but laughed anyway. I would have done the same thing. Tom held out his hand as I walked by.

"Nice shot," he smiled and whacked my ass. I sat down and took a sip of my drink. The whack on the butt was a brotherly way of saying 'don't worry about it and by the way your boyfriend is an ass for saying that out loud'.

We had a great time bowling. At least Tom, Vicki, and I did. Matt was trying so hard but he just wasn't very good, which of course made us all laugh. He played along but I knew it was killing him. He was so competitive, and with coming in last every game, his ego was taking a pounding. Vicki was hilarious and had Tom and I in stitches the entire night. She was prime time Vicki, and Tom was eating it up. I watched the two of them closely. They would steal glances and slight touches. Nothing overt. Nothing showy. Just moments. Small moments that shut out the noise of the bowling alley. The screaming of the kid who wanted more candy. The whiz and bang of the ball return. Moments that stopped the world. The moments became their world. They definitely had a connection. A strong one.

Matt on the other hand took every chance he could to grope my ass or kiss me openly. Tom kidded him once to 'stop feeling up his sister in public', but Matt didn't get the hint and I was getting annoyed. Finally, I just ignored his advances and concentrated on my bowling. I didn't just want to beat him; I wanted to crush him. I knew it was wrong and petty but I didn't care. I had to win.

"Look out," Tom said, "Alex has got that crazed look in her eyes. I haven't seen that since we raced go-carts at the cottage. She's out to win tonight!"

Vicki and exchanged glances and both started to laugh. She knew why I had the look.

"What's so funny?" Matt asked.

"Don't even try to understand it man," said Tom. "They've been doing that since they were kids. They have their own special telepathic language going on. Get used to it."

"I'd rather not," Matt answered as he whipped another ball into the gutter. "Damn it! I think there's something sticky on these shoes."

Vicki was dying, and had to pretend to get a drink of water from the fountain.

"Honey, don't throw it so hard," I said trying to help. "It's sort of like golfing. It's not how hard you swing but the motion and smoothness." Wayne had told me that once when we were dating.

"This is nothing like golfing. This game is ridiculous," Matt said taking off his shoes. "I'm done."

We all just looked at each other in shock.

"Well I have a few more frames to go and I'm finishing," I said.

"Go ahead. I like the view from behind anyway."

"You are such a pig Matt!" I said throwing a perfect strike. "It's too bad your shoes let you down isn't it?" He just smiled. That handsomely devilish smile. I looked away before its spell reached my senses.

We finished up and walked down the street for dinner. It was a great restaurant with a wickedly splendid patio. It was evident as I watched Vicki and Tom interact that they were friends. I wasn't so sure about Matt and me. We slept together but were we really friends? I don't think I could tell him something serious or personal without fearing he would pass judgment or make fun of me. I'd been down that road with Luke, and I didn't have the stomach to go it again.

I watched Matt during dinner. He was so good with people. Almost too good. Always saying the right thing. Always playing the part. He dominated the conversation and was forceful with his ideas and opinions. I saw both Tom and Vicki roll their eyes more than a few times. I said nothing. Tom was very patient with Matt but I could tell Vicki was about to blow her stack. She would hold her tongue in public only out of love and respect for me. I was fairly certain I'd be getting an earful though the minute we were alone.

"So how's work Vic?" I said trying desperately to divert her attention from the current conversation of investing in stocks and bonds.

"It's going okay. I'm a little bored though. They have me doing ad campaigns that are just ridiculous. If I want a job, I have to do them. It's frustrating."

While she was speaking, I'd accidentally dropped my napkin on the floor and as I bent over to retrieve it, my necklace popped out from under my shirt. Vicki noticed it right away.

"Holy shit Alex where did you get the diamond pendant? It's freakin' huge!" she said.

Matt stopped mid-sentence and looked over.

"Ya it's new…" I said uncomfortably. I could sense Matt's eyes boring deep on my face. I had to say something spectacular. "Matt gave it to me the other day. Isn't it great? And isn't he great?" He met my smile with a kiss on the cheek.

"Anything for my baby," he said. "I know how attached Alex is to that Bobby guy…can't figure it out for the life of me. She really is way too good to be hanging around a bar full of losers. Anyway, I figured since she wouldn't take the necklace off, I'd spruce up his blue-collar gold with a little high-class diamond. Look how it sparkles in the candlelight."

I was crushed and furious all at the same time. How could he say that about Bobby? He'd never even met him. I couldn't bear to look at Tom and Vicki. I was too ashamed.

"Well Matt," Tom said finally breaking the silence, "it's beautiful. A great choice!" God bless Tom, always the gentleman, trying to help me out when I knew he must have been fuming on the inside. There's nothing he hated more than blatant discrimination.

"I need to use the ladies room," I said getting up quickly.

"Me too," Vicki chimed in.

"Don't even say it Vicki. I know what you're thinking," I said pushing the bathroom door open.

"No you don't Alex."

"Fine then. Tell me what you're thinking."

"Honestly…I like him…sort of. I mean he's definitely good looking and he seems smart enough," she tried to hide a grimace. "He's just a little arrogant…and I totally didn't like what he said about Bobby. I'm trying Alex but I just can't see it." She flushed and joined me at the sink. "I'm so sorry honey."

"Don't be sorry. I agree with you. Sometimes he drives me insane. Like tonight, I just want to smack him up side the head. Then other times, especially when we're alone, he's totally different. Sweet and kind. I was so pissed when he cut up Bobby."

"Why didn't you say anything then?" Vicki asked.

"I don't know…I guess I didn't want to cause a ruckus in the middle of the restaurant. And did you see the pendant? I mean c'mon. It's huge! I don't even like it. What am I supposed to do?"

"It is pretty large," she said pulling it out from under my shirt. "Almost gaudy…" she giggled, "I'm sorry for laughing."

I rubbed my face in my hands and laughed. "I know. It gives me a sore neck when I wear it. He'd flip if I took it off and only wore the necklace."

"I agree. What if you only wear it when you're together?" she asked.

"I like the necklace though. Bobby put a lot of thought into it and I don't want to hurt his feelings."

"But it's okay to hurt Matt's?"

"I don't want to hurt either, Vicki. And Matt has this stupid idea that Bobby has this thing for me. Which is totally bogus. Bobby is like a brother, nothing more."

"I know Alex. Listen settle down. It'll be all right. Let's just go back to the table."

"You go. I'll be there in a minute."

"I'm not leaving you alone in here. The guys would wonder. What am I supposed to say? You're constipated or something?"

"It's like the more we see each other, the less time I want to spend with him. Does that make any sense?" Vicki nodded as I continued to rant. "Don't get me wrong...the sex is fantastic. I mean really good...despite the dress up games, but I'm not sure it's enough. Here I am finally dating a gorgeous looking, financially successful man, and I'm still unhappy. What is wrong with me? Seriously Vic, should I be seeking counseling?"

Vicki gave me hug. "There's nothing wrong with you and you don't need counseling. Maybe you two just need to spend some time getting to know each other without always hopping in the sack. I realize this might be difficult for you, now that you've become you know, 'dependent on the penis' and everything, but I think you should try."

I could always count on Vicki to supply me some good advice spiced with humor. "I'm not dependent on sex. I just enjoy it tremendously!"

"I bet you do!" she laughed.

We went back to the table only to discover that Matt had paid the entire dinner bill, much to the dismay of Tom. His treat he said. I think he just enjoyed being the big man with all the bucks. I could only smile at Tom and he understood that it certainly wasn't my suggestion. He shrugged his shoulders and led Vicki out of the restaurant. I followed close behind leaving Matt to pocket all of the peppermint candies.

"We need to do this again sometime," he said as we stood outside.

"Ya definitely. We had lots of fun," Tom lied.

"So what's up now babe? Back to my place for a little night cap?" Matt asked as he kissed my neck. I could see Vicki giving me the stern eyes, like 'don't give in Alex. Be strong!'

"I'm actually kind of tired tonight Matt. Maybe you could just walk me home?"

"Alright...if that's what you want," he answered.

"Well we're going to head," said Vicki. "It was nice to meet you Matt, and Alex…I'll talk to you later."

I knew exactly what she meant by that. If Matt even stepped inside my front door, Vicki was going to give me hell. Tom and Matt shook hands and exchanged pleasantries while Vicki and I communicated an entire conversation with our eyes. I watched them playfully disappear into the misting night, holding hands and talking wildly like two teenagers.

"What's so funny?" Matt asked as we walked home. "You've got this funny grin."

"I'm just so happy for Tom and Vicki. They've both been through so much over the years…I'm glad they've finally found each other."

"Tom seems like a decent guy…but Vicki! Man, that chick is a piece of work. Did you see her bowling? Acting like she was queen shit or something. I don't know how you stand her. She would drive me crazy after a while."

I was furious. It was one thing to make a few comments about Bobby. I understood that. In fact, there was a time when I may have judged Bobby the same way, like when I was young and stupid. But to cut up Vicki, my best friend was too much. And right to my face! Did Matt think I was an idiot?

"Matt you don't even know Vicki and I can't believe you just said that. Sometimes you can be such a jerk!"

He seemed genuinely surprised at my reaction. "Alex, I'm so sorry. I didn't mean to hurt your feelings. I just meant that I prefer people who aren't quite as goofy or over the top. I'm sure Vicki's great. She has to be if she's your friend. I really didn't mean anything by it. Honest." He tried to kiss me but I backed away. "Oh c'mon Alex. I said I was sorry." We'd reached my front stoop. "Baby I don't want to fight."

"I don't want to fight either Matt, but sometimes the things you say make me really angry. You don't think you could be hurting someone else's feelings."

"You're being a bit sensitive aren't you? Half the time I'm joking. I thought you enjoyed my sense of humor?" he said.

"I do. But you have to understand that not everything you say is funny."

"Okay, I'll try harder if that's what you want."

"I don't know what I want," I mumbled.

"Let's go upstairs to your apartment and figure this out Alex."

"I don't think so Matt. Not tonight. I'm suddenly not feeling that well."

"Whatever Alex. You don't have to make excuses. I get it."

"It's not an excuse Matt. I really am not feeling that well. Maybe it was something I ate." I don't think he believed me but I wasn't lying. My stomach was gurgling and my head was starting to ache.

"Now that you mention it, you do look a little pale and you were pretty quiet during dinner. Do you want me to take you up and help you into bed?" he said pouring on the charm.

"No, thanks anyway, but I think I'm just going to sit here for a minute and catch some fresh air," I said.

Matt looked at his watch. "It's still early, maybe I'll see if I can still catch the guys at Flannigan's for a game of pool…if you don't mind?"

"I don't mind. Go have fun."

"Are you sure?"

I nodded and let him kiss me goodbye. He hailed a cab and was gone. I was glad. Vicki would be proud of me. I hadn't given in to the seduction of the penis. It was a step in the right direction. I sat on the steps for a while and let the crisp fall air cleanse my lungs. Another season. Changing leaves, changing temperatures, changing lives. Where did the time go? Why couldn't it slow down so I had time to think; time to breath. I put my head in my hands and closed my eyes. I just wanted time to stop. Just until I could catch up and be at the place I needed to be. Problem was I didn't know where that place was or what time I needed to be there. Life didn't come with an itinerary.

"Alex, are you okay?"

"What?" I said lifting my head at the sound of Shirley's voice.

"Are you okay?" she asked.

"Ya I'm fine. Why do you ask?"

"Well besides the fact you're sitting out here all alone…you're crying."

I hadn't even realized it. Shirley sat down next to me. "Mort and I were out for a walk. I've already sent him inside. Tell me what happened. Did you and Matt have a fight?"

"Not really a fight. A disagreement maybe. But I don't think that's the reason I was crying. I don't even know why I was crying." She looked at me with those eyes that could penetrate any wall I'd try to throw up. "It's just that…I don't know what I'm doing Shirley. Everything is happening and I can't seem to stop it." I started to cry again. Shirley put her arm around me. "It's always so much work you know? And I'm just feeling so tired. I don't know if I want to do it. Is it wrong for me to not even want to try anymore?"

Shirley was quiet for a moment. "Alex, you are what I like to call my little wild stallion. My free spirited friend. You don't like to be held down. Be forced to do things that you're not comfortable with. You love your freedom. It's okay not to go through life in the traditional sense. Marriage…kids. The most important thing is that you are happy with yourself. Do something for yourself. Find an empty field and run to your hearts content. If Matt doesn't like it, or can't handle it, then he isn't the man for you."

"But I want those things Shirley…marriage, kids."

"Of course you do."

"Then how do I get there?" I asked.

"You don't get there. It finds you Alex. Haven't you ever watched a cowboy movie? Even the wildest of horses slows down at some point. She drops her head to the ground to chew on some fresh grass…and bam! The cowboy loops the bridle around her and she's caught. Now she might kick and scream a bit at first until the cowboy gains her trust. But if it's the right cowboy, with the right touch and encouraging words, she'll settle down just enough for them to become partners."

"So you're saying I should wait for John Wayne?"

"No, I'm saying you need to wait for the cowboy that understands you can't totally tame a true wild horse. If he respects you, he won't even try. He'll love you the way you are."

I put my head on her shoulder.

"Alex you are burning up?" she said feeling my forehead. "Are you feeling okay?"

"Not really, I started feeling crappy a little while ago. I thought maybe I was just stressed out."

"Honey, I don't think this is stress. We need to get you inside." She helped me up and I had to admit I was feeling very lightheaded. "Go slow Alex. Hang onto my arm."

We got upstairs and into my apartment. Shirley wanted to stay but I told her I was fine. She would be back in the morning to check on me. Somehow I managed to change into my pajamas and climb into bed. My head was spinning like a crazy man on fire and I'd almost regretted sending Shirley home. She must have somehow sensed my apprehension because when I woke up in the middle of the night, she was sitting at my side holding a cold cloth on my forehead.

"I was worried about you honey. I used the key you gave me to get in. I hope you don't mind."

I mumbled something incoherent even to my own brain. I couldn't think. I was hot, I was shaking, and my body ached terribly. I tried to sit up and talk to Shirley but found that apparently my head weighed as much as a concrete block.

"Shh," she said, "don't sit up. I'm not here to chat. Go back to sleep. I'm not going anywhere." She gently stroked my hair. "You missy have what I think is a very bad case of the flu. It's going around you know. Leslie on the third floor was sick all last week. And with the hours you've been keeping lately...I see you slinking home at night...way past your bed time if you ask me...You need to start taking of yourself Alex. I worry about you like you were one of my own...actually you're more like my mine than my own kids...I remember once when I was younger..." She rambled on about this and at that, her soothing voice slowly lulling me back to sleep.

I awoke with a start sometime later. Shirley was draped uncomfortably on my chair fast asleep. I didn't want to wake her but I needed to go to the bathroom and be sick. I attempted to throw back the covers but I was like Superman in the presence of kryptonite - useless. My strength eluded me, and my limbs felt and acted like wet spaghetti noodles. It was hopeless. Shirley with her Spidey senses was at my side before I could muster enough moisture in my mouth to ask for help.

"What is it Alex?"

"I think I'm gonna be sick."

"Hold on, let me get the bucket."

"I can probably make it to the bathroom."

"No you don't. Stay right there. It's easier for me if you barf in this bucket then having to pick you up off the floor." She shoved the bucket under my chin just as I felt my stomach wretch. It seemed to go on forever but Shirley was a trooper, holding both the bucket and my head at the same time. By the time I was finished, I was certain that my entire intestines and both lungs would be in the bucket along with last night's meal. I flopped my head back on the pillow, closed my eyes, and sighed. I heard the toilet flush. Bless Shirley's heart. I was glad she had come over. While I considered myself an independent woman, it's times like these, when I hated being alone.

I wasn't feeling any better the next day. I sent Shirley home for a while to get some sleep, promising to call her right away if I needed her. I drifted in and out of sleep the entire day not really remembering too much of anything. Shirley came back and tried to feed me some soup but my stomach wasn't giving an inch. She wanted to take me to the hospital but I didn't want to go. I'd rather be sick snuggled in my bed then sick sitting in a hard plastic chair in the waiting room. She understood but told me she was calling my mother just in case. I didn't object, in fact it'd be kind of nice to have my mom around. I missed her. It's so easy to take advantage of your mother while you're growing up. You just assume she'll always be there, to pick up your clothes and nurse you when you're sick. The first time she isn't, is when you realize what being an adult is all about. Sometimes being an adult sucks.

The phone rang a couple of times while I was dozing and I heard Shirley taking some messages. She didn't want the machine to pick them up in case one of the calls was my mother. "She'd worry if she couldn't get a hold of you Alex," Shirley had said. She of course was right. Mom would assume the worst, hop in the car, rush down here in a panic, and get in an accident. I wasn't at death's door, just a few rings up the ladder.

"Your friend Vicki called," Shirley said as she shoved the thermometer under my tongue. "I told her you were sick. She's going to stay with you tonight if that's okay. Mort and I have this thing to go to at the Lodge. I don't really want to go but it's an annual get together and Mort's looking forward to it." She held the thermometer up to the light. "My gosh child, you're still running a fever. I'm going to get you some more aspirin. You need to try and at least drink something. What if I give you some ice cubes to suck on? That'll help bring down your temperature and give you some liquids. I'm also going to get a fresh face cloth from the freezer. Alex I really don't like your fever. Promise me you'll go to the doctor if it doesn't start dropping soon?"

I nodded and tried to lick my lips but I think my tongue was stuck to the roof of my mouth.

"Let me get you those ice cubes and a glass of water for the aspirin."

She helped me sit up and held the glass of water while I tried to swallow the pills. I didn't get them down fast enough and they started to melt in my mouth leaving a taste somewhere in between a dead rotten fish and an overused dishrag. I started to gag, my face contorting like a rubber man on acid. Shirley grimaced along with me.

"Quick drink some more water," she said tipping back my head. It didn't help.

"Let me suck on one of the ice cubes," I whispered, "maybe that'll help."

Shirley propped up my pillows so I wouldn't choke and handed me an ice cube. The instant it touched my tongue I felt a momentary coolness throughout my body. It was like diving off the dock into the lake on a July day, when the air was blistering hot but the water still felt like mid-May. The shiver started from my tongue and traveled all the way down to my toes. It felt good. Shirley wouldn't let me close my eyes while I was sucking on the ice cube in case I fell asleep and made me open my mouth and show her when the ice cube was gone.

"Alright, you can sleep now," she said tucking the covers under my chin. It's almost five o'clock so I'm going to head home and get ready for tonight. Do you need anything before I go? No? Okay then, I'll leave the front door unlocked for Vicki. She should be here soon." She leaned over and kissed my forehead. "Now you take care. Mort and I shouldn't be too late, so you have Vicki call me if she needs me."

"Thank-you Shirley," I whispered.

"Don't mention it and quit trying to talk. You'll strain your throat even more than it already is." She fussed with my blankets one more time and placed the phone within arm's reach on the bed. "I'll see you tomorrow sweetie." She waved and walked out of the bedroom door.

It was oddly quiet when she was gone. Normally I enjoyed the silence but I was hoping Vicki would arrive soon. I really did feel sick, and was starting to worry that I had a bit more than the flu. I turned on the television to catch the day's news but the light hurt my eyes. All I wanted to do was sleep.

By the time I woke up, the sun had set and the sky was dark. My throat was so dry and swollen I could hardly swallow. I needed to go to the washroom but honestly didn't know if I could make it. I eased my head off the pillow, stopping mid-way to catch my bearings but still felt a wave of nausea sweep across my body. I managed to get my feet on the floor but the true task would be taking that first step.

"I thought I heard you in here." Thank God, Vicki was here. "I was just coming in to check on you." I pointed to the bathroom. "I'll help you. Geez Alex, you look awful." I tried to smile but wanted to cry. "What hurts the most?"

"At the moment my throat," I whispered, "but just about everything."

She helped me to the bathroom then sat on the edge of the tub and waited for me to finish like only a best friend would. "Are you hungry? I can make you something."

"I'm just thirsty."

"How about a Popsicle? I stopped on the way and picked up some 'sicky' foods. You like banana right? Finished? Let's get you back to bed. Actually, sit back down for a minute. Shirley wanted me to take your temperature again."

"Was she over?" I said.

"Ya, she stopped by on her way out. She's worried about you and frankly so am I. I've never seen you this sick."

"I don't think I've ever felt this sick before."

"Stick out your tongue." We waited in silence for the thermometer to beep. "You're still running a fever. Let's get you back to bed but I'm taking off some of those covers and opening your window. We need to cool you down."

"Thanks Mom," I said climbing back into bed. "You're the best."

Vicki just smiled, "It's because I love you! I'll be right back with a Popsicle."

While I sucked away on my Popsicle, Vicki proceeded to wash my face with a cold cloth. She was so kind and compassionate and I loved her for everything she was doing.

"Tom said he might stop by later," she said just making conversation, "he had a late meeting tonight with a client and wasn't sure what time he would finish up. So...I have to ask...and I feel bad doing it because you're sick and everything, but did you sleep with Matt the other night?"

"No, we had a fight, and then I started to feel really sick. He didn't even come up stairs."

"Good for you. Did you fight about dinner?"

"Sort of. I told him I didn't appreciate some of the things he says." I didn't want to tell her that we fought because of her. "It wasn't a big one. Just an argument, that's all. We made up before he went home. Only a kiss though, nothing more."

"I'm sure the horn dog wasn't pleased with that," she said wiping my face again. "You close your eyes now and sleep. I'll be right here or in the living room. I brought some work so I'm fine and I'll make myself a bed on the couch. You holler if you need me okay?"

I was so restless all night long, Vicki ended up throwing some blankets on the floor in my bedroom and sleeping there. I was cold, then I was hot, then I was cold again. My body couldn't make up its mind. Vicki was there each time to help me throw back the covers or tuck me in. She must have been exhausted in the morning because I know she didn't get much sleep.

"I'm fine," she said the next day. "I'm just going to have a shower before work. Shirley said she'd be over later and I think your mom is driving in today as well. Whether you like it or not, you're going to the doctor. Tom said last night that your mom already scheduled an appointment for you."

"I'm not going to complain. 'Cause this aspirin just isn't cutting it."

"By the way Matt called last night when you were sleeping. I told him you were really sick. He said he'd call back in a few days to see how you're doing."

"A few days?" I said, "Glad to see he's so concerned."

"You said it Alex, not me. He said he couldn't afford to get sick. Sorry."

Vicki showered and was out the door in a flash leaving me alone to either ponder my life or count the number of tiles in the ceiling. I chose to count the tiles. Twenty-four full and ten half pieces. I was completely bored. Nothing to do. Didn't want to think, watch television, or even turn on the radio. Maybe I'd try to get some more sleep. It couldn't hurt. I closed my eyes and snuggled under the covers. I loved my bed, it gave me more warmth and comfort than apparently my boyfriend was willing to offer. Truth was I didn't want to deal with Matt right now anyway. I didn't want to pretend to be feeling better; in fact, I was just plain tired of pretending.

I had almost dozed off when I heard the most annoying buzzing by my ear. I waved my hand but the fly wouldn't go away. It zipped back and forth across the room like a dart always seeming to pause for a quick rest on my head.

"Son of a bitch! Get out of here you little bastard!" He flew to a safe perch on the nightstand and stood there watching me. Mocking me. Daring me to play his little game. I stayed still and hoped the stupid thing would go away. Buzzzz! He whipped in front of my face and I distinctively thought I heard him laugh. That was it! It was war. I grabbed the newspaper Vicki left me and readied my position. Little Bastard was flying around the room building up speed and momentum. I sat up and pretended to read the paper, all the while keeping a close watch on him. He circled once more around the room then dove for the puddle of leftover Popsicle juice on the nightstand. I let him land and taste the sweet nectar of his last meal. Slowly I raised the paper. Little Bastard was oblivious. Smack! Little Bastard was dead. I flicked him off the nightstand with the paper, his remains left to decompose with the other creatures living on my bedroom floor. Satisfied with my achievement, I tossed the paper and wriggled under the covers, content to sleep in peace.

The doctor diagnosed a serious bacterial infection in my lungs that had migrated to my throat. He prescribed some heavy drugs and complete bed rest for which I was happy to oblige. My Mom, Shirley, and Vicki took turns staying with me until I was well enough to get out of bed and tend to my needs on my own. Bobby was so sweet and stopped by one day to bring me some soup. He didn't want to stay (I think he felt a bit uncomfortable because I was in my pajamas and had very scary hair) but it was the thought. Even Wayne came by a few times to bring me the news from the office and drop off some work. No sign of Matt though. He called a couple times but I was always sleeping.

"So, you feeling any better?" Wayne asked during one of his visits.

"I'm starting to. I'm not as tired and my throat isn't quite as sore. I'm still coughing up some green stuff but other than that, I think I'm on the mend," I said.

"That's nice. Very visual."

"I thought so."

"Do you feel up to a cup of tea?" he asked.

"That sounds wonderful. I can make it."

"Don't you get off that couch. That's why I'm here…to help and cater to your every need. After everything you've done for me, making you a cup of tea is the least I can do."

"What have I done for you?"

"More than you'll ever know. Now stay here and I'll be right back." He fluffed my pillow before heading into the kitchen. "By the way I fixed the hinge on your cupboard door the other day. It was driving me crazy every time I went for a glass."

"Thanks," I said. "I've been meaning to do it but well you know, things come up and I get distracted."

"No problem. Is there anything else that needs fixing? I can do it before I go."

"No…I think that was it," I lied. I didn't want Wayne feeling obligated to be my handyman. Matt had said one night that he'd help me fix the cupboard door but like I said, I was easily distracted.

"Here you go sweetie. A nice cup of steaming hot tea. This should help your throat."

"Thanks," I said taking a sip. It did feel soothing on both my throat and my stomach.

"Well Alex I've got to get going."

"Are you sure? I mean can't you stay for a while?"

"No I'm afraid not. I've got a meeting tonight with some guys."

"A story?" I asked.

"Something like that."

"Well thanks for the tea. It's delicious. I didn't think a man knew how to make a good cup of tea."

He just smiled. "There are a lot of things about me you don't know. Anyway, I'll talk to you later." He kissed me on the cheek and left.

The tea was perfect. In fact, everything about his visit was perfect. Wayne was such a kind and gentle man, very considerate and giving. He didn't have to fix the cupboard door but he did. That was just him. That was just the way he was. I sat on the couch and finished my tea in silence. Wayne had said that someone had called a while ago but he didn't feel right in answering and let the machine pick it up. I pressed play.

"Hey baby…it's Matt. I'm just wondering how you're feeling? I've been missing you lately. Give me a call if you feel up to it."

I didn't. As I let the last sip of perfect tea drizzle down my throat, I realized I wasn't really missing Matt at all. I felt a sense of peace and accomplishment as I pressed the delete button. I was ready to move on but I also knew it was one thing to delete a message and quite another to delete a relationship. I put my mug in the dishwasher and headed back to bed. I was exhausted just thinking about it.

CHAPTER FIFTEEN

"I thing I'm going to break up Matt," I said handing Vicki a muffin. "These past few weeks that I've been sick have certainly shown me a lot about his character and his level of commitment. I just can't deal with him anymore. I'd rather be alone. Less hassle, less worry."

"So he hasn't stopped by at all?"

"Nope. He called yesterday and left me a message. Said something about missing me...but please, you know what he was missing."

Vicki smiled. "I don't think it was the conversation."

"Exactly!"

"Well at least you seem to be feeling better. You've got your fire back," she laughed.

"I am. I think the drugs are finally kicking in. You know, now that I think of it, I really hadn't been feeling that great all month. I chalked it up to relationship stress."

"Alex if it's a good relationship, it shouldn't be stressful."

"Then apparently, I've never had a good relationship!"

"So when are you going to break up with Matt?"

"Next time I see him. I'd like to be a coward and do it over the phone but I won't."

"Well I think it's a good thing Alex. He just doesn't seem very genuine to me. Besides, he has really bad taste in jewelry. If you two got married you'd look like a friggin' mafia princess."

"No kidding. Well he didn't like you either," I said.

"Ya I'm not surprised. I caught him giving me some dirty looks when we were out. What an ass!"

"Well if he thinks I'm choosing him over my best friend, he's sorely mistaken."

Matt called later in the day and since I was feeling better, we made plans for dinner the next night. I wanted to go somewhere neutral but Matt talked me into having dinner at his place. He said he'd been planning this elaborate spread for a while now. I fully intended to break up with him before dinner even started, so I secretly hoped he didn't go to too much trouble.

It felt good to put on something other than pajamas for a change. I dressed a little bit more conservatively than I normally did for a date with Matt because I didn't want him getting any wrong ideas. This was going to be our last date. I was sticking to my guns - at least I would try.

The night was drizzling as I stepped outside to catch a cab. I was still on antibiotics and didn't trust myself behind the wheel of my car. In my purse I carried a letter I'd written just in case I froze up during my break up speech. I know it was lame but it couldn't be helped. I was horrible at face-to-face meetings like this. I didn't know how Matt was going to react, so if worse came to worse I could throw the letter at him and run out the door. I'd be gone with the wind before my unsuspecting ex-boyfriend even got through the first paragraph.

"Hey baby," he said opening the door. "How you doing? I missed you?" We hugged. "Geez, you've lost weight."

"Well, I was pretty sick you know," I answered.

"Ya I know…Vicki told me more than once. Look Alex, I'm so sorry about not coming over to see you. I wanted to but I just have this aversion to sickness. I hate seeing people when they're like that. I like things to be healthy and happy and good, you know?"

"Ya sure. It's fine. I wasn't great company anyways."

I wasn't sure why I let him off the hook so easily. Maybe I just didn't want the night to be harder than I was already anticipating. He took my coat and let me into his monochromatic living space.

"I hope you're hungry. I made an Italian feast," he said pouring me some wine.

"Sorry Matt, I can't have any wine, I'm still on antibiotics."

"It can't hurt to have a little? Relax put your feet up."

"No seriously, I can't have any. Do you have any juice or something?"

"I think I might have some mango juice."

"That's fine," I knew I wasn't myself. I was nervous and being a bit of a bitch. Whatever makes the job easier. "Look Matt, we have to talk."

"About what? Here come and sit down. Dinner's ready."

He took my hand and led me into the dining room. The room glowed with the soft, romantic light of numerous candles. In the center of the table was an enormous vase of flowers. I was overwhelmed.

"Oh Matt this is beautiful." He pulled out my chair and waved me to sit down. "This must have taken forever to do."

"No, not really. Besides, I told you before…anything for my girl."

I almost choked on my mango juice. How was I supposed to break up with him now? I had to at least wait until after dinner. The lasagna was delicious and I found the conversation during dinner to be light and fun. Matt was on his best behavior and being incredibly romantic. He even opened up a little bit, telling me some funny stories about his childhood. After dinner, I helped him clear away the dishes and blow out all of the candles. It was now or never.

"Matt," I said taking a seat on the couch. "I don't think this is going to work out."

"What's not working out? I thought dinner was great."

"It was. I don't think we're working out. I just don't get the sense that you and I are on the same page most of the time. I really don't know what to do…"

"Just give it some more time Alex. We've just had this incredibly romantic dinner and we haven't spent any time together in ages." He started to kiss my neck. Here we go again. Be strong girl! Don't give in!

"Matt stop…we need to talk about this! We never talk…"

"Talking is over rated. Look we get along. We have fun." He kept on kissing. "All the other stuff will come, I promise."

"Matt you can't make that kind of a promise. You have no idea what the future holds."

"Neither do you, so quit trying to pretend you do." His voice was soft, smooth, and sexy. He had moved into caressing mode. I was having trouble resisting. I must! I must! I couldn't… He carried me to the bedroom and we made love. I knew it was for the last time and I think deep down Matt did too. It was a beautiful night.

With Matt snoring away beside me, I had to make my escape before he woke up. He looked so handsome and surprisingly innocent as he slept but my mind was made up. I was determined. I didn't want to hurt him but I had to. I quickly dressed, fetched the letter from my purse, and set it on the pillow. I reached around my neck, undid the clasp on my necklace, and let the pendant fall into my hand. I had to return it. It wouldn't be right to keep it. I didn't want to keep it. It would only serve as a reminder of everything that was wrong with our relationship. I set the pendant on the letter, took one last look at my sleeping beauty and left.

I slept in late the next day, exhausted from the events the night before. Matt was going to be angry and he probably had a right. I don't think he's the type of guy that girls run out on in the middle of the night. I felt bad about doing it, but for me it was the only way. I couldn't have risked him trying to talk me out of it. And he would have tried. I was weak when it came to Matt. I would only be kidding myself if I believed I could resist him. He was the Pied Piper, the Charmer, and the Suave Persuader. I let him control the relationship when it should have at least been an equal endeavor. I was ashamed about slinking away in the middle of the night like a two-bit hooker, but not enough that I wanted to go back. I had some pride. Then again, I did once wear fish net stockings and strip naked like a psychotic snake.

I didn't answer the phone the entire day. Matt called twice and wanted to talk. He sounded upset but I just couldn't deal with him right now. I needed a 'special me' day. Time to reflect, rejuvenate, and convince myself that yes indeed, I did the right thing. I put on the kettle and planned to spend the day writing, not necessarily working- just writing. Maybe I'd start that novel that had been festering in my brain for so long. I felt like being creative. I needed to release that spirit caged inside the sensibility of my life. Maybe my story would be about the taming of a wild horse, or maybe it would be about the possibility of just allowing the horse to be free.

I reached up to get my mug and found a screw sitting on the shelf. Wayne must have left it there when he fixed the cupboard door. What a wonderful guy. He helped me not because he expected something in return but because he wanted to. He was probably the best male friend a girl could ever want. There'd be no pressure to be anything other than friends; in fact, in all the time since we dated, Wayne never treated me like an ex, only a friend.

I sat down at my desk with my steaming cup of tea and stared at the blank screen, waiting for the words to come to me. Something wasn't right. I wasn't feeling the vibe yet. What was missing? I had my tea, I was wearing my 'special me' pajamas? Suddenly it hit me! I rolled back my chair and sprinted to my closet. Taking a deep breath, I reached in between the laughable bridesmaid dress I wore to my cousin's wedding, and the pair of pants I was fully intending to fit into again. There it was waiting for me like a weathered friend. My old pink housecoat. I wrapped it around me and instantly felt the warmth and comfort that radiated from the semi-tattered cloth. I was me again. I was whole.

I wrote like a fiend the entire afternoon, only leaving my desk for the odd bathroom break or snack. I was on fire. I didn't know if what I was writing had merit but it didn't matter because for the first time in a long time, I felt free to express myself. Who I was and who I wanted to be. The female character wasn't me of course. She was so much stronger. She would have flipped Matt off the first time he made an offensive remark about one of her friends, and she definitely wouldn't have been a slave to his or any mans' charms. She was bright, funny, and articulate. Too bad Wonder Woman already had dibs on the invisible jet...my girl would love an invisible jet. She deserved an invisible jet. Didn't we all?

The phone rang off and on all afternoon but I was too engrossed in my writing to answer or even check my messages. Nothing was going to distract me. Probably just Matt wanting some answers to questions I didn't want to hear. It was over. I dumped him. End of story. It felt good to say that. I dumped him. Ya that's right honey, I dumped you! It can never be construed any other way. I'm sure he'd tell his friends something different. Of course he would, he couldn't stand to lose. And he just lost.

I was a machine for the next couple of days, banging out chapter after chapter of what was sure to be a masterpiece. I was mid-sentence when the doorbell rang.

"Shit! That better not be Matt." I tip toed to the door trying to make as little noise as possible and peered through the peephole. Vicki was standing in the hallway looking rather annoyed.

"Hey what's up," I said opening the door.

"Where the hell have you been? I've been calling and calling but you're obviously not answering. It wouldn't hurt to check your messages sometime. I've been worried. By the way, you look like hell. What's wrong?"

"Nothing's wrong."

"You're still in your pajamas at three o'clock in the afternoon."

"I've been writing," I said.

"Oh that explains the lack of hygiene. You need a shower honey."

"Thanks for the compliment."

"So why didn't you pick the phone up? I thought maybe you'd had a relapse and were sick in bed."

"I thought the calls were from Matt. We broke up Saturday night. Actually, I dumped him."

Vicki was trying not to smile. "Are you okay?"

"Ya I'm fine. No remorse whatsoever. I just didn't feel like talking to him. He's already left a bunch of sappy messages."

"Good for you! So what happened? Tell me the details."

We sat on the couch and recounted the break-up. I wasn't going to mention the sex part but it was Vicki and I couldn't lie. Besides, I thought dumping him after sex was rather heroic on my part. Vicki thought laying the pendant on the note was a good touch.

"It's almost like in a movie," she laughed. "You slinking off in the middle of the night. Were you wearing the fishnets?"

"No. I don't know where the outfit was and I couldn't care less."

"Well I'm glad. You're way too good for him. I think we need to go out and celebrate," she said.

"You just want me to have a shower."

"That too. You smell a little stale."

"Fine…I'll have a shower and get dressed. Give me ten minutes."

"Ten minutes? It'll take ten minutes alone to run a brush through that mop on your head. Take your time, I'm in no hurry."

When I came out ready to go, I found Vicki sitting at my computer. "Hey, what are you doing? Don't read that. It's not finished yet." I ran over and turned the monitor off. Vicki just stared at me. "What? I know it's bad. I need to edit and rewrite…that's why I don't want anyone reading it yet."

"Bad?" said Vicki, "You think it's bad?"

"No I don't think it's bad, just not worthy of a read yet."

"Alex, what you wrote is phenomenal! I mean it. I'd buy just the way it is right now."

"Thanks Vicki but you don't count. You're my friend. I don't think you're reading with a critical eye."

"Still. It's good. Really good."

We stepped outside into the brilliant sunshine of the afternoon. The green leaves were trying to fend off the infusion of orange, red, and yellow to no avail. Time was passing, the seasons changing, and soon the howling whistle of an early December wind would replace the rustle of leaves. We bought a coffee from the old vendor on the corner and walked to Thompson Park to sit and relax. School was out for the day but the park seemed empty except for a few teenagers smoking who knows what on the swing set.

"Remember when we were kids, you couldn't wait to get home from school and go outside to play?" I said. "You'd throw your school bag on the floor, change into your play clothes, grab a snack and you were gone until dinner. Look at this park. It's practically empty."

"That's because all the kids are at home eating chips, watching television or playing video games. It's a different world nowadays," Vicki answered.

"Why though? I mean does it have to be?"

"I think parents are so afraid to let their kids be kids," Vicki said taking a sip of coffee. "It's like as soon as they can walk and talk, they're little adults. If they're not hovered over by their over-protective parents, then they're forced to face things…adult problems at such a young age. Sometimes I think the kids are more mature than the parents."

"You were forced to grow up pretty quick though Vic."

"I know…which is why I know what I'm talking about. It isn't fair to lay such heavy issues on a kid. It screws you up for life."

"I don't know about that…you turned out okay."

"The only reason my life is semi on track these days is because of you. You saved me. You and your family. You took me into your apartment that night, no questions asked. You have no idea what it meant to me when you grabbed my shirt and stopped me from running away. I was praying that you would but didn't want to admit it. I had nowhere else to go. I treated you so poorly back then. I was wrong. I know I've said it before but I'm so sorry."

"Oh Vicki, you have nothing to apologize for. We were kids. I knew you were going through a terrible time. All I wanted to do is help. I only picked you up off the floor and steered you in the right direction. You did the rest. I don't think you realize how much respect I have for you. Having the courage to go it alone for so long like you did. I'd be a mess without the support of my family."

"Well it's a safe bet that your family would never abandon you. Your parents actually seem to love you unlike mine."

I hesitated before I answered. "I don't think your parents stopped loving you. I just think maybe they stopped caring…about each other, their lives, their marriage, and unfortunately, you were caught in the middle. Neither one wanted to take responsibility for their problems, and you were a constant reminder of the life they used to share."

"Good theory but I don't buy it."

"It's my Mom's actually. That's how she explained it to me when I was

263

younger. I sense now that she was just trying to protect me from the reality of the situation. To be honest, I think she was horrified at what your parents did to you. I heard her once tell my Dad that your parents ought to be sent to prison for abandonment."

Vicki laughed, "Ah your Mom....bless her heart. I love her to death. She's been so great to me. Putting up with all my crap over the years."

"She loves you too Vicki. She believes in you and only wants what's best. She knows your past, and really does look forward to your future."

"I think that's why Tom and I get along so well. He knows my baggage and he accepts me anyway. It's like this enormous hurdle has already been crossed. It takes the pressure off. Every other guy I've dated seriously always wants to know the intimate details and let's face it, there's some things I've done in my past that I don't feel comfortable sharing with anyone." She looked at me and grinned. "Well you know pretty much everything…"

"And I'm honored that you told me…especially the detailed version of the guy on the beach in the middle of winter."

"Ahh!" Vicki moaned, "Don't ever bring that up again. I was fifteen and hopped up alcohol and some stupid pills that he gave me. I was such an idiot!"

I was laughing by now. "I have to say I was pretty shocked when the story hit the school."

"Shocked?" Vicki said, "I think mortified would be a better word. I could tell by the look on your face every time we passed in the hall. I knew. You didn't have to say a word. I knew you were disgusted with me. I think your reaction hurt so much because deep down inside I was disgusted with myself. Truth hurts, isn't that the saying?"

"It is, but still…I'm sorry about that. I shouldn't have reacted the way I did. I just couldn't help it. I was a naïve teenager who lived in this protected little world."

"You weren't naïve Alex…just uncool!"

She slapped my leg and took off running for the jumbo slide in the playground. I threw my cup in the garbage and ran after her. It felt good to run and to laugh at old jokes with my best friend. We took turns going down the slide laughing and screaming and I'm sure the passerby's thought we had to be mental patients. Neither of us cared. It was a beautiful day and we were having fun.

"Guess what?" Vicki said plopping herself in a swing, "I'm thinking about leaving my job and heading out on my own."

"What? Are you serious this time?"

"Yep. I've always wanted to. I love what I do but I hate the company I work for. We're never on the same page when it comes to ideas. They're so damned conservative with no vision for the future. I feel trapped. They know I'm the one that brings in the big contracts but they're never willing to compensate me above and beyond. I do all the work and they get all the cash and usually take the credit."

"I think it's a great idea Vic. You'd be fantastic. I bet a lot of your clients would follow you."

"So I was thinking…I could use a good partner. You know, someone to take care of all the writing, editing and shit like that."

"Have you tried looking on the internet?" I said trying to keep a straight face. "There are some great writers on there looking for work." I pretended to be interested in the ant crawling on the cup."

"Oh…okay," Vicki stuttered.

"I can post a note at work too if you want me to?"

"No that's okay…I can probably manage on my own."

"Vicki?"

"What?"

"I'm just joking! I'd love to be your partner!"

"You bitch…I couldn't tell if you were joking or not and I didn't want to assume you'd want to be my partner." She pushed my swing with her foot and sent me flying forward.

"Just for that I change my mind," I said.

"Really Alex…You'd seriously think about going into business with me?"

"I don't have to think about Vicki. It'd be so much fun."

"It doesn't have to happen right away or anything. I think we should take our time to plan. We'd need some equipment, office space. Maybe a little start-up capital."

"I know just where to go," I said.

Vicki met my grin with a gleaming smile of her own. "Bobby?"

"He'd help us in a second if we needed it. And as far as office space goes, he wants to fix up the warehouse. If we promised to help him with the planning and that, I bet we'd get to customize our space from the ground up."

"Oh Alex...it'd be perfect."

"It might take some time to get the project together," I said.

"But we could always start planning and setting aside some cash. I don't care if it takes a year or so as long as know I don't have to stay with my company forever." She reached over and took my hand. "Are you in?"

"I'm in! Now we just have to run it by Bobby."

"He'll do it for you Alex. He loves you to death."

"Ya I know. I love him too."

We talked for a while longer about the future and were both terribly excited. It'd be great to be on our own. I loved writing for the paper but sometimes it wasn't enough. I had deadlines and story restrictions. Working with Vicki would allow me even more freedom than I had right now. I could tell she was pumped. She didn't stop smiling the entire walk home.

"Uh oh," she said. "You've got some company waiting for you."

Sure enough, Matt was sitting on the stoop. "Shit!" I said.

"What are you going to do?"

"Talk to him I guess. There's no other way up."

"What about the parking garage?" Vicki asked.

"I don't have my parking key with me. Besides I think he just saw us."

"Do you want me to stay?"

"Maybe for a minute if you don't mind."

"Hi Alex," Matt said. "Vicki."

"Hi Matt," Vicki answered.

"Alex, I have to talk to you."

"Matt, there really isn't anything more to say."

"There's a hell of a lot more to say. Just let me come up so we can talk and work this thing out."

Vicki was giving me the evil eye. "I don't think that's a good idea," I said.

"Why are you scared of me?" he asked moving closer towards me and even though he smelt like a dream, I wasn't giving in.

"Matt I'm not scared of you. I just don't want to be with you anymore. Why can't you accept that? We don't talk, which means we never communicate. We want different things, and I'm not going to waste any more time working on a relationship that clearly is going nowhere."

"I think you've been getting some stupid advice," he said glaring at Vicki.

"Vicki had nothing to do with this Matt."

"Ya whatever. Can I at least talk to you alone?"

"I've got to get home anyway Alex. There's some dreaming to do." She gave me a hug and whispered to call her later.

"Seriously Matt, why are you here?"

"I've missed you. I've been calling like crazy but you're not answering. I don't want to leave things the way they are."

"I like things the way they are right now Matt."

"What being alone?"

"I'm not alone."

"So you'd rather hang out with Vicki than be with me?"

"Truthfully? Yes I would. At least we talk."

"But we have so much chemistry baby," he said trying to put his arm around me. "You can't deny that. We're good together."

"I'm not denying that Matt," I said pushing him away. "But I can't live my life between the sheets. There's more to it than that."

He turned away for a minute and stared into the street. "It's that Bobby guy isn't it. You're in love with the cable guy."

"I'm not in love with Bobby. I love him ya, but I'm not in love...there's a big difference. Besides my relationship with him is none of your business."

"Are you sleeping with him?"

"God no Matt. We're just friends. Good friends. A lot better friends than you and I could ever be."

"Good friends?" he snorted. "That's the universal code word. I'm not stupid you know."

I was getting angrier by the minute. "Matt you need to face the facts. I don't love you. I don't want to be with you. You're arrogant and have no respect for anyone including yourself. If you did, you wouldn't be standing here drunk making all these ridiculous accusations. You're such a little boy! Grow up!"

"I'm not drunk."

"You know...I don't even care. Please go away. I'm done talking." As I turned to walk up the stairs, he grabbed me forcefully by the arm. "Ow, Matt let go, you're hurting me."

He pulled me close to his chest. "Here's what I'm going to do," he said loosening his grip slightly. "I'm going to give you a chance to cool down and think about it. I know you'll reconsider. Remember, a guy like me doesn't come along that often. But, I forgot you seem to enjoy slumming. Trust me Alex...it doesn't suit you. You'll see the light, and when you do...let's hope I'm still around. For your sake, I'd hurry up. Time's a ticking baby...tick...tock...tick...tock." He let go of my arm and smugly pushed me away.

"Matt," I said gathering all my courage. "If you fucking grab me like that again, so help me I'll call the cops. You need some help. Some serious help. Slumming might not suit me but alcohol definitely doesn't suit you. Go home and sober up. And here I thought you were a nice respectable guy. Boy am I ever a shitty judge of character." I strutted up the steps and went inside, leaving a confused looking man alone on the street.

CHAPTER SIXTEEN

A few days passed since the incident with Matt. He called the next day and apologized for his behavior but I still wasn't taking him back. The streak of violence I'd witnessed scared me. I know he didn't mean to grab my arm that hard but he did and it hurt me. I'd tolerate many things in a relationship but being afraid my partner was going to explode and take a swipe at me wasn't one of them. After our telephone conversation, I think he finally understood we were done. I was proud of myself. I didn't sway even when he showered me with compliments, apologies and a slight choking of his voice. He actually sounded quite pathetic and I felt sorry for him. Rather I felt sorry for the next woman he was going to woo. And guaranteed there would be another woman. Good luck to her.

It was Saturday night and we were having a party at Wilkins Place to celebrate Ben moving in with Bobby. The whole gang was there: Bobby, Carrie, her son Michael, Ben, Vicki, Tom and of course all the regular Wilkins guys. Everyone was having a blast. The taps were open and the beer was flowing just like old times. Ben and Michael seemed to be getting along great as they played pool in the corner under the watchful but still sparkly eye of Bobby. Carrie was draped on his arm and the two of them looked like they'd been together for years. I was so happy for Bobby. He was in heaven. Every once and while he'd look over and smile. He didn't have to utter a word, I knew what he was thinking.

The music was blaring and the room began to dance. Everybody was up, shaking their groove thing. Even Tom who I'd always thought was too cool to dance was laying down some serious moves with Vicki. She motioned for me to come join them, but I was quite content to sit at the bar, watch, and enjoy the fresh lime margarita the bartender placed in front of me. I hadn't let loose in a long time, and considering the stress I'd been under with the break-up, I was ready to have some serious fun.

"Hey darling," Big Dave said as he sat down beside me, "you take it easy with those drinks. I know what happens when your blender gets too full."

"I know I know...I'm being careful," I laughed. "I'd hate to make you guys clean up another mess."

"Like I've said before, your mess was nothing!" He took an enormous swig of beer, draining his glass. He set the glass on the bar and when the bartender went to refill it, Dave put his hand across to stop.

"I'm taking 'er easy Jimmie. Don't you know beer's fattening? I won't keep this sexy figure I've got, if I keep filling my gut with brew. Unless of course I work each drink off!" He grabbed my arm and pulled me off the stool and onto the dance floor. "Whoa ho! Shake it girl, shake it!"

With the margarita's pulsing through my veins, I danced almost like I was alone in my living room. I said almost. I wasn't drunk enough to try the front scissor kick in public. Maybe later. Dave kept grabbing my hand and twirling me around this way and that, under his arm, around his back, whichever way he felt. Vicki and Tom were killing themselves laughing, but Big Dave seemed oblivious to the fact that my arms were now in the shape of a pretzel...and not the straight kind.

The song ended and the music slowed. Dave pulled me close and we swayed to the beat.

"You know," he said. "You're quite a woman. What you've done for Bobby is amazing. He's a different guy since you first walked into this bar."

"Thanks Dave...but Bobby did all the work. I just helped a little."

"You're selling yourself short Alex. Bobby's a respectable guy now because of you. And he's shamed all of us into wanting to be better and not settling for stuff. He never talked like that before. He has dreams now. Things he wants to do, and I think he's capable of doing them. I couldn't have said that a year ago." We twirled to arm's length and then back. "Seriously Alex...I know I'm always seen as the joker, the big guy, but you know there's some stuff that I'd like to do to. Maybe lose some weight and meet a nice woman like that Carrie. Bobby said we all deserve happiness but we can't always wait for it to find us, sometimes we need to help it along a little."

"Well that Bobby's a smart man," I said with pride.

"Oh shit Alex, Bobby'd never think of something like that on his own. Those words come from you. Don't you see? You've affected us all. Every man here is captivated by your smile. You've put a spell on us girl. There's no going back now! We're moving on up. You taught us that it's okay to dream. And I thank you."

I didn't know what to say so I snuggled into Dave's arms and let his sweater soak up my happy tears. The song ended, I kissed Dave on the cheek and went back to my drink.

"You okay Alex?" Bobby said placing his hand on my shoulder. "I saw you dancing with Dave there. Did he say something to upset you? 'Cause if he did I'll take him down."

"No, it's nothing like that. He was saying some really nice things. These are happy tears Bobby. You don't have to beat up Dave for me."

"I would you know. I'd do anything for you."

"I know you would."

"C'mer, give me some loving."

I got off the chair and gave him a big hug. It must have been the margarita's because the tears started to flow again. Bobby pulled me close and caressed my hair like only a big brother would. I lifted my head and kissed him on the cheek. He smiled and kissed me back.

"I'd better get back before Ben hustles Joe out of another pack of Skittles. I'll see you later."

"I knew it!" A familiar voice whispered in my ear. "I knew you were fucking both of us at once."

"Matt! What the hell are you doing here?" I was in shock.

"I can't believe you Alex! You left me for this jack ass!"

"Matt...calm down. Nothing is going on between Bobby and me. Not that I need to explain anything to you. Why are you here? Have you been following me?"

"No I went by your place and the old guy told me where you were. I just wanted to see you. I miss you Alex."

"Matt we've been through this."

"I know but I need to know your answer."

"Answer to what?"

"Whether or not we have a shot together?"

"God Matt are you dense? I don't want you back."

"C'mon baby…you know you want me." He came closer and I held up my arm to keep him away. "Look can we just go somewhere a little more private."

"Fine," I said looking around, "follow me." I walked to another part of the bar with Matt hot on my heels.

"Alex, I'm so sorry about everything." He said reaching for my hand but I pulled it away. "I've been a mess without you."

"Matt first of all I'm not going to talk about this when you've been drinking heavily."

"I've only had a few beers," he said trying to put his arm around me.

"Matt stop. I don't want you to touch me."

"I miss you. I haven't been with anyone else since we broke up." He could hardly stand up and almost fell over when he leaned in to try and kiss me. I told him to stop but he wouldn't listen. He grabbed my arm and pulled me close. "Let's get out of here." His grip was hard. I tried to pull away but he was too strong. I looked around the bar and caught Vicki's eye. She immediately grabbed Tom's hand and headed across the bar to my rescue. "C'mon baby." Matt slurred as he kissed my neck.

I was totally creeped out and shoved him away with all my strength. I pushed him so hard, he tripped over his own feet and began to fall. As he fell, he managed to reach out and snatch hold of my arm taking me down with him. I felt like I was falling forward in slow motion. I saw him laughing. I saw the corner of the table. The hard wood ripped against my head. I heard Vicki scream. Or was it me? I felt the blood trickle down my face. A white cloud shaded my eyes and everything went dizzy…then dark.

"Oh my God! Alex are you okay?" I could hear Vicki talking but I couldn't comprehend the meaning of her words. "Someone get a wet towel. She's bleeding like crazy. It's okay sweetie. Everything's going to be fine. You've cut your head on the table." I could feel her stroking my hair and the side of my face. Suddenly I felt something cold and wet on my face.

"How is she?" Tom's voice fluttered in.

"See for yourself." Vicki lifted the towel. "She's going to need stitches for sure."

"I'm gonna kill the bastard," Tom said looking over at Matt.

"Stitches…seriously…" I mumbled.

"Hey Alex…you had me worried there for a minute," Vicki said. "You passed out on us here."

"I'm fine," I said sitting up a little. "Just a bit of blood."

"Actually, it's cut pretty bad. You hit your head on the side of the table when Matt pulled you down."

"Is he alright?"

"Do you care?"

"Not really."

"He's fine except for the fact that I think Bobby and Tom are taking turns beating the crap out of him at the moment."

"What? Tell them to stop," I yelled. "I don't want anyone else hurt." Vicki helped me up so I could see what was going on. All of the guys had Matt cornered by the door. He looked scared.

"It was an accident. I swear," he yelled. "I would never hurt her."

"Somehow I don't believe that," said Tom. "Now why don't you just leave quietly."

"How's Alex? I want to know if she's okay," Matt stammered.

"She's cut her head and will need stitches, so no, she's not okay."

"Just let me see her." Matt took a few steps but Bobby intercepted before he could get near me. "Get your hands off me you dirty low life."

He pushed Bobby hard. "I don't know what Alex sees in you…she could do so much better."

You could see the steam pouring out of Bobby's ears. "Listen here you stupid prick. Alex and I are not sleeping together despite what you may think. But that's not even the issue. I don't respect a man who thinks he can bully a woman into doing what he wants, and you pretty boy are a bully. So why don't you take your sorry ass, and get out of the bar before you get hurt."

"What are you going to hurt me?" Matt teased.

I'd had enough. "Matt don't! Just leave," I said stepping out from behind Vicki.

"Oh God baby, look at your head. I'm so sorry."

"I'm fine but I'm not changing my mind. We're over. I don't want to see you again. Goodbye." I turned around and walked away with Vicki. I could hear Matt and Bobby arguing about something but I didn't care. My head was pounding and I was feeling queasy.

"Holy shit!" Vicki screamed excitedly, "Bobby just punched Matt and sent him flying."

"Good," I mumbled.

"Big Dave and Joe just picked him up and threw him out of the bar," Vicki laughed. "Matt must have said something really stupid. Those guys are pretty mild mannered." I only nodded. "Shoot Alex, we've got to get you to the hospital."

I ended up with ten stitches along my hairline. The emergency room nurse questioned me about the cut and I told her I'd accidentally been pushed into a table at a bar. I didn't lie, I just didn't tell the whole truth. I wanted my association with Matt to be over with, and if I pressed charges or made a fuss, he would still be a part of life and I didn't want that. Vicki backed me up although I think she would have preferred I told the nurse a drunken ex-boyfriend caused the gash.

"You should have told her Alex," Vicki said after the nurse had left the room.

"I know but…he didn't actually hit me."

"That's not the point. He had a pretty good grip on your arm. I could see the panic on your face."

"I don't want to talk about it anymore. I just want to go home."

Vicki took me home and stayed the night. The doctor was concerned that I may have suffered a slight concussion since I passed out right after it happened.

"You're awfully quiet Alex. What's the matter?" Vicki asked as she brought me a glass of water. "I don't think you have to worry about Matt coming back again. Tom said the boys threatened him with his life if he ever came near you again. You're safe."

"I'm not worried about that."

"What then?"

"I guess I'm just really embarrassed about the whole thing. The guys are probably wondering why the hell I went out with him in the first place. I just feel so stupid that everybody had to come to my rescue and defend me. I should be able to take care of myself."

"Alex stop that. There's nothing to be embarrassed about. You had no idea Matt had a temper when he drank."

"But he didn't Vic...that's what's been bothering me. There were many times we both drank too much and he was never anything but sweet and kind...and maybe a bit obnoxious...but never a hint of violence. I don't know what happened. Did I trigger it?"

"Maybe he has trouble dealing with rejection. He only started to change after you broke up right?"

I nodded. "Who knows...I don't even care anymore. I just want to go to bed."

"I have to meet with a client tomorrow morning so I might be gone when you get up," Vicki said climbing in beside me.

"On a Sunday?"

"I know. It's the only time they could meet. Apparently, he has a flight to Cuba later that afternoon for holidays. The office thought I wouldn't mind meeting with him before he left."

"That was nice of them," I said.

"Ya no kidding. Let's make a pact. When we're on our own…no Sunday meetings. Deal?"

"Deal."

I awoke the next morning to a clanging of dishes in the kitchen and the smell of bacon and eggs. I threw on my housecoat and slowly ventured into the kitchen. My head was throbbing and I still felt dizzy.

"Alex," said Shirley. "My dear, how are feeling?"

"I'm sore this morning. I must have wrenched my back and neck a bit when I fell." I took a sip of the coffee that Shirley handed me. "What are you doing here anyway Shirley? Not that I mind of course."

"Vicki knocked on my door this morning and told me what happened. She didn't want you to wake up alone. Let me look at that bandage. Vicki said we needed to change the dressing. Here Alex, you'd better sit down."

I sat at the table while Shirley carefully peeled back the tape and even though I was still under the influence of some damn good painkillers, it hurt.

"Well this doesn't look too bad," Shirley lied.

"It's okay Shirley, I saw the cut last night when they were cleaning it up. I know it's not too pretty."

"I wouldn't say that. At least it's right along your hairline. Once it's healed it shouldn't be too noticeable."

"Thanks for trying to make me feel better and for coming over Shirley. I don't know what I'd do without you."

"Neither do I Alex," Shirley laughed. "Neither do I. You might want to hang on to something sweetie. I need to squirt the area with some of this antiseptic spray they gave you. It's leaking a little puss and blood."

"Great…this shouldn't hurt too much," I said sarcastically. I grabbed hold of the chair with both hands, closed my eyes, and took a deep breath. "Okay I'm ready." The instant the liquid hit my head I wanted to cry. "Holy Mary Mother of God!"

I'd never felt something so painful before in my life. And I thought using vinegar to clean a scrape I'd gotten after wiping out on my bicycle was bad. Talk about a fucking sting! This was a thousand times worse and then some. Normally I had a high pain tolerance but this was different. And the smell. There's nothing worse than the smell of dried blood, especially when it was in the process of being liquefied and cleaned by a powerful yet unpleasant chemical spray. I'm not afraid to admit I'm weak when it comes to smells. That and hitting a bone, or seeing someone get hurt. Nothing gets me on the ground faster than witnessing someone else's injury. My blood fine. Your blood? You'd better send for two paramedics because I'm definitely going down.

"Sorry Alex. I'm so sorry…geez does this stuff ever bubble. It's soaking the puss right up. How you doing?"

"I think I'm going to pass out." Shirley quickly wrapped her hands around my waist and led me to the couch. "Here lay down for a minute. I hate to say this but I'm supposed to dab up the excess then reapply the spray. Do you want me to wait?"

"No just do it now and get it over with."

The second time didn't hurt quite as much but I think that's only because all of my senses were numb. She put on some fresh gauze and kissed me on the cheek. I knew she felt bad for causing me so much pain. It wasn't her fault. I was the one who dated the loser. Maybe I deserved it and why didn't I see it coming? He was too good to be true. That should have raised a red flag but no…I was too content in the knowledge that I was banging a prize winning tiger on a regular basis. And let's face it, that's all it really was. There was no relationship. Just sex. And all I had to show for my torrid little affair was ten stitches to the head. At least he didn't give me genital warts.

Once the searing pain passed, I joined Shirley at the kitchen table for breakfast. I was surprised at how hungry I was. Sometimes nothing feels better in your gut than a big plate of greasy bacon and eggs.

"So are you up to telling me what happened?" she asked between bites of toast. "Vicki just said that you had a fight with Matt and somehow fell into a table. She was very vague."

"She was probably in a hurry. Early meeting with a client. Did she say if she'd be back later?"

"Yes she'll be back as soon as she's done. Do you want more bacon?"

"No I'm fine. This is great. Thanks Shirley."

I told her what happened at the bar and she was mortified.

"How did he know where you were?" Shirley asked.

"Matt said that my old neighbor guy told him."

"Mort! I'm gonna kill him!"

"Oh Shirley it's not Mort's fault. He had no idea that Matt and I had broken up. Please don't get angry with him. I'm sure he was only trying to be nice and helpful. I saw him on the way out last night. He asked where I was going all spiffed up, so I told him. He had no idea that Matt was going to be a twit."

"A twit? That's a bit tame isn't it Alex? There are a few other choice words I'd like to say to that young man and twit isn't one of them. I can't believe him. He seemed like such a nice guy...but didn't I tell you there was something about him I just couldn't put my finger on. Something about his personality that just wasn't right."

"Well apparently he becomes a fucking spazz when he drinks heavily and doesn't get his way. Not the most attractive quality in a man but then again I seem to have some trouble picking men...so what do I know?"

Shirley shook her head and laughed, "Oh Alex. What are we going to do with you?"

Our special moment was interrupted by a knock on the door. My first thought was Matt had stopped by to apologize. I couldn't deal with him ever again. Shirley must have sensed my apprehension.

"You stay in here," she whispered. "I'll get it. I won't let him in. I promise."

I was nervous as she went to the door and looked through the peephole. She let out a huge sigh. "It's your mother. Thank goodness." She opened the door and my mother flew in like a wolf on fire.

"Hi Shirley. Where is she? Is she okay?"

"Mom...I'm fine," I said.

"Oh Alex," she ran and gave me a humungous hug. "Tom called me this morning. I was so worried. I came right away."

"Well, I'm going to head home," said Shirley picking up her purse. "Call if you need anything Alex."

"Thanks Shirley." I watched her exit the apartment then turned my attention back to my mother. "Do you want some coffee or anything Mom? Shirley made a full pot." I was trying to avoid talking about the situation as long as I could.

"Sure. I can get it though. You probably shouldn't be moving around too much honey. Why don't you have a seat on the couch? I'll get the drinks." She fiddled around in the kitchen as I made myself comfortable on the couch. "Does it hurt much?" she said handing me my mug.

"It just sort of throbs, and I have one killer of a headache."

She grimaced. "Tom told me what happened at the bar but he didn't go into much detail. I don't think he really knew what was going on except that you needed help. Do you want to talk about it?"

I took a sip of my coffee and settled into the couch. "It was an accident. Not that I'm defending him because I'm not...but I seriously don't think he meant to pull me down. I think he was grabbing hold of my arm for balance and it didn't quite work. I whacked my head on the table and passed out."

"Tom said you were knocked out instantly. That's one of the reasons they were so concerned. That and the amount of blood. Do you think Matt will try and see you again?"

"I don't know. I hope not."

"Do you think you should file a complaint with the police?" she asked.

"He hasn't really done anything to warrant one. I don't think it would help. If he comes around again, I'll consider calling, but until then I'm not going to worry about it."

"Okay Alex, if you say so. I trust your judgment."

"I'm glad someone does," I replied.

"What do you mean?" she asked.

"I beginning to think I have terrible judgment. Look at my track record. I feel like such a failure. All your other kids are successful and in good relationships. Janey's married with the kids. Tom's with Vicki...and then there's me…always picking the village idiot. I'm trying Mom, I really am." I could feel my throat begin to swell.

"Oh Alex," she said embracing me. "Don't cry."

"I just don't know what I'm doing wrong."

"Honey you're not doing anything wrong, and don't ever let me catch you saying you're a failure again. You have no idea how much I admire you and how proud I am of you. You are the kindest most loving girl there is, and any man is crazy not to want to be with you."

"Well Matt wanted to be with me but it turns out he was crazy," I sniffled.

Mom laughed. "You have so much to offer the world Alex. More than you give yourself credit. It's not about the man. It should never be about the man. It has to be about you. If the man doesn't make you happy then kick him to the curb. Don't settle for anything. You're better than that."

"I just don't want to let you down."

"Let me down? What are you talking about? You could never let me down. I don't care if you're single, married, gay or whatever. As long as you're happy and you're who you want to be. That's all that matters to me."

"Well I'm not gay, I can assure you of that, although sometimes I think with my luck maybe it's time to switch teams."

"You're starting to feel sorry for yourself and I won't allow that. I didn't raise you that way. Life isn't about choosing sides. It's about being about to being about to handle the pitches thrown at you."

"Are we going with the baseball analogy here Mom?"

"Yes we are. Now be quiet and listen. So you get a few curveballs thrown at you. No big deal. Just foul them off until you get a pitch you like and knock it out of the park. There's always at least one hittable pitch in every at bat…you know that. Be patient and wait for yours. It'll come."

"What if I strike out swinging?" I laughed.

"You'll at least be content in the knowledge that you gave it your all. It's better to go down swinging than to be caught with the bat still on your shoulders."

"That was very good Mom. Having you been saving that one," I asked.

"As a matter of fact I have. Been working on it for years. Just never got the chance to use it until now. Did it sound all right?"

"It was perfect."

"All kidding aside Alex, you know it's true."

"I know. And I'm not really upset about the breakup, honestly. Ask Vicki. I think maybe the pain medication is making me sappy. That and the fact that you're here. I miss you Mom. We haven't spent that much time together lately. It's my fault. I feel like we're drifting apart a little and I don't ever want that to happen. We used to talk all the time."

"I miss you too Alex. I want to call more and stop by, but I don't want to seem like I'm interfering or checking up on you. You're an adult and have your own life to live. I have to respect that."

"Please Mother, I still sleep in flannel pajamas with sheep on them. I can't be that grown up."

"What about we make a pact to have lunch or get together, just the two of us, say at least twice a month?"

"That sounds wonderful. And I promise to drive out to the house more to visit you and Dad. I take you guys for granted…that you'll always be there and it bothers me because I should know better. Look at Vicki. She's lived her whole adult life without the comfort of loving parents. I'm so lucky. I forget that sometimes and I'm sorry."

"Oh Alex…my baby girl. I love you so much."

"I love you too Mom."

We sat on the couch and talked for hours. She whipped up some lunch and we had a mother and daughter picnic in the family room just like when I was a kid. We talked of old times and our plans for the future. She told me some things I never knew. Some unfulfilled hopes and dreams she had as a young girl. But she was okay with that because new ones replaced the old unfulfilled hopes as her life progressed. She said it's called living. You can't stay in one place or be static. You have to keep in motion, keep moving. And since there was never any point in going back, the only real solution to any situation was to move ahead. Look to the future. Be excited about the unknown. Be willing to take that chance. That leap of faith. You can't change the past but you can definitely shape your tomorrow. Wake up every morning with a smile on your face, she said. It can't hurt your chances. My mother was a smart woman. Too bad the genetics seemed to skip a generation. I thought that was only supposed to happen with twins.

CHAPTER SEVENTEEN

It had been over a month since the episode with Matt and thankfully, I hadn't seen or heard from him at all. Life was getting back to normal and I was glad I hadn't had any lasting effects, except of course the nasty scar both on my head and in my heart. My sole salvation during the past few weeks was my writing. Working at a feverish pitch, I was pleased with the progress. I'd also spent some more quality time with my mother rediscovering our relationship. I was happy.

I hadn't seen or talked to Bobby much. He was busy being a Dad and a boyfriend, two roles that suited him perfectly. Ben was adjusting to his new life and relishing the fact that not only did he have a new dad around, he also had a mother figure in Carrie, and a brother in Michael. It was such a change for him and Bobby was delighted at his progress, especially in school. All the kid needed was a little stability to feel safe enough to spread his wings. Then again, don't we all?

It was Sunday afternoon and having just wrapped up a marathon session at the computer, I decided to take a walk and enjoy the fall colors. Passing Wilkins Place on the way, I stopped in to see some of the guys but the place was empty of faces I knew. A skinny little man who needed a shave and a sandwich was sitting in Big Dave's chair, and Joe, who I think had a bed in the back, was nowhere to be seen. The bartender said the old guys only drop in once and a while these days. All of them seem to have found other things to do. They still hang out he said, in fact he was fairly sure they met once a week at Bobby's for a game of poker and a few beers.

I declined the drink he offered and went on my way. It's funny how things change and evolve. All it took was for Bobby to step up, show some responsibility and the others followed like a pack of sheep. It was good to see. They were all great guys and offered so much in their unique ways. For me, Wilkins Place held many good memories and one incredibly bad one. Unfortunately, the bad one stared back at me every time I looked in the mirror. But seasons change, and we're forced to move on whether we like it or not.

Not feeling like going home yet, I strolled leisurely down to Thompson Park to people watch. It was a beautiful day and I was content just to sit and gaze at the sun reflecting on the changing leaves. It had been one hell of a year. Meeting Bobby, meeting Matt, helping Bobby, losing Matt. My life had changed in so many ways, yet here I was, sitting alone on a park bench once again. I was right back where I'd been after Luke left. Or was I?

No. I was a different woman these days. I was stronger, more independent, and definitely willing to face whatever my future might hold. I had friends and I had family, which was more than most. I was writing and generally living my life the way I wanted to. I couldn't ask for more. So many things were out of my control, and I decided right then and there sitting on that bench that I wasn't going to worry about the future. I would control the things I could and not be concerned about the rest.

"Hey good looking!" said a voice breaking the silence and almost sending me flying off the end of the bench.

"Geez Wayne, you nearly scared me half to death. What are you doing here?"

He sat down beside me. "Actually, I was on my way over to your place when I noticed you sitting here. What's up?"

"I'm just taking a writing break and enjoying the afternoon sunshine. You were coming over to see me?"

"Ya...I've got some news," he said excitedly. "I've quit my job and I'm taking a post in Africa. I've been planning it for months but didn't want to say anything until everything was finalized. It's something I've always wanted to do. What do you think?"

What did I think? I couldn't think because all the blood in my body was now residing in my toes. He couldn't leave. It was Wayne. He was my guy...the one that was always around just in case. My friend.

"Wow that sounds wonderful Wayne," I lied. "Congratulations." I couldn't say anything else. I tried but the words wouldn't come out.

"You don't sound too excited," he said laughing.

"I'm sorry. You caught me off guard. I'm in shock. It's not the news I was expecting."

"I know, and I'm sorry to spring it on you like this. It's all come together in the last few days. Alex it's the right thing to do for me. I love reporting on sports but there's so much more, you know? My sympathies for professional athletes only run so deep, and Africa…gosh, it's just full of stories. Stories the world needs to hear. I want to do something more. Something important. I'll be working with an international news organization as a freelancer so I'm free to go and do as I please and report on the things I want. Imagine the choice and the challenge! It's gonna be great."

He rambled on for a while about the benefits of going to Africa yet I found myself not hearing a word he said. Wayne was leaving. I couldn't believe it. Nobody just stops by one day and says they're quitting their job and moving to Africa for God knows how long. He couldn't go. I hadn't decided how I felt about him yet. I needed more time.

"You hungry?" It was all I could say. "I've got some chili cooking in the crock pot if you're interested. It's nothing fancy."

"I'd love to Alex. Let's go."

He took my hand and together we wandered out of the park and onto the concrete sidewalk. The path was strewn with red and gold maple leaves and as hard as I tried not to, I found myself playfully kicking them as I walked.

"I'm going to miss you Wayne."

"I'm going to miss you too sweetie," he answered softly.

"I'm sorry if I'm not better company right now but I still can't believe it. How long will you be gone? I mean it's not forever is it?"

"No it's not forever but I signed a three year contract, so…"

"Three years? Holy shit! That's an eternity."

"You could come and visit me," he said.

"Maybe I will. Africa…I've always wanted to run with the giraffes. They're so graceful unlike myself."

He laughed and squeezed my hand. "What are talking about? You're graceful."

"Oh shut up," I said opening the apartment door.

"Mmm, I smell chili."

"Want a beer or something?" I said giving the chili a quick stir, "It's not quite ready yet. Are you in a hurry?"

"Never in a hurry when it comes to you. And sure I'll take a beer."

I cracked open two beers and sat down on the couch beside him. Normally I hated beer but it seemed like a fitting drink for the moment.

"Alex before I go, there is one thing I need to ask you."

"Sure," I said taking a drink.

"Why didn't it work for us? We seem so compatible…have so much in common. Why couldn't we have made it work back then?"

"It's funny Wayne because lately I've been asking myself the same question, and I can never come up with a good answer. It was probably me…not knowing what I wanted…being stubborn…being stupid."

"I'm sure it wasn't just you Alex. Didn't we try hard enough?"

"I don't know. I thought we did," I said. "I think we thought we'd be better as friends you know? But then you had to go and kiss me in my office that day and fuck everything up. Why did you do that?" I laughed.

"Well to be honest, I've wanted to do that for a long time. If you can recall our relationship wasn't all that physical when we dated. A few pecks here and there and then it was over. I needed to kiss you. Were you angry?"

"No I wasn't angry, just confused. I felt some things I never thought I would."

"Me too. That's why I had to do it. I'm a different man than I was when we dated. Not so shy…more open to risks…more open to change."

"So why didn't you say anything after the kiss?" I asked.

"You were seeing Matt and seemed happy. Once again, the timing was wrong. I wasn't going to complicate your life even more." He kept getting closer as he talked and I felt my heart begin to flutter. He brushed back my hair and noticed the scar. "I'm so sorry that had to happen to you...that you had to go through that whole ordeal. You didn't deserve it, and Matt certainly didn't deserve you. Any of you. It makes me sick to think of it. I would never hurt you. I could never hurt you. You mean too much."

He lifted his chin and gently kissed my scar. I could hardly breathe. "Why did you have to do that?" I said.

"Sometimes," he said, "scars need a little loving to help them heal. But they will heal. I promise."

He kissed the scar again so tenderly, I couldn't help myself. Overwhelmed with emotion, I took his face in my hands and kissed him passionately on the mouth. He returned my kisses and more. I'd never felt this way before. My entire body was shaking uncontrollably, and I began to cry. He held me close and kissed my tears. I felt so safe, so comfortable in his arms.

"Alex...I want more. If only for tonight, I want to be more than friends."

I nodded and led him to the bedroom. Matt and I had sex. Luke and I had obligation. Wayne and I made love. It was the most wonderful moment I'd ever experienced. Not just the physical aspect but the emotional one. I'd finally found my puzzle piece and now he was going away.

"Do you smell something?" Wayne said brushing the hair out of my eyes as we lay in bed.

"Smell what? The chili!" I jumped out of bed and raced to the kitchen, "Oh shit! It's burnt."

"Although I enjoy the view, I thought maybe you'd want this," he laughed handing me my pink housecoat. I didn't realize I was standing there naked stirring the chili. It must have been a sight.

"Thanks. Sorry I burnt the chili."

Wayne kissed my neck from behind. "It's not burnt, just charred. It's looks good to me, where's the plates?"

"You're too sweet." I plopped a spoonful of chili into a bowl and handed it to him. "I won't be offended if you don't eat it. We could always order in."

"Never." He took the bowl, sat at the table and proceeded to shovel the chili in his mouth like he hadn't eaten in years. "Seriously Alex, it's not that bad. A little aftertaste but that's all. Sit down and have some." I filled my own bowl and sat down beside him at the table. "By the way, I love your housecoat. You look so damn sexy right now I can hardly chew."

"I know it's old and ratty. What can I say?"

"No, I really do like it. It has character just like its owner. Stains. Little rips. It's perfect. I wouldn't expect you to wear anything else."

"How do you feel about silk?" I said.

"Hate it. It's cold against your body. Not very comfortable."

"But don't you think it's sexy? I mean wouldn't you rather have a woman dressed in fishnet stockings with a silk teddy?"

"What do you think I am a pimp?" he laughed. "No...stuff like that isn't for me. It's too formal. You can fart in an old cotton housecoat but in silk...not so much. It wouldn't even sound the same."

"You're gross," I said putting my empty bowl in the sink.

"Like you've never farted. Please I've heard you a million times."

"I never fart. It's not ladylike."

"Whoever said you were a lady?" he said pulling me onto his knee. "You really think I'm the type of guy who wants a lady? No way. I want a woman who's not afraid to get dirty or break a nail."

"Well I'm not afraid to get a little dirty..." I whispered in his ear.

"I bet you aren't."

"C'mon then farm boy, I've got a load of dirt in that back room that's just a itchin' to be shoveled. I could use a pair of strong hands if you know what I mean." I sauntered down the hall and dropped my housecoat midway. Thank the Lord I'd been doing my Pilates lately because my white ass shone like a beacon in the night.

"Oh I know what you mean," he said practically falling off his chair. "Who needs a shovel? I've got a perfectly good front-end loader that's just been refueled and raring to go."

He chased me into the bedroom and we spent the rest of the night repositioning the dirt until it was just right. It was exhausting work, but I have to say that the farm boy was certainly up to the task. Talk about a green thumb. Everything was coming up roses.

I awoke the next morning entwined with Wayne like an overgrown weed. I found it quite unusual since normally after sex, I kicked the guy to his side of the bed so I could get some quality sleep.

"Good morning gorgeous," he said kissing me softly.

"Oh man," I laughed, "your breath smells like chili."

"So does yours, so kiss me anyway."

We kissed and snuggled for a minute before we got up and made some breakfast. It was still early and I had to go into the office later for a staff meeting. Wayne had to go home and finish some packing.

"When do you fly out?" I said walking him to the door.

"Early tomorrow morning."

"Tomorrow morning? You can't go that soon. I'm not ready for you to leave yet."

"Me neither…but I have to. I have no choice. I'll write when I can."

"I know and I understand. I don't like it but I understand." I gave him a hug and we kissed once more. "I'm glad we at least had last night. A chance for two very good friends to say goodbye in their own special way. It can't be anything more than that. It'd be too hard." It almost killed me to say the words.

"I agree. Not that I don't want to try you know."

"I know…but it's Africa Wayne. You're not just moving up the street. You're going to have all these exciting adventures and experiences and that's great…I don't want you not to do this because of me. It's your dream. I could never take that away from you. You'll write and tell me all about it. It's the only way."

He smiled, brushed back my hair, and kissed my scar one last time. "You be good Alex. No more crazy men or I'm coming home to set you straight."

"Promise?" I said trying not to cry.

"Promise." He held me tight and I could tell that he too was fighting back tears. "I love you Alex Hanson," he whispered.

"I love you too." We kissed once more and he was gone.

I shut the door behind him and crawled back in bed. Wayne was gone. It was funny because I'd never felt so alone yet so satisfied in all my life. I'd found and lost my great love all in one day. That had to be a record. I guess I didn't really lose him, but I would. I think that's why our goodbye was so special. We both knew that our future consisted of right now, and we couldn't change that. He wasn't going to cancel his job in Africa, and I would never have asked him to. That would have been selfish and wrong. We had our chance and we blew it. That's just the way life was sometimes. It didn't mean I had to like it. And it certainly didn't mean I couldn't crawl under the covers and cry about it.

Wayne had been gone for almost three months and winter was firmly entrenched in the cityscape. I'd spent the passing days working on my novel and generally getting on with my life. Vicki and I had started to make formal plans for the business and with Bobby's capital and office space in the warehouse, the future seemed bright. Although he hired an architect to help finalize the structural design for the warehouse, the three of us pretty much drew up the concept of the plans ourselves. There was going to be loft apartments upstairs, with office space in the bottom, along with some space for future expansion. It was an exciting project and I was to glad to have the distraction.

I wasn't going to deny that I missed Wayne terribly. Going to the office just wasn't the same, and I found myself working from home more and more. I liked the solitude. Vicki of course was worried I was isolating myself, and maybe I was, but I didn't care. She was the only one I'd told about my night with Wayne, so her concern was well founded. I'd been asked out on dates a few times but declined. My heart just wasn't into it. Wayne left a void that wasn't going to be easily filled, nor did I want it to.

It was hard to describe, losing something you never really had, but that was under your nose the entire time. All the 'what ifs' and 'maybes'…it was enough to drive you crazy if you let it. I wasn't going to let it. In the time since Wayne had gone, I'd grown up. I was no longer that cynical girl who just waited for the bird poop to land on her head, and got angry when it did. Instead, I realized that a little bird shit wasn't going to kill me, it was the anticipation, and getting angry that would. I needed to chill. Relax. Take what life threw at me each day and deal with that only. My mother's good advice. No sense in worrying about things I had absolutely no control over. I woke up each morning with a smile on my face, and the determination not to waste a minute of my life. You never knew when the bird was going to have diarrhea.

I received a letter in mail from Wayne almost every other week. He was having a fabulous time and had already gone on a few safaris. There was an incident with a baboon but he didn't elaborate. He loved Africa and found the country, and his work fulfilling. He said he'd met a bunch of fantastic people and spent the New Year in a rented cabin on the Coast. I could tell reading between the lines he'd met a woman. He didn't want to come right out and say it but it was there. He'd mentioned her in one of his first letters. A woman from France who was a freelancer like him. He said they'd essentially been working on the same story, and decided to pair up and split the credit. He told me they were only friends but I knew he was just trying to protect me.

He asked about my love life and said he was sorry he couldn't be there to screen all the potential suitor's that must be lining up. That Wayne…what a funny guy. Thinking of him with another woman almost made me sick to my stomach but I could never let him know that.

Although lately, I'd been feeling sick quite often. I thought at first it was stress over Wayne, but I was truly at peace with the way our relationship ended. Sure, I wished it had worked out but I wasn't upset like I'd been with Luke or Matt. I was only sad. Really sad. Vicki thought maybe I was having a relapse of the flu and urged me to go to the doctor. It didn't feel like a relapse but I made an appointment anyway. It'd been a while since my last full-fledged medical, and at least Vicki would stop nagging me.

My personal diagnosis was an allergic reaction to the foot of dust that had accumulated in my apartment. The dust clogged my sinuses', which prevented me from breathing properly, which in turn somehow made me feel queasy. It used to happen all the time when I was a kid. I wasn't worried.

The nurse made me strip naked and since I knew there wasn't going to be any sex, I wasn't all that excited. I put on the gown and sat on the chair to wait for my doctor. She ran the full gamut of tests and blood work and sent me on my way. Nothing jumped out at her, except a bit of mucus in my lungs but she said she'd get back to me when the results came in. At least there was no sign of a flu relapse, and the stuff in my lungs could easily be traced back to the dust. I didn't want to be sick all winter long. I had things to do, people to meet, and an apartment to clean.

When I got home from work the next day there was a message on my machine asking me to call the doctor's office right away for a follow up appointment. When they told me they could squeeze me in first thing the next morning, I become concerned. It must be something serious. They only squeeze you in if it's serious. I'd been a bit tired lately but nothing out of the ordinary. I didn't feel sick. Maybe they'd misdiagnosed my sickness in the fall, and it was just a precursor to something worse. Normally, I wasn't one to worry, but I was worried. Cancer of all kinds ran in my family. Was I next on the hit list?

I hardly slept at all that night, my mind racing faster than the wind. What would I tell my mother? She'd be devastated. Maybe the stuff on my lungs was more than just mucus, or something must have shown up in my blood work. I tried to calm myself down but couldn't. I was cold, I was hot, I was sweating. My heart pounded and I couldn't breathe. I wanted to call someone and talk but it was the middle of the night, and I wanted to keep whatever it was I had a secret until I knew I could face it.

"Good morning Alex, how are you today?" the doctor said looking over my chart.

"Not so good," I said, "I'm a little worried. I don't usually get a call back."

She smiled knowingly. "Have a seat."

"I've got cancer don't I? It runs in the family. Oh gosh."

"Alex calm down," she said reaching for my hand. "You don't have cancer."

I let out a deep breath. "That's good to know. What then?"

"You're pregnant."

I almost fell off my chair. "I'm pregnant? But I haven't had sex in...oh my God...Wayne."

"You're almost three months along. You had no clue?" The doctor having to ask made me feel stupid.

"No, I mean my period isn't very regular during the best of times and it's been even more off kilter since I was sick in the fall. I'm pregnant? Holy shit. The nausea...the tender boobs...and I chalked it up to having a dusty apartment." It all began to make sense now.

"Well this has nothing to do with a dusty apartment," she laughed. "Now there's a few things we need to discuss and some more questions I need to ask. Now that we know it isn't cancer, we can start to take of you and the little one."

The little one? The words hit me like a ton of bricks, and I began to zone out and feel queasy.

"Alex are you alright? I think you should lie down." She helped me up on the examining table and placed her hand on my stomach while she summoned the nurse. "We need a cold cloth here and a glass of orange juice."

"Is she alright?" the nurse asked placing the cloth on my head.

"She'll be fine. Just a little dizzy. Don't worry Alex, you're not the first woman to be shocked by the news that they're going to be a mother."

"Oh, congratulations," said the nurse.

"It's obvious you weren't expecting this, which begs the question is this something you want? Because if it isn't we can discuss those options as well," the doctor said helping me sit up.

"God no," I said. "I want this baby...more than you know. I'm just overwhelmed right now, and am feeling really stupid because I didn't see the signs. Normally I'm so careful with birth control but it happened so fast...the father was going away...we both forgot." I was rambling.

"You said the father was going away?"

"He's in Africa working. We were friends. He came over to say goodbye. It's a long and complicated story."

"How long is he gone for?" the doctor asked.

"I don't know really. At least three years but then again he may never come back."

The doctor gave me some final instructions, and had me make a follow up appointment for the next week. She was also kind enough to let me lie on the couch in her personal office until I could get my head together enough to leave. I was going to have a baby. Wayne's baby. He'd be so excited. But what was I thinking? I couldn't tell him. He'd feel obligated to come home and the last thing I wanted was to feel guilty. Going to Africa was his dream. Having a baby was mine. The way I saw it, we both won. Besides, he was with someone new. I wouldn't spoil that for him. No one would have to know who the father was. I'd say I'd been planning it along and went to a fertility clinic. Only Vicki would know the truth. I'd have to tell her. She'd figure it out anyway.

"Hi Alex," the doctor asked. "I just have to grab a few files and finish my morning fix of caffeine. Are you feeling better? You're looking better. The color's returned to your face."

"Ya, I'm feeling much better. Thanks. Sorry about that. I was expecting a diagnosis of death, and here you give me a diagnosis of life. It's taken me a while to wrap my head around it all."

"Well you have nine months to figure it out. No sorry…in your case six." She sat down beside me on the couch. "You have nothing to be afraid of Alex. I've known you for a long time now. You'll make a great parent."

"But will I make a great single parent? That's the question."

"There's no chance that the father would come home?"

"Oh he'd come home but I can't ask him to. It wouldn't be fair. He's not there for a vacation. He's already started a whole new life. I may never see him again."

"It's none of my business but do you love him?"

"I think I'll always love him, but we've both moved on."

"Well I can't tell you what to do, and right now my only concern is for you and the baby. The less stress you have the better. You understand? You need to take care of yourself. Do you have anyone to talk to? Because that's important too. You need support."

"You don't have to worry about that. I've got plenty of people to talk to. I'm sure they'll be more than happy to share their opinions," I laughed and got off the couch. "I'd better get going. Thanks so much for taking the time to talk to me. I really appreciate it."

"I'm here if you need me Alex. Don't be afraid to call."

"Oh I'm not afraid. I'm not afraid at all. Not of the pregnancy or being a mother. I'm ready for it. In truth, I think I've waited for this moment my entire life. I just had to let it sink in. I'm going to be a mother. Wow."

I left the office feeling great. I could do this. I could raise this child on my own. So the situation wasn't conventional, but really what had been conventional in my life lately? At least I knew the child was conceived in love and not the result of some stupid one-night stand. I wasn't ashamed of what happened between Wayne and me. We were two consenting adults that knew the risk we were taking when we made love. When we made this child. I still couldn't believe it. I knew I'd eventually have to tell Wayne, was the right thing to do. I would never want him to hate me for concealing his child from him. I couldn't bear the thought. I would tell him in my own time. Not today or tomorrow, not even next week but when the time was right. The doctor said right now I needed to concentrate on me and my baby, and that's exactly what I was going to do.

The January air was cold and crisp as I walked out of the office. I stopped and took a deep breath. "Did you feel that air little person growing inside my tummy? That's mommy breathing. That's mommy breathing in fresh air for her fresh start. For our fresh start." I put my hand on my stomach. "I can't wait to watch you grow and I'm so happy that you decided out of all the people in the world, you wanted me to be your mommy. Did you here that baby? That little click. That was a piece of the puzzle snapping into place. We'll do this together little one. I promise. I may not always do the right thing but I'm going to try my best. You'll see."

I pulled my jacket tight around my waist to shut out the cold and headed home. I had a skip in my step that had been absent for a long, long time. I was going to be a mother. I couldn't stop saying the words and the more I said them, the wider my grin grew. All the hurt and disappointment I'd ever experienced in my life disappeared. Shit like that just didn't matter anymore. I was going to be a mother. Me…Alex Hanson. I was going to be somebody's mother.

My skip turned into a jog and then a full-fledged sprint. I wanted to shout it from the mountaintop. I didn't care if the world thought I was crazy. Hell I was crazy. But there's nothing wrong with a little crazy in your life. It makes things interesting. It makes it worthwhile, and I was worthwhile. I deserved to be happy and I deserved this child. I wanted to sing. I wanted to sing a song about life. My life. Because it was a good life and it was only going to get better. I knew that now. It had taken me awhile to understand, and I had to endure a few bumps and bruises along the way, but I knew that now. I couldn't ask for anything more than what I had. I didn't need to. My landscape would hang on this child's wall and one day in the eve of my being, it would be complete. A testament to my struggles and my successes. My triumphs and my trappings. My loves and my losses. My puzzle would have them all. Maybe there'd even be a pair of fishnet stockings hanging on the clothesline, blowing in the wind. One day I'd look back and laugh. What a story that would be.

ABOUT THE AUTHOR

Trish Faber was born in Markham Ontario, Canada, the youngest of five children. She began to write at the age of five, using her family as characters in her first epic novel, "The Rabbit Family". Although never formally published, the single, handwritten, and self-illustrated copy of "The Rabbit Family" did make appearances at the local school, grocery store, bowling alley and bridge club meetings, courtesy of an enthusiastic mother and her large purse.

Trish is grateful to her family for allowing her to develop her imagination and creative flair without ever passing judgment. She realizes that at times this must have been difficult. Trish holds an Honours Degree in English and History from the University of Western Ontario, and a life degree in the trials and tribulations of being a restaurant owner, an academic tutor and life skills coach, as well as a business owner. She likes music, sports, tomato soup, and has secret aspirations of one day becoming a rock star. Most of all, she loves spending quality time with her friends and family.

TITLES
"Songs About Life" (1st Edition 2006, 2nd Edition 2016)
"I Was, I Am, I Will Be" (2010)
"Pierre's Story" (2013)
"Ghost – The Rick Watkinson Story" (2016)

Connect with Trish Online:
My Website: www.trishfaber.com
Facebook: www.facebook.com/pages/Trish-Faber-Writer
Twitter: @trishfaber
Wonder Voice Press: www.wondervoicepress.com

www.ingramcontent.com/pod-product-compliance
Lightning Source LLC
Chambersburg PA
CBHW060535180626
46817CB00002B/582